The Best
AMERICAN
SHORT
STORIES
1976

The Best AMERICAN SHORT STORIES 1976

And the Yearbook of the
American Short Story

Edited by Martha Foley

 1976

Houghton Mifflin Company Boston

Library of Congress Catalog Card Number: 16-11387
ISBN: 0-395-24770-5

Printed in the United States of America

C 10 9 8 7 6 5 4 3 2 1

"Roses, Rhododendron" by Alice Adams. First published in *The New Yorker*.
Copyright © 1975 by The New Yorker Magazine, Inc.
"Terminal Procedure" by M. Pabst Battin. First published in *American Review* #22.
Copyright © 1975 by M. Pabst Battin.
"The Boy Who Was Astrid's Mother" by Mae Seidman Briskin. First published in
Ascent. Copyright © 1975 by Mae Seidman Briskin.
"Beautiful, Helpless Animals" by Nancy Chaikin. Reprinted by permission of *The
Colorado Quarterly* and Nancy Chaikin. Copyright, 1975, by The University of Colorado, Boulder, Colorado.
"The Actes and Monuments" by John William Corrington. First published in *The
Sewanee Review* 83 (Winter 1975). Copyright 1975 by the University of the South.
Reprinted by permission of the editor.
"A Chronicle of Love" by H. E. Francis. First published in *Kansas Quarterly*.
Copyright © 1975 by *Kansas Quarterly*.
"Pontius Pilate" by John Hagge. Reprinted from *The Carleton Miscellany*, copyrighted by Carleton College, October 14, 1975.
"Dietz at War" by Ward Just. First published in *The Virginia Quarterly Review*,
Autumn 1975. Copyright © 1976 by Ward Just.
"John Henry's Home" by John McCluskey. Reprinted from *The Iowa Review*.
Copyright © 1975 by John McCluskey.
"Grubbing for Roots" by Stephen Minot. First published in *The North American
Review*. Reprinted in *Crossings*, published by the University of Illinois Press. Copyright
© 1975 by Stephen Minot.
"Looking into Nothing" by Kent Nelson. First published in *The Transatlantic Review*. Copyright © 1975 by *The Transatlantic Review*.
"A Mercenary" by Cynthia Ozick. First published in *American Review* #23. Reprinted in *Bloodshed and Three Novellas*, by Cynthia Ozick. Copyright © 1976 by
Cynthia Ozick. Reprinted by permission of Alfred A. Knopf, Inc.
"Broad Day" by Reynolds Price. Copyright © 1975 by Reynolds Price. Reprinted

TO BARRY TARGAN

Acknowledgments

GRATEFUL ACKNOWLEDGMENT for permission to reprint the stories in this volume is made to the following:

The editors of *The American Review, Antaeus, Ascent, Carleton Miscellany, The Colorado Quarterly, The Iowa Review, The Kansas Quarterly Review, The New Yorker, The North American Review, Salmagundi, The Sewanee Review, Shenandoah, The Transatlantic Review, The Virginia Quarterly;* and to Alice Adams, M. Pabst Battin, Mae Seidman Briskin, Nancy Chaikin, John William Corrington, H. E. Francis, John Hagge, Ward Just, John McClusky, Stephen Minot, Kent Nelson, Cynthia Ozick, Reynolds Price, Michael Rothschild, Barry Targan, Peter Taylor, John Updike.

Foreword

"HE FLUNG HIMSELF on his horse and rode madly off in all directions." Ever since I was a child I have cherished that description in a Stephen Leacock nonsense novel but never did I feel like Lord Ronald until this year when I tried to decide the trend of American short stories. Their variety is astonishing. They can be innovative or traditional, realistic or romantic, light-hearted or tragic, concise as a fable or long as a novella. By the thousands they have been published in weeklies, monthlies, bimonthlies, quarterlies and semiannuals, ranging in format from cheap, unbound newsprint pages through more conventional layouts to sumptuous productions on quality paper with stitched bindings and lavish illustrations. Their authors are equally various. They may be world-famous men and women or promising young beginners but only merit wins them a place in the literary magazines.

Unfortunately most people never see these magazines because few ever appear on newsstands, owing to a monopolistic distribution system and the usurpation of all the media by advertisers in the last half-century. The invisibility of the good magazines, with their abundance of fine reading, fiction and non-fiction, has resulted in a widespread impression that short stories and the novel are dying. Some reviewers, isolated on the East Coast, have been led to encourage the false assumption. This when there is greater literary activity throughout the entire United States than ever before!

Stories are timeless. The *Jakata*, an anthology published in 483 B.C. in India, includes five hundred short stories. With our Western one-hemisphere minds we forget there were civilizations with great literatures thousands of years ago in the East. Long before the Arabs adapted and adopted them, in the early years of this millenium, the *The Arabian Nights' Entertainments* were popular in Persia and India. Our college English courses hail Defoe and Richardson for writing "first novels" in the eighteenth century. Lady Murasaki wrote a novel, *Genji*, in the eleventh century in Japan. And how many know that it was not Gutenberg who invented the first printing press but a Korean whose name is unknown?

The Greeks and Romans were writing stories in classical times. The oldest Latin story manuscript of which fragments have survived is the *Satyricon* by Petronius who was master of ceremonies in Nero's court in the first century A.D. Another first century Roman whose influence on Boccaccio, Cervantes, Fielding and Smollett has been traced, is Apuleius, who wrote *The Golden Ass* with its immortal love story of Cupid and Psyche. Lucian, a prolific Greek author of the second century, wrote *The True History*, a prototype of *Gulliver's Travels*.

As it was then so it is now. All around the world wonderful stories are being written. Many foreign stories have appeared in translation in our literary magazines. Charles Angoff, especially, for years has given over whole issues of *The Literary Review* he edits to fiction from foreign countries. Daniel Halpern, one of whose two summer issues of *Antaeus* carries four hundred pages of stories, is another editor who has given us translations of splendid foreign stories, as has *The New Yorker*. One of my most pleasant evenings this year was spent enchanted by the contemporary Greek stories James Boatwright chose for his Fall 1975 issue of *Shenandoah*. As for American stories, the new edition of the *American Short Story Index*, published by H. W. Wilson Company, covering 1969 to 1973, inclusive, lists 11,561 short stories published in book collections during those five years. Added to the 96,336 stories recorded in previous volumes of the *Index*, it makes a total of 107,897 stories printed in books since the republic began. The *Index* does not count folk tales, humorous sketches, character sketches, stories for children under twelve and the thousands of stories printed only in magazines.

When they are not being ignored, American short story writers are being insulted. There have been angry comments by writers about an egregious interview in the *Wall Street Journal* in which a young reader at *Esquire* expatiated upon her martyrdrom as "arbiter of the slush." I know she did not invent the label but terming unsolicited manuscripts "slush" does denote a lack of literary awareness and empathy. No matter how bad some may be, much effort went into them and much hope — oh, the longed for and at the same time dreaded arrival of the mail! Years ago I founded *Story* magazine in Europe. At the time it was the only magazine devoted solely to the short story. We received more than a hundred unsolicited manuscripts a day. Many of their authors are now celebrated. Unheralded and un-agented, tucked unpretentiously in those tall stacks of mail had been stories from two writers who were to be awarded the Nobel Prize. *Story* was moved to America about the time *Esquire* was started and that magazine had not yet received any of the important fiction it was later to print. Arnold Gingrich, the editor-in-chief of *Esquire*, came to my office and asked if he could look at the manuscripts I was rejecting to see if there were any he could publish. I liked Arnold and told him sure. I don't remember his calling them slush.

American fiction has always see-sawed between realism, or naturalism, and romanticism. Realism used to shock — it still does, a number of readers. Every year I receive letters complaining about sexual frankness in some story in this collection. Or, in the tone of Villon's "Mais où sont les neiges d'antan?" comes the plea, "Aren't there any more happy endings?" to which Max Beerbohm's famous rejoinder, a cliché by now, is still the perfect answer. "What's all this talk about happy or unhappy endings when it is a question of the inevitable ending?"

Today it is not the realistic but the romantic which startles, so unused to it have American readers become. It comes under the name of "Innovative," a free-wheeling, invented kind of writing which, whenever the author wishes, forsakes characters, narrative and natural laws and even allows the long-tabooed *deus ex machina* to reappear. A term apter than "innovative" might be "free fiction," just as the poets who first abandoned meter and rhyme called their writing free verse. A striking characteristic of many of the Innovative writers is their resemblance to the old Dadaists with their love of parody. Dada was a sensation from the time of its founding in the middle nineteen-tens until its disappearance in the early twenties. It was an anarchistic art movement started by writers and painters in the United States and Switzerland to express their utter dissatisfaction with the world. An anthology of Innovative short stories, *Superfiction*, edited by Joe David Bellamy, was published in the past year.

Of the two literary forms, realism and romance, to write the latter is much safer. Romance is considered by the powers that be as "made up." But let Stephen Crane write *Maggie, A Girl of the Streets*, or Dreiser *Sister Carrie* or Caldwell *God's Little Acre* and there is trouble. All three authors were punished: Crane by having his writing damned as "too grim"; Dreiser by his publisher's burying *Sister Carrie* in a vault for twelve years after it had been printed and made ready for distribution; and Caldwell by being hauled into court for his vivid description of impoverished Georgia sharecroppers. Four times the United States Post Office burned as obscene issues of *The Little Review* because it was serializing Joyce's *Ulysses* and the publishers, Margaret Anderson and Jane Heap, were arrested, finger-printed and fined. Joyce's other masterpiece, *Finnegans Wake*, probably would not have been harrassed in even those prudish times because it is such a romantic melange of wildly imaginative word games. No passages in it are as realistic and easily understood as Bloom's wanderings and Molly's soliloquy.

Both romantic and realistic writers are attracted by the novella. It is a marvelous length for writing though a difficult one for publishing, too short for a book and too long for most magazines. Henry James' *The Turn of the Screw* and Thomas Mann's *Death in Venice* are only two examples of the many magnificent novellas. Once they were called "novelettes," an inaccurate name and a diminution of their importance. To me it sounded like pirouette, coquette, etiquette and similar frivolities. When *Story* began receiving such splendid long stories as Eric Knight's *Flying Yorkshireman* and Richard Wright's *Bright and Morning Star*, I refused to damn them as novelettes and in desperation lit upon novella. I knew it was far from perfect but it did not have the shoddy connotation of novelette, was more musical sounding and won acceptance from dictionary makers. Every year sees the publication of splendid novellas and it saddens me that I am unable to reprint as many of them as I would like.

If Turgenev had not pre-empted the title, a very thick book called *Fathers and Sons* could be assembled from the number of deeply moving short stories about that relationship of father and son. I don't know what has happened to the Oedipus complex, for these stories are full of filial love. Thank heaven "Mom," as portrayed in Philip Wylie's once too popular *Generation of Vipers* has just about vanished from the writing scene. Stories about mothers and daughters, however, are not as numerous as those about fathers and sons. Ivy Litvinoff, the Englishwoman married to a Russian commissar, who wrote stories for *The New Yorker*, said something interesting in one of them. "A woman matures when she forgives her mother." As a woman writer myself, I felt that opened a long vista of story possibilities.

Knowing all the difficulties of starting and continuing a literary magazine in a pragmatic land, I want to stand up and cheer whenever I can announce the anniversary of one. There have been at least four noteworthy magazine anniversaries in 1975. *The Virginia Quarterly* is marking its fiftieth year and readers who have followed *The Best American Short Stories* know how many masterly stories that magazine has published. *The Chicago Review,* one of the most fearless, is thirty years old. *Salmagundi,* truly an intellectual feast, has become ten years old. *Antaeus*, one of the most independent of the newer magazines, celebrated its fifth birthday. And *The New Yorker*, founded in 1925? Ever since Tess Slesinger told me that in discussing one of her stories with the *New Yorker* editors she said "I thought this was a humorous magazine" and was rebuked with an indignant "Definitely not! *The New Yorker* is a *serious* magazine!" I am afraid to use any descriptive term for it. So let's simply say, "Congratulations, *New Yorker*, and thank you for the many beautiful stories you have published during your long life."

As this book goes to press, the United States of America is reaching the end of its second century and the American short story, the first one written in the American colonies, is two years older than the Declaration of Independence. As the country goes into its third century, our future writers will have a throng of glorious predecessors, Irving, Hawthorne, Poe, Melville and many, many more to keep them company. We may not be leaving them and their readers a country without problems but we can rejoice that their literary heritage is so splendid. May they enjoy it and prosper!

I am grateful to all the editors who have kept this anthology supplied with copies of their magazines and to their authors for generously granting reprint rights. The editor of any new magazine is urged to send copies to me.

The editors and staff of Houghton Mifflin are entitled to gratitude for their help. Finally, tribute is paid to the memory of Edward J. O'Brien who founded this anthology in 1915.

MARTHA FOLEY

Contents

The Best
AMERICAN
SHORT
STORIES
1976

ALICE ADAMS

Roses, Rhododendron

(FROM THE NEW YORKER)

ONE DARK AND RAINY Boston spring of many years ago, I spent all my after-school and evening hours in the living room of our antique-crammed Cedar Street flat, writing down what the Ouija board said to my mother. My father, a spoiled and rowdy Irishman, a sometime engineer, had run off to New Orleans with a girl, and my mother hoped to learn from the board if he would come back. Then, one night in May, during a crashing black thunderstorm (my mother was both afraid and much in awe of such storms), the board told her to move down South, to North Carolina, taking me and all the antiques she had been collecting for years, and to open a store in a small town down there. That is what we did, and shortly thereafter, for the first time in my life, I fell violently and permanently in love: with a house, with a family of three people, and with an area of countryside.

Perhaps too little attention is paid to the necessary preconditions of "falling in love" — I mean the state of mind or place that precedes one's first sight of the loved person (or house or land). In my own case, I remember the dark Boston afternoons as a precondition of love. Later on, for another important time, I recognized boredom in a job. And once the fear of growing old.

In the town that she has chosen, my mother, Margot (she picked out her own name, having been christened Margaret), rented a small house on a pleasant back street. It had a big surrounding screened-in porch, where she put most of the antiques, and she put a discreet sign out in the front yard: "Margot — Antiques." The store was open only in the afternoons. In the mornings and on Sundays, she drove around the countryside in our ancient and spacious Buick, searching for trophies among the area's country stores and farms and barns. (She is nothing if not enterprising; no one else down there had thought of doing that before.)

Although frequently embarrassed by her aggression — she thought nothing of making offers for furniture that was in use in a family's rooms — I often drove with her during those first few weeks. I was excited by the novelty of the landscape. The red clay banks that led up to the thick pine groves, the swollen brown creeks half hidden by flowering tangled vines. Bare, shaded yards from which rose gaunt, narrow houses. Chickens that scattered, barefoot children who stared at our approach.

"Hello there. I'm Mrs. John Kilgore — Margot Kilgore — and I'm interested in buying old furniture. Family portraits. Silver."

Margot a big brassily bleached blonde in a pretty flowered-silk dress and high-heeled patent sandals. A hoarse and friendly voice. Me a scrawny, pale, curious girl, about ten, in a blue linen dress with smocking across the bodice. (Margot has always had a passionate belief in good clothes, no matter what.)

On other days, Margot would say, "I'm going to look over my so-called books. Why don't you go for a walk or something, Jane?"

And I would walk along the sleepy, leafed-over streets, on the unpaved sidewalks, past houses that to me were as inviting and as interesting as unread books, and I would try to imagine what went on inside. The families. Their lives.

The main street, where the stores were, interested me least. Two-story brick buildings — dry-goods stores, with dentists' and lawyers' offices above. There was also a drugstore, with round marble tables and wire-backed chairs, at which wilting ladies sipped at their Cokes (this was to become a favorite haunt of Margot's). I preferred the civic monuments: a pre-Revolutionary Episcopal chapel of yellowish cracked plaster, and several tall white statues to the Civil War dead — all of them quickly overgrown with ivy or Virginia creeper.

These were the early nineteen-forties, and in the next few years the town was to change enormously. Its small textile factories would be given defense contracts (parachute silk); a Navy preflight school would be established at a neighboring university town. But at that moment it was a sleeping village. Untouched.

My walks were not a lonely occupation, but Margot worried that they were, and some curious reasoning led her to believe that a bicycle would help. (Of course, she turned out to be right.) We went to Sears, and she bought me a big new bike — blue, with balloon tires — on which I began to explore the outskirts of town and countryside.

The house I fell in love with was about a mile out of town, on top of a hill. A small stone bank that was all overgrown with tangled roses led up to its yard, and pink and white roses climbed up a trellis to the roof of the front porch — the roof on which, later, Harriet and I used to sit and exchange our stores of erroneous sexual information. Harriet Farr was the daughter of the house. On one side of the house, there was what looked like a newer wing, with a bay window and a long side porch, below which the lawn sloped down to some flowering shrubs. There was a yellow rose-bush, rhododendron, a plum tree, and beyond were woods — pines, and oak and cedar trees. The effect was rich and careless, generous and somewhat mysterious. I was deeply stirred.

As I was observing all this, from my halted bike on the dusty white hilltop, a small, plump woman, very erect, came out of the front door and went over to a flower bed below the bay window. She sat down very stiffly. (Emily, who was Harriet's mother, had some terrible, never diagnosed trouble with her back; she generally wore a brace.) She was older than Margot, with very beautiful white hair that was badly cut in that butchered nineteen-thirties way.

From the first, I was fascinated by Emily's obvious dissimilarity to Margot. I think I was also somehow drawn to her contradictions — the shapeless body held up with so much dignity, even while she was sitting in the dirt. The lovely chopped-off hair. (There were greater contradictions, which I learned of later — she was a Virginia Episcopalian who always voted for Norman Thomas, a feminist who always delayed meals for her tardy husband.)

Emily's hair was one of the first things about the Farr family that I mentioned to Margot after we became friends, Harriet and Emily and I, and I began to spend most of my time in that house.

"I don't think she's ever dyed it," I said, with almost conscious lack of tact.

Of course, Margot was defensive. "I wouldn't dye mine if I thought it would be a decent color on its own."

But by that time Margot's life was also improving. Business was fairly good, and she had finally heard from my father, who began to send sizable checks from New Orleans. He had found work with an oil company. She still asked the Ouija board if she would see him again, but her question was less obsessive.

The second time I rode past that house, there was a girl sitting on the front porch, reading a book. She was about my age. She looked up. The next time I saw her there, we both smiled. And the time after that (a Saturday morning in late June) she got up and slowly came out to the road, to where I had stopped, ostensibly to look at the view — the sweep of fields, the white highway, which wound down to the thick greenery bordering the creek, the fields and trees that rose in dim and distant hills.

"I've got a bike exactly like that," Harriet said indifferently, as though to deny the gesture of having come out to meet me.

For years, perhaps beginning then, I used to seek my antithesis in friends. Inexorably following Margot, I was becoming a big blonde, with some of her same troubles. Harriet was cool and dark, with long, gray eyes. A girl about to be beautiful.

"Do you want to come in? We've got some lemon cake that's pretty good."

Inside, the house was cluttered with odd mixtures of furniture. I glimpsed a living room, where there was a shabby sofa next to a pretty, "antique" table. We walked through a dining room that contained a decrepit mahogany table surrounded with delicate fruitwood chairs. (I had a horrifying moment of imagining Margot there, with her accurate eye — making offers in her harsh Yankee voice.) The walls were crowded with portraits and with nineteenth-century oils of bosky landscapes. Books overflowed from rows of shelves along the walls. I would have moved in at once.

We took our lemon cake back to the front porch and ate it there, overlooking that view. I can remember its taste vividly. It was light and tart and sweet, and a beautiful lemon color. With it, we drank cold milk, and then we had seconds and more milk, and we discussed what we liked to read.

We were both at an age to begin reading grownup books, and there was some minor competition between us to see who had read more of them. Harriet won easily, partly because her mother reviewed books for the local paper, and had brought home Steinbeck, Thomas Wolfe, Virginia Woolf, and Elizabeth Bowen. But we also found in common an enthusiasm for certain novels about English children. (Such snobbery!)

"It's the best cake I've ever had!" I told Harriet. I had already adopted something of Margot's emphatic style.

"It's very good," Harriet said judiciously. Then, quite casually, she added, "We could ride our bikes out to Laurel Hill."

We soared dangerously down the winding highway. At the bridge across the creek, we stopped and turned onto a narrow, rutted dirt road that followed the creek through woods as dense and as alien as a jungle would have been — thick pines with low sweeping branches, young leafed-out maples, peeling tall poplars, elms, brambles, green masses of honeysuckle. At times, the road was impassable, and we had to get off our bikes and push them along, over crevices and ruts, through mud or sand. And with all that we kept up our somewhat stilted discussion of literature.

"I love Virginia Woolf!"

"Yes, she's very good. Amazing metaphors."

I thought Harriet was an extraordinary person — more intelligent, more poised, and prettier than any girl of my age I had ever known. I felt that she could become anything at all — a writer, an actress, a foreign correspondent (I went to a lot of movies). And I was not entirely wrong; she eventually became a sometimes-published poet.

We came to a small beach, next to a place where the creek widened and ran over some shallow rapids. On the other side, large gray rocks rose steeply. Among the stones grew isolated, twisted trees, and huge bushes with thick green leaves. The laurel of Laurel Hill. Rhododendron. Harriet and I took off our shoes and waded into the warmish water. The bottom squished under our feet, making us laugh, like the children we were, despite all our literary talk.

Margot was also making friends. Unlike me, she seemed to seek her own likeness, and she found a sort of kinship with a woman named Dolly Murray, a rich widow from Memphis who shared many of Margot's superstitions — fear of thunderstorms, faith in the Ouija board. About ten years older than Margot, Dolly still dyed her hair red; she was a noisy, biased, generous woman. They drank gin and gossiped together, they met for Cokes at the drugstore, and sometimes they drove to a neighboring town to have dinner in a restaurant (in those days, still a daring thing for unescorted ladies to do).

I am sure that the Farrs, outwardly a conventional family, saw me as a neglected child. I was so available for meals and overnight visits. But that is not how I experienced my life — I simply felt free. And an important thing to be said about Margot as a mother is that she never made me feel guilty for doing what I wanted to do. And of how many mothers can that be said?

There must have been a moment of "meeting" Emily, but I have forgotten it. I remember only her gentle presence, a soft voice, and my own sense of love returned. Beautiful white hair, dark deep eyes, and a wide mouth, whose corners turned and moved to express whatever she felt — amusement, interest, boredom, pain. I have never since seen such a vulnerable mouth.

I amused Emily; I almost always made her smile. She must have seen me as something foreign — a violent, enthusiastic Yankee (I used forbidden words, like "God" and "damn"). Very unlike the decorous young Southern girl that she must have been, that Harriet almost was.

She talked to me a lot; Emily explained to me things about the South that otherwise I would not have picked up. "Virginians feel superior to everyone else, you know," she said, in her gentle (Virginian) voice. "Some people in my family were quite shocked when I married a man from North Carolina and came down here to live. And a Presbyterian at that! Of course, that's nowhere near as bad as a Baptist, but only Episcopalians really count." This was all said lightly, but I knew that some part of Emily agreed with the rest of her family.

"How about Catholics?" I asked her, mainly to prolong the conversation. Harriet was at the dentist's, and Emily was sitting at her desk answering letters. I was perched on the sofa near her, and we both faced the sweeping green view. But since my father, Johnny Kilgore, was a lapsed Catholic, it was not an entirely frivolous question. Margot was a sort of Christian Scientist (her own sort).

"We hardly know any Catholics." Emily laughed, and then she sighed. "I do sometimes still miss Virginia. You know, when we drive up there I can actually feel the difference as we cross the state line. I've met a few people from South Carolina," she went on, "and I understand that people down there feel the same way Virginians do." (Clearly, she found this unreasonable.)

"West Virginia? Tennessee?"

"They don't seem Southern at all. Neither do Florida and Texas — not to me."

("Dolly says that Mrs. Farr is a terrible snob," Margot told me, inquiringly.

"In a way." I spoke with a new diffidence that I was trying to acquire from Harriet.

"Oh.")

Once, I told Emily what I had been wanting to say since my first sight of her. I said, "Your hair is so beautiful. Why don't you let it grow?"

She laughed, because she usually laughed at what I said, but at the same time she looked surprised, almost startled. I understood that what I had said was not improper but that she was totally unused to attentions of that sort from anyone, including herself. She didn't think about her hair. In a puzzled way, she said, "Perhaps I will."

Nor did Emily dress like a woman with much regard for herself. She wore practical, seersucker dresses and sensible, low shoes. Because her body had so little shape, no indentations (this must have been at least partly due to the back brace), I was surprised to notice that she had pretty, shapely legs. She wore little or no makeup on her sun- and wind-weathered face.

And what of Lawrence Farr, the North Carolina Presbyterian for whom Emily had left her people and her state? He was a small, precisely made man, with fine dark features (Harriet looked very like him). A lawyer, but widely read in literature, especially the English nineteenth century. He had a courtly manner, and sometimes a wicked tongue; melancholy eyes, and an odd, sudden, ratchety laugh. He looked ten years younger than Emily; the actual difference was less than two.

"Well," said Margot, settling into a Queen Anne chair — a new antique — on our porch one stifling hot July morning, "I heard some really interesting gossip about your friends."

Margot had met and admired Harriet, and Harriet liked her, too — Margot made Harriet laugh, and she praised Harriet's fine brown hair. But on some instinct (I am not sure whose) the parents had not met. Very likely, Emily, with her Southern social antennae, had somehow sensed that this meeting would be a mistake.

That morning, Harriet and I were going on a picnic in the woods to the steep rocky side of Laurel Hill, but I forced myself to listen, or half listen, to Margot's story.

"Well, it seems that some years ago Lawrence Farr fell absolutely madly in love with a beautiful young girl — in fact, the orphaned daughter of a friend of his. Terribly romantic. Of course, she loved him, too, but he felt so awful and guilty that they never did anything about it."

I did not like this story much; it made me obscurely uncomfortable, and I think that at some point both Margot and I wondered why she was telling it. Was she pointing out imperfections in my chosen other family? But I asked, in Harriet's indifferent voice, "He never kissed her?"

"Well, maybe. I don't know. But of course everyone in town knew all about it, including Emily Farr. And with her back! Poor woman," Margot added somewhat piously but with real feeling, too.

I forgot the story readily at the time. For one thing, there was something unreal about anyone as old as Lawrence Farr "falling in love." But looking back to Emily's face, Emily looking at Lawrence, I can see that pained watchfulness of a woman who has been hurt, and by a man who could always hurt her again.

In those days, what struck me most about the Farrs was their extreme courtesy to each other — something I had not seen before. Never a harsh word. (Of course, I did not know then about couples who cannot afford a single harsh word.)

Possibly because of the element of danger (very slight — the slope was gentle), the roof over the front porch was one of the places Harriet and I liked to sit on warm summer nights when I was invited to stay over. There was a country silence, invaded at intervals by summer country sounds — the strangled croak of tree frogs from down in the glen; the crazy baying of a distant hound. There, in the heavy scent of roses, on the scratchy shingles, Harriet and I talked about sex.

"A girl I know told me that if you do it a lot your hips get very wide."

"My cousin Duncan says it makes boys strong if they do it."

"It hurts women a lot — especially at first. But I knew this girl from Santa Barbara, and she said that out there they say Filipinos can do it without hurting."

"Colored people do it a lot more than whites."

"Of course, they have all those babies. But in Boston so do Catholics!"

We are seized with hysteria. We laugh and laugh, so that Emily hears and calls up to us, "Girls, why haven't you-all gone to bed?" But her voice is warm and amused — she likes having us laughing up there.

And Emily liked my enthusiasm for lemon cake. She teased me about the amounts of it I could eat, and she continued to keep me supplied. She was not herself much of a cook — their maid, a young black girl named Evelyn, did most of the cooking.

Once, but only once, I saw the genteel and opaque surface of that family shattered — saw those three people suddenly in violent opposition to each other, like shards of splintered glass. (But what I have forgotten is the cause — what brought about that terrible explosion?)

The four of us, as so often, were seated at lunch. Emily was at what seemed to be the head of the table. At her right hand was the small silver bell that summoned Evelyn to clear, or to bring a new course. Harriet and I across from each other, Lawrence across from Emily. (There was always a tentativeness about Lawrence's posture. He could have been an honored guest, or a spoiled and favorite child.) We were talking in an easy way. I have a vivid recollection only of words that began to career and gather momentum, to go out of control. Of voices raised. Then Harriet rushes from the room. Emily's face reddens dangerously, the corners of her mouth twitch downward, and Lawrence, in an exquisitely icy voice, begins to lecture me on the virtues of reading Trollope. I am supposed to help him pretend that nothing has happened, but I can hardly hear what he is saying. I am in shock.

That sudden unleashing of violence, that exposed depth of terrible emotions might have suggested to me that the Farrs were not quite as I had imagined them, not the impeccable family in my mind — but it did not. I was simply and terribly — and selfishly — upset, and hugely relieved when it all seemed to have passed over.

During that summer, the Ouija board spoke only gibberish to Margot, or it answered direct questions with repeated evasions:

"Will I ever see Johnny Kilgore again, in this life?"

"Yes no perhaps."

"Honey, that means you've got no further need of the board, not right now. You've got to think everything out with your own heart and instincts," Dolly said.

Margot seemed to take her advice. She resolutely put the board away, and she wrote to Johnny that she wanted a divorce.

I had begun to notice that these days, on these sultry August nights, Margot and Dolly were frequently joined on their small excursions by a man named Larry — a jolly, red-faced man who was in real estate and who reminded me considerably of my father.

I said as much to Margot, and was surprised at her furious reaction. "They could not be more different, they are altogether opposite. Larry is a Southern gentleman. You just don't pay any attention to anyone but those Farrs."

A word about Margot's quite understandable jealousy of the Farrs. Much later in my life, when I was unreasonably upset at the attachment of one of my own daughters to another family (unreasonable because her chosen group were all talented musicians, as she was), a wise friend told me that we all could use more than one set of parents — our relations with the original set are too intense, and need dissipating. But no one, certainly not silly Dolly, was around to comfort Margot with this wisdom.

The summer raced on. ("Not without dust and heat," Lawrence several times remarked, in his private ironic voice.) The roses wilted on the roof and on the banks next to the road. The creek dwindled, and beside it honeysuckle leaves lay limply on the vines. For weeks, there was no rain, and then, one afternoon, there came a dark torrential thunderstorm. Harriet and I sat on the side porch and watched its violent start — the black clouds seeming to rise from the horizon, the cracking, jagged streaks of lightning, the heavy, welcome rain. And, later, the clean smell of leaves and grass and damp earth.

Knowing that Margot would be frightened, I thought of calling her, and then remembered that she would not talk on the phone during storms. And that night she told me, "The phone rang and rang, but I didn't think it was you, somehow."

"No."

"I had the craziest idea that it was Johnny. Be just like him to pick the middle of a storm for a phone call."

"There might not have been a storm in New Orleans."

But it turned out that Margot was right.

The next day, when I rode up to the Farrs' on my bike, Emily was sitting out in the grass where I had first seen her. I went and squatted beside her there. I thought she looked old and sad, and partly to cheer her I said, "You grow the most beautiful flowers I've ever seen."

She sighed, instead of smiling as she usually did. She said, "I seem to have turned into a gardener. When I was a girl, I imagined that I would grow up to be a writer, a novelist, and that I would have at least four children. Instead, I grow flowers and write book reviews."

I was not interested in children. "You never wrote a novel?"

She smiled unhappily. "No. I think I was afraid that I wouldn't come up to Trollope. I married rather young, you know."

And at that moment Lawrence came out of the house, immaculate in white flannels.

He greeted me, and said to Emily, "My dear, I find that I have some rather late appointments, in Hillsboro. You won't wait dinner if I'm a trifle late?"

(Of course she would; she always did.)

"No. Have a good time," she said, and she gave him the anxious look that I had come to recognize as the way she looked at Lawrence.

Soon after that, a lot happened very fast. Margot wrote to Johnny (again) that she wanted a divorce, that she intended to marry Larry. (I wonder if this was ever true.) Johnny telephoned — not once but several times. He told her that she was crazy, that he had a great job with some shipbuilders near San Francisco — a defense contract. He would come to get us, and we would all move out there. Margot agreed. We would make a new life. (Of course, we never knew what happened to the girl.)

I was not as sad about leaving the Farrs and that house, that town, those woods as I was to be later, looking back. I was excited about San Francisco, and I vaguely imagined that someday I would come back and that we would all see each other again. Like parting lovers, Harriet and I promised to write each other every day.

And for quite a while we did write several times a week. I wrote about San Francisco — how beautiful it was: the hills and pastel houses, the sea. How I wished that she could see it. She wrote about school and friends. She described solitary bike rides to places we had been. She told me what she was reading.

In high school, our correspondence became more generalized. Responding perhaps to the adolescent mores of the early nineteen-forties, we wrote about boys and parties; we even competed in making ourselves sound "popular." The truth (my truth) was that I was sometimes popular, often not. I had, in fact, a stormy adolescence. And at that time I developed what was to be a long-lasting habit. As I reviewed a situation in which I had been ill-advised or impulsive, I would reënact the whole scene in my mind with Harriet in my own role — Harriet, cool and controlled, more intelligent, prettier: Even more than I wanted to see her again, I wanted to *be* Harriet.

Johnny and Margot fought a lot and stayed together, and gradually a sort of comradeship developed between them in our small house on Russian Hill.

I went to Stanford, where I halfheartedly studied history. Harriet was at Radcliffe, studying American literature, writing poetry.

We lost touch with each other.

Margot, however, kept up with her old friend Dolly, by means of Christmas cards and Easter notes, and Margot thus heard a remarkable piece of news about Emily Farr. Emily "up and left Lawrence without so much as a by-your-leave," said Dolly, and went to Washington, D. C., to work in the Folger Library. This news made me smile all day. I was so proud of Emily. And I imagined that Lawrence would amuse himself, that they would both be happier apart.

By accident, I married well — that is to say, a man whom I still like and enjoy. Four daughters came at uncalculated intervals, and each is remarkably unlike her sisters. I named one Harriet, although she seems to have my untidy character.

From time to time, over the years, I would see a poem by Harriet Farr, and I always thought it was marvellous, and I meant to write her. But I distrusted my reaction. I had been (I was) so deeply fond of Harriet (Emily, Lawrence, that house and land) and besides, what would I say — "I think your poem is marvellous"? (I have since learned that this is neither an inadequate nor an unwelcome thing to say to writers.) Of course, the true reason for not writing was that there was too much to say.

Dolly wrote to Margot that Lawrence was drinking "all over the place." He was not happier without Emily. Harriet, Dolly said, was travelling a lot. She married several times and had no children. Lawrence developed emphysema, and was in such bad shape that Emily quit her job and came back to take care of him — whether because of feelings of guilt or duty or possibly affection, I didn't know. He died, lingeringly and miserably, and Emily, too, died, a few years later — at least partly from exhaustion, I would imagine.

Then, at last, I did write Harriet, in care of the magazine in which I had last seen a poem of hers. I wrote a clumsy, gusty letter, much too long, about shared pasts, landscapes, the creek. All that. And as soon as I had mailed it I began mentally rewriting, seeking more elegant prose.

When for a long time I didn't hear from Harriet, I felt worse and worse, cumbersome, misplaced — as too often in life I had felt before. It did not occur to me that an infrequently staffed magazine could be at fault.

Months later, her letter came — from Rome, where she was then living. Alone, I gathered. She said that she was writing it at the moment of receiving mine. It was a long, emotional, and very moving letter, out of character for the Harriet that I remembered (or had invented).

She said, in part: "It was really strange, all that time when Lawrence was dying, and God! so long! and as though 'dying' were all that he was doing — Emily, too, although we didn't know that — all that time the picture that moved me most, in my mind, that moved me to tears, was not of Lawrence and Emily but of you and me. On our bikes at the top of the hill outside our house. Going somewhere. And I first thought that that picture simply symbolized something irretrievable, the lost and irrecoverable past, as Lawrence and Emily would be lost. And I'm sure that was partly it.

"But they were so extremely fond of you — in fact, you were a rare area of agreement. They missed you, and they talked about you for years. It's a wonder that I wasn't jealous, and I think I wasn't, only because I felt included in their affection for you. They liked me best with you.

"Another way to say this would be to say that we were all three a little less crazy and isolated with you around, and, God knows, happier."

An amazing letter, I thought. It was enough to make me take a long look at my whole life, and to find some new colors there.

A postscript: I showed Harriet's letter to my husband, and he said, "How odd. She sounds so much like you."

M. PABST BATTIN

Terminal Procedure

(FROM THE AMERICAN REVIEW)

MUCH IS NOT CLEAR about the way the dogs died. Events on the periphery of the deaths, like points on undulating, outward-moving circles, recede into liquid uncertainty. The origins of the event are obscure, and its effects dwindle onward into indeterminacy. Causality cannot be established, and responsibility becomes a meaningless conceit, of no concern and no question.

Yet at the center remains the event itself, and it is fully clear: the dogs died.

Phase 1

If we look, we can see the place where the dogs died: a small laboratory, assigned to an associate named Boaz, in a sprawling research institute. The place has not changed; it is the same simple, almost square room, hidden in an obscure wing of an old building far to one side of the institute's grounds. We see the usual furniture of science: two bulky wooden desks, an untidy bookcase, and a flimsy file cabinet cramped together on one wall; on the other side of the room, flanked by its recording and control apparatus, the soundproof experimental box. On the floor beside the box, centered on a stained and yellowed newspaper, is a small tin water dish.

The lab has not changed since the dogs died there, except that the stack of data tapes grows no higher, and a half cup of black coffee left in a mug marked Maia has dried into a thick brown crust. And there is a small stain, left by a few drops of blood-tinged fluid on the tile floor, which the janitor, if he has come at all, must have missed.

The lab has not changed. There is no one there now, but if we look back we can distinguish two figures: the researcher Boaz, and his assistant, a girl named Maia. They move, they talk, they look together at the clock, though that is all we see; the causes are obscure. We cannot tell, for instance, what brought Boaz to neuropsychological research: whether he was groomed, as the eldest, most promising son of a well-established family, in the finest schools for an eminent career in science; whether he was impelled to the study of mental phenomena by a scrupulously sublimated attraction to a particular professor; whether he chose psychology simply to spite his nervous mother; or whether his penchant for experimentation was born in the alley, nailing half-conscious rats to the boards of the tenement fence. Nor does it matter: he is here. We can watch him in his laboratory, though his past be indeterminate and his future uncertain: we see him not as the product of any painstaking development, nor as a process toward some ineffable goal, but simply as himself.

We see what Boaz does before the dogs die: we see him in his laboratory, shuffling through stacks of graphs, drawn meticulously on green-ruled paper, running his fingers down the index columns in the back of a thick black-bound book; we see him sprawling in a swivel chair, talking with his assistant, the girl Maia, or perhaps by telephone with his wife; he sprawls back, his hand hanging idly over the arm of the swivel chair. One of the dogs is sleeping beneath the chair; Boaz's hand finds the dog, and his fingers play beneath the rope lead around the dog's neck. The dog moves just enough so that Boaz's fingers can scratch all of its neck, no more.

There is only one window in the laboratory, and it is obscured at the top by an uneven venetian blind, at the bottom by an old and noisy air conditioner. They will turn the air conditioner on in the afternoon, Boaz and the girl Maia, even though it is not summer: it will grow hot in the small square room with the door closed, hot and heavy with the odors of the dogs. They will have to keep the door to the lab closed so that the office workers across the hall do not see, and so that the dogs do not break loose and escape down the long colorless corridors. And they will think too, that the throaty hum of the air conditioner will cover the noise of the dogs, so that the office workers across the hall do not hear.

But the office workers asked anyway, when Boaz and Maia came back afterward to the lab, what they had done to the dogs.

"We had to give them a little shot," said Boaz.

"Oh," said the office workers. Uncertainly, some of them smoothed thick hands across the flat planks of their girdles. "We thought something was wrong."

"Nothing is wrong. It was just a little shot," repeated Boaz.

"They don't seem to like it very much," said the worker whose office door is just to the right across the hall from the lab. The worker whose office is directly across the hall is ill; her door has remained closed for a month now, maybe more. "They made a lot of noise."

"It's not getting the shot they mind so much," counters Boaz, his hand involuntarily pulling at his chin. "It's what's in the shot. When the fluid is forced into the tissue, it creates pressure. . . ."

The office workers understand. Some of them remember from the inoculations they had to have when they went to Europe, or from the preoperative injections given them when they had their root canals or their hysterectomies. They are not sure just how they know, but each is certain of the prick-pain of the needle itself, then the slow hard swelling within the flesh . . . yes, they understand, the needle does not hurt so much as the fluid. That is why the dogs made so much noise.

The office workers nod, and turn back into their separate rooms.

Phase 2

There we have it, some of the scene the afternoon the dogs died. We saw the researcher, Boaz, as he parried the anxious questions of the women who work across the hall, but we missed the girl Maia, his assistant. Perhaps she had just stepped out, down the long corridor to the bathroom, to comb her straight black hair back out of her face — when she came to work that morning her hair was hanging loose, but by the time the dogs were dead she had bound it back, severely, with a thin rubber band — or perhaps when we looked she was hidden by the door of the soundproof experimental box. The box, after all, is very large, a double-walled cube of steel, insulated so well that even a dog, whose sense of hearing is much more acute than any man's, can hear nothing, nothing at all outside the box, nor can anyone outside hear even the loudest noise of a dog within. Maia might have easily been standing behind the box. Beside the box is the recording and control apparatus, a complex construction of knobs and dials and levers, displaying a small oscilloscope screen and twin reels of recording tape. She might have been watching from behind the apparatus, peering out between its irregular protrusions. Or perhaps she had stepped behind the box to put the rubber band in her hair, for she is always just a little shy of Boaz's gaze and is not eager to invite any intimacies. In any case, she was there the afternoon the dogs died.

Of course she was there: it was part of her job. She must have known; she must have been told when she was hired to be Boaz's assistant what would happen to the dogs. Surely the institute's personnel officer, a conscientious man exactingly aware of the protective regulations, had felt obliged to tell her that the job involved handling experimental animals on which terminal neurological studies were to be performed. Or maybe Boaz had told her.

"Sit down, Maia," Boaz may have said, a gruff edge exposed in his low voice. "I am going to tell you exactly what these experiments are about, so you won't have any questions and so you won't say I didn't tell you."

She sat, crossing her thin legs, in the swivel chair, and smiled just slightly at him.

"The man in Personnel said you were doing basic research in comparative conditioning. Using dogs. My job would be to take care of the dogs and run the conditioning experiments. That's all he said."

"Let me explain," Boaz begins, rather stiffly. "There has been a lot of neurological research done on how the brain codes things. And there's been a lot of research on how animals react and learn in particular situations, but that kind of behavioral research says nothing about what happens in the brain. Not many attempts have been made to correlate a specific behavioral event with a neural event."

"And that's what you're trying to do."

"Yes," said Boaz. "It's worth doing."

She tosses her head lightly. "Well, I'm glad of *that,*" she says, a little fliply.

He leans forward in the swivel chair. "You must understand that this research is significant," he warns, "and that it's important that we do it just this way."

She does not answer, and he begins again to explain. "What we're trying to find out is what patterns of electrical activity occur in the brain during certain types of conditioning or learning. So we have electrodes implanted in the dog's brain, and then we record the population of neural cells that fire while the dog is being conditioned."

Boaz must have watched her as he talked; he must have noticed how small a girl she is, small and slender, made smaller by the large swivel chair. Perhaps she was wearing her thin black hair free that beginning day, or perhaps it was knotted up with a long paisley scarf, but surely Boaz must have noticed her eyes: wide eyes rimmed in black mascara, eyes so wide she looked as if she might cry at any moment.

"Each dog spends an hour in the experimental box every third day, learning how to react to a given stimulus situation. It will take the dogs three or four months, maybe longer, to complete their conditioning, and then —" He hesitates, watching her wide eyes.

She looks at him, saying nothing.

"Stereotaxic implantation is very difficult," he says distantly, "because you never can be sure just where the electrodes are."

She sits silent, listening.

"An electrode is nothing but a piece of conductive wire, inserted directly into the brain through a tiny hole bored in the skull. The shaft end is cemented to a terminal for the monitoring equipment, called a pedestal, and the pedestal itself is affixed to the skull directly over the cortex region. The pedestal anchors the electrodes, and —"

"Do they hurt?" Maia interrupts.

"What?" he stops, a little annoyed.

"The electrodes. Do they hurt the dog?"

"There are no pain receptors in the brain," Boaz answers flatly. "Does it bother you?"

"No, I just wanted to know." She pulls a long strand of hair out of her face. "I just wanted to know, that's all. Go on with your story."

"This is not a story, Maia."

"I know," she answers quickly. "I'm sorry."

"The problem," he begins again, "is to determine just where the electrodes are. It's not easy to implant them precisely, and there's only one way to determine exactly where they are."

"What's that?"

"By direct inspection of the neural region." He talks more quickly, enunciating the syllables almost too clearly, as if to conceal in scientific jargon something he does not quite want her to understand.

She sits still, saying nothing.

"The procedure is terminal," he says at last.

"I knew that," she says flatly, and Boaz realizes that she is not going to cry, that her eyes are wide all the time.

"I am going to tell you how we are going to do the termination," he says, "just so you'll know."

Maia sits motionless. "All right."

"After the dog has completed its conditioning program, we give it a double or triple dose of anesthetic. Then we open the chest cavity while circulation is still functioning, and by inserting a tube directly into the heart, we can pump fluids up into the capillaries in the brain. We use a saline solution first to flush the blood out, and then a Formalin fixative. The Formalin prevents decomposition."

"Keeps it from spoiling," Maia translates, partly to herself and partly so that Boaz will know she understands.

"Then we remove the head, and put it in a preservative. Anytime after that we can remove and section the brain."

Maia sits quietly, as if forming questions. "Do you do all this?" she asks finally.

"No, no indeed," says Boaz, almost amused by her suggestion, "not when there are people around the institute who are really experienced at that sort of thing —"

"Who?"

"Some physiologists in the animal-surgery laboratory, over on the other side of the institute. It's all arranged."

"All we do is bring the dogs?"

"That's all."

She still sits quietly, though her fingers comb unevenly through her long thin hair, or twist the ends of the paisley scarf.

"Why are you telling me all this?" she asks, after a long time, her voice even and clear. "Not just so I'll know."

"Yes," he said, "so you'll know. So you won't ever have to say you didn't know what we were doing."

"I'm not a coward," she says slowly, deliberately.

"Good," says Boaz, his mouth achieving a smile.

She smiles easily back.

It is possible that sometime after the experiments were terminated and the dogs were dead Maia came back to the lab, perhaps still employed, to help Boaz write up the results of the experiments, or just to retrieve the little china pot she had used to brew coffee. Perhaps she came for no reason at all, just wandering in, opening the door by chance, to see the small square room again. Her eyes must have traveled over the walls, over the neat graphs Boaz had drawn of the dogs' performance in the box, graphs he had tacked to the walls, graphs with the dogs' names, Mustard, Monroe, Egg-yolk, Isabel, graphs with the dogs' names, Frenchfry, Faulkner, Yoghurt, Trotsky, Theresa, 23 dogs, 23 names, Hubert, Pablo, Pianissimo; her eyes must have wandered over the untidy book-case, the flimsy file cabinet holding old research proposals and reprints of other neuropsychological studies on dogs, mostly brown mongrel dogs, dogs with names, for it is customary in the biological sciences to name laboratory dogs, though cats and rats and mice are given only numbers, over the cabinet full of electronic scraps, bits of electrode wire and odd-numbered dials and snipped lengths of exposed film, over the old brown desks where she and Boaz had sat, talking or not talking while the dogs ran their trials in the experimental box. And when she came back, Maia may have stepped across the stained floor to the soundproof box, put a thin hand out to touch the metal sides of the huge box; she may have opened first the outer door, pressed the heavy handle down, and then the inner door, as heavy as the first, and perhaps she stepped inside the box, as she would have with a dog, any dog, with Mus-tard or Muffin or Petunia, to see one last time the stout canvas harness in which she would have strapped the dog, Pablo, maybe, or Theresa, the dangling wires ready to connect to the pedestal cemented to the center of the skull, and other wires to be taped to the dog's wrist to administer graduated levels of electric shock;

perhaps she would finger the slender bar to which the dog's foreleg would be tied so that when the dog lifted its leg in the response expected of it, the bar would move and record the leg lift on the dual spools of tape turning slowly at the top of the recording apparatus outside. Perhaps Maia, her eyes still rimmed in black and her hair falling free, would sit motionless in the soundproof silence of the box, or perhaps she simply turns away, steps down out of the empty box, and lets the door bang heavily shut behind her.

Or perhaps she did not come back.

Still later, much later, Maia shows someone a photograph, though the circumstances are so remote from the center that almost none of the details are clear. It may be in responding to the courtship of a new lover that Maia takes the small, square photograph, its corners bent, from her purse, as if by that one picture to explain herself; or perhaps she reminisces with her family, leafing through a dusty album of her single years. Perhaps she shows the photo to a colleague, laughing over cocktails at a convention of neuropsychologists, where Boaz will be honored for his work; or perhaps she sits alone, on the hard edge of a hospital bed, and shows the picture to herself. But the photograph itself, since it was taken much closer to the center, is quite clear; it is a snapshot, taken presumably by Boaz, of Maia on the lawn behind the lab, running in from the kennels with two of the dogs. The dogs strain ahead on their leads, their noses to the ground, but Maia is only allowing herself to be tugged, her head tossed back, her hair loose in the wind, her face laughing.

As she studies the photograph, Maia binds her black hair back with a rubber band. But she is too far from the center now, and we cannot see if there is any expression on her face.

Phase 3

Still, some things are already clear. It is certain, for instance, that both Boaz and the girl knew what they were doing. Boaz knows because he designed the experiments, or at the very least took them over from some other researcher; in any case he knows: exact determination of the location of the electrodes is essential to correct analysis of the experimental data. That is what he knows.

And Maia knows too, knows that the dogs she runs through the experiments will eventually be put to sleep, have fluids perfused through their brains, have their heads severed, soaked in preservative, and their brains removed. But Maia also knows that however protracted the surgeries, the dogs will feel none of it; their conscious end will be swift, sleepy, painless. She finds nothing wrong with the plan.

And the dogs? Do they know? No, they are just dogs; they do not know anything more complex than immediate attention or actual pain. They are just dogs, common mongrel dogs, their coats dull and their markings irregular. Their breath is sour from the standard kennel diet, and the electrode pedestals protrude like plastic cancers from their heads. But their tails beat against the sides of the wooden desks when Maia brings them in from the kennels, and one jumps up to lick her hand.

Ah, yes, the one that licks her hand is Mustard. He is just a little smaller than most of the dogs, but smarter, sharper, and his coat is an almost yellowish brown — which is why, of course, Maia named him Mustard. She has just brought him into the lab; they have run breathless together across the wide green lawn, and after his hour in the box, they will run back again, loping free across the green grass to the kennel. But now Maia has looped the rope lead through the handle of the file drawer. Mustard paces nervously, keeping as far from the experimental box as possible; the rope pulls the file drawer out, then back, then out again. Annoyed, Boaz drums on the surface of his desk.

Maia presses a button on the recording apparatus; she speaks into it, her voice small but clear: "Now running Mustard. Avoidance conditioning. Number of trials: 50. Prestimulus interval 2.0, poststimulus interval 5.0 seconds." As she speaks, she twists the numbered dials on the face of the control apparatus, setting it to sound the stimulus tone and record the dog's behavior. "Shock duration .5, shock intensity 2.25 milliamps . . ." Then it is ready, and she turns toward Mustard.

She loosens the rope lead from the file cabinet, and pulls the dog toward the box. He struggles back, but the rope lead tightens, like a choke, and he has no choice. Maia lifts him up onto the platform inside the box; he struggles, but she is stronger, and she straps the canvas harness around his body. He struggles still, but now he cannot escape. She ties his right foreleg to the movable leg-lift bar; he pulls on it a few times, as if he remembers what response is expected of him, and the bar makes a little clicking noise outside the box.

Then Maia reaches for a thin coil of wire hanging from the ceiling of the box; there is a flat patch at the end of it, a sensor to measure electromyogram potentials in the muscles, and with adhesive tape she fixes the patch to a shaved area on the side of Mustard's leg. Finally, she tapes two small silver disks, attached to the end of a red wire, to the wrist joint of Mustard's foreleg, just above the footpad and below the dewclaw. It is the terminal that will give him the shock. She tightens the stomach strap.

"Good doggie," she murmurs, and she rubs the underside of his neck, just for a moment, before she puts the head restraint on him. Finally, when the restraining collar is in place and his head is secured so that he cannot move it, she plugs the wire leads into the pedestal in his head.

She stands back, checking: Mustard is strapped firmly in position, unable to move anything except his right foreleg and his tail.

"Good doggie," she says to him again. He is the cleverest of all the dogs. "Do a good job, Mustard, and you'll be the first one through." She hesitates, suddenly aware of her own words, and looks at Boaz. He looks back, as if to call her bluff.

She takes it. "Do a good job, Mustard," she promises, "and you'll be the first one to get your head cut off."

Boaz smiles into his papers, and Maia closes the inner door of the box. Mustard barks, but the sound is very flat, muffled by the door; after Maia has closed the outer door, she can hear nothing more. She looks in through the triple-thick window; Mustard, she can see, is still barking, but the straps are holding well. She turns to the control panel; it is all set, and she flips a single switch. The two tape reels at the top of the recording apparatus begin to turn, in unison, and the conditioned stimulus, a single clear tone, sounds. Then there is a clicking noise, the noise made by the bar as Mustard lifts his leg, and finally the rapid clatter of the printer, recording the data of the trial.

Then it is quiet. If we look in through the window, we will see Mustard standing motionless, his tail still and his eyes fixed dully on the wall of the box in front of him. The tone sounds again; this time he fails to lift his leg, and after precisely five seconds the shock is presented. He jerks his leg rapidly, since that is the only movement he can make, and then holds his leg up, unaware that the terminal is taped to his wrist and cannot be avoided. He struggles in the harness, but the canvas is tough, unyielding, and he cannot free himself. He drools heavily.

It is difficult to tell just how much more time elapsed before the end came, though surely Maia could figure it out from the dogs' records, from the protocol sheets or the data tapes or even the learning graphs taped to the walls. And it is hard to say just when they realized that the end had come: that some of the dogs had learned as much as the design of the experiment required, and that the experimental data on them was complete.

It may have been Boaz, sitting engrossed over long columns of figures recorded by the apparatus, who sees first that three of the dogs are finished. Or it may have been Maia, watching each of her dogs through the thick window of the box, who sees the end: Mustard, frail Theresa, and Pablo. Or perhaps they did not realize it at all; perhaps Boaz simply telephoned the animal surgery laboratory.

He swivels outward from the telephone. "Tomorrow," he says to Maia, "be here early. We'll do them first thing in the morning."

She is puzzled. "I thought you said the physiologists were going to do it."

"They will," Boaz assures her, "all except for the anesthetic. We do that, here."

"How can we do it here? Wouldn't it be easier to do it there, then we wouldn't have to carry them . . .?"

"No. Besides, that's the way we made the arrangements. We anesthetize the dogs here, and once they're out, put them in my car, drive over to the main building, and load them on a gurney at the shipping door. That way the physiology people won't have live dogs running around their sterile laboratory, and they won't have to waste a lot of time waiting for the anesthetic to take effect. It doesn't always work, you know."

"Why not?"

"You calculate the dosage according to the weight and condition of the dog. But you have to be sure not to give it too much, otherwise you'll kill it outright, so sometimes you end up giving it not quite enough."

"What happens then?"

Boaz smiles, tolerant of her question. "You just start all over

again, that's all. That's another reason we're doing it here, in case
we have to do any of the dogs twice."

Maia thinks for a moment. "I suppose it's nicer for the dogs to let
them go to sleep in a place that's familiar, not with a lot of strange
people standing around," she muses.

"I suppose so," says Boaz, without interest.

"Do I have to go with you to the surgery?"

He looks at her, and his gaze is suddenly kind. "No, Maia, you
don't, not if you don't want to. I'll just need you here in the morning to help with the anesthetic."

She does not respond.

"Just hold some paws, that's all. It's just one little shot."

"All right," she says finally.

You see that they were quite calm about it beforehand, Boaz and
the girl. After all, there was nothing unusual about the situation;
their procedures were perfectly routine in experimental psychology, and they were executing these procedures as well as they
could.

But afterward, after they had anesthetized the dogs and loaded
them into the back seat of the car, Boaz saw that his hands were
shaking.

Maia too may have seen his hands tremble, but she said nothing;
she sat beside Boaz, immobile and silent. He knew the roads of the
institute grounds well, and he had tried the great curve down the
hill at every speed from 30 to 80, but his hands shook too much, he
did not really see the road, he missed the turn. The car spun back
off the road and slid, tilted, into a ditch; as it stopped Boaz heard a
sliding noise, and then the heavy thump of a body falling to the
floor. He turned quickly; it was Theresa, her leg bent back double
beneath her body. He lurched over the seat to help her, but then he
realized it made no difference. And he realized that Maia had not
moved during the accident, not at all; she sat unmoving, her eyes
glassy and hollow.

At the same moment Boaz saw a car pull off the road behind
them, to help. He leapt out, strangely alarmed, as the car pulled up
toward them. No, he thought, go away, and he ran toward the
approaching car, "I'm all right," he yelled, his voice cracking, to the
would-be samaritan, "I'm all right," his arms flailing, "go away, I'm
all right," flailing, beating off the samaritan, and then, just for a

moment, he saw himself: a madman, protecting an almost catatonic girl and three half-dead dogs.

Then he caught himself. "Thank you," he said to the driver, a bewildered student. "I think I can get it out of the ditch myself."

The record does not show how they got to the surgery lab: whether the student towed them out of the ditch, or whether Boaz scraped together branches from the woods and forced them into the mud under the wheels for traction; it is not important whether they took the usual route or another, back behind the pond; it is not clear how long Maia's state lasted, or when Boaz's hands stopped shaking, but the chief physiologist, a severe woman, said later that they were both present for the perfusion and termination procedure. She did say, when asked, that they were both rather quiet during the procedure, that she had expected Boaz, in particular, to be more interested in the findings — though of course they would all be recorded in detail and he would be able to study them later. She had attributed their silence to the natural squeamishness of those not accustomed to observing surgery, she said, and she quite understood. Besides, she guessed that Maia had grown fond of the dogs.

Phase 4

It seems, then that something must have upset them. Boaz was calm beforehand, calm and completely scientific, but afterward he ran his car off the road — a road he knew well — in broad daylight, without speeding.

And Maia? Wasn't she calm? She had been calm with the dogs that morning: she had done nothing unusual. She went out to the kennels, out behind the building, just as usual, quietly stepping through the early grass; the dogs heard her coming, and all 23 began to bark. She opened the wooden gate to the fence surrounding the kennels; the dogs leapt up, each in its own wire pen, to greet her. She began her duties at once, going from one pen to the next with the long-handled shovel, scooping out the little piles of excrement; then she hosed out the floors of the cages. Last she filled the dishes with water and with food, though she did not fill the dishes in the cages of Mustard, or Theresa, or Pablo. She walked the three back, each tugging in a different direction on its leash, across the lawn to the laboratory.

But Boaz was not ready. He had not been able to find the right kind of needle for the syringe. He had left a note for Maia, saying he'd gone over to the surgery lab to get a new needle. He might not be back until after lunch: she should wait.

So Maia was alone in the laboratory, with Mustard and Theresa and Pablo. She opened the drawer of her desk, and took out her sandwich. Ham sandwich, made from ham she had baked for someone, her boyfriend perhaps, or her father, or just herself. She folded out the square of waxed paper, opened the sandwich. Three slices of ham. Three heavy slices of thick, old ham, mottled with sinews that seemed to shimmer green. She wasn't hungry. Maybe the ham was spoiled; maybe the dark yellow mayonnaise was spoiled too. It would make her sick; no, she would not eat the ham, she would give it to the dogs; it would make them sick too, it would make no difference. She wasn't hungry, not at all.

She was suddenly aware of a dog's head in her lap. It was Pablo, nuzzling in between her knees, attracted by the sandwich. He was not an affectionate dog, but now he nuzzled up, his long flat head in her lap, his limp ears falling loosely over her knees. His smell surrounded her, the thick, sour smell of unclean animal. His eyes stared at hers, as if to plead for the sandwich, and her own eyes fixed on the pedestal in his forehead. Her hand moved up through the dirty fur to stroke the back of his head, but her eyes remained on the pedestal: a plastic cap as big around as a dime, protruding almost an inch from his skull. The skin had been slit lengthwise along his head, but it had not healed well; it had remained spread apart, like half-open lips, for about four inches. She could see the sloping base of the pedestal, where it was cemented to the exposed skull; she could see edges of light-red flesh beneath the retracted skin. Pablo had had several infections, and even now a thin yellow pus oozed out from beneath the open skin, collecting in dirty black clots at the edges of the wound. She had tried to keep the opening as clear as she could, and from habit she reminded herself to put on more of the antibiotic ointment, but she realized there was no point in it: within an hour, or at the most two, she would see Pablo's head sitting not in her lap but in a stainless steel basin.

Almost reluctant to touch them, she lifts the slices of ham from her sandwich. She gives one to Pablo, the second to Theresa; Mustard jumps up and snatches his from the desk. She steadies herself against its edge, unwilling now to scold.

She considers the bread of her sandwich, not the ham, just the bread; she wonders if she ought to eat the bread, if she ought to eat something, so that she won't feel weak later on, later on at the surgery lab, when they are cutting into the chests of the dogs, when they are inserting the thin tube into the heart, still beating, into the heart still beating, so that it can pump the fluids into the brain, beating, beating slowly . . . she must eat the bread, she decides, so that she won't feel weak, so that . . .

Then she hears Boaz returning. Her stomach knots sharply, and she is glad she has eaten nothing. She gives the bread, too, to the dogs.

Boaz brings the new needle. He unwraps it, fits it carefully onto the syringe, and from his pocket takes a small rubber-sealed bottle: Nembutal. He has already calculated the dosage; it will be three times the normal amount. He picks the bottle up in one hand, inverts it, and pierces the needle upward through the rubber seal; he draws the plunger out, watching the syringe fill slowly with the clear fluid. When it is full, he withdraws the needle from the bottle, and puts them both on his desk.

"Ready, Maia?"

She looks at him; his face is firm, impassive, strange, and she wonders if she has ever seen him before. She wonders suddenly where he came from, if he was a rich child or a tramp, whether he could conjugate a Latin verb or skin a rat, whether he ever thought of death, and if he ever had a dog.

"Ready, Maia?"

She starts. "Yes, I'm ready," she answers, and together they begin. It is not easy; Maia must hold the dog, while Boaz injects the anesthetic. They do Theresa first, as if to practice on the weakest of the dogs, then Pablo and finally Mustard, and by the time they have finished with Mustard, the drug is already beginning to affect Theresa.

Afterward, there is nothing to do but watch; Maia pours two mugs of coffee from the little china pot, and she and Boaz sit in the chairs at their desks, swiveled outward. The dogs move free around the room, though always at a distance from the experimental box, as if they do not understand why they are not tied to the file drawer or harnessed up inside the box. Theresa is already distinctly slower, as if burdened by some weight; she lies for a moment

on a pile of rags in the corner, and Mustard sniffs uncertainly
beneath her tail. She struggles up again, but her hind legs drag; she
pulls herself forward a little, then turns and drags her legs back
toward the pile of rags. She does not reach it. Maia sees her fall;
unsure, she stands, aware that Boaz is watching her, and pulls
Theresa gently over to the rags, so that her head and forepaws rest
upon them. Maia looks into the dog's eyes, as if perhaps expecting
gratitude, but they are growing glassy. Theresa pulls for breath in
short small shallow gasps, but as the drug overcomes her, her
breaths grow long and wholly automatic. She does not move again.

"One down," observes Boaz, his voice flat.

"And two to go," answers Maia, her tone equally artificial. They
do not look at each other.

Mustard and Pablo, heavier, healthier dogs, take longer to succumb; they stumble and dance, they slide down and fight back up,
their legs slipping out from under them as they stagger sideways;
they slurp water from the tin dish until they can no longer control
their tongues, they whimper and thrash their tails and roll their
heads, and in the end they too go down in motionless forms, their
eyes glazed, their tongues hanging thick and still, their respiration
so slow and even that it can barely be detected.

"Let's go," says Boaz finally, and Maia says nothing. She moves
mechanically to open the door of the lab, and Boaz carries first
Theresa, then Pablo, and then Mustard past the open doors of the
office workers, outside to his car.

Phase 5

Wait. We saw, fairly clearly, what happened just beforehand: how
Boaz misplaced the syringe and Maia fed her sandwich to the dogs,
and we observed them together afterward, sitting silent in the lab,
watching the dogs struggle down. But we have missed something
between; we must have flinched, as one does in the face of the sun,
letting our eyes close and turn away. If we are to see clearly, we
must look back one last time.

We have seen them moving toward the center, Boaz and the girl,
Maia. They have glanced at the clock, though they have not read it;
it is early afternoon now, and on the other side of the campus

people are waiting for them. Maia has loosened Theresa's leash from the drawer of the file cabinet; she has stood for a moment, uncertainly, in the middle of the room; now she sits, slowly, on the floor beside the dog. The filled syringe lies waiting on the desk; Boaz takes it and squats on the floor beside them. He puts the syringe on the floor, aware there is no need for sterile precautions, and looks just once at Maia. Together, they turn Theresa over so that she is lying on her back, Maia at her head, Boaz at her tail. Maia places her own thin leg over the dog's chest, to pin her down, and grasps her forelegs tightly, just above the elbow joint. Boaz shifts, uneasily, from sqautting to kneeling, and picks the syringe up from the floor.

Watch: we see Boaz at the center now, as he kneels over Theresa, positioning the syringe over her belly. We see his back first, clearly; a small red mole on the back of his neck, then the fine creases of adult skin; we see the cross-woven threads of his cotton work shirt. We circle around his collar, and we count three anomalous whiskers, not more than an eighth of an inch long, that his razor has missed this morning. We see each separate stub of hair, closely shaven, we note the tiny pocks and minute lines of his skin, drawn in tight lines toward his mouth. We see small round beads of sweat across his upper lip, and others on his temples. If we are still, we sense the anxious pace of his heartbeat and feel the tight constriction of his breath. And then we see what he sees: the uneven edges of his fingernails, the coarse and calloused surfaces of his fingers, gripping the slim barrel of the syringe. He sees the slant-sharpened needle, poised. The drug must be injected directly into the peritoneum, he knows, and he chooses a place to the side of Theresa's abdomen and low, just above her back leg, where there are no internal organs that might be punctured. The hair on Theresa's belly is thin, and the needle rests directly on her pale skin. Her body moves a little as she struggles, but we see Maia holding her, her thin bare leg clamped across Theresa's chest, her small hands tight around the forelegs.

And we see Maia, too, we see the separate strands of her black hair, falling now into her face, into the face of the dog beneath her. It is thin hair, without curl or gloss. We see her round black-rimmed eyes, but they do not answer: they watch the floor, the cold tile floor, see the inexact angles of the edges of the tiles and the small fissures cracking between them; they study the scuffs and scratches, the streaks of dull gray color, the tiny pits and dents, the uneven seepages of mastic, the yellowed film of ancient wax. She looks once at Boaz and finds him watching her, his eyes wide, staring; her eyes recoil.

Her eyes recoil from his, and then she feels the dog jerk, she can almost feel the needle through the dog, the needle plunging into the soft belly, and she clamps her hands more tightly as the dog's throat arches back, yelping. She is afraid she will lose her grip, that the dog will struggle free and bite her, and she looks once more at Boaz, sees him fight to keep the dog's hind legs clamped between his knees, sees the syringe flap in the thrashing stomach, sees that it is still full, sees Boaz break, sweating heavily now, sees him break, lose hold of the syringe. It flaps wildly, and he grabs it, pulls it out.

The syringe is still full; the fluid is not in Theresa.

Boaz draws back, wipes his arm across his forehead. "I thought it would be easier," he says, unsure, afraid. His eyes plead.

But her eyes do not answer his. "Don't you know how to do this?" she asks, deliberately, almost coldly.

"Inject the anesthetic directly into the peritoneum," he recites mechanically, like a rote-learning schoolboy. "Be sure to avoid the internal organs. . . ."

"Haven't you done this before?" she asks, her voice kinder now.

"No."

"Then could we get somebody else to do it for us, somebody who knows how?" Maia's thin voice is hopeful.

Boaz turns on her. "I thought you weren't a coward."

She does not answer. She sees him pick the syringe up off the floor, the tip of its needle tinged with blood, and as she tightens her grip on the dog, she sees him hold it high, then thrust it hard into the abdomen. The dog howls again, hard and long. Maia's arms are suddenly weak, and she sees Boaz, his face sweating, his eyes narrow. She sees his hand move around on the syringe so that his thumb is on the plunger and he can press the fluid out of the syringe; she sees it, sees Boaz's thumb press the plunger, slowly, sees the Nembutal move slowly out of the syringe, through the needle, into Theresa, and she looks down into Theresa's face, sees the brown eyes wide and motionless with terror, feels the huge howl of pain welling up from her throat, from her bowels, a constant, motionless howl, frozen, frozen in pain, and Maia sees for-

ever down in Theresa's open mouth, sees the brown-stained teeth
and the flattened tongue, sees all the soft pale-red glistening surfaces of her throat, motionless in an eternity of pain.

No, much is not clear about the way the dogs died. Events on the
periphery of the deaths, like points on outward-flowing circles, recede into ambiguity. The origins of the fact are obscure, its effects
indeterminate. Causality has not been traced, at least not securely:
dare we impute responsibility? Responsibility? To Boaz, or the thin
girl Maia? No, responsibility is an empty conceit: of no concern, no
consequence.

At the center there is only the fact: the dogs died.

MAE SEIDMAN BRISKIN

The Boy Who Was Astrid's Mother

(FROM ASCENT)

IN A BOX headed "advertisement" on page four of the paper, was a small photograph of a smiling young girl. Below it was the message, "Astrid, I miss you. Please contact me. Mother." It was summer's end, 1972, a time of runaway children.

Pictures of Astrid's mother formed in my mind, changing as I imagined varied chains of events leading to Astrid's departure. Through all the many changes, however, the face of Astrid's mother was always a face of sorrow. Repeatedly, the next few days, I thought about her. Then I forgot.

Weeks later I stopped at the high school, in search of a student looking for yard-work.

"Just today a boy asked about jobs," a counselor answered, "but I told him no one comes to us for boys — they go to the State Employment."

"This boy — is he reliable?"

"I couldn't say — he's new, a transfer from the city. But if you want to meet him, check our library. He's always there."

"Always?"

"Always after school."

"And his name?"

"Clark something. Some easy last name, like Smith or Jones. You can't miss him — he's the boy with the beautiful hair."

And that, to be sure, was true.

Clark was at the table nearest the door, so that as I entered he was directly before me, his back toward me, his elbows on the table and both his fists supporting his large head. His hair was glossy as cornsilk and trimmed neatly in line with his earlobes. It was hair the color of autumn — yellows and golds and burnt orange, all intermingled. I walked softly to the far side of the table and stood opposite him silently until he looked up at me.

The poor boy's genes had tricked him. They had given him a face that could bring only disappointment to anyone who saw first his hair and then his face. His skin was pasty and pimpled, his nose blunt, his grey-blue eyes small and close-set. Even then, in that confusing moment, I knew, too late, that I had let him notice my response.

He followed me outside, and we arranged for him to work the coming Saturday. Throughout the conversation he never smiled, and as we said good-bye, I thought of Astrid's mother. It was weeks before I thought of it again and understood why.

He came to work at one o'clock. At three I rolled apart the large glass doors that separate our family room from patio and asked him in for milk and cookies. He hesitated, and as he did his eyes went slowly to the book-filled shelves. He seemed to have forgotten what I'd said. Then he looked at me, thanked me and refused.

At five he stopped, his eyes anxious as I surveyed the yard. "It's very nice, Clark," I said. "Would you like to come every Saturday?" He said he would.

At one the following week, I found him working. It was clear he needed no continuing supervision. He had remembered my priorities, and he worked steadily and with great concentration. Again at three I offered and again he refused refreshments.

"Clark, if you were working at a store you'd get a coffee break by now, and this work is harder."

"I get enough to eat," he said, continuing to work, but he said it with the smallest trace of emphasis on the word "eat," so that the inevitable next question was, "What don't you get enough of?" I hesitated a few moments, then asked it.

Without interrupting the motion of the rake, he said, "I need a place to stay."

I was immediately sorry I had ever gotten involved with him, and because of that, and because I had no intention of taking him in, I find it hard to explain why I asked him any more.

"Where do you stay now?"

"I have a room on Bryant."

"With your parents?"

"No."

"With relatives?"

"No." Then, suddenly, he stopped raking and fixed me in place with his eyes. "I pay for it," he said firmly — though with no hostility. "I work every night, six nights, busing tables. I make good money, and I always pay my way."

He stood there waiting for my answer, holding me with his solemn eyes until discomfort forced me to withdraw. "I have something on the stove," I said.

At five I said, "No one's ever done the yard so well in four hours, so I'm paying you eight dollars instead of six. But as for the other thing . . ." He was concentrating on my words, squinting from the effort, so that his eyes grew even smaller, and creases formed between them. He knew what I was going to say.

"Could I come back next Saturday anyway?" he asked.

"Well, yes, I guess so," I said. "That was what I agreed to." As he turned to go, however, I added, "If for some reason I wanted to contact you, like if I didn't need you — just one Saturday, I mean — how could I reach you?"

The creases reappeared between his eyes. I was sure he knew I planned to send a note, with polite excuses, ending his employment. He shrugged, slowly. It was an utterly despairing gesture. "Phone the school," he said. "They send messages to classrooms."

I felt ashamed to my very core.

All week I wished he would never come again — that he would in fact not even notify me, but rather just stand me up and relieve me of the responsibility I had begun to feel for him. I told no one of his request, however, fearing my husband would himself take the initiative in sending the necessary message. That would have added to my incipient guilt, and unnecessarily, I felt, since I had a vague hope of resolving the boy's problem without becoming personally involved. When my husband, therefore, looking at the well-groomed yard, remarked that that new boy was a winner, and my son scowled at the insult to himself implied in any praise of any other young man, I merely said, "He doesn't work like a boy at all."

The boy came again, as I had feared he would. I was waiting where we kept the garden tools. "I want to talk to you." I said gently.

"I really want to work here," he said, "and I won't talk about living here, never again."

Finally I asked, "How old are you?"

"Seventeen."

"Why did you leave home?"

"My mother's new husband says he wanted a woman, but not her kid besides. My father has a different wife too. He says I'm old enough to shift for myself, why do I bother him?"

"But why did you come all the way down here?"

"Because I heard your school is better. It's harder, but maybe here I'll get to be an educated man."

That last phrase was too much for me. I suggested he get started and perhaps we'd talk more later. I went indoors to try to analyze the ache in my heart. It was that phrase — "an educated man." I was convinced he was utterly sincere.

I myself had two sons, and I was sure I had never heard either one of them use those three words together. The phrase was archaic, or perhaps the very aspiration was archaic and alien to the world of the seventeen-year-olds I knew. Clark himself seemed archaic, and again I remembered and this time understood why he had reminded me of Astrid's mother. His eyes were slow and sorrowing, as hers must be. He seemed old, buffeted, experienced — not of Astrid's generation, but of her mother's and therefore of mine. He spoke in tones that set up resonances deep inside of me from feelings I had forgotten were there. To aspire to be an educated man — I could understand that.

I poured a glass of milk, cut a slap of pound cake and took them to the table on the patio. Clark, preparing to mow the grass, was rolling the mower across the patio.

"Sit down," I said familiarly, and somewhat sharply, too, "and drink that milk."

He stopped, and still holding the mower, he stared at me a long time — long enough for me to realize that the sharpness with which I'd spoken we normally reserve for those we love.

He let go of the mower, and his eyes still on mine, he lowered himself slowly into the chair. His nostrils widened, and I was afraid tears would come next, but they didn't. Instead, he turned to the table, obediently picked up the glass and brought it to his lips. His hand began to tremble, however, and a rivulet of milk tumbled over the rim of the glass and ran down its side and over his fingers. He kept his eyes on the glass, and his jaw hardened, perhaps from the effort to control his trembling hand, and still he couldn't bring himself to drink.

"Oh, Clark, I'm sorry," I said. "I wanted you to be young." His eyes went to my face, and it was obvious he didn't understand. "Don't drink it," I said. "I mean do, if you want it, but not if you don't. Or leave it for later — whatever you want."

I turned my back on him and hurried indoors, and all afternoon I avoided looking out. I had succeeded in upsetting us both, but we never referred to the incident again.

At five I went out, and again I paid him eight dollars.

"The room you have on Bryant — what's wrong with it?"

"You read books," he said. "My landlady's an old woman. She doesn't know much, and when I need help with my homework, there's no one there to help me."

A wave of relief engulfed me. "Is that all? You can get help from the teachers. Tell me whom you have." He was shaking his head. "Please tell me," I said.

He told me, counting off the names on his fingers.

"Oh, Clark, they're the dogs of each department. When you transferred in, they put you in the smallest classes with these marginal teachers."

The creases were again between his eyes as he labored to understand these complexities.

"I'll go to school for you on Monday," I said. "I'll get your program changed." He began shaking his head again. "I do that for my own son. I'll get you Mr. Cohen for math and Mrs. Turner for English. They'll help you after school — they do that — and you won't need a new home."

"No," he said. "I don't belong down here. The principal will think I'm a bother and make me leave."

"We don't need the principal. A counselor can do it."

"No," he said. "I don't want to be a bother to anybody." He paused. "But can I still come back here on Saturdays?"

"Of course," I said.

He mounted his bike, and, chin down, he rode away in the cold autumn dusk, under the elms, which were the colors of his hair. I remembered the food on the patio table and got a sponge from the kitchen. Both cake and milk were still on the table, but the exterior of the glass had been wiped dry, and the table was clean. He had set the cake plate over the glass and the inverted saucer over the cake, surely so that both would still be usable and so that he would not have been a bother.

On Monday I phoned the counselor and asked that she send him a message to come to my house on Wednesday, if possible, to do a small job. He didn't appear till Saturday.

Without greeting, he said, "I can never come weekdays. I have to do my homework and then go straight to work."

"When do you have dinner?" I asked.

"I eat at the restaurant. It's part of my pay."

"Do you need this yard-work money for your rent?"

"No," he said. "This is for a luxury."

I smiled. "Would you tell me what luxury?"

Simply, without malice, but without apology either, he said, "No."

That night I asked my husband if Clark might live with us. He was incredulous. "Tom's room is vacant anyway," I said, "and the boy would pay for it.

"Who wants his money?" he answered. "A boy you don't even know? Aside from having a stranger intruding on our privacy, we have problems enough with our own kids — who wants *him*?"

"No one," I said. "That's the point." I told him everything I knew of Clark and pointed out we'd seldom even see him, since he worked six evenings out of seven. He heard me out entirely and then refused.

I dropped the subject. I knew the conflict he was facing. I was sure that what this dull archaic boy had done to me he must be doing also to my husband. I knew my husband was comparing — bitterly — Clark, seventeen and striving toward his manhood, with our older son, twenty-one, shacked up in Berkeley and making candles. Or with the younger one, eighteen, lazy and sullen. We said nothing further on the subject all week.

The following Saturday my husband returned from his office at two. It was something he rarely did, and then only after phoning me first.

"Are you ill?" I asked.

"No," he answered. "I wanted to see that boy."

He didn't, however, go out to meet him. He sat in a chair in the bedroom, brooding, and watching Clark from the window. It made me uneasy. I was afraid Clark would notice and reproach us, if not in words, through his old sad eyes. I went out, rearranged some chairs and looked toward the bedroom. With the strong sunlight outdoors and the dimness within, my husband was not visible.

In a little while, he joined me in the kitchen. "If he came to live with us," he said irritably, "in addition to everything else, Dave would be jealous."

"I'd bend over backward to minimize that," I said. "And besides, Dave's never at home till dinner-time. That girl he spends the afternoons . . ." My husband waved his hand, cutting me off with his gesture. He didn't want to be reminded of any of his son's friends, and least of all that girl.

He went to the doors of the family room and watched for a while from there, where Clark could see him. Suddenly he rolled apart the doors and shouted, "Clark! Get in here!"

I was appalled by my husband's tone, but I could see Clark clearly, and I know he wasn't cowed. If anything, he stood taller in preparation. With no haste at all, he set the pruning shears atop the table, slapped the legs of his jeans and stamped his shoes free of dirt. Deliberately he met my husband's eyes and passed before him into the room. Inside, he looked around the room while the doors were being shut.

"Sit down," my husband ordered. The boy did. "Do you still want to live here?"

"Yes," he answered — instantly, as though he had known all along that the offer was coming.

"Then give it to me from the top. If I said yes, what could we expect of you?"

"At my room now I pay the lady twelve dol . . ."

"No," he interrupted. "I'm not talking about money. I mean when would you be here, and what would you do?"

"I get up at seven. I go to school till three. Then I'd come back here to do my homework, and I'd need some help from your wife. I go to work at five, and I get off at say ten, ten-thirty, and I go right home. Saturday morning I do my laundry, and I clean my room. Saturday afternoon I work here in the yard. Saturday night in the restaurant. Sunday is my day off, and I go out."

"Do you have a girl-friend?" my husband asked. For the first time, Clark balked. "Well, do you?" my husband demanded.

The boy's face became belligerent. "Yes. I sure as hell do."

"Good," my husband answered. "You're entitled to it."

Suddenly Clark smiled. In all the previous weeks, despite all the gentleness I had shown him, he had never smiled. My husband was at him once again: "You spend two hours a day on homework. How the hell can you improve at school on two lousy hours a day?"

Clark laughed, suddenly, loudly, and as though a child would know the answer to that one. "I do two hours in the after*noons*. I finish at night, or Saturday morning or Sunday night. Hell, you don't think I could stay in *this* school on two hours."

"You had *better* finish," my husband said. He rose, told Clark he was leaving the terms of the contract entirely to me and left for his office.

I, in turn, left those terms to Clark. He knew to the dollar, it seemed, the rates for rooms in different parts of town for homes of different quality and vintage. He told me what our older son's now-vacant room was worth and made it clear that he was giving more for it than he was paying for his room on Bryant. It was, however, worth it, he said, because he had "improved" himself.

That phrase, and that quarter-hour, marked the turning point in my perception of him. A new alert look had come into his eyes, and I perceived he could be strong and self-assertive.

He would not, for instance, be persuaded to let me cook any breakfast for him or agree even to cook his own. Kitchen privileges, he informed me, cost extra, and he couldn't afford that yet. He did, however, expect a little space in my refrigerator, rationalizing it was something I should yield, considering the rent that he was offering. With the food he kept there, he assured me, he'd assemble by himself his lunch and breakfast, avoiding contact with the stove.

He next negotiated for the washer and the dryer, which he'd use on Saturday mornings while he cleaned his room. Prices at the laundromat were thirty cents a load, and this was what he meant to pay. When I said I couldn't take his money for a thing like that, he told me, patiently, retailers take a hundred per cent mark-up, so laundromat costs must be fifteen cents a load, and he would compromise at fifteen cents, take it or leave it. I took it.

As he rose to resume his work in the yard, he said, "Can I move in tomorrow?"

"Why, yes, I suppose so," I said. He turned toward the family room, and I added, "Clark wait. My husband spoke roughly to you before. Were you offended?"

He stared at me a few moments. "He didn't speak roughly," he said. Then he added, "But if he did, when I get you to help me, I'll have my reward."

He went back to his work, and I sat a long time wondering what had ever made me do this. I had become fearful. This was not the boy I had meant to help. I didn't know now whether I liked him or not, and I surely didn't know whether he had suddenly changed, or whether I had merely not known him before. I, however, had put us on this path, and I could see no way of turning back.

Clark arrived at ten Sunday morning, his meager possessions on the handlebars of his bike. He went directly to his room, closed the door and spent the morning there alone. I was by now extremely apprehensive, but my husband was utterly calm, and I could not admit my second thoughts. At one, Clark showered, spent a long time in the bathroom, dressed and left. I opened the door to his room and looked in. It was in perfect order. He had left his towel to dry on the desk chair, but he had protected the chair with a sheet of plastic. I checked the bathroom. He had scrubbed the tub and washstand and had polished the mirror, too. Clark came in late that evening and said only "Good-night."

With each passing day I had reason to feel increasingly assured. Mornings, Clark was out of the kitchen before I was in it and before my son was even stirring. He cleaned the bathroom, kept his room in order and left no crumb or drop on the kitchen counter. On Friday morning, therefore, as he left for school, I said, "Clark, I want you to know you're no trouble at all. You keep my house clean, and the bathroom, in fact, cleaner than the way you find it."

"It's your house," he answered. He didn't smile, or shrug, or do anything but, simply, in those few words, define our relationship.

Clark had established that relationship on an exchange of goods and services of equivalent value as he himself assessed their value. As we worked on his homework during that first week, I wondered if he was capable of relationships based on anything else. He gave no clues. I wondered also why he was accepting my time without repayment, because this was the flaw in the arrangement he had otherwise so carefully thought out.

My question was answered on Saturday. When I returned from the beauty salon at noon, Clark was washing windows. "We didn't talk about windows," I said, wondering if he'd know I was teasing. "Do you charge the same for windows as for yard work?"

"No charge for windows," he said evenly. "I don't pay you for tutoring."

In the weeks that followed, Clark took on all the heavy janitorial work that I had normally done and much that I had always left undone. He simply would not accept my gift.

And yet this did not detract from the pleasure I took in teaching him, and pleasure it was as soon as we had passed the second day.

Clark was so poorly educated that he could not write three consecutive words without spelling errors or a paragraph with other than simple sentences. I felt inhibited at first, fearing I would hurt him with my criticism. By the third day, however, I was convinced that I would not. He seemed to see his ignorance — though he never used that word — as no reflection on himself, but only as a temporary state to overcome — and quickly at that, now that I was helping him. He believed without reservation in my superior knowledge, and though his progress was slower than he deserved, he cherished it.

At the end of the first week, I asked if he felt he had made significant gains. "I always do," he answered. "I been learning all my life. I can do janitorial work, yard-work, and bus and wait tables. But this!" he added emphatically, tapping his notebook, "this especially, this is knowledge, this I have to learn, because knowledge is power."

I almost laughed. "And when you have this power," I said, "what will you do with it?"

"Protect myself."

I thought more about that in the following days. It was, after all, not the most depressing thing he might have said, but it raised again the question I had asked myself a hundred times: "What had they done to this child?"

He had told me nothing of his past. Our tutoring sessions were strictly that. No confidences were exchanged, and on the one occasion when I took a cue from his assignment to ask about his family, he said straight out we had no time to waste on that.

Once, however, in a moment of rare intimacy, when in the flush of pleasure at grasping a grammatical concept, he confided that he kept a diary. Since he had such difficulty expressing himself in writing, the diary, he said, had in the past been more "like lists."

"For instance," he said, "I had codes. Like TINU meant 'things I now understand,' T,I,N,U, see? And when I know something I didn't know before, I used to write it in the TINU list."

"You mean like now, when you learned something in grammar?"

"No, when I learn something about. . . ." He was groping, I thought, for a word to categorize his discoveries.

"About what?" I asked. "People? Relationships? Consequences?"

Suddenly his expression changed, as though he knew he had revealed too much. "Forget it," he said.

"Clark, diaries are good, but they're no substitute for people. Do you have any friends?"

"Yes," he said. "I once told you I have a girl. But please, I'll have to go to work soon."

That was as much as he'd say. One thing, however, greatly encouraged me. Clark had begun to imitate my husband. He seldom saw him, and when he did, it was for the briefest of periods, but he was alert to his every word and movement. The expression "in my judgment" was one that my husband picked up in the days of John F. Kennedy, and by the second contact with my husband, Clark had adopted it too. My husband also had a minor facial tic, and before long Clark had affected his tic. It was an imperfect rendition, an exaggeration, and out of keeping entirely with the rest of Clark's movements, but it gave my husband something his own sons withheld from him.

I tried to take advantage of it. I proposed to my husband that he take a little time on week-ends for helping Clark with math. This was a subject in which I felt inadequate, and it was the one, therefore, in which he wasn't getting help. Though I didn't say it, I also hoped that through this, the boy would form another friendship. My husband thought a moment and refused. He felt, he said, that we were even then too much involved with Clark.

The following day I went to school to speak with Mr. Cohen. I told him only that a student, Clark Smith, was living with us, that he needed tutoring in math but wouldn't ask a teacher's help. I asked if he would coach me as he did his poorer students, so that I, in turn, could do the same for Clark. In a gesture far more typical of Clark than of myself, I offered him a fee.

"Don't be silly," he said. "Come during lunch when the kids come. Like I have time for them, I'll have time for you."

During lunch hours the next two weeks, he worked with me.

Between his help and my stubbornness, I learned to use the text, and I became of use to Clark even with math.

Then, one afternoon, Mr. Cohen phoned. "I'm calling to confess. I was proctoring, and I met Clark Smith. I said, 'So *you're* the boy.' He got terribly pale. He said, 'Who told you about me?' and all I could think of was the truth."

"And?"

"He insisted I tell him how may hours we'd put in on it — exactly how many. And how were you paying me? And since you hadn't, he said he would pay me."

"I'm sorry. I should have told you more about him. He's a good, hard-working boy, but this principle of his he carries to the point where it's almost sick."

"Sick's too strong a word, I think," he answered. "He takes himself a bit too seriously, but on the whole his attitude's a welcome change. For me, that is. What I said was, 'Look, Clark, don't make a federal case out of it. I gave Mrs. Kaye a few hours of my time, because I wanted to help her out. She gave a few hours of *her* time, because she wanted to help *you* out. Now, whenever the time is appropriate, and you find someone who needs a few hours of *your* time, you'll help *him* out, and that's the way it all gets paid back.' "

"What did he say?"

"Nothing. He just stood there trying to understand. In any case, now you know what happened."

And if I hadn't known from Mr. Cohen's call precisely what had happened, I'd still have known that it was something critical. Clark came in at the usual time, looking, at best, weary. He avoided my eyes and said, "I can't do homework today."

"There are days like that," I said.

He went to his room and soon came out and asked, "Would you mind if I lay down on the lawn?"

"Of course not," I said.

He went out the family room doors, crossed the patio, and lowered himself, face down, to the grass. He had most likely never touched that grass except to mow, edge, rake, feed and water. Now he was caressing it. I turned away.

I hadn't planned on anything but working with him during these hours, and now, without him, I sat at the kitchen table probing my memory for a clue to the consequences of his encounter with Mr. Cohen. In all these weeks, however, he had given me no sign of friendship or trust and no hint of what I could expect now that he knew I'd done a deed contrary to his wishes.

Shortly before five, I tiptoed out. He was immobile on the grass, his face turned away from the house. I walked around him and saw he was asleep, his face dusty and streaked with tears.

I kneeled down and called his name softly. He started and sat bolt upright, staring at me.

"You fell asleep," I said. "It's almost five."

He needed a few moments to collect his thoughts, then he rose without a word, went in, and soon left.

The following day Clark said, "I worked on homework by myself last night. And I don't want to do any now. There are things I have to think about. Yesterday I fell asleep and didn't."

He put his books in his room and went out to the patio, this time without asking permission. He removed the plastic cover from the chaise and sank down into the cushions. As he did, he glanced toward me. At five, he left.

That night something woke me, and I went to check. The house was quiet, but from Clark's room light was visible below the door. I assumed some noise from there had wakened me.

I returned to bed, but now I couldn't sleep. All kinds of possibilities offered themselves to me. In the most maudlin of these, a disillusioned boy was weeping over my betrayal of him. At that moment, I heard a faint scraping sound from Clark's room, and I was sure he'd hanged himself. I ran the hall's length, but then, instead of plunging in, I stopped, and softly tapped. I heard the scrape again, and then Clark's footsteps, and when he'd edged the door ajar, I grabbed the jamb, close to fainting.

"What's the matter?" he whispered. "You drunk?"

"No, I stood up too fast after lying down — that's all. I saw your light and thought maybe you were sick."

I returned again to bed, aware of my foolishness, calmed down and fell asleep. In the morning I overslept and didn't see him. I went, however, to investigate one of the more sinister possibilities that had occurred to me — that he'd defaced the room or something in it. I was relieved to find he hadn't, and I tried to rationalize my suspicions.

That day, when Clark returned from school, he came directly to the kitchen table with his books, as he had always done before the incident with Mr. Cohen.

"I did an extra-credit assignment," he said. "For English." He handed me a thick sheaf of paper. "It's a short story. I wrote it last night."

I riffled through the pages. "In one night?" I asked.

"Yes."

It was a story titled "Duncan and Zazu."

"A humorous one," I said. He shook his head. "The name Zazu," I explained. "The only Zazu I ever heard of was an old-time movie comedienne."

"I know all about her."

"That name suggests a funny story."

Helplessly he said, "But her name was really Zazu."

A flicker of intuition came alive in me. "Was his name really Duncan?"

"No," he said. "But it was a handsome name."

"And was he himself handsome?"

"When he was little."

"And Zazu — was she pretty?"

"Why don't you just read the story?" he said.

And so I did. From the first paragraph I knew it was indeed Clark's writing, and his most recent work at that. Errors were numerous, but the compound sentences were a subtlety of which he'd been incapable several weeks earlier. For me the manuscript was easier to read than it would have been for someone unfamiliar with his quirks of style, and I read quickly through the pages.

It was a story of two children, a brother and sister. The boy was older by three years, though their ages were never specified. Nor was it clear how long a time span the story covered. Only the incidents were clear — the whole succession of incidents. They held my attention so completely that I forgot about all the technical criteria for which I had previously read Clark's papers.

The incidents involved Zazu primarily. Duncan appeared when he was a party to an incident, or when a reference to him helped in describing her. Thus it was clarified that Duncan knew how to clean toilets, and Zazu did not. Duncan learned fast and remembered. Zazu did not. Duncan was wary of danger, and Zazu was not. Nor did Duncan feel the need to protect Zazu. It appeared he did not. He merely observed what befell Zazu, and he learned.

And what, precisely, befell Zazu is more than I can repeat. It is enough that I remember. It is enough that Ivan Karamazov memorialized for all time children victimized by their parents. I will let his words suffice for Zazu as well and say only that the neglect, the deprivation, the humiliation, the abuse and the torture of Zazu ended when the child was flung from a window. And still — despite what I have said — I must repeat Clark's own final words: "till one day Zazu was thrown to death from the fourth floor window. And she is buried."

I covered my eyes and wept. Clark said nothing, and I will surely never know what he did during those minutes when I finally understood what they had done to him.

When I had stopped crying, he said, "Now please help me fix the mistakes."

I took the pencil and started to read. Only then did I see a problem I never had had before.

"I'll show you the punctuation and spelling," I said, my voice still quavering, "but that's all."

"But why?" he said. "What about all the other mistakes?"

What I had to explain was that I could touch nothing else. I had to tell him that the brokenness of the language was like the brokenness of the lives it described; that he, Clark, writing for once without inhibition, had poured out in one night a volume of words that on any other subject would have taken him a week to write, words that were inevitable and unalterable.

"Did you ever read *Huckleberry Finn*?" I asked.

He shook his head. I went to the bookshelves and took down our copy.

"Here," I said. "This is for you to keep. I mean that — I will not let you refuse me. Read it, and you'll see what I mean. The way these people spoke, that's the way Mark Twain wrote it down, even though he knew the right words to say and how to pronounce and spell them. Now, in your story, all of it is written that way. What I mean is, there are mistakes, yes, but they're appropriate to the circumstances."

He was shaking his head. "I'll get points taken off," he said. "She expects good English, you know that."

I was suddenly tired, and I hadn't made him understand.

"Why can't you do what you always do?" he pleaded. "You always help me with the words. You give me better words."

"I could no more change your words," I said, "than I could disturb that child's grave."

He drew back in his chair, staring at me. After a long time, he lowered his eyes. Something in his gesture told me that although in one way he didn't understand me at all, in another way he did. He finally did.

"We have to risk this," I said. "We have to trust that this teacher will see that these words are right for this situation. And if she can't, the worst that can happen is you won't get extra credit."

He was nodding. "All right," he said. We rushed through the manuscript, fixing up the spelling and the punctuation. It was almost five when we finished.

As he slipped the papers into his binder, I said, "How many people know the story of Duncan and Zazu?"

"Only you," he said. A moment later he added, "Why did you cry?"

It was the first personal question Clark had ever asked me. He waited for me to answer, and when I didn't he asked, "Should Duncan have helped Zazu more?"

"How old was Duncan when Zazu died?" I asked.

"Seven," he said.

"No," I answered. "You couldn't expect him to. Seven is a little child, and powerless." He sighed. "In your last sentence," I added, "write it in. Where it says 'and she is buried' write in 'since the time when Duncan was seven.' "

"But see?" he said, "they weren't really so bad to Duncan. He was just always afraid that they *would* be."

"Still," I said, "he was a little boy. You can't ask such strength of a little boy. Please, make sure you write that in. 'And she is buried since the time that Duncan was seven.' "

"All right," he said. "I'll write it in when I copy it."

Those were the only words I gave him.

He was about to leave the kitchen when, thinking better of it, he sat down again and, gripping his loose-leaf binder in both hands, he lowered his eyes and said, "I want to tell you something else."

I sat waiting for what Clark was finding very hard to say. Suddenly, in the garage, there was a click, a rumble and a shattering slam of the heavy door, and then the sound of boots with metal taps on heel and toe stamping across the concrete floor. Before I could assimilate the knowledge that my son was home an hour earlier than I'd expected, there he stood before us, tall and bent and white with rage, glaring at Clark, shrieking, "You mother-fuckin' son-of-a-bitch! You two've been balling!"

Clark was silent. Then I heard him answer quietly, "Yes."

I can't remember when I rose, or when Clark did, or how I came to be standing at one end of the room while the boys were at the other, circling the kitchen table. I remember only the awareness, as I watched them, that my own son had accused me of this and that the boy whom I had befriended had confirmed his accusation. I heard a click, and all my attention became focused on the boys. They had stopped moving. Clark was a little to my left, his back toward me. My son was about five feet from him, facing him, and in my son's hand was a switchblade knife. I was rooted to the spot where I stood, and as had happened before in dreams, I tried to scream but couldn't.

"Every goddam Sunday you've been screwing her," my son shouted.

Clark answered evenly. "With me she came. With you she never did."

Only then did I understand they had not been referring to me.

"She only made you think she came," my son shouted. "She liked the things you buy her."

Clark was still calm. "I pay my way, but I know she came."

My son was making menacing movements with the knife, and this time I shrieked, "Put it down," but neither boy so much as glanced in my direction. They only became silent and resumed their circling, my son's knife poised for an attack.

Clark's eyes flicked to the rack of knives on the counter that divides the kitchen in two, and I knew that when he had circled around to where he could reach it, he would equalize the odds. The decision became mine. Clark lunged the last segment of the circle, and, his eyes still on my son, tapped the vertical rack onto the counter, spilling the knives to within his reach. I moved forward, and in one long sweep of my arm across the counter I sent the five knives flying in all directions, striking wall, window, refrigerator and then clattering, rattling, echoing, trembling in all parts of the room. Our eyes followed the sounds. Both boys then saw my face as though for the first time and in some alien world. Their two faces wore the same bewildered expression, and the major difference between them was the knife in my son's hand. In an uncanny instant, both sets of eyes moved to my arm, and both their faces took on an expression of something akin to but less than horror. I had felt no pain, and felt none even then, but when I looked down I saw my blood running in a broad, insistent stream from the crook of my arm toward my fingers.

Slowly, my son lowered his knife and then averted his eyes. He walked deliberately and silently past Clark through the part of the kitchen in which I stood and on toward his room. Clark, however, fixed his eyes on mine for a long time, in a message of reproach, and finally he too passed through the kitchen, but turned back, took his books from the table and proceeded to his room. A few minutes later he left the house, and I assumed he had gone to work.

It was clear that the girl with whom Clark had been spending his Sundays was the girl with whom my son had been spending his weekdays. She was also, I felt sure, the luxury for which Clark had been doing our yard-work. I wondered momentarily whether Clark had known all along that she was my son's girl, and if so, what that meant, but I never asked, and I still don't know.

That evening, when my husband returned home, we tried to face our problems. It was plain he was feeling equal parts of guilt for our son's deed and of bitterness for Clark's intrusion upon our lives. Unable to determine what to do about our son, he solved instead the question: what to do with Clark? Clark must go. We must appease him, pay him somehow to his satisfaction — since he knew a price for everything — and then be rid of him. No sooner had he said all this than he was saying, "My God, what am I saying?"

We started again. I had told him only the events beginning with our son's arrival. I now went back two hours earlier and told him Clark's story and our subsequent conversation. I said I knew we couldn't keep the boys together now, but to pay Clark off — even to suggest it — would be to cheapen every moment I had offered and deny that I had ever given something genuine.

My husband listened. He tried a bit to argue, but halfheartedly, and because he was uncertain about the kind of boy Clark was, there was nothing left for him to do but worry.

That night I waited up for Clark, alone, for though my husband offered to be with me, it was easier alone. Clark arrived at midnight.

"I got a little worried about you," I said.

"Why?"

"This late, and you out on a bicycle. Someone might have hurt you."

He shrugged. "Good-night," he said.

"Wait," I said. "Sit down. Please."

He remained standing. "I have to move out, don't I?" he asked.

"Clark, what he did today was terrible, I know that. But I couldn't let you get a knife too. And now I can't keep you both here. He's my son, and even though I'm ashamed of what he did, I can't throw him out. I have to do something about him, and I don't even know what, but I can't throw him out."

I had seldom been able to read Clark's eyes, and surely not then.

"Good-night," he said and turned his back on me.

I couldn't sleep. I kept hearing sounds from Clark's room. Perhaps there had always been sounds, but that night I was hearing them.

Some time near dawn I fell asleep. I woke to the alarm, unnerved. Unsteadily I walked and stopped and listened at Clark's door. I tapped and waited. Finally I turned the knob.

He was gone. The linens were folded neatly and stacked on the chair. The furniture was freshly polished, the scent strong in the room. In the dresser drawers and closet there was nothing left to show that Clark had ever lived there.

I phoned the school at nine and was informed he'd not attended class at eight o'clock. At noon I learned he hadn't been at school all morning. Why was I inquiring? they asked. Who was I? Fearfully, I scanned the evening papers.

News, however, came the following day, in the mail, addressed to me, in Clark's handwriting. There were Xeroxed copies of two pages from a diary, and neither of them was a list.

Today S. told Dave she has been balling with me. Dave came home and pulled a switch-blade on me, so I tried to grab a kitchen knife, but Mrs. Kaye stopped me. She knocked them on the floor and cut her arm, but then I didn't need the knife, because Dave got shook and put down his.

Now she says I have to move. I saw it coming.

                                                        3:20 A.M.

It would really not be good to stay here any more. I see that now, even though at first I didn't want to have to go. Dave is not like me, and she

*could not tell him to go away and shift for himself. He would not be
able.*

Besides, she does not send away sons. It is a thing I now understand.

*4:00 P.M. (I always write
at night, but today I want to Xerox it, and mail it first, before I go to
work.)*

I have my room on Bryant back. It was empty all this time.

*I missed the morning, but I went to school in the afternoon, and during
lunch I talked to Mr. Cohen. I told him Dave and I were fighting, so I
moved.*

*I asked if he would help me out with math, and he said he would be
glad to. He also said, "Continue getting help in other subjects too," and I
should ask the teachers. I will.*

*I also think I better not go back to do the yardwork. Besides, I don't
need all that extra money now.*

*Some day though, when I think the time is right, but not too long from
now, I'll write a letter to her. I'll tell about the things I'm doing, and then,
if she still wants, and she invites me to their house to come and see them,
I will be glad to go.*

NANCY CHAIKIN

Beautiful, Helpless Animals

(FROM THE COLORADO QUARTERLY)

"So, YOU FLUSHED ME OUT!" As indeed she had. Coming around the turn in the corridor as he bent to lock the door of his office, she had surprised him only moments before she might have lost him for the single day she meant to spend in this town.

"You might put it that way." And now, entering the office, after eight years, scarcely touching him, she was almost overwhelmed by the profusion of detail she had forgotten: the sharp spice of his after-shave lotion, unchanged in all this time; the dry smell of his dusty corners and his old untended wing-backed chair; a sense of spring, defiant of his inaccessibility, rising from the campus below; and, overlaying all, strongest of all, the acrid odor of the ink with which, in tight, forbidding script, he made his comments upon a hopeful page — his purposeful triumph over all the sensual diversions he could not control.

No student might ever forget, despite the distractions of spring, of spice, of dust risen from hidden corners, the ultimately orderly nature of one's business in this room. For Marius Fleming might fail to subdue the sources of such distraction; but he would never spare from the black tyranny of his pen the unfortunate author of a dangling participle, a misplaced antecedent, a rashly exuberant phrase. Though his huge form had stormed like a rampant colossus through all her dreams of this college town, he was a creature (still!) of inflexible order, incomparable control.

And how well his precision still served him! Even Anne, so long free of that unerring sense of language, so far beyond the limits of his marksmanship, grew curiously clumsy under the obliquely degrading suggestion that she had flushed him out. "You make me sound like a bird dog." She smiled, but her voice, like her body, was uneasy. "Was it so gauche of me to have come looking for you?"

Even passing only briefly through Avalon, hoping to find tolerable the inevitable changes in the campus, she had thought it the logical thing to do. His brief, cryptic notes at Christmas-time each year had seemed somehow binding in their constancy. And neither the intervening time, nor her children, nor her sense of separation from that old college self had ever dispelled his image. It had seemed to her, looking backward to the inordinate satisfactions of having met his standards, the ambiguous intimacy of their tutorial debates, to the wistful pleasure he had taken from her Honors and her degree — his great, grey eyes appraising almost sadly the effect of her four-cornered hat and long black gown — that he might welcome her now.

"Oh, my dear Annie," he shook a head only slightly more bald than she remembered, only lately peppered to match his tweeds, "you must know that I am pleased you came! Besides, I love bird dogs. Have you forgotten my compassion for beautiful, helpless animals?" He threw back his head in a laugh which showed all the yellowed surfaces of his large teeth, and she knew that the joke was still, somehow, on her.

Still, she leaned forward to meet his amusement.

"Human beings are more vulnerable than animals," she offered softly, "and recover more slowly. From wounds as well as from love." So she, too, she thought with some pleasure, might take aim, fire, and hope at last to reach her mark. "But I suppose if it is helpless dogs that evoke your kindness, then I should be grateful to be counted among them." She smacked her lips, surprised by her own agility. But beneath the energizing glow of this slight success, there seared the deeper, the more familiar pain: the acid self-diminishment of having (still! still!) to keep up with him, to be his sharpest, his brightest, his most nearly equal student.

"Oh, damn!" and she pushed back angrily upon the swivel chair, only to find her feet flying up before her, her arms flapping, reaching at balance like a pair of crippled wings. "Oh, Marius," now her feet found the floor again and she maneuvered toward him on the dangerous wheels, "you always make such a fool of me." She was on the verge of tears. "Even now, after eight years, and nothing but those miserable Christmas crumbs. Where have you been?"

For it was true that in certain corners of her married life, his shadow had hovered like some old, unbidden dream, his inaccessibility as much a challenge as ever it had been when, shrunken small beneath his watchful eye, his towering form, his large hand upon her shoulder, she had written her Humanities papers to gain him glory. Only his brief, faintly contemptuous inquiries had reached across the miles. Had she worked any more with Donne, he had prodded once, and she had responded with shameless joy to the cold, familiar angularity of his script beneath the classic wreath, the embossed phrases of the season. Where had he been?

"Trapped in this dreary office." He did not seem to resent the implication of her claim upon him, but rolled his eyes heavenward in mock despair. "But waiting, nevertheless, for someone like you!" Oh, but there were things about him she had forgotten, despite the work of her thrifty squirrel-memory, with its industrious hoarding of detail: the way his mockery disfigured him, his tongue thrust so far against a fleshy cheek that even his jaw seemed swollen; his grey eyes, behind their magnifying lenses, seeming almost to pop from the dark hollows beneath his brows; his large hand suddenly limp, dangling from its long wrist like something broken, disavowed, severed from the rest of him. Still, it had been these isolated glimpses of ugliness, clumsiness, that had always fascinated her, made her heart turn over and warm with pity for his unsuspected weakness. For, merely to point out how foolish his mockery made him would, she knew, disarm him with frightening efficiency; he had no idea that he ever seemed pitiable and vulnerable to the most primitive thrust. And it had always been, she remembered now, like carrying a loathsome weapon: all his harsh attacks upon her work, upon her lack of conviction and disordered mind, had never quite succeeded in pushing her to the point at which she might meet his mockery with ridicule, might dare to brandish so cruel a club before him. And now, determined to disturb his unfortunate posture, she placed a cigarette between her lips and leaned across the desk for his light.

So, he had been waiting for someone like her! Apparently, then, she said, he had grown tired of waiting and would have left, finally, without seeing her, had she not happened by just as he was preparing to lock up.

"Apparently." He smiled, leaned back, leaving her to apprehend: that there was some question about her claim, though he would not openly contest it. Perhaps, in spite of her brief note of the week before, he had never meant to see her at all. Perhaps he meant to give no more than he had once given, eight years before: the uncommitted message on the flyleaf of his graduation present ("To Anne, my finest student, my fondest hope!"), the cold ceremony of his farewell at the railroad station, the offhand answers to her letters, neither encouraging nor rebuffing her tentative plans to return as a fellow.

Then it was she who must be bold and dare to risk now, as she would never have dared then, the ultimate definition, the casting of a cold, analytical eye upon the nature of their affinity, the possible knowledge that there had not, nor ever might have been, more between them than this clinical challenge, this cautious, orderly playing of an old, unprofitable game. She had always feared that ultimately he would destroy her doubtful dream; but even that destruction — some final act of violence, some devastating assault — would be sweet, would be tolerable, when measured against the heavy silences, aborted gestures, and glances that had locked like limbs: that terrible, tangible ambiguity which, even in memory, had shaken, excited, confused, and finally exhausted her. How stubbornly he had avoided the disorganizing effort of commitment! How much she had suspected, how little confirmed!

And there, there! still beat the heart of it, behind her own incorrigible, remembering heart: that the pauses between them had been more powerful than any contact, any accident of proximity, or of affection. And all that they had narrowly avoided being to one another mocked and challenged, like an echo behind it, the equivocal comfort of all that they had been. It was not for love, she knew suddenly, that people took their own lives, but for the knowledge of having just missed it.

Now, therefore, at however great a risk, she would hurl herself suicidally against that question, against his strength, his order, his confusion of ugliness and beauty, against his old, sweet promise of destruction. It was his nature to deny and hers to be denied; in this curious complement, this negative transparency of love, lay the delicate balance between them. If, like someone returned to make a compulsive check of the premises, she dared to disturb that balance and violate his sense of order, might she not at least dispel forever the prospect of what might have been? Might she not, once and for all, exorcise the spirit that had stalked like a giant down all the corridors of memory, loomed over all she could salvage from that cherished academic past and, even now, claimed all credit for her alliances with Keats, with Mozart, Milton, Pope, with all the voices of order in a disordered world?

"You needn't muster your defenses," he added now; "I'm glad you came. What's more, I intend to prove it by taking you out to dinner." "Sweets to the sweet," he had mocked at that long-ago railroad station, proffering a bar of candy for her long trip eastward. Cold comfort, against the pain she most dreaded — of abandonment, of separation, of loss. (Foolishly, she had kept the candy bar so long that when, at home, she took it from its wrapper it had looked diseased.) He had retained a posture of gallantry, a deep bow from the waist, until she could no longer see him from the window of the train.

And now, again, cold comfort! For on this occasion he would, she knew, devote himself to proving what she most feared: that nothing, alas, might ever have changed between them. Even his food preferences, she imagined, would have remained the same! Over how many cuts of rare roast beef had he outlined critical principle and calculated, while the meat grew cold, the number of students who would miss, as she was perpetually in danger of doing, the subtle rewards of disciplined response? And all this while she, like the meat, grew cold, went dry and colorless under the overwhelming effort of knowing that she must not, dare not reach across the untouched plate to him nor make known (her palm against the broad back of his hand, where it rested on the table), the longing which stirred and quivered with a life of its own beneath her pale, impassive surface.

Now, across the desk from him, she felt herself in danger of doing the unforgivable, seduced as she was by the stubborn, inexplicable concentration of all his strength in that heavy, hair-fringed wrist, the broad thick-boned hand that jutted from beneath blue cuffs and links of cat's-eye and gold. How she might alarm him! Grasp the wrist, turn the hand, and press submission like a prayer. But he had offered only dinner, and even now, almost surely aware of the danger in which she found herself, he offered nothing more. "Dinner would be lovely," was all she said at last.

And, "Your husband?" he wondered offhandedly, only incidentally — an afterthought.

"Meeting me in Chicago. Tomorrow." Equally offhand, she offered neither a smile nor a photograph to suggest that there was, indeed, some more pressing reality, that she was, after all, the wife, the mother she seemed to have left behind. "But perhaps you have some other commitment! I wouldn't want to steal your evening."

"You have stolen nothing. My commitment, now, is to my stomach and to you."

"In that order." But she went with a smile through the door he had, with a deep bow (his old, mocking gallantry), opened wide for her.

Nothing, apparently, had gone awry in the dronelike consistency of his attention to physical detail, the demands of his metabolism still being met, like the demands of his work, in a kind of joyless routine. There could be no doubt that the comb went through his thinning hair, the cat's-eye links through his starched cuffs at precisely the same moment each morning. He wore consistency like a sacred medal, a talisman with which he might ward off the harbingers of havoc that chattered like crows at every door. And her arrival, however flattering, however brief, could only be flattered by his forbearance, the generosity of his willingness to alter the unalterable. It gave her a sense of power!

Was there possibly some vengeance in her self-assurance? Walking to the Mermaid's Tavern beside him, reduced by his long strides to breathless silence, she wondered whether she only meant, after all, to pay him back for the long, mortifying silences of their past, for the dinners at which she had been tongue-tied, shrunken, bludgeoned by the morality of his control? There had been no question, then, or at their tutorial conferences, as to how one conducted one's self: emotion, like poor grammar, was something covered by rules and corrected by them; one simply did not yield to one's feelings any more than to the falsely warming candlelight on the tavern table, and life's longings were as easily dispatched to order as the components of a compound sentence. Perhaps, now, she thought, she meant to rip wildly through the old rules, leaving participles and bright ribbons of hope, unfinished phrases and unanswered questions, dangling, floating, flying dangerously between them!

Still, she only followed like an obedient child as he chose their table in a corner, and, still the child, she sat passively as he ordered their drinks, and observed her own quiet reflection in the leaded, diamond-paned window at her left. As he studied the menu, then, she studied him: inscrutable, she thought with amusement! For the

large, grey eyes certainly slanted sharply at their outer corners, and
the slight, closed smile below them just missed being cynical, just
missed being sweet.

"So you are finally returned, Anne Detweiler Ames!" Even in
welcome, his smile seemed slightly crooked, his glance ambiguous,
his head tilted to study her, to reserve decision upon her. And it
seemed to her that behind the smile, behind his heavy-limbed
solidity, in the opposite chair, something strained, some small but
powerful muscle worked desperately to hold that posture. Had she,
then, jarred him awake to the disturbance of that old safe balance?
Was it a shifting for which he had ever, even mildly hoped? Oh,
never! never! she reminded herself; only *order! moderation!* Down
that straight, double-tracked path he had seemed to glide like a
great machine, leaving, behind him, only a clean path, trium-
phantly clear of excess — that great dark chasm toward which all
human rituals seemed finally doomed to yield. Surely he would not
now be lured by the subtle danger of giving when she, herself,
might give anything he wished. Still, that muscle worked mightily
behind his composure; she wondered whether it had been only
youth which prevented her from seeing before with what effort he
sometimes preserved his limits.

"Anne Detweiler Ames," he chanted her name like a litany, giving it and her a kind of unexpected grace. "Anne Detweiler Ames,
what have you become?"

Should she have tried to answer him, pretended that that was
really what he wished to know? She shrugged, laughed, raised her
glass, preferring the oblivion of pleasant incoherence, the prospect
of some future courage, to the sobering challenge of trying to
explain herself. Her fugitive eye revisited the dark portraits on the
panelled walls: Shakespeare, Jonson, Essex, the stiff-necked Elizabeth in her great pleated collar; none had turned from his silent
study of the past, nor aged, nor faded in the semi-darkness of that
gothic corridor. But her eye lit with sudden horror upon the unmistakable outlines, just beyond the archway, of a jukebox, brazen,
flashy, which had replaced the tavern's old player-piano. Its colors
shone obscenely through the archway and above it, on the wall, a
quaintly lettered sign announced that twenty-five cents would coax
from its clever insides a treasury of authentic ballads. "Really,
now," her eyes sought refuge in the receding amber depths of her
glass, "isn't that awful, that machine? How dared they?"

Marius shrugged tolerantly, but his wry smile implied that, like her, he deplored this final, definitive assault. "Everything changes," he said dryly, "as you have surely discovered. At least it's authentic Elizabethan music, somewhat bawdied up." He signaled for a second pair of drinks. "Apparently only you, my dear, have resisted time."

"And you." Again, she took refuge in her drink and raised her glass to click against his own. But to what might they drink, when her tongue had already thickened and numbed in her mouth and what she had thought she hoped for, the indefinable change of which she even now despaired, was also, alas! what she seemed to fear the most?

"To immutability," his eyes still on her, "however rare. You still blush easily, I see."

"And you still talk like a college professor." She held both palms to her burning face.

"Then how should I talk?" But his amusement was clearly tainted with contempt. He picked up a menu, signaled to the waitress, and left her holding her foolishness as though it were an embarrassing bit of underwear from which they might both do well to avert their eyes.

Perhaps, she thought, through a maze of alcohol and anger, he was only bored with her, had always wearied at the ambiguity which had so excited her. Perhaps he was thinking, even now, of another woman, someone who waited for him, whose gifts of love connoted no childish charade. It was all she deserved: to sit in wounded silence while he, shifted away from her, ordered for both, studied the half-empty dining room, drummed nervously upon the old, scarred tabletop. She moved anxiously in her seat, fingering and releasing things, knife, fork, spoon, in an agony of isolation.

Years before she had sat in this room, isolated as she was now, and heard his oblique pronouncements on morality, though it had seemed, then, that he spoke to her of art. "One must go up in an airplane, so to speak, in art as in life," he had told her. "Only thus can we observe with a balanced glance, with the fine advantage of perspective, which supersedes all feeling, all personal regard." It had been, in a way, his final word to her, and she recognized it, now, when he came so close to abandoning it, as the foundation of his forbearance. Now, as then, it paralyzed them both.

And, what had she become, he had asked her. What, indeed? If she had snatched her children's pictures from her purse, invoked her husband's name, catalogued the realities of the past years, might she, then, have persuaded him that, though she dizzied and flushed on two drinks and the prospect of commitment, she was, in fact, no longer his student; might she persuade him that a kind of love might prove more basic than commitment, a kind of chaos more beautiful than order? Had her chemistry betrayed her, just at the point of courage, so that, all purpose diffused and equanimity lost, she could submit only to his impatient silence, his marked absence of response? All hope abandon! Somewhat gratefully she sank softly into the limbo of intoxication; all effort blurred, and she shared his relief in the arrival of their dinner.

She felt weak, pale, dizzier now than ever, and could not really focus on her plate. But Marius, revived by the prospect of food, had returned to her with a smile. "Their roast beef, at least, hasn't changed!" There was something infuriating in his earthly appetites, his sudden expansiveness with the arrival of the food.

"Well, thank heaven for that." But the reassuring pleasure of rare roast beef, the solid baked potato, the homely green beans, came to her through a haze of panic. She was not thinking clearly, she knew, and her cheeks burned like coals, and something just beneath her scalp was tightening, twisting, whirling her into confusion. In some danger of passing out, she could feel cold droplets of fear forming on her forehead, was alternately stifled and nauseated by the possibility that she might, at any moment, slide like a soft, stuffed dummy to the floor. Very carefully, therefore, she contrived to lift her glass (how heavy it had grown), sip water from it, and then, quite casually, as though without design, to slide its coolness back and forth across her forehead, press it to her perspiring brow, even to dip her fingers (so cleverly surreptitious!) into it and apply them to the soft hollow at the base of her skull — all of this, so casually, so calmly that he could not have known in what danger she had suddenly found herself. And, at last the coolness quieted and comforted her and she was safe.

But she need not have been so tricky, she saw now, for Marius, oblivious to her discomfort, would not have noticed. Wordlessly, methodically, he dug at the soft center of his baked potato which sat, vulnerable (as she did), defenselessly exposed, torn open in the center of its shiny foil jacket. This conceit vaguely pleased her, and

she smiled slowly at the almost metaphysical precision of her restored senses. She was tempted to tell him of her cleverness, the
creative juxtaposition: Anne-Potato, equally vulnerable. For it was
he, wasn't it, who had trained her to perceive, in the most unlikely
places, the subtle affinities between man and matter. Smiling
broadly at him, enjoying a sudden and pleasant sense of freedom,
she made a great stab at the baked potato on her own plate and
slashed it cleanly at its center. (Potato-Marius, possibly?) She was,
after all, rather hungry!

"Well, Annie," his voice diagnostic, like a doctor's voice, "it seems
that I have got you drunk! Such silence! Such pretty, flushed
cheeks!"

She placed her palms lightly against her face, smiling sheepishly
from the frame of her hands. "Tony says that it's a low threshold
for intoxication; adorable, he says, before marriage, but deplorable
afterward. He's nice, my Tony; too bad you don't know him." But
even as she recommended him, she could neither see his face nor
hear his voice. With a tremor of alarm, a shocking sense of delin-
quency, she drew her husband's picture from her purse and placed
it between them. The smooth, sweet features smiled reliably up at
her, but it was the face of a stranger.

"Very handsome, very nice." But the blandness of his compliment betrayed his indifference. And her anger, mobilized to meet
his arrogance, brought Tony's image, Tony's voice (whose resonant
warmth she remembered, after all) into the gap between them, to
illuminate, as in a flash fire, the cold, flat, amnesiac failure of her
heart.

"But he's special, really special!" she heard her high-pitched ar-
gument, as though she had to convince him, had desperately to
persuade him of the reliable, point-by-point catalogue of those
dear virtues with which she might now hope to hold off the terrible
lapse of her own. Still, even as she struggled (her words coming
back to her strangely, as though spoken under water), she felt the
onrush of some frenzied, hopeless battle: beneath the surface of
her urgency she felt its slow seeping — desire flowing through her,
as she leaned across toward him. And she knew that even to have
evoked her husband's name, at this moment of separation from
him, was a gesture of obscene hypocrisy. Reaching to retrieve his
photo, she sensed that Marius, awakened at last from the contemplation of his needs, began to understand the urgency in her man-

ner. Soon, very soon, she told him wordlessly, she would be on her
way to Chicago; soon, very soon, that critical point to which, perhaps, even these eight years had only meant to lead them, might be
beyond them, passed by, like something only briefly glimpsed from
the window of a train.

"Finish your coffee," he said, at last, as to a child.

And, somewhat perversely, she drank it slowly, quite happy,
now, to put off that moment; enjoying even the prospect of submission, of being impaled, as she had hoped, upon his curious
strength.

Still, it offended her to see how easily he managed it, how per-
functorily (as with the signal to their waitress, the careful paying of
the bill), he apparently proposed to settle their old account. For
obviously, she told herself uneasily, it was what he meant to do: to
take her home, to have it over with once and for all (in an organized fashion, of course) and send her, finally, on her way.

But, "We'll go to your hotel," he was saying as he opened the
door for her. His fingertips, quite firm upon her arm, seemed to
imply some vague disapproval, something cold and punitive that
was not being said. And even this excited her, though she knew it to
be demeaning, unworthy of the role she had so often dreamed for
herself and seemed, now, to be approaching at last. She allowed the
excitement to mount, to draw in her limbs and flame upon her
cheeks until, like a child delighting in an old game, she had dispelled all that offended or confused her pleasure. And, thus delighted, thus made younger than she was, she dared to tease
him.

"You're such a terrible prig," she laughed, "such an impossibly
stuffy prig."

"I know, I know." But he did not smile, or even break his stride.

"And a bore!"

"Certainly a bore." Still, his stride unbroken, no smile, to betray
even a flicker of compassionate humor.

"And too goddamn orderly." She had turned to face him now
and, like a child, was walking backward along the street to her
hotel.

"Always orderly. Above all, that." And now his voice had taken
on a lightness to match her own — his relief, possibly, at ending
this long charade?

"And now," she stopped, threw both arms wide in wonder, "in spite of all that, you are taking me to my hotel?"

He halted, too, drawing close to her: "It's what I seem to be doing."

"Hallelujah!" and briefly, just very briefly, she embraced him. Now they walked together, side by side. "But what does this do to your sense of order?" But they were passing Mackay Hall, its white, moonlit columns even more sentinel than once they had seemed to be. "The scene of all our crimes!" she cried in delight, for she remembered every word of every meeting there. "All those sterile tutorials! All that wasted time!"

Still, they walked on, past the diagonal with its twin ghinko trees, each circled by a bench. How many times had she sat there, waiting to see him pass? And how many times had he passed, noticed, and merely nodded. While she, poor thing, had watched without words, had even imagined that it was her indiscriminate love of Shelley, of Renoir, of Tschaikowsky (each, for his lack of discipline, the object of Marius' contempt) from which he possibly recoiled. How he had stripped her of her old loves, all her old enthusiasms! With what might she have replaced them, if not with the cold, distant, even unattainable prospect of his approval? She had felt so diminished by his control, by the scorn with which he had wrenched her from them; how could she possibly have imagined that, despising them, he could, nevertheless, love her?

And could he? Or was this episode, too, to end in the triumphant exercise of something he called discipline? She had always imagined that his strength lay in control; but now, walking at last through the lobby of her hotel, she wondered whether, in fact, it had all been a masquerade, paralysis passing for discipline, detachment for control. In that quiet, carpeted old place, she turned and faced him again.

"Why did you never love me back?" And the words so stunned her, coming from her own lips, that she found herself trembling, leaning against the elevator door. "Why, Marius?"

He glanced away, apparently unwilling, even now, to come to terms with the ambivalent nature of their past. And then, "There were other considerations," he said, still looking away from her. "Other factors."

But she would not let him off: "Other factors? You mean

scruples? protocol? or simply order? Surely you knew that I would have stayed. One word, Marius, and I should never have left Avalon that spring!"

"It wouldn't have mattered — then." But he had met her eyes at last and there was something in him she did not recognize, something which hinted of dark recesses of disorder, despair. Perhaps he did not know, either, what those other factors had been. Perhaps ambivalence was so basic to his nature that without it he would perish. Perhaps there was some balance better left undisturbed.

But, too late! For they were already at her door, and entering, with the hesitancy of newlyweds, that charming, corner suite with its climate of old-fashioned, unimproved grace. It was only then, as she caught a glimpse through the open bedroom door of the white candlewick counterpane, that she understood how far they had come. Surely not too far, after eight years of preparation for this time, and yet, surely too far to let the mechanics confound her. Besides, she reassured herself, he was apparently no stranger to hotel bedrooms, and she, mercifully, still loosened by the magic of alcohol, felt herself quite capable of anything he might require.

Actually, he required very little. Practiced, perfunctory, yet surprisingly effective, he brought her quickly to the point of what sometimes passed for love; and when she lay, quiet, untroubled, against his great warm bulk, she even forgot to wonder what those other factors might have been. The great dissembling leaps of longing and of love had seized and finally released her; it no longer seemed important to know why it had taken eight years to reach this condition.

Still, she would have liked to tell him, though he would surely scoff, that even without this time together, she had somewhere given herself to him: for there was continuity in a woman's life, long skeins of feeling that trailed out of the past and bound her, illogically, to old loves, old letters, old furniture no longer useful, faces unclearly seen. Men like Marius might deprecate or cynically dismiss as sentimental what most women knew to be a most profoundly feminine power of evocation, but they would never erase its oddly pleasurable pain. For even its signals, though fragile, were strangely binding: songs, fragrances, textures, all so ephemeral that one might well wonder to learn that in each of them, over and over again, one gave one's self away.

So she might have told him that evening: that from the past she had brought with her all the unanswered questions evoked by the textures of this day, by the air of the town, the sounds which came from it, the murmurs traveling like smoke through its long, dark corridors, the shock beneath her hand of the knob that had opened an old door.

She would have told him, too (had it seemed to matter to him), that even now, with him sleeping beside her, nothing had changed between them: not because he had, in fact, given so little of himself away, but because she had not really wanted him to. Somehow, she had feared, more than he had, that he would betray that old, essential sense of order. He had, of course, managed to avoid making any major alterations; even in the act of love, he had somehow avoided her. And for this, she was strangely grateful.

When she left in the morning, she thought now, it would be as though she had never come back at all, nor sat, nor dined, nor slept with him, here, in this hotel bed. They would have an easy, effortless goodbye; he would not, she felt sure, even try to persuade her to take a later plane.

And somewhere between this room and her destination, on that plane that rushed her toward another life, she would retrieve from the past all she wished to save. Having left her Marius, at last, having gone safely past his tyranny, it was with his old image and ambiguity that she would travel to her home.

JOHN WILLIAM CORRINGTON

The Actes and Monuments

(FROM THE SEWANEE REVIEW)

AFTER THE CORONARY I quit. I could have slowed down, let things go easier, taken some of the jobs where little more than appearance was required. But I didn't do that. I like to believe that I cared too much for the law. No, I *do* believe that. Because if I had cared nothing for the law, I would have played at being an attorney — or else simply stopped being involved with law at all. But I did neither.

Rather I let go my partnership and began looking for some way to use all I knew, all I was coming to know. I was thirty-eight, a good lawyer by any standard — including the money I had let collect in stocks. A bachelor and a one-time loser on the coronary circuit. What do you do? Maybe you settle down in Manhattan and have fun? Maybe you don't. There is no room in Manhattan for fun — not in the crowd I knew, anyhow. You are either in it or out of it; that was the rule, and everybody understood and accepted. Poor Harry wasn't in it. So Harry had to walk out of it. Who needs to be pushed?

So Harry comes on very strong. Much stronger than anyone can credit, believe. Who knows where I caught the idiot virus that took me down there? Maybe it was *Absalom, Absalom!* which once I read, not understanding a word of it, but living in every crevice of time and space that the laureate of the Cracker World created.

It is no overstatement to say that my friends paled when they received postcards from Vicksburg. It was much too much. They were old postcards. Pictures in mezzotint of the Pennsylvania memorial, of the grass-covered earthworks outside the town. Post-cards which must have been printed at the latest in the early 1920s and which had been in the old flyblown rack waiting for my hand almost a half century. I cannot remember what I wrote on the cards, but it must have been wonderful. I can say it was wonderful, because outside of one slightly drunken phone call from Manhattan late at night about a week after I arrived, I got no answers to those cards at all. Perhaps they never arrived. Perhaps they slipped back into the time warp from which I had plucked them at the little clapboard store outside town where there was a single gas-pump with a glass container at the top, and which the proprietor had to pump full before it would run into the tank of my XKE.

Should I tell you about that man? Who sold me gas, counted out my change, made no move at my hood or windshield; told me in guarded tones that he had seen a car like mine once long ago. A Mercer runabout, as he remembers. Never mind.

I rented a place, leased it. Almost bought it right off, but had not quite that kind of guts. It was old, enormous, with a yard of nearly an acre's expanse. I came that first day to recognize what an acre meant in actual extent. I stood in my yard near an arbor strung with the veiny ropes of scuppernong, I looked back at the house through the branches of pear trees, past the trucks of pecan and oak strung with heavy beards of that moss that makes every tree venerable which bears it. My house, on my property. Inside I had placed my books, my records, my liquor, what little furniture I had collected in the brownstone I had left behind.

My first conclusion was that the coronary had affected my mind. I could have committed myself to Bellevue with my doctor's blessing. Or, secondly, had I found in some deep of my psyche a degree of masochism unparalleled in the history of modern man? Is it true that Jewishness is simply a pathology, not a race or a religion? Perhaps I had, in the depths of my pain and the confusion attendant on my attack, weighed myself in the balance and found my life and its slender probings at purpose wanting utterly. Could it be that a man who in the very embrace of probable death can find no reason for his living except the sweating grab of life itself housed in a body, looks at all things and condemns himself to Mississippi?

Or finally, grossest of all, was there an insight in my delirium whereby I saw Mississippi not as exile, not as condemnation, but as a place of salvations? Must we somehow search out the very pits and crannies of our secret terrors in order to find what for us will be paradise? Consider as I did, in retrospect, that no man of normal responses raised in Manhattan is going to look for himself in the deep South. And yet how many of those men of normal responses are happy? How many die at the first thrust of coronary, dreaming as life ebbs of a handful of dusty dark-green grapes, a sprig of verbena, the soft weathered marble of an old Confederate monument within the shadow of which might have lain the meaning of their lives? I offer this possibility only because we are, most of us, so very miserable living out the lives that sense and opportunity provide. I wondered afterward, when I came to understand at least the meaning of my own choice, if we do not usually fail ourselves of happiness — of satisfaction anyhow — by ignoring the possibilities of perversity. Not perversion. Those we invariably attempt in some form. No, perversity: how few of us walk into the darkness if that is what we fear. How few of us step into a situation which both terrifies and attracts us. If we fear water, we avoid it rather than forcing ourselves to swim. If we fear heights, we refuse to make the single skydive which might simultaneously free and captivate us. If we cannot bear cats, we push them away, settling for a world of dogs. You see how gross my insights had become.

In order to live, I thought, standing there staring at the strange alien house which was now my legal domicile and the place where I was determined to create, as in a crucible, the substance of my new life, it may be essential to force, to invade, to overwhelm those shadowed places we fear, and fearing, learn to ignore as real possibilities even when we know them to be real, to be palpable, to be standing erect against a hot sky windless and blind to their own beauties, realizable only to those of us who come from distant places.

A simpler explanation was offered me later by one of Vicksburg's most elegant antisemites, a dealer in cotton futures who, loathing my nation and my region, my presumed religion and my race, became a close friend. He suggested that Jews, for their perfidy, are condemned to have no place, to strike no roots. Don't you live always out of a moral and spiritual suitcase? he asked slyly. Isn't it notable that there has never been any great architecture of the synagogue? How many of you speak the language of your great-grandfathers? Isn't placelessness a curse?

Yes, I told him in answer to his last question. Indisputably yes. But think of the hungers of a placeless man. Can you even begin to conceive the mind of a man who has suffered a failure of the heart once, who had fled all ordinary lives and come to Mississippi? No, he said, no longer joking or arch. No, I can't conceive that mind. But I expect there must be riches in it. You'll be using your talents, he half asked, half stated. You'll be going to help niggers with the law, won't you?

Yes, I told him. That certainly. Not that it will mean a great deal. Only the reflex of the retired gunfighter who no longer hopes to purge the world of good or evil but whose hand moves, claws at his side when pressed, out of a nervous reaction so vast and profound that the very prohibition of God himself could not stop it.

Good, he said. Not about the niggers. Everybody in the country wants a try at that sack of cats. But not your way. We've never had a man who came loving, needing, down here to do that kind of thing. I want a chance to see this. It has got to be rich.

What, I asked. What will be so rich? Why, seeing a yankee Jew fighting in the South because he needs her, because he loves her. Did you ever in your life hear the like of that?

How could I help loving? Where else could I come across such a man? but he was the least of it. There was, at the garage which saw to my car, an avowed member of the klan who asked me why I had come so far to die. My answer satisfied him: Because, if you have got to die, it is stupid to die just anywhere and by accident of some valve in your heart. If it comes here, I will know why and maybe even when.

He looked at me and scratched his head. My Christ, he said, I never heard nothing like that in all my life. You are a nut. How do you like it, I asked him over the hood of my Jaguar, now dusty and hot with April sun. Why, pretty well, he said, grinning, putting out his hand without volition or even I suspect the knowledge he had extended it. I took it firmly, and he looked surprised. As if the last thing on earth he had ever expected to do was shake hands with some skulking yankee kike determined to stir up his coloreds.

By this time you have dismissed me as a lunatic or a liar or both. Very well. You only prove that the most profound impulses of your spirit can find their fulfillment in Fairlawn, New Jersey. Good luck.

But if your possibilities are . . . what? More exotic — then I want to tell you the proving of what I found here in Vicksburg, Mississippi. I want to tell you about Mr. Grierson, and the cases we worked on together.

At that time I was handling now and again the smallest of cases for certain black people who had heard that an eccentric yankee lawyer had come to town and would do a workmanlike job of defending chicken thieves, wife-beaters, smalltime hustlers, whores, and even pigeon droppers. This alone would have drawn me little enough custom, but it was said further and experience proved it true that the yankee did his work for free, a very ancient mariner of yankee lawyers doomed to work out his penance for bird-mangling or beast-thumping by giving away his services to whatever negro showed up with a likely story. It was at first amazing to me how a negro was willing often to take a chance of six months or a year of prison to avoid a fifty-dollar fee, even when he had it. For some reason I could not at first grasp, my own logic had no purchase with them. Think: suppose a man offered you free legal service. Wouldn't you, like me, presume that the service would be about worth the price? Yes, you would. But how do you suppose the blacks reasoned? One of my chicken — actually a pig — thieves explained why he trusted me. You got a nice house, ain't you? Yes, I said. You out of jail yourself, ain't you? Yes. You look like you eats pretty good. I do, I eat very well. Except no pork. No saturated fats. Huh? Never mind. Oh, religion, huh? All right. Anyhow, if you got a good house, if you look like eating regular, and if the judge let you stand up there, you got as much going for you as any jackleg courthouse chaser I seen.

It was that very pig robber who carried me down one day in search of a law book. Something to do with statute of limitations on pig thievery. It seems that my man was charged with having stolen a pig in 1959, the loss or proof of it having come to light only in the last few days. I wanted to make absolutely sure that there was not some awful exception to ordinary prescription in Mississippi law when the subject was pigs. There are some oddities in Texas law having to do with horses. I had never had much practice connected with livestock in Manhattan. I thought I had better make sure.

So I was directed by a deputy who was everlastingly amused by the nature and style of my practice to the offices of Mr. Grierson.

They were on a side street just beyond the business district. Among some rundown houses that must have been neat and even prime in the 1920s but which had lost paint and heft and hope in the 1950s at the latest, there was a huddle of small stores. A place that sold seed and fertilizer and cast-iron pots and glazed clay crocks that they used to make pickles in. Just past the pots and crocks there was a flat-roofed place with whitewashed doors and one large window, heavy curtains behind it, across which was painted

FREE CHURCH OF THE OPEN BIBLE

There was a hasp on the door with a large combination lock hanging through it. I wondered what might be the combination to the Open Bible.

Just past the church there was another storefront building standing a little to itself. There was a runway of tall weeds and grass between it and the church, and it was set back a little from the sidewalk with a patch of tree lawn in front. On either side of the door was a huge fig tree, green and leafy and beginning to bear. Through the heavy foliage I could see that there were windows behind the trees. They seemed to have been painted over crudely, so that they looked like giant blinkered eyes which had no wish to see out into the street. Above the door itself was a sign made of natural wood hanging from a wrought-iron support. On it was graved in faded gold letters cut down into the wood

W. C. GRIERSON
ATTY AT LAW

The door itself was recessed fairly deeply and I got the notion that it was not the original door, that it had nothing really to do with the building which was, like those nearby, simply a long frame affair, what they — we — call a shotgun building, although much wider and apparently longer. I stood there in the early summer sun looking at that door as if it were the entrance to somewhere else, another place. Why? I rubbed my chin and thought, and then I found, back in the fine debris of my old life, back behind the sword edge of my coronary, the recollection of another summer afternoon spent with a lovely woman at some gallery, some wealthy home — somewhere. We had gone to see paintings, and there had been one among all the others that I could not put out of mind. It had been by the Albrights, those strange brothers. Of a door massive and ancient, buffed and scarred, the very deepest symbol both of a life and of the passage through which life itself must pass. On its weatherbeaten panels hung a black wreath, each dark leaf pointed as a spike, shimmering in the mist of its own surreality. My God, I remembered thinking, is death like that? Is it finally a door with a wreath standing isolated from air and grass — even from the materials which are supposed to surround the fabric of a door? And then I thought, the lovely woman beside me talking still about a Fragonard she had spotted nearby, of Rilke's words: "Der grosse Tod. . . . The great Death each has in himself, that is the fruit round which all revolves." But the title of the painting was "That Which I Should Have Done, I Did Not Do," and I could find neither sweetness nor rest in that.

Yes, I am standing still in front of that frame building in my town of Vicksburg, and, yes, looking at the shadowed door which now after all looks only the least bit like the other one, the weather, the light, the substantiality of all things about being so much less dense. Reality spares us; we do not have to know what else there is very frequently, do we? A colored boy no more than twelve walked by in a polo shirt and worn corduroy pants. He exchanged a quick glance with me and stepped on past, a transistor radio hanging from his neck, a tiny tinny thing which crooned:

> . . . *looks like the end, my friend,*
> *got to get in the wind, my friend,*
> *These are not my people, no, no,*
> *these are not my people. . . .*

Surely he had his radio aimed at me. How could he tell? And was the announcer a friend of his? He was an agent of the station which had discovered me, an alien, waxing in their midst. All of this I thought in jest, putting sudden flashcuts of the Albrights' door out of mind, reaching for the knob, and stepping inside.

I do not know why I was not prepared. I should have been. No reason for me to suppose that a lawyer's office here, in an old frame building, would have the sort of Byzantine formality I remembered from New York. Receptionist, secretary, inner office — with possibly a young clerk interposed somewhere between. But the mind is stamped inalterably with such impressions when we have done business a certain way for a very long time.

So I was not prepared when Mr. Grierson turned in his chair and smiled at me and said:

— Well, this is nice. Mighty nice. I don't know as I expected it.

— I beg . . . I began. Then I tried again. Best not beg. — I'm sorry. Have we met? Is it better to be sorry than to beg, I thought instantly. Too late.

— You'd be the lawyer just come down. Got you a house and everything.

My God, I thought, even a B-movie would tell you that things travel like lightning here. He probably saw the deed, the note of transfer on the title. Knows what you paid for the lease, what you owe on the house if you pick up the option. Knows your last address, your last place of employ. Knows about your little chicken-thief cases, your car . . . I almost thought coronary.

— Yes, I said, putting out my hand as he rose and offered his. — I'm Harry Cohen.

He motioned me to a chair near his desk and I sat down, trying as I did to begin the task of seeing him, of seeing this place in which he worked. Trying at the same time to put out of mind the impressions I had created, had begun to suppose from the moment the deputy had told me where to come. If we could only stay free of our own guesses, what would ever make us wrong in advance?

He walked over to a large safe against the wall to the left of the door. It was taller than he was, and the door opened slowly as he turned the handle. He stood reaching into its dark recesses, his back to me. I wondered what he was looking for as his voice came to me, small talk like a magician's patter, over his shoulder.

— Yes, Mr. Cohen. It's kind of you to pay a courtesy call. A custom languishing. Not dead, but in a bad way. A fine custom. Men who stand to the law shouldn't meet for the first time arguing a motion before Basil Plinsoll or one of the other boys on the circuit here . . .

I scanned the room as he spoke. I would deal with him later. It was a bright room — almost the opposite of what the door suggested. Or was it only the opposite of what the Albrights' door suggested?

On the wall over his flat desk, the shape and design of which had vanished long ago, I suspected, beneath a welter of papers and books, there were three old tintype portraits. Only they were not tintypes. They were fresh modern reproductions of tintypes. In the center, in a military uniform I almost recognized, was that stern beautiful face one recognizes without ever even having seen it. It was Lee. To his right, left profile toward me, hung the other one, that crafty rebel whose religion had almost severed the continent, Jackson. I did not know the third. He had a Tatar's face, long, bony, richly harsh. His beard was a careless Vandyke and the effect was that of seeing the man who had last closed the Albrights' door, nailed the wreath on it, and walked away, hands in uniform pockets. Whistling.

Mr. Grierson turned from the safe, hands filled with two tumblers and a dark brown bottle without a label. It had no cap. There seemed to be a cork stuck in it. He set all of it down on the edge of his desk and pulled the bottle's stopper with his teeth. The liquor was the lightest possible amber, a cataract of white gold as it twinkled into the glasses.

He smiled up at me. — You'll like it, he said. — Maybe not this time. But you let me send you a couple bottles. You'll come to like it.

— Corn, I said.

— Surely. Comes from upstate. Costs more than it used to. Bribes are just like the cost of living.

I sat back and sipped a little. It was peculiar, nothing like whiskey, really. it was a shock in the mouth, vanished as you swallowed. Then it hit the pit of your stomach and paralyzed you for the briefest moment. Then great warmth, a happiness that spoke of cells receiving gifts, of veins moving to a new rhythm, muscles swaying like grain in a breeze-swept field. It was lovely. Nothing like whiskey. More like sipping the past, something intangible that could yet make you feel glad that it had been there.

Mr. Grierson sat watching me now. As I took another swallow, deeper this time, I watched him back. A man of middle height, aged now but hale. Steel-rimmed glasses revealing large innocent blue eyes that seemed never to have encountered guile. He had that almost cherubic look that one associated with country doctors — or, in certain cases, with southern politicians. He wore an old suede coat cut for hunting. I had never seen anything like it. It was a soft umber and fit as if it had been his own pelt originally.

— Your jacket, I couldn't help saying, feeling the whiskey lift me and waft me toward him, toward his smile. — Could I get one . . .

— At Lilywhite's, he said.

— Here?

— London, he said apologetically. — And even there back in 1949. I wouldn't reckon they make 'em like this anymore.

He wasn't putting me on, I could tell. But I could tell too that he enjoyed that level of conversation. It pleased him to please with pleasantries. One moves from a series of set exchanges to another. An infinite series, and when the last series is exhausted, it is either time to go, or you have lived out your life and death clears its throat, almost loath to interrupt, and says that it is time. I thought I would not want to go on like that.

Coronary. O God how that word has come to press me with its softness, its multiple implications. Corona. Carnal. Corot. Coronary. A place, a name, the vaguest warm exhalation glimmering from an eclipsed sun. Shivering golden and eternal around the glyph of a saint. Called then a Glory. I lay for weeks thinking Coronary, wondering when it would reach into my chest once more and squeeze ever so gently and bring out with its tenderness my soul, toss that gauzy essence upward like a freed dove to fly outward, past morning, past evening, past the blue sky into the glistening midnight blue of deep space, and past that even to the place where souls fly, shaking great flakes of their own hoarded meaning outward, downward on all suns and the worlds thereunder.

— Another little drink, Mr. Grierson suggested. — I believe you've already found something in it.

— I was thinking . . . of martinis.

— No comparison. Next step from corn would be . . . perhaps a pipe of opium.

I did not even wonder if he spoke from experience or from some book by Saxe Rohmer. I wanted to go on.

— Mr. Grierson, I wonder if you have the *Southern Reporter* from —

He poured each of us another glass. — I have it all, he said. — I think my . . . library will fill your . . .

I looked around. There was a single bookcase across the room, and only a handful of books in it. I must have looked doubtful. He gave me the oddest of small glances, and I took refuge in my whiskey.

— Maybe we should go into the library, he said, rising and walking toward a door at the back of the room which I had not even noticed until now. It was painted the same dull color as the rest of the office. There was a hook nailed badly to it with coats and jackets and what looked like an old fishing hat hanging from the hook.

I followed him and stepped ahead of him as he opened the door. What shall I say? I have to tell you that Coronary fluttered not far away, and I stepped in and turned in the new room slowly, slowly, taking it in, feeling, thinking in a simultaneity resembling that first moment of the attack:

So this is what lies behind them, southerners. There is always that front room, the epitome of the ordinary, a haven for bumpkins. And behind, in one way, one sense or another, there is always this.

Because it was, properly speaking, not a room. No, many rooms. It went on, back at least four more rooms, and perhaps side rooms off each of the main rooms toward the back. And I knew without even entering the others that they were all more or less like this one I was standing in:

Filled from floor to roof with books. Thousands upon thousands of books. Books in leather and buckram, old, new, burnished bindings and drab old cloth. Behind and around the shelves the walls were paneled in deepest cherry wood. Before me was a beautiful nineteenth-century library table surrounded by chairs. It was like the rare book room of a great private library. I moved spellbound toward the nearest shelf. It was . . . religion. What was not there? Josephus. The Fathers in hundreds of volumes. The Paris edition of Aquinas. Was this a first of the Complutensian Polyglot? Scrolls in ivory cases. Swedenborg, Charles Fort. A dissolving Latin text from the early seventeenth century. The *Exercises* of Ignatius, Marcion, Tertullian. And I could see that the rest of the room was of a kind with those I was looking at.

— I had a house once, Mr. Grierson was saying. — But even then it didn't seem fitting to have all this stuff out where my clients could see it. Folks here can abide a lot of peculiarity, but you ought not to flaunt it. You want to keep your appetites kind of to yourself.

This in a depreciating voice, as if possession of books, especially in great number, was somehow a vice — no, not a vice, distinctly not a vice, but an eccentricity that must disturb the chicken thief or the roughneck with a ruptured disk. Was it a kindness to spare them this?

— I think you'll find most anything you'll need here, Mr. Grierson said softly. — Except for science. Not much science. Darwin, Huxley, Newton — all the giants. I kind of gave up when they went to the journals. They stopped doing books, you know.

— Yes, I said. Still thinking, this is where the southerners have stored it all. You ask, how could Faulkner . . . how could Dickey . . . down here, in this . . . place . . . ? This is how.

I knew that this was madness. I did not question that. This time, had there been a psychiatrist close by, I would have gone to him at once without a doubt. Because, after all, this was not what I thought, but worse: what I felt. I *knew* it was not so, and still I *believed* it.

— This is where I do . . . my work, Mr. Grierson was saying.

— Work, I repeated as we entered another room filled with Literature. All of it. My hand fell on a shelf filled with French. Huysmans, Daudet, De Musset, Mérimée — and a large set of portfolios. They were labeled simply Proust. I took one out. It was bound in a gray cloth patterned in diamond-shaped wreaths, each filled with starlike snowflakes, smaller wreaths, featherlike bursts gathered at the bottom, nine sprays flaring at the top.

— It was the wallpaper, Mr. Grierson was saying. — That pattern . . .

I opened the portfolio. In it were printed sheets covered with scrawling script, almost every line of print scratched out or added to.

— Proofs. Of *Du Côté de chez Swann*. I was in Paris . . . in 1922. Gide . . . Anyhow, I came across . . .

— Of course. You've studied them?

— Oh yes. The Pléiade text isn't . . . quite right.

We went on for a long time, shelf by shelf. But we did not finish. We never finished. It could have taken weeks, months, so rich was his treasure.

I left at dusk with Grierson seeing me to the door, inviting me back soon, offering me the freedom of his library. I was back home sitting under my arbor with whiskey and a carafe of water on a small table beside me before I recalled that I had never gotten around to checking in the Mississippi code as to its position on pigs and those who made off with them.

The pig had prescribed, sure enough. But on the way out of court, I found myself involved in another case dealing, if you will, with similar matters.

They were bringing in a young man in blue jeans, wearing a peculiar shirt made of fragments, rags — like a patchwork quilt. He had very long hair like Prince Valiant, except not so neat. He was cuffed between two deputies. One, large with a face the color of rare steak, kept his club between the young man's wrists, twisting it from time to time. There seemed somehow to be an understanding between them: the deputy would twist his club viciously; the young man would shriek briefly. Neither changed his expression during this operation.

— What did he do? I asked the other deputy who looked much like a young Barry Fitzgerald.

— That sonofabitch *cussed* us, he told me with that crinkly simian smile I had seen in *Going My Way*. — We should of killed him.

— Local boy, I asked.

— You got to be shitting me, he answered, watching his partner doing the twist once more. — He's some goddamned yankee. Michigan or New York, I don't know. We should of killed him.

— Did you find anything in his car?

— Car, your ass. He was hitching out on U.S. 80. We better not of found anything on him. I know I'd of killed him for sure. I can't stand it; nobody smoking dope.

— What's the charge?

— Reviling, he said, eyes almost vanishing in that attenuated annealed Mississippi version of an Irish grin. — Two counts.

— Two?

— We was both there. He was vile to Bobby Ralph and me both.

— What did he say?

— Wow, Barry Fitzgerald's nephew crinkled at me. — We should of killed him and dumped him in Crawfish Creek.

— What?

— Pigs.

— Sorry?

— You heard. Called us — Bobby Ralph and me — pigs. My God, how do you reckon we kept off of killing him?

I think it was a question of free association. Pigs. I had had luck with pigs so far. Maybe this yankee sonofabitch — pardon me — was sent for my special care. God knows the care he would get otherwise. Just then Barry's partner gave the young man a final supreme wrench. He came up off the floor of the courthouse hallway at least three feet. He squealed and looked at me with profound disgust.

— You old bastard, he drawled, hunching his shoulders. — Would you let' em book me so I can get these things off?

— I'm a lawyer, I said.

— You're fucking bad news, the young man said wearily.

— See, Barry said, as his partner shoved the young man down the hall toward the booking room. — Reckon we ought to take him back out an' lose him?

— No, I said. — You don't want to do that.

— No, Barry said, walking after his partner and their day's bag. — No, you lose him and the feds shake all the feathers out of your pallet looking for him. Christ, all you have to do to make him important is lose him. Or paint him black.

— You leave the ninety-nine lambs and seek the one that's lost, I said, striving for his idiom.

— Anyone does that is a goddamned fool, Barry said over his shoulder. — And he's going to be out of the sheep business before he knows it. Lost is lost.

Later — you guessed it — he sent for me. On the theory that I seemed to be the only one in town able to speak English as he knew it, as opposed to lower Mississippian. We talked in a corner of his cell. There was a sad Mexican and a local drunk in the cell with him. The three had reached a kind of standoff between them. None could understand the other. Each seemed weird to the others. Since they had no weapons and were roughly the same size, an accommodation had been arranged. No one would begin a fight which could not be handicapped.

His name was Rand McNally. He might have been a nice-looking young man if he had wanted to be. But he was not. His eyes were circled, his skin dry and flaked. I could not tell precisely what color his hair was. He had a small transistor radio the size of a cigarette pack stuck in the pocket of his shirt. It was tuned to a local rock-music station:

> *She's got everything she needs,*
> *She's an artist,*
> *She don't look back . . .*

— The spic stinks and the redneck keeps puking over there in the corner, Rand McNally told me. — But that's all right. I've got it coming. I deserve it. Jesus, I wish I'd kept my mouth shut.

— Or stayed out of Mississippi.

— It was an accident, Mississippi.

— Some say that, I told him.

— Oh shit. I mean being here. I was running away from a . . . girl. It come up Mississippi.

— Where are you from?

He sat back and fingered his essay at a beard. It was long and a kind of dark red. I supposed his hair was probably the same color if it was washed. The beard was sparse, oriental. Above it, he had large green eyes which somehow gave me a start each time I looked squarely into them; I am not used to being put off by a physical characteristic, but those eyes, deeply circled, seemed to demand a concentration and attention I had no wish to muster. They seemed, too, to require the truth. Not knowing the truth, I evaded such demands whenever possible. I wished I had let him pass on with Barry Fitzgerald's kinsman and his partner. No, I didn't.

— I don't know, Rand McNally said. — From one place after another. I just remember motels and rooming houses. The old man was an automobile mechanic. I never had the idea it started anywhere. I mean, it had to start somewhere. I got born, didn't I? But I remember it being one dump after another forever. Al's Garage, Bo-Peep Motel; Fixit Tire Company, Millard's Auto Court; Willie's Car Repair, Big Town Motor Hotel. Somewhere the old man had a woman and she had me — told him I was his — and then on to the next place. She dropped off somewhere. I think he whipped up on her. I seem to remember something. About money? Sure, probably. I don't remember her.

I saw his father, a great tall harried man with grease worked permanently into the skin of his knuckles, under his fingernails, with the soul of Alice's white rabbit, an ancient Elgin running fast in his pocket and a notebook listing all the small towns, garages, and motels he was obliged to move through before it was done. One entry said: *Get Son.* Another said: *Son grown. Leaves.* There were faded smeared pencilled checks beside each entry. Life lived between Marvin Gardens and Baltic Avenue.

— How do you want to plead? I asked him.

He shrugged. — Make it easy on yourself. I've got a couple of months to do here. Price of pork.

I had not thought him intelligent enough to have a sense of humor. We smiled at each other then. The transistor was quacking another of its vast repertoire of current tunes:

These are not my people,
No, no, these are not my people.
Looks like the end, my friend,
Got to get in the wind, my friend . . .

— I'm going to plead you innocent. No malice.

He tossed his hair back and smiled up at me. His green eyes seemed to hang on mine for a long while. It surprised me that someone so worn, so ground off by the endless procession of new people in his life, could reach across to the latest in that anonymous parade with even the appearance of interest.

— No malice, he said. — That's true.

It was late that evening when the phone rang. At the other end was Billy Phipps, one of the county attorney's assistants. His voice was lazy with an undertone of something like amusement or exultation. I did not like him. He was provincial as a Bronx delivery man and took pleasure in the webbing of paltry law as it snared those who had not the slightest idea of its working. His own ignorance made him delight in that of others.

— Well, what do you think of your boy Rand McNally, he asked.

— Not a lot, I said, wondering why he would bother with a call on such a matter. — It seems silly to put him on the county for a little mild name-calling. Hadn't you ought to leave room for rape-murderers?

At the other end of the line, I could hear Phipps draw in his breath.

I pause only to say that I neither believe nor disbelieve in magic, precognition, spiritualism, and so on. I come to feel that all we do in the four dimensions of our world is like the action of water beetles skating on the surface of a still lake, turning our tricks between water and air, resident truly, fully, in neither, committed vaguely to both. Are we material — or other? I receive hints from varied sources. If you have loitered at the gates of Coronary, you must wonder. Is a massive seizure only a statistically predictable failure of meat mechanism? Could it be counted a spiritual experience? Who, what seizes the heart? Who, what attacks the heart? Could it be an entrance into the indices of those currents which play above and below the beetle, in the great eternal world where there are neither serials, sequences nor statistics? Where forever,

possibly, dear God and his precious Adversary choose to disagree
as to the purpose of their copulation? At my worst — or best? —
moments, I seem to hear, like a radio signal from the most remote
reaches of time and space, the voice of the Entities making their
cases over and over, yet never the same, because each permutation
is a case unto itself. Is it the voice of God one hears, arguing point
by point, A to B to C, coolly, without rancor or regret — like Her-
man Kahn? Is it Satan who sobs and exults, demands, entreats,
laughs, chides, tears a passion and mutters sullenly? Or are those
voices reversed? Maybe I am gulled believing in polarities. Why
not? Could not God howl and sob the Natural Order of Normal
Occasions? While Satan urges quietly the Stewing Urgencies of
Madness? Why not? And why should we not in one way or another
receive darts and splinters from those agelong and intricate arguments?

So much to explain my mind as I heard Phipps draw in his
breath. *Jesus,* I thought, *a message.*

— What did he tell you? Phipps asked quietly, his normal sneer-
ing country manner gone altogether.

— Nothing, I said. — What do you mean?

— Counsellor, we got a telegram from Shreveport. They want to
talk to Pig Boy. About a rape-murder.

— Ah, I said, and felt those faintest stirrings in my chest. Not
even a warning, only the dimmest — can I say, sweetest — touch of
recollection, of terrible nostalgia, from the distant geographies of
Coronary. Like the negative of a photograph of a memory, saying:
This twinge, this whisper, is what you felt without noticing before
you came that day for the first time upon the passage to Coronary.
Be warned and decide. It is a landscape you wish to visit again? Is it,
pulsing once more, a place where gain outmeasured loss? Stroke
the contingencies and wonder your way to a decision. You have
been once across the bourn from which few travelers return. Do
you have it for another trip? And will that trip too be round?

— Ah, I said again to Phipps. — Let me get back to you, all right?

It was all right. Spatially, Rand McNally was fixed. This allowed
certain latitude with time. Tomorrow would be just fine. Since the
rape-murder, evocation of a nameless victim cooling after life's
fitful fever 350 miles away in north Louisiana, was fixed irrevocably
in time and there could be, for those to whom its being was announced, no moving from it even as it receded backward and away

now, once more permutation in the patterns spoken of in that bower where God and his Demon Son ramble on to no probable conclusion.

Is it strange to say that after the call from Phipps I found myself thinking less of the long-haired boy than before? Before I had been searching for a way to free him from, at most, a three months' term in jail. Now, when he might stand within the shadow of death or a lifetime in prison, he seemed somehow less a point of urgency. Perhaps because I believed not only that he had committed that rape-murder in another place and time, but that he had, in passage from one serial point called Shreveport to another called Vicksburg — both noted as mandatory in a book such as his father had been slave to — placed upon that act, called rape-murder by authorities who have the legal right to give comings-together names and sanctions, his own ineradicable mark: a fingerprint, a lost cap, one unforgettable smile caught by a barmaid in a cafe as he passed toward or from the fusion with another — presumably female — in that timetable inherited from his father, and for all either I or he could say, from the very Adam of his blood. However that might be, there was no hurry now. Ninety days in the county jail, so implacable only a little while before, no longer mattered. Which called to my mind, making me laugh inordinately, that on the day of Coronary I had developed a painful hangnail. It is a question of magnitudes. When Coronary came, I was transformed into one who, having disliked mosquito bites, now used the Washington Monument for a toothpick. Mosquitoes, landing, would fall to their deaths in the vastness of a single pore. And later, drinking off my bourbon and water and sugar, I slept without dreams. Or, as I am told, dreaming constantly, but remembering none when it came time to awaken.

— I hear you reached in for a kitty and caught yourself a puma, my telephone was saying.

It was Mr. Grierson calling. He wanted to know if he could be of assistance.

— Seeing you hadn't figured on anything quite like this, he said blandly.

Yes, I told him. Hell yes. Only small boys and large fools stand alone when they might have allies. Anyhow, I thought, McNally will barely have representation anyhow: a heart patient obsessed with the exotica of his complaint; an old man gone bibliophile from sheer loneliness. We would see.

We did. It was noon when we got in. Rand McNally stared out at the jailor in whose eyes he had obviously gained status. When he opened the cell, he loosened the strap on his ancient pistol. *This here bastard is a killer,* I could almost hear him thinking.

Mr. Grierson hitched up his pants, passed his hand over this thin hair, and sat down on a chair the jailor had provided for him. I made do with the seat of the toilet. Mr. Grierson studied the boy for a moment, then looked at me expectantly, as if protocol required that I begin. I nodded, returning the compliment to my elder. I had divined already how such things would move in Mississippi. Mr. Grierson returned my nod and cleared his throat.

— Well, sir, it appears that clandestine hog-calling is the least of your problems.

Rand McNally stared at him in astonishment. Then he laughed, looked at me, saw me smile despite myself. He went on laughing while Mr. Grierson sat quietly, an expression bemused and pleasant on his face.

— I'm glad you got such a fine spirit, son. You're gonna need it.

Rand McNally took the earplug of his transistor out and hung it through the spring of the empty bunk above his. The Mexican and the farmer were gone now. Perhaps released to the terrors and punishment of sobriety; perhaps simply transferred to other cells in honor of Rand McNally's new status.

— Huh, McNally said to Mr. Grierson.

— If you did to that lady in Shreveport what they say you did, you're gonna have a chance to stand pat whilst they strap you in the electric chair. Shave your head, I believe, before you go.

Rand McNally shuddered. Whether it was the standing pat, the chair, or the head-shaving I could not tell.

— Well, Mr. Grierson asked him. — What about it?

Yes. Well, he told us. He was glad it was over; was tired of running. ("Son of a bitch only did what he did three days ago," Mr. Grierson observed later. "What do you reckon? Think he's been reading *Crime and Punishment*?") He had gone to work for an elderly widow in Shreveport, had cut the yard for a meal, had hung a shelf for a dollar, and came back the next day to whitewash a fence for two dollars. He had whitewashed most of the day with her looking on from her kitchen past the blooming wisteria and lazy bees. Near sundown, covered with sweat and whitewash, he had gone inside to get a glass of ice water and his two dollars. As he drank, the woman squinted out at the fence, saying, "It'll take another coat." "Huh," Rand McNally said. "Another coat. Then I'll pay you," she said softly, smirking at him, some last wilted, pressed and dried wisp of her ancient femininity peeking through. At the very worst time.

She said something else that he could not remember and he picked up a knife with which she had been dicing peaches and pushed it into her throat. Then he pushed her over on the kitchen table, pulled off her clothes and down his pants, made with that agonized and astonished crone the beast with two backs, blood, coughing, and great silence between them. In retrospect he was mildly surprised by it all. It was not, he told us, a planned happening. He was curious that, following the knife, he had discovered himself erect. Why he pressed on with it, distasteful and grotesque as it was, he could not say. But when he was done — he did get done, by the way — he found that she was still very much alive, admonishing him with one long bony liver-spotted finger.

So he got the remainder of the whitewash, dragged it back into the house in a huge wallpaper-paste bucket while he held up his pants with one hand. While she lay there mute, violated, bleeding, he whitewashed the kitchen: the walls, floor, cabinets, stove, icebox, calendar, and four-color lithograph of Jesus suffering the little children. Chairs, hangers, spice rack, coffee, tea, sugar and flour bins, breadbox, and cookie jar. All white. At last he rolled her off onto the floor, whitewashed the table, and put her back in the middle of it. After studying it all for a moment, he decided, and whitewashed her too. Which, so far as he could remember, was all he could remember.

— Ummm, Mr. Grierson said. — So she was alive when you were done with your fooling?

— Alive and kicking, Rand McNally said without smiling. — You see I got to die, don't you?

— Well, Mr. Grierson said, looking at me — you ain't done much by way of making a case against that. Do you want to die?

— Everybody wants to die, Rand McNally said. He was picking his toes, disengaged now, considering certain vastnesses he had talked himself to the edge of.

— Right. At the proper place and time. How do you like the chair?

— Ride the lightning? What a gas, Rand McNally almost smiled. — Anybody'd do that to an old lady has got to pay the price. You know that's so. The price is lightning in this state.

— Well, Mr. Grierson said, getting up stiffly. — Let me study on it, son. I'll see you.

As we left, Rand McNally was screwing the transistor's plug into his ear. — Christ, he said. — A sonofabitch would do that has *got* to die.

Outside we passed Billy Phipps talking to a couple of police we didn't know. Phipps nodded to us. I suppose they were from Shreveport.

— Do you smell Rand McNally . . .

— Sneaking up on an insanity plea, Mr. Grierson finished my sentence. — Indeed I do.

— It looks good. From slimy start to filthy finish, doesn't it?

— Ummmm, Mr. Grierson hummed, smiling. — All he's got to do is convince a jury he's Tom Sawyer . . .

— And she was Becky Sharp . . . ?

He looked at me sorrowfully and shook his head as if only a yankee would have pressed it that awful inch. — Thatcher, he said — But there is a question still . . .

— Yes?

— If he *is* trying to get himself decked out with an insanity plea, the question is: Why *did* he kill the old lady, and then do that to her? If he hadn't, he wouldn't need any kind of plea at all, would he?

That afternoon under the scuppernongs I felt as if I were waiting for some final word, some conclusive disposition of my own case. There was a dread in me, an anxiety without an object. I thought ceaselessly of Rand McNally and his insane erection in the midst of an act of violence. I thought of his surprise at it. I thought of my own prophecy over the phone to Phipps. What had brought him to this place, this conclusion? He had stepped from life into process: extradition, arraignment, indictment, trial, sentencing. I came to feel that he had ceased to exist, to be a human being owed and owing. He was no longer a proper object of feeling. No one only *thought* about him. One took him into account along with Dr.

Crippen, Charles Starkweather, Bruno Hauptmann, Richard
Speck, and the others of that terrible brotherhood whose reality is
at once absolute and yet mouldering day by month by year in
antique police archives or grinning dustily in the tensionless
shadows of wax museums.

It was just after supper when Mr. Grierson appeared. He pulled
into the drive in a 1941 Ford Super DeLuxe coupe. It was jet black
and looked as if it had been minted — not built, minted — an hour
or so before. He wore a white linen suit and a peculiar tie: simply
two struts of black mohair which lay beneath and outlined the
white points of his narrow shirt-collar. It was not that his car and
clothes were old-fashioned; it was that while they were dated, they
were not quaint or superannuated or amusing. As if by some shift,
Mr. Grierson had managed the trick of avoiding the lapse of time,
of nullifying it so that what had been remained, continued unchanged. Could one pile up the past densely enough around himself so as to forbid its dwindling? And what would happen if the
rest of us shared that fierce subterranean determination to drag
down the velocity at which today became yesterday? It would fail,
of course. You cannot disintegrate the fabric of physics. But what
would happen?

We spoke of the weather, hot and dry, the bane of planters
hereabouts. No sweet June rain. Only scorching sun, the river lying
like a brown serpent between us and those like us in Louisiana. It
was the mention of Louisiana that Mr. Grierson chose as his pathway past the amenities.

— He's crossing the big river tomorrow. Waived extradition.

— Oh? Did you . . . ?

— Talk to him again? O yes. Surely. Shreveport detective
showed up while I was there.

He smiled at me, knowing what thoughts had crossed my mind
and instantly been dropped as I asked my question.

— I'll speak to him in the morning — apprise him of his rights.

— He was forcefully apprised of his rights. Not once, but several
times. And he repudiated every one of them in obscene terms.

— What? I don't . . .

— He said it was a goddamned piss-poor legal system that gave
all these rights to a . . . fucking pervert.

Mr. Grierson looked embarrassed for the sake of the quotation.

— Jesus, I said, almost dropping the bottle of sourmash from which I was pouring our drinks. — Christ, he *is* crazy. He *must* have been reading Dostoevsky.

— I don't know, Mr. Grierson said. — He gave me this. Said it was your fee.

He handed me a greasy fragment of oiled paper — the kind they wrap hamburgers in. There was what looked like a quatrain scrawled on it in no. 2 pencil:

> *It's bitter knowledge one learns from travel,*
> *The world so small from day to day,*
> *The horror of our image will unravel,*
> *A pool of dread in deserts of dismay.*

— What's that, I asked Mr. Grierson. He smiled and sipped his whiskey.

— You can come over to my place and look it up, he said. — The idea is interesting. Wine don't travel well.

— The horror of our image . . .

— Seems what broke him up was that business after he stabbed the old lady. He didn't seem much concerned about the stabbing, you know. It was . . . the other.

— And the finale . . . ?

— The whitewashing? Oh, no, he liked that fine. You can't make up for it, he told me. But you do the best you can. That boy is a caution . . .

We sat drinking for a while. I shook my head and said, not so much to Mr. Grierson as to myself:

— It's . . . as if Rand McNally was a . . . historical figure.

— Well, yes. That's so. But then, we all are.

— Yes . . .

— But history ain't like grace, is it? It has different rules. Which is to say, no rules at all.

I stared at him. Grace? What might that be? Luck? Fortune? I had heard the word. I simply attached no meaning to it. Now this old man set it before me as an alternative to history. I felt that dread again, some low order of clairvoyance wherein I imagined that Coronary might open once more: at first like the tiny entrance to Alice's garden — then like the colossal gates of ancient Babylon. It struck me at that instant with ghastly irrationality that grace was the emanation of vaginal purpose and womb's rest. Is grace death?

— Is grace death? I heard myself asking aloud.

— It could be, Mr. Grierson answered. — I can imagine in a few years I might ask for that grace. But not altogether. History is the law. Grace is the prophets. History comes upon us. I reckon we have to find grace for ourselves. The law works wrath rather than grace, Luther said.

— That line . . . the horror of our image . . .

— Yes. Well, that's what brought grace to my mind. I think that boy has just broke into and out of history.

— Yes?

— Something else I remember from Luther: certain it is that man must completely despair of himself in order to become fit to receive the grace of Christ . . .

— I didn't know you were a Lutheran.

— Hell, I'm not. Never could be. Most often, I quote Calvin. But you always go for water out of the sweetest well, don't you?

— No and yes. He cares all right. He wants to get on with it, don't you see? He's sick of problems. But no, there won't be any more motor courts and repair shops for old Rand McNally.

— Problems . . .

— What happened to him that evening in that old woman's kitchen? Do you know? How is it that killing moved to something like what they call an act of love? Neither fits the hour's need. What happened? That's the problem.

I felt very warm, my face flushed, my hands wet as if I had just climbed out of the river. Believe me. I was afraid. I thought it was another attack. Tryst might be better. Liaison, assignation.

— You feeling bad, Mr. Grierson asked, pouring us both a little more whiskey.

— No, I lied. — I'm fine. Just thinking. Was it grace that came on Rand McNally? Is that what you want to say?

— Lord no, Mr. Grierson smiled depreciatingly. — That'd be crazy. Grace to kill and rape an old woman? Naw, I never said that. I wasn't speaking *for* grace, you know.

— He's insane. They'll find him insane.

— Sure. So was Joan of Arc. So was Raymond of Toulouse . . .

— Raymond . . . ?

— A hobby of mine, he spread his hands. — I take on old cases sometimes. Not Joan. She's all right, taken care of. But Raymond . . .

Who was an Albigensian — or at least no less than their defender
in his province. Tormented by orthodox authorities most of his
life, he died outside that grace which Rome claimed to purvey
exclusively, and lay unburied in the Charter house of the Hospi-
tallers for four hundred years. Mr. Grierson told me much more —
told me that he had written a three-hundred-page brief in Latin
defending the acts and character of Raymond of Toulouse as those
of a most Christian prince. But that was, he said, with a perfectly
straight face, ancient history. He was working now on the defense
of Anne Albright, a young girl burned during the Marian perse-
cutions at Smithfield in 1556. It was to be a class action, aimed at
overturning the convictions of all those Protestants burned under
Mary Tudor.

— What about the Catholics, I asked sardonically, draining my
whiskey.

— Fisher, Southwell, Campion? No need. The world's good
opinion justifies them. As well waste time on More or Beckett. No,
I go for those lost to history, done to death with no posthumous
justification.

— That's a mad hobby, I told him. Somehow his pastime made
me angry. At first I supposed my anger came from the waste of
legal talent that so many people needed — like Rand McNally. But,
no, it was deeper than that. Could it be that I, a child of history,
descendant of those whom history had dragged to America, resented Grierson's tampering with the past? How many of yesterday's innocents, perjured to their graves, can we bear to have thrust
before us? Isn't the evil in our midst sufficient unto the day?

— The past is past, I said almost shortly.

Mr. Grierson looked disgusted. — My Christ, he said. I had
never heard him speak profanely before. — You sit under an
arbor in Vicksburg, Mississippi, and say that? You better get hold
of history before you go probing grace.

We were quiet for a long while then, Grierson's breach of manners resting on us both. At last he left, walking slowly, stiffly out to
that bright ancient automobile that came alive with the first press of
the starter. I stood in the yard and watched him go, and found
when I went into the house that it was much later than I had
thought.

I found myself gripped by a strange malaise the next day, and
for weeks following I did no work. I walked amidst the grassy

parkland of the old battlefields. I touched stone markers and tried to reach through the granite and marble to touch the flesh of that pain, to find what those thousands of deaths had said and meant. It was not the northern soldiers I sought: history had trapped them in their statement. It had to do with the union, one and indivisible, with equality and an end to chattel slavery. That was what they had said, whether they said it or not. But the southerners, those aliens, outsiders, dying for slavery, owning no slaves, dying for the rights of states that had no great care for their rights. In the name of Death which had engulfed them all, why?

But I could find nothing there. It was history, certainly: the moments, acts frozen in monuments, but it told me nothing. I could find nothing in it at all. One evening as the last light faded, I sat on a slope near the Temple of Illinois and wept. What did I lack? What sacred capacity for imagining had been denied me? Could I ever come to understand the meaning of the law, much less of life itself, if all history were closed to me?

Or was it not a lack but a possession which kept me from grasping the past as it presented itself, history as it laid down skein of consuming time about us all? I imagined then that it was Coronary. That I had been drawn out of history, out of an intimacy with it by that assault. What was the time or space to an anchorite who stared at forever? How could consequence matter to one who had touched All at Once? When I tried to concern myself with practical matters, I would remember Coronary and smile and withdraw into myself, forget to pay the net electric bill on time, suffering afterward the gross. Surely, I thought, I cannot care or know within history because I am beyond it, a vestal of Coronary, graced with a large probable knowledge of how I will die. Knowing too that superflux of certain action can even preempt the day of that dying. I know too much, have been too deeply touched to succumb to history. I have no past, no particulars, no accidents. I am substance of flesh tenderly holding for an instant essence of spirit. I am escaping even as I think of it. Surely, I thought, a vision of one's dying must be grace. Yes, I am in grace, whatever that means.

Toward the end of some months of such odd consideration, I saw a small notice in a New Orleans paper that announced — purported to announce — the judgment of Louisiana on Rand McNally. He had been found incompetent to stand trial. Yes. The people had adjudged him insane. Not culpable. Simply a biological misstep within history. To be confined until the end of biology corrected the error of its beginning.

I found that I was sweating. As if in the presence of something immutable, and preternaturally awful. It had no name, and I could give it no shape. I began to reduce the feeling to an idea. Was I sorry? How is that possible? Capital punishment is a ghastly relic from that past barbarism. To place a man in such state that he knows almost to the moment the time of his death is . . .

Is what? The blessing of Coronary? My God, is it punishment or grace? I sat with my face in my hands, feeling my own doomed flesh between my fingers, trying to plumb this thing and yet trying not to let the juices of my body rise stormlike within, carrying me toward that dark port once more.

One evening a few weeks later, I drove downtown and bought two dozen tamales from a cart on a street corner. It was an indulgence, the smallest of sneers behind the back of Coronary. It was possible to go on with bland food and a rare glass of wine, so long as the notion dangled there ahead that one day I would buy tamales and beer and risk all for a mouthful of pretended health.

I carried home my tamales, opened a beer, and began to eat with my fingers. The grease, the spices, the rough cornmeal, the harsh surface of the cheap beer. Before the attack, in New York, I would never have dreamed of eating such stuff. But to live in grace is to dare all things. Then I looked down at the faded stained palimpsest of the old newspaper in which the tamales were wrapped. Above Captain Easy, next to the crossword puzzle, was a short article. It told of a suicide, that of a mad rapist-killer about to be sent to the state hospital, how he had managed to fashion a noose of guitar strings and elevate himself by a steel support in the skylight.

It was Rand McNally, of course. No doubt enraged by a system so blind and feckless as to suffer his kind to live, a self-created lynch mob determined to do justice to himself. My hand trembled, spilling beer. A rapist-murderer will lead them, I think I thought. A little later that evening, my second cardiac arrest took place.

Dr. Freud, with the most fulsome humility I say you should have been in there. You would have forgotten physiology: it was not the smooth agonized tissue of my heart which sent tearful chemicals upward to trek the barren steppes of my brain. No, in there, within the futureless glow of Coronary, I was constructing my soul. What, precisely, occurred there? Why should I not smile like Lazarus and

suggest that the price of such knowledge is the sedulous management and encouragement of your own coronary involvement? Because I need to tell it. That is why we do things always, isn't it?
Because we must. Not because we should.

But never mind. That is part of what I have to tell you. I saw
Rand McNally in there, and Joan of Lorraine, Raymond of Toulouse, and Anne Albright. All in Coronary, yes, Dr. Freud. Being a
man dead, there is no reason one must honor time or space,
chronology or sequence, in his hallucinations.

It was the Happy Isles, where I was, looking much like the country around Sausalito. There was worship and diversion, of course,
and the smoky odor of terror. Two Mississippi deputies dragged
Raymond before the Inquisition. Anne Albright was condemned
once more for having denied the doctrine of Transubsegregation.
They claimed that Joan had stolen something: Cochon, pig? A
Smithfield ham! Mary Tudor curtseyed to Lester Maddox as they
sat in high mahogany bleachers in Rouen's town square. Agnew
preached against the foul heresies of all spiritual mediums while
shrouded klansmen tied Rand McNally to a stake, doused him with
whitewash, and set him afire.

I think I saw Jesus, now only an elderly Jew, in a side-street
weeping, blowing his nose, shaking his head as the Grand Inquisi-
tor passed in triumphant procession, giving us both a piercing
stare, blowing us kisses. Behind him in chains marched Giordano
Bruno and John Hus, Mac Parker and Emmett Till. Savonarola
was handcuffed to Malcolm X, and Michael Servetus walked pain-
fully, side by side with Bobby Hutton. The line went on forever, I
thought, filled with faces I did not know: those who had blessed us
with their pain, those suffering now, those yet to come. I wondered
why I was not among them, but old Jesus, who was kind, and whom
they ignored, said that there were those who must act and those
who must see. It was given, God help me, that I should see.

There were other visions which I have forgotten or which I must
not reveal. I saw then the ecstasy of Coronary, the end of all things,
and was satisfied. It was only important that nothing be lost on my
account. What does that mean?

— What does that mean? I asked Mr. Grierson when he came to
the hospital to visit me, as soon as they allowed anyone to come
at all.

— Ah, he said, his pink scalp glistening in the weak light above my bed. — Economy. You got to note all transmutations. Correct all falsehoods. Don't you see that? Lies, falsehoods, perversions of reality — those are man's sovereign capabilities. Only man can rend the fabric of things as they are. Nothing else in the universe is confused, uncertain, able to lie, except man. And through those lies, those rifts in reality, is where all things are wasted. But . . .

— But what . . . ?

— Well, Mr. Grierson smiled. — That's what my hobby is about.

— Your . . . cases . . . Anne Albright . . . ?

— Sure. No lie survives so long as the truth is stated. Those are the terms of the game.

— I don't see . . . what if people *believe* the lie . . . ?

— It doesn't matter. Tell the truth. Sooner or later that mere unprovable undefended assertion of the truth will prevail.

— How can you believe . . . ?

Mr. Grierson shrugged. — How not? We got all the time in the world. When the profit goes out of a lie, nobody wants to bother defending it any longer. That's where grace joins history, you see?

I did. I *did* see. He was right. A lie *couldn't* stand forever. Because there is no history so old, so impervious to revision, that the simple truth doesn't establish itself sooner or later. Like gravity the consequences of truth can be avoided for a while. Sometimes a little while, sometimes a great while. But in the end that which is false crumbles, falls away, and only the truth is left. So long as that truth has been once stated, no matter how feebly, under whatever pain.

— Yes, Mr. Grierson said quietly, taking a sheaf of yellowed papers out of his briefcase. — What with all the time you've got on your hands just now, I reckoned you just as well get started . . .

— Started . . . ?

He handed me the file. — In southern Texas, summer of 1892, there was this Mexican woman . . . they gave her something like a trial, then they went ahead and lynched her which was what they had in mind all along. It was the late summer of 1892. There was a panic that year, a depression, some trouble in Pullman Town . . .

I lay back, eyes closed, veteran of trances. Why not tell you of one part of my final vision? Why not? Yes, I saw, larger than the sky, what they call the Sacred Heart, burning with love for all the universe. I saw its veins and arteries, how we every one moved through it and away again, the sludge of lies and torture and deceit choking its flow like cholesterol. I saw that heart shudder, pulse

erratically. I saw the fibrillation of God's own motive center, and I
cried out that I should share His pain, and rise to the dignity of
sacrifice.

Grace is history transcendent, made true at last. And faith is the
act of embracing all time, assured of renewing it, making the heart
whole once more.

— It's an easy one, Mr. Grierson told me. — They did Rosa
Gonzales wrong. You won't have any trouble . . .

I smiled and reached for the file.

— I don't think I'll ever have any real trouble again, I told him.

H. E. FRANCIS

A Chronicle of Love

(FROM KANSAS QUARTERLY)

THE CLUB WANDERER is always in near darkness. Lights burn from invisible places. A crystal globe revolving over the dance floor sends out shafts, steady as a light at sea. Against the sunken glow the band becomes four living shadows. Front spots now and then thrust them close. During breaks, the juke blinks on for ten minutes, coiling blue-green-yellow-purple-orange over the faces clustered around the tables. At the entrance three figures, two women and the doorman, come stark against the lights whenever the door swings open. Through an arch, dim lights over the bar glitter — bottles and glasses, sometimes the flash of eyes or teeth.

The dancers are dark against the lights, silhouettes whose motion the music dictates as if with unseen strings, now leaping and veering, now drifting, swaying, or standing in a quivering freeze — but always moving, moving. The pianist's arms leap, the guitarists sway, the drummer goes frenzied, the vocalist breaks into the flood. Sounds drown over. From all the country around — and all the way from Nashville or Birmingham or even Atlanta, when there is a big-time guest star — the swingers come to hear the country western of the SOUNDS.

The day he was twenty-one, Lawton Wingfield's buddies said, "Field, tonight we're carrying you to a real place. Wow! We'll celebrate this here birthday like it's the *last*. If you don't get you a good drunk and fun and laid all to one time, we been sure miscalculating. . . ." And Field did. Then, come every Friday, he was back at the Wanderer as regular as work or church, a thing not to be omitted without breaking his new rhythm. His whole self came to be attuned to it. Going to the club was how he knew it was the end of work week and the beginning. That's what he told every-body: "Man, when you walk in there, it's the be*gin*ning."

(*John Paul Vincent*: When I heard Field's sick in the city, I went; but he wasn't in no room. Mrs. Warner said he didn't hardly stay there a minute after he come from work, got him a shower and changed clothes, and gone — she didn't know where — cept she knew he drank, but never said a word to him cause he was good and quiet, paid on the button, and she knew something was bugging him. You all right, Field? she'd say. Right as the day I was born, was all she'd get out of him. Field never was much for talking, after Alice. Don't believe nobody ever heard him say that name, Alice, one time neither, after, like the name died with her too, or her name's just for him, I don't know. Can't be far, Mrs. Warner said, he's got no car. Had a wreck, Field did, and lost it. But you know, she said, I don't think he had no wreck. I think, the way he looks sometimes, I think he let that car go, just let it go, she said. What his friend Hadley said was: he didn't even hear sometimes; and Field told Hadley: I don't know, Had, if it was accident nor not, it just hap-pened like I wasn't there. I seen — But he'd never tell what he seen. That's how come I think he didn't have no accident. I went looking — Field wasn't far: that club one block off, the Wanderer, that's where. Says: Well, John *Paul*, agrabbing me, and I seen that whole place come up in his eyes like he's not going to make it, like I was something I wasn't or maybe all of Greenville come in with me and surprised him, maybe like it was Alice; but in a minute he's turned on again — gone, way out, sailing like I never seen nobody. And *skinny!* Only I was afraid to say, but after I did: you got to take *care* now, Field, I said. Hooo, I'm in the best shape I ever been in, not a ounce of fat and all hard's a rock, he says, never was this way on the farm — *feel* that. But his face was like jaundice, no matter what he said; like a ha'nt he was; and I thought, He'll die right here this night, he ain't going nowhere or moving in about a hour, but he's on his pins, high up like a jack, and Je-*sus*, you should of *seen* that mother! I sure in a hurry changed my mind. And he didn't stop neither. He went at it till the last lick, only I don't know what happened, he all of a sudden went, passed out. We had to carry him home, they got a doctor, he said You bring him around in the morning; but there wasn't no disease nor nothing *he* could see, but says That boy's so weak he maybe won't get up again if you don't see that he gets to the hospital in the morning. The doctor began to ask about family and all. I told him too, but looked like they'd do him no good here. Only Field come round after — I sat watching him like he was going to fade out — he said You better sleep, hoss — hear? The boys pick me up for work at six. And I slept too — I didn't mean to — and when I come to he was gone. Jesus, who'd of believed it — gone to work and back and that night dancing again! I had to go to Greenville. I had to tell his folks. He couldn't go on too much like that.

Reta: Where are you *going,* Field? I'd ask him, cause he was already smiling, he was on his way — like doped up or loaded or Jesus-bit. I couldn't think of anything else to say. He looked like traveling, he'd never stop, his eyes were seeing things — he had that look — and I wanted to reach up and jerk his head down and tell him Me me me, look at *me,* but he'd study that globe or the long lights. His eyes followed like they were real and he'd lose them. He made me feel like a *thing,* just nothing. I hated him. I did, I did, I did.

Marylou: Nobody ever danced like Field. I followed him around. I'd sit and watch all night, thinking he'd ask me, but once he picked somebody it was her all the time, he most never let up, held onto her like she's his life, and dance dance dance. When the band took a break, it was the juke, and he'd even bend and bob when he wasn't dancing, aswaying, like he was rubber and couldn't stop. Sometimes it was funny — I wanted to push him like one of them toy clowns with a round bottom.

Reverend Bullard: Lawton used to come to Greenville, to the church — I'd see him from the rectory window — never when there was service, always Saturday — and stand outside and stare. He'd be there a long time, walk around the grounds, and go back and look at that door, then go away. He never set foot in the church. Perhaps he'd stay fifteen minutes, half an hour. He never looked sad, no — but quiet and natural, a bit at home even. I never went out to disturb him.

Wendy: Call me his Tuesday girl. Every Tuesday, like clockwork. And all night. How'd Field ever get to work? Who knows? He'd

leave me in bed. I don't think he even knew who I was by then.
Sometimes he'd slip and call me Alice. Who cares? He gave me a
good time and if I had to be Alice for him to make it that good,
okay, so I'm Alice.)

Friday night

FIELD: Like it says in the Bible, Alice, I come to a city over five
months now, only it ain't like you think. Oh, it's all shining all right,
them neons make it so bright you see it miles, yeah, it makes a great
big whale of a light in the sky, a mountain you're going to big as a
promise, like driving fast to, only when you get there, it come
down, you're on it and can't see *it* anymore, just a couple of miles of
neons, and they're pretty, they sure are, like an invite to anything
you ever dreamed could be, you know, like the sun at home daytime only this here's here, makes you feel the things are so close
you can grab them. Grab what? Well, I had to find out, you gone
and all, and came here. It's a stone city, and days, when the neons
are gone, it's like they just died quiet come morning, and the city's
not even there, not the same one, it's a whole different thing, like
it's got a mind of its own and a body too, you know what I mean?
And days I get a hankering for green and dirt under my feet, not
cement, stone, asphalt and all — makes your feet hurt, cept when
you're dancing. I'm dancing all the time now, Alice, like I'm with
you and loving dancing the way you did, and I got me some prizes
even, they're yours, they really are; if it wasn't for you, I'd never of
danced anyway, not one time, I don't know — maybe that's a lie,
but how do you know? Anyway I'm *telling* you, that's how come you
know. *You* taught me — remember? Daddy said no, not to go, he'd
give me the farm, always said I'd be him someday and my kids
standing in that same doorway and looking at the view, and I swear
to God I can see the view right now bigger than the ceiling and high
and wide and so fresh with air, Alice; and Momma she said I'll not
have a body to cook for f-you go, son, and that almost broke me up.
I couldn't tell them why, why I was going, and you got to hand it to
them, they didn't prize it out of me, not even try cept Momma's
hangdog look when she wants to get her way, only I still wouldn't
tell them, in their heart they know I guess, I don't know, and I'm
getting letters all the time — oh, it ain't but a hour from here,

sometimes Daddy comes in to business, I seen him bout a month
ago, and he said Son, you looking bad, you better come home, this
life ain't doing you no good, but I said Got me a steady job in
construction almost five months now, I can't go back on that, and
he said Guess you cain't if you feel that way, son. It's that *son* got
me. Daddy he don't use it like that all the time, son son son, like he
got a hankering to. Well, ain't we all? And he give me all the news,
said the Hansons moved to town, mister got too old to keep things
going; Whip McCord gone to college — imagine, Whip! — and
Bethanne McCune married ole Jimmie Haley — *Jimmie,* what
never settled down one *minute* in his life; and Willa Mae took a job
as a librarian in town; seven boys gone to Vietnam; and Wick —
you remember how he pestered me to go with him hunting all the
same times I was sneaking off with you? — the Viet Cong got him;
and all the news, only nothing from your house — that's how come
I know Momma and Daddy's sure why I come here without one
time saying it; it made me feel better I tell you, Alice, only cept
when Daddy went; he said I'll tell momma we had a long talk; and I
give him a linen handkerchief for momma I bought one time for
when she'd go to church, you know when she gets to hacking and
one of Daddy's won't do; and then he got in the truck, he said
Better be careful, boy, you looking mighty bad, I won't tell your
momma that; and I almost couldn't see him when he said that, but
it don't matter none's long's I can dance, I got to keep dancing, it's
the time you're there, Alice, I feel you — you know that — and you
know something, Alice — course you do! — you know that ball
hangs right smack there in the center of the dance floor, it makes
colored lights moving slow, every color, and when it hits, you see
faces just one sec, like it's all a dream and you drifting like water's
carrying you past everything far far. Last night I sure got going
good, you know, I mean that music tore right through me and
made my blood sing so it's going like that rhythm abeat and abeat
taking me right up there, agoing so my feet's dancing on fire and
my arms touching the sky and me like getting longer and longer till
my hands near touched that light and it come in my eyes and made
me feel all lit up inside and about to bust into it all and — you know
what, Alice! — them faces bobbed and bobbed, I got like dizzy and
that light white as fire and I seen your face just as clear, it tore me
up, and I reached out quick and all that music saying *Alice* and me
too *Alice, Alice,* and I must of passed out, I couldn't dance any

more, or I fell or something, but my whole heart's to bust I'm so happy cause I seen you, I seen your face.

*

Six nights a week the band plays. They give the place a soul, slow and fast, always loud, a vibrating voice that trembles everything. All the place keeps moving, the juke instantly merging into their last struck note. One of the three owners is always at the entrance, a smile of welcome. Weekends Jaw sells tickets, fifty cents cover charge, for the whole long night; and Willyjo, the doorman, a kind-faced ox-broad man not very tall, pounds his fist into his palm rhythmically, and taps, and rolls on heels and toes, arock half the night in a partnerless dance. When the door swings out, the neon freeway pours scorching bright light in. "Hey, Freddie!" "What say, Jimbo?" "You're sure lookin' cool, honey." "Man, get a load-a that!" "You'd cream just lookin' at her!" "Which side is up?" They laugh in the warm, near air and cigarette smoke and wafted alcohol. From a side room, especially during band breaks, comes the familiar clack of pool balls. Cries, laughs, jeers fill the room — Joe PeteMiriamWaltBickWillaMaeLoisJimmieMurphAngieRoberta.

Each entry shuts a door. Outside, a hundred rooms vanish. The world recedes into deep and endless dark. The Wanderer holds its own lights, faces, past — familiar. Ben, one of the owners, smiles. "Ready, Will? Say, Gert, another screwdriver here." The bartender, Bob, knows them all inside out and backwards ("You heard about ole Harry's pullin' a gun on that drummer last night? One o'clock in the a.m. the cops come, askin' where he headed —"). And the waitresses, Gert and Eula, are faces constant as drink, despite the shifting wigs and eyes and lashes and gewgaws and rage of outfits. And the other constants are there: the half-drunk little carpetlayer hanging on the end of the bar; the NASA engineer; the Fayetteville carpenter; the long-haired, dark girl from the Studebaker place; Alton, the Vietnam vet; Paul, the bootlegger from New Hope.

Whenever Field looked around they were all there. He breathed it all in deep. "*Hey*, Field!" "Hey, Ben. Hey, Eula," he said. "Bud?" Bob said, bottle and glass ready. "And a double shot of E.T.," Field said. He relaxed — back, as if at home, a family. Light glowed. The dark burned.

(*Roanna:* Met him downtown by Grant's this one Friday morning
and I don't know what but something just stopped him cold when
he saw me like he thought I was *some*body — you know, somebody
not *me*. He near flipped when he came to. Me, Roanna Wilcox, I
said. *I* know Roanna, he said, looking like he still didn't but looking
hard too, and I put it out for'm to see too. Sure don't look like no
country girl right now, he said. Pure country, I said, you *know* it —
he ought to, coming from right down my way there by the Piggly-
Wiggly sign — and I touched his arm, quick: You doing all right,
Lawton? And just that quick li'l ole touch did it, he came round, he
came right close like he's going to have me right there against
Grant's window, and I laughed and said Now, Lawton, and quick
he said How bout dancing tomorrow night, it's Sat'dy, and we can
go down to the River Club after and never stop, what say? Why,
Lawton, I said. Only he ain't so dumb; this time he reached out and
touched my shoulder and his hand hard and rough-skinned it just
sent shivers down me. You're from my town, he said, like it was the
sweetest thing. And he made it that way all night too at the club and
me thinking every minute Pretty soon we'll leave, we'll go it somewhere — in the car or the grass or back of my place, or he got a
place, about to die with him rubbing me like that sometimes, and
when it's over, him near passing out from dancing and drinking,
and fell asleep on me and me on top of him to wake him up and go
at it, I couldn't stand it, and drove back home alone without a
thing, Goddamn it.

Reddick Farr: His daddy was the only one came. Mrs. Warner
couldn't say a word to him. I said Field wouldn't have nobody
around, a loner he was since he came here, only he didn't seem
alone, he had something in his head, I don't know what. His daddy
just looked at him. Said How'll I tell his momma? And it Sunday
too. Jesus!

Kim: Always did prefer ectomorphs, and he certainly was that.
Field was on the construction crew for the new building. He told
me how he went dancing at the Club Wanderer. I got the hint and
couldn't resist. And he *did* dance. You're a little out of my class, he
said. And you out of my orbit, I said. He laughed, a rather boyish
innocent laugh too. There was something terribly moving about
him. I wanted to hold him and comfort him, tell him it was all right.

And in bed when he was sleeping, I did hold his head, so thin and long his face, with long dark lashes, and long brown hair. But the rest of him was all hard, wiry, all energy — maddening in bed, with a terrible impersonal drive. I felt used, used, with an enormous indifference by him — and I wanted that.)

Saturday night

FIELD: Oh, Alice, I'm telling you this every night, honey, only what can I do, me not wanting to talk to nobody, everybody's you — I can't help it — I'm looking at them, but it's you. Pretty soon I'm dancing up a storm. I know how it is: I try — I say I'm going out with Sue, Alice wouldn't want me to just moon like this; but it's because *that* — you wouldn't want me to do it — that's why I do it: if you wanted me to it wouldn't mean the same thing, now would it, Alice, honest? It's cause you *don't.* Maybe that don't make no sense, but it's the onliest way I know. Mornings — not just one time, Alice, but every morning — since you gone I been waking up like I died and come back and it ain't real. First thing, I think The bed's *real,* I ain't dead, Alice's here; and for a sec I believe it too, I leap out and get in my clothes — it's like back on the farm with Daddy and Momma, and I know if I look out the kitchen window I can see straight out to the sun smack on your bedroom window just the way I could nighttime fore you put your light out, and me watching, like it's the moon right inside your room shining for me — you saying Field, I'm never going to pull the shade down so's you can't stop seeing me — ever. And I ain't — I ain't stopped *one* second since I seen you in the river. Ohjesusgod, Alice, why why *why?* Oh, don't, *don't* answer me, Alice, I can't stand that: I know it's me, I did it, but you got to know: I'm trying, I'll make up for it, I *will* too, Alice. You won't be ashamed your Field's just gone and forgot with no shame for what he done. Listen here, Alice, I ain't never gonna stop till it's done, and I reckoned with it, and it's right by you, if it takes twenty years — hear? You *hear* me, Alice? Why don't you answer me? Alice! I been waiting all day for your voice, just one *sound* since last night, cause I seen your face, Alice, and now I'm waiting for you to say it so I'll know I'm getting there cause I can hear it in my head, I *been* hearing it day and day and day, like never stopping, only I want to hear it *out,* I'll know I'm *with* you, in the

same place, I done it, and you forgive me and we'll be together. I
work like a dog, Alice, yes — you believe it? ole Field the farmer's
son working like a dog in the city! Ain't it a joke? But I got to, I stop
one minute and you're there and then I'd of had to leave work and
start looking for you, there ain't no *way* to stop if you get in my
head. It's all I can do to keep you back — *Till five* I'd tell me, *Till
five*. That's all I could do, even when you was there, say *Till five,
don't think about* — I'd not even say your name, but I heard it and
I'd work harder, *Till five,* and come five o'clock I'd be in my room
and washed and changed, only now I'm not even doing that, I just
come straight here to the club and get me that cool beer and a
double shot to begin and another cool beer and, oh man, I can say
it *Alice,* like free — and you're right there. You come floating up,
far — I see you, just like you was, only you're *now,* in your white
dress, all of you so small, and all your legs showing, that little mini,
and all your shoulders, I'm smelling your long black hair on me. I
want to put my hand right in the mirror and tell you Alice, come
dance with me, honey. And you know: I'm already dancing, my
heart's dancing thinking about you and you coming with that white
dress, and my feet's starting. That ball of light — you see it,
Alice — it hits them colors round and round, it goes and goes, and
band time it beats with the band, they send the old rhythm right
into them lights and pretty soon they're going right into you, like
they're touching and warm, and getting warmer, and your blood
goes, it begins, it starts abeating, abeating, and your blood beats,
abeating; and it's your legs beating, and your toes, and your arms;
and it's all of you pretty soon abeating. I got to get up. I got to go
get Alice. She's sitting there in the dark. She's at one of them tables.
She's all alone waiting for me. She knows I'm coming. I see her
eyes, all the light in her eyes, in the dark and holding it for me, yes
she is. And I go right to her close, and I feel her hand and take her
. . . and quick as anything it's you, Alice, you're right there against
me so good it hurts, I'm about to bust, and a minute I shiver like,
standing there and swaying, swaying, and I can feel it already going
right into you, my hot and my blood like my skin's yours, and you
come back into me, and me into you, and you can't tell which, and
then moving and swaying like we're all alone, moving round in a
circle, standing still and moving; and dipping, dipping; moving
and moving; and the lights going round and round till it's like
carrying, the music's lifting us and carrying. And I ain't letting you

go, Alice, never a time: nothing going to stop us even with you klack-klack-klacking to a fast one and your arms legs and whole body and hair swinging and throwing and flying high and your bubs shaking and hips wiggling and legs leaping, and when I close my eyes feeling you I see you just the same through my eyelids, yes I *do,* that light comes right through, I can feel it — you believe that? — and you, I see *you* in it, waiting for you to come down, your face, and kiss me, only it don't. I keep thinking it will, I feel me getting longer and longer, I try, I keep reaching only it's like I ain't long enough, but if I got up enough steam and danced harder, I could move, I'd get so light I'd float up on the music, right smack up to you, and I'd feel your face against mine; and I get afraid, Alice: comes a minute — I *know* it's coming — and it's going to make me want to cry and yell, but I can't he'p it — I think if I open my eyes, I won't see it, but if I do it'll be gone, don't go, Alice! And it's water, everything's water, I'm looking, and there's your face, and all your hair, and the willow branch almost touching it, and a leaf floating by, and you still, looking at me out of the water, and I got to touch your face, Alice, I got to put my hand in the water and touch your face, both of my hands, I can't stand it, I'm reaching and quick my voice's saying *AliceAliceAliceAliceAliceAlice,* my blood's crying it, and all of me beating, and I open my eyes and a minute it's me under, and hands reaching down, but they're mine, going like *mad* like *mad* like *mad* like *mad* and you're there and you going like *mad mad mad mad mad,* your hips and arms and legs and hair and hair and hair hair hair hair hair drum drum drum drum drum woweeeee, we going and leaping leaping and pretty soon close rubbing and sliding, sliding and rubbing, oh baby Alice you going to make me come right here on the floor, slow slow grinding slow slow grinding grinding, and I'm getting there, getting on high, I feel it riding that music, that rhythm coming with a long slow heave, long long long now, and pulling pulling, and I'm getting there slow, slow moving up, up, oh Alice I'm going to, I'm going to, going to touch, right out and reach your face that's coming down to me. And then I'm waking up it's bright light I can't stand, sun, morning sun, and the walls all dirty wallpaper, them flowers like dead and dried in a winter field gone to seed, and dark ribbons straight down the walls, and that light, and them blinds making dark bars on the floor, my eyes're wet from the sun and the night before and I got to get up quick, I wish I was dead, my head's

bustin, Jake'll pick me up in a minute. Good thing I'd moved close
to the club or I'd be up the creek, only Alice I couldn't stand it,
thinking it's the only place I'd get to you, and here I am dancing
with you again, I'll never stop, no never till I'm with you 'one
minute past eternity,' yes *our song:* and there I go, it's your face
coming up close to the water, only like if I look long *I'm* under and
looking up and you looking down at me, it gets all twisted and I
wanted to get out from under the water and *to* you. Sometimes I
want to move my arms only I can't, like the water's holding them
down, I want to scream then, only the water's filling my mouth and
then quick the water moves and you gone, gone, Alice, and I can't
see or yell or touch, thinking I'll never see you again, about to go
crazy thinking that, and thinking you're getting even for all them
girls I'm dancing with and kissing and screwing, but Alice, you
know something: I get dancing and get me going and feel them
warm and begin to *go,* up, high, up up up, and — I don't know how
come — but I ain't *here,* I'm floating, oh baby I'm going fast so fast
sucked up in a thing so strong I know I'm going to hit, I know it —
going to hit and *pow* explode and go everywhere, smithereens, and
then all of a sudden it's you: *pow* and it breaks like fireworks and
then honey it's so quiet and you come so clear, clearest light I ever
seen, like you're close as that ball turning round in the ceiling and if
I reach up I'll touch your long hair and face I love: only somebody's crying, it's my momma — *yes,* momma — and I say Momma,
what's making you cry? like I *know* only don't, and Poppa's standing
there with his hand on her shoulder and looking at me like when
my dog Wilbur got runned over, and I *know:* you said to me It'd
get dark forever if I couldn't see you no more, Field; you said
There's no man in this here world for me but you, Field, you know
that, Field; you said I'd not live a day without you if I thought you
believed Andrew Phelps ever come *near* me cept that one kiss he
snuck and me not knowing he was there, it didn't mean a thing, I'd
of run, I *did* slap him too; you said Nobody touched me the month
I was at my cousin Willa Mae's, nobody ever would but you, Field,
and the letters are from a boy likes me but you *know* I won't look at,
I swear it, I'll swear on the Bible, I'll swear before Reverend Bullard and the whole church, Field; you said What's in my belly's
yours, Field, gonna look like you, you wait, then you'll be ashamed
you ever said a word, you'll take it all back and love me all your life,
you will, just you wait and see. And oh, Alice, I do, I love you now

like never before; never knew I'd love you so much I couldn't stand
even to live without you. I got to go where you are. I had to find the
way, Alice. I come one night and danced and there you was. You
was in my arms, apressing and agliding, like a miracle come in me,
and I knew I couldn't let you go: when I woke up it wasn't you, but
I knew I'd had you for a minute, maybe a hour, maybe all night,
and I'd get you back: so I come here, I danced, I danced, I kept
dancing, I couldn't stop dancing, I can't now: I'm getting to you,
Alice, I know I am, and I won't stop, never, till I'm with you — you
hear me? And maybe you'll tell me it's not doing any good, but you
just wait till you see this time I mean it, I do, I'll never stop dancing
till I'm in your arms forever and you can't let me go, I won't let you,
only sometimes I can't make it, Alice, you know I get to falling, I
get so weak — me — go ahead, *laugh!* — me, ole Field, getting so
weak he almost can't stand up, but something pushes me, keeps me
going till the last song and then go on like I'm dancing out the door
and in the car and in bed even and sleeping too, it never stops, the
room's still athumping when I wake up and all day that music's
pounding in me when I'm banging nails and lugging boards. Come
five o'clock it gets strong, stronger every minute, till I'm back in the
dark and that light going round and the band comes *one minute past
eternity;* it's like you, I'm near you, that place; like I lay my head
right down in the dark against your skin, the dark's all warm, and
you say Come on, honey, come onnnnn, Field, we'll dance, honey,
and me getting up feeling you all soft and warm and cool too agin
me, and fore I know it I'm dancing, I'm swinging and swaying and
leaping and bouncing and jerking, keeping time, keeping the beat
with you and that music and that hot air touching like it's water and
your face under water, it comes, it's looking at me, ohjesus it's
looking at me, and if just one time you'd say Field, it's your fault;
but you never did, nobody ever accused me but me, and Momma
and Poppa looking at me so soft and pitying like looking at my own
dog, and Reverend Bullard's soft voice and all them people and
nobody not one accusing, saying a word to me but me me me me *me*

*

The neon sign CLUB WANDERER burns around the clock. In the
sun it fades a sickly blue and red, but with nightfall it beckons, stark
and beautiful in the empty sky. With each opening of the door,

some soul loosed from the sounds spills onto the freeway. From outside, in the night traffic, you would not suspect the seething rhythm, the collective beat like a heart throbbing deep in the night; only the parking lot, filled to overflowing, tells you something is happening close by. During the week it is the lone pool player, seeking, who comes, and the isolate couple, the vagrant drinker, the so-called perpetuals; weekends it is the lovers, mates — couple time, rest and desire, escape and search — commingled with the usuals. The regulars know that if you go away for days, weeks, months, even years, and come back, some of them will be there; it is the place to find them; sit long enough and the missing will walk in, no longer phantoms from the past, for sooner or later nearly all return. "How's everything on the West Coast?" "Hey, man, ain't seen you since Vegas." "Lauderdale! Too empty. Nothing doing!" The truckdrivers make the Wanderer known all over the country. "Wilson struck a hydrant on US 1, off Elizabethtown." "Heard about Field?" "Heard about Bess Wickham's shooting all the way up to Dayton." "What's Larry doing now?" "She's making it in New Orleans, got guts that girl." Inside, they wait — for dates, loan, two-timer, wife-stealer, thief, friend. Nobody is forgotten. Away long enough, he comes up in the conversation. "Can't stay away too long, it's in the blood." They have every confidence. When the moment comes, the light is burning outside, a stark, beckoning sign.

(*Walt Everst:* I got there too late. His landlady said Field just got took away — to Greenville. Had to turn me around directly and go back home.

Sue: Why was he dancin' that way, for *what?* I wanted him — yes, I did, me, and I went through all that with him, drinking and dancing. My God, I'm sick of dancing; I never want to see a floor in my life, after him. Near killed me with his dancing. *What for?* He'd not answer, he'd look through me, he'd look like I wasn't even there. It'd make me madder'n hell. Sometimes I even hit him and then he'd smile or laugh and grab me, and what could I do then, I wanted him so? I don't go near the Wanderer now. I hate that place, *hate* it.

Mrs. Wingfield: His daddy stops and stands in the fields. I see him from the kitchen. He stops work and looks, like he's waiting. Only

he ain't waiting. He al'ays did. But he cain't now. He keeps lookin'
into the ground, and sometimes up. Then he gits mad and works
like you never seen him go. But I know he'll sell it. He's waitin' for
me to put my foot down and say no. He knows I will too: he cain't
stop workin' and sit. He knows that'd kill him sure. Used to be he'd
look out there like it'd just go on, somebody else'd come, and
somebody else, somebody he *knew,* and he'd die comf'table knowin'
it was one-a his, like he had somethin' to do with it even after he
was gone. But seems like to me now he just stops and looks up like
he got no place to go.)

Sunday night

FIELD: Alice, you're talking to me, baby, I know you are — there's a
sound I never did hear before in that music, like somebody
touched the guitars in a way not before, and the piano and the
drums and all together they got a extra sound never come before,
makes my blood tingle and hum, me all humming, Alice, never
hummed like this before; a sound come. What you think of that? A
sound — it's taking me to you, I'm riding it, I sure am, Alice, taking
me to you like it's your voice in my blood trying to tell me and if I
open my mouth it'll come out — I will too, I'll open it — and *you'll
say it,* me talking and you talking like one sound; then I'll know I
got you, I'm touching you like that ball of light come to my hand at
last, and I'll kiss your face happy out of my mind, blow it, and never
leave you, whole hog. Only, Alice, sometimes my hand don't do
what I tell it, or my legs, I'm dancing in my head, only legs slow or
dragging and arms flopping — how come?— I *can't* fall off now,
honey; it's time, been too long; and Momma come last night right
in the middle of the night and said Field? Field? You hear me,
Field? and I was saying Yes, Momma, only seemed like she'd not
hear, saying Field? and my eyes wide open's could be in the pitch
black cept for the light over the city. I come to a city, Alice, and
Momma's in the city atalking, Field, son, we want you home, you
got to come home or there'll be nothing left-a you, Field honey,
and then what'll your poppa do, going along with you the way he
done so you could try yourself out and then hopefully come home
and take over the way he says you're supposed to, ain't no life this
city life for a boy's got so much country in him, pure country your

daddy says, says How come he's wasting pure country in the city,
I'd like to know. Field, honey? And Momma's right there, only my
eyes filled with that big dark and I can't touch her; and it's morning
and Daddy he's standing there but real, says You going to a hospital, Field, or you ain't living long, and it's the first time I ever seen
like a shadow of water in my daddy's eyes, and you know, Daddy he
ain't never showing it, but this time ups and shouts at me A hospital, a hospital, you hear me, Lawton Wingfield? And you know,
Alice, I had to out and laugh loud's I could to hear my daddy talk
thataway, for a minute it was like *you* caring; and me getting up and
putting on my clothes; Alice, I had to hang onto the bureau — you
believe that? — and fell, I couldn't he'p it, but had to get out fore
they called somebody, I ain't going to no hospital, and it's Sunday
and the sun out and burning; everything's so green I think I never
seen things before, a tad of grass around the house, but them *trees*
swinging over the houses with wind, like you in it, Alice, it's *that*
good: and Daddy's shouting at me, and me back at him, I couldn't
he'p it, Alice, he don't understand, I'll *go* back home, Daddy, but
you let *me* do it, I'll decide and then pop I'll be there one day on the
stoop — okay, Daddy? and him standing there, but I know he's
going to do something, I know it. So I got me away, I got to Bill
Wamp's place by the church and sat in the fi'ty-six Ford up on
blocks, up there on Ninth Street, cause I got this thing to do, my
legs are abeat with it even when they ain't moving, Alice, like dancing in my head even when I ain't dancing, it never stops, *I* ain't
never stopping cause long's I'm dancing I'm with you, honey, no
matter what, come hell or high water: and your face in the river,
the water's over it, only I feel water, air's all water, touching, only
how can I see your face and it's mine too, I feel the water, only why
don't you let me have it? — you ain't never accused me, only your
eyes looking out of the river at me are worse than anything, Alice;
if only one time you'd say Field, I done forgive you, one time Alice,
I'd maybe sleep a minute and rest and think She's beside me, I
don't worry none; but everywhere I go I'm seeing your face and
eyes in the sky and trees green and the sidewalk and through that
there Ford windshield and working in the cement and on bricks
and in the dark worse, the only thing, like your eyes are that big
white light over the city come down and holding me and never
letting me out, Alice honey, only please please *Say* it one time: You
done it, Lawton Wingfield, you killed me, so it'll be like I got down

on my knees before Momma and Poppa the first time and said I did
it, I can tell it all now, I did it, I didn't mean to, and to all my
buddies don't know and all the church and all the town and God
even, like as if *He* didn't know too, Alice; like it's this here Sunday
and I made it to the Sunday afternoon jazz session and they're all
here — like it is, Alice — they *are* here, every one of them — and
you give me the word, just say it, *the* word, Alice, and I can throw
me down right in the middle of all that music and rhythm and
pumping and tell it like it was: I killed Alice Falls, my wife even if
we didn't tie the knot yet, and I was wrong playing around like she
wasn't even mine to make her jealous and love me more and not be
able to stand one minute away from me, and thinking she'll come
round when *I* want her, and she did, she did it like I told it, and
carrying mine and me not knowing a while and then when she says
it, thinking *she* been cheating the way I'm doing and wanting to kill
her and *did* — just by walking off and telling her I'll never see you
again, I don't want to see your face, never want to look at you, hope
it's born dead and you gone with it; and packing my things and
telling them I'm going on construction in Huntsville, I'm going
there and beginning; beginning, yes, Alice, and it was the ending;
Lonnie he come telling me first thing I's in a room and making
money and thinking Maybe I'll die and never have to think about
her again cause, honest, Alice, I never thought of anything but you
on the walls and in the mirror and in the bed till I'm thinking I
can't never sleep in no small box like this room, no box of no kind,
without I'm tight in with her and going crazy out of my mind with
her. Momma said She's the sweetest thing this world knows, why'd
she do a thing like that? and Daddy and Momma and everybody I
know at the church and then Field, How come you stayed away?
old Bickley says, and me *blind* with you, Alice, ready to die, and
couldn't stay away from that church one day after and that night —
you know what, Alice? — I went there — sure you remember —
and slept all night right beside you, me near dead too, wishing I
was beside both of you, and not knowing, never knowing now, who
it'd be, like me or you, a boy or a girl, or what'd it bring with it,
maybe it'd have kids and its kids like forever, and it cut off with you
in the river and I'm me wanting to know where you done it, how —
you jumped off that Runkley bridge way up where we'd go nights?
or just slip and let yourself not move or fall? maybe you did fall?
Jesus, Alice, God help me, it'll drive me crazy you don't tell me or

just come down, come down from that light going and no don't tell
me, just yell it out It's your fault, Lawton Wingfield, just yell it out,
yellllllll, it's in my blood, I can hear it all beating, oh Alice baby, you
feel that rhythm, man there never was a band like the SOUNDS, and
you dancing like you never danced before tonight, like we never
was together thisaway, so close you're ole Field hisself, and that
light it's getting so bright almost to blind me but I ain't taking my
eyes off it one time, noooooo, Alice, you ain't leaving me tonight,
you coming down, you coming close, you going to touch down with
that white face and smiling and say Field honey, I love you, Field
honey, don't never leave me; and I'm going to touch your face with
both my hands, Alice, you so close you'll never get far from Field
again, you feeling it now, Alice? that beat like it's your heart, feel it?
It's abeat and abeat, uuuuuuuuhhhhhhhhh, man, Alice, it's bout to
swell right out of me, it's moving and moving, it's leaping like it's
going to bust out and go into this here room, like water, your face,
come down, Alice, and kiss me and tell me it's all right, just one
time, please, Alice, my heart's to bust if you don't, oh man, *lis*ten to
that, that sound, that sound like them SOUNDS *never* made before,
never, no, they going to carry me, oh that sound, Alice, it's going to
carry me; look at that light, look, I'm looking: it never been so
bright; Alice, if I reach I'm going to touch it, and I'll do it too,
Alice, make my arms stretch out I don't care how long if you'll just
one time come closer, say it; I been trying so hard, Alice, I never in
my life tried so hard to do anything like dancing till I can't no more
and every bit of me's going to you, I can't stop cause if I do, you
won't be there; I'm afraid, Alice, yes I am, I got to tell you that,
without you I'd die and I don't know how, this here's the only way
to get to you, Alice, and be near you and never stop without you're
in my arms, oh Alice you hear that beat, it's going, it's getting there,
it's moving up up up, mannnnnnn, feel it a beat beat beat, my
heart's going, it's going so fast, it's making — listen to that, that
sound, Alice it's coming, it's coming yes from down in me, it's in my
blood, it's coming from my heart going to you, Alice; you hear it?
yes you do, you do, I see it, I see your face, it's coming, Alice,
jesusgod you *do* hear, you coming down, that light's getting there, I
getting to it, I *am,* Alice, ohjesusgod it's beating beating abeat like
never, abeat-abeat-abeat woweeeeeeeeee going, I'm going to make
I'm going to come right in my britches, Alice, if you, if you . . .
yessss, bust out into the air, it's going to go right through my skin

and into air and sweat and water and smoke and that light, it's so
bright, and you, Alice, I see you, *Alice!* yes ohmygodjesus, Alice,
thank you, baby, come on, come onnnnnn, we going to make it, we
going to make it together, going to *be* there, I feel it coming, it's
burning up up up, oh my blood and that heart's beating beating
and this whole room growing and all light and you coming down,
and now, Alice honey, your face, it's so close I can touch if I reach
out with my hands, yes I will, I will, my heart's beating and my head
and all this room, my heart busting out into this whole room, Alice,
Now, now, tell them, *tell* them I done it and I made up for it, Alice,
in the only way I know how, dancing, dancing, and to get to you,
tell them. I'm burning, Alice, and yes I can now I will touch you;
see, honey, my hands, they're moving, my arms, they're going right
up to that light, reaching to touch, I'm going to touch you, I'm
going to touch, I'm going to

JOHN HAGGE

Pontius Pilate

(FROM CARLETON MISCELLANY)

IF YOU LIVE IN NEW MEXICO, you go to bed in the summer, and it is cool and dry and the only sound you hear is the constant scraping of the cicadas sending out their mating calls, and if you go outside and stand under the streetlamp and look for the cicadas, you can never find them. But if you attend summer school in Minnesota, it is hot and humid, and you lie in bed naked as sin and float on a sticky film of sweat; and you cannot get to sleep because your mind jumps from one thing to another like drops of water bouncing off a larded pan when you test whether the griddle is hot enough to pour the pancake batter in. Mainly you think about sex. The only way you can stop thinking is to listen for thunder because then you know something will happen: the air will cool and you can sleep. Perhaps it will rain. And it is pleasant to listen to rain when you don't have to get wet. But after it rains, next day is hotter.

Next morning after the rain when you drag yourself out of bed, the sun is burning the dew off the grass, and the earthworms lie smashed, the impress of a tire or heel left carelessly on them, and the faint miasma of their death hangs in the air and mingles with the steam from the grass. But that Saturday I paid no attention to the odor of the earthworms or the steam from the grass.

As I was cleaning my room, my two best summer school friends dropped in. Both were pre-seminary students. One was handsome, stupid, and believed in the literal truth of the word of God. The other was ugly, brilliant, and believed what he wanted about the truth of God. The ugly one had grown uglier because he had shaved his head totally bald during the break between sessions when I had ridden the bus to northern Minnesota to see Becky, and had broken the sixth commandment in the back of her minister father's station wagon parked in an alley after seeing Noel Coward's *Private Lives*. When I had returned to school, I had gone into Thomas Leeward's room and had seen him shaving off the last remnants of his hair with an electric razor.

"Why the hell are you doing that?" I had asked. He had mumbled something, but the truth was, I think, that he did not have the foggiest notion why he had done that but at the moment shaving his head seemed the thing to do, just as it had seemed the thing to do to have Becky in her father's car.

To put off studying, my friends and I would do anything. Mostly we played cards or had great theological discussions in which I participated little but smiled a great deal because I thought I had the truth of the universe balled up in my hand: and the truth was there was no truth.

"Cleaning your room for her?" observed Leeward ironically, because he had gotten an engagement broken off and was living out the rest of his days in heroic despondency. Maybe that was why he shaved his head.

"When's she coming?" asked Lief. Lief Erickson was his name, and although he could not help it, maybe that was what made him stupid. I thought he glanced around uneasily, and I could see a vague notion rising inside his head like bread dough without enough yeast: where was she going to sleep? Then I saw something beat down the dough because Lief was a simpleton who could find no wrong whatsoever in anyone. You could shake his hand while you snatched his wallet and all the time he would say what a fine fellow you were and how he believed in you, and that if only you believed in yourself and Jesus, the world would come up roses and the lion would walk with the lamb. He was the perfect Christian, and everyone hated him for it.

"Around noon."

Queenie called at twelve o'clock. She was waiting at the bus depot downtown.

The sun was scorching the grass. It was humid and there was no place for the sweat to go so it clung to you like it was your girlfriend who was afraid of the thunder and whom I was running madly to see. I was running madly to see my Queenie: and I'll take her back to my room and then we'll . . . And on the way I thought about the days we had spent in love.

This. I waited at the truck stop and got in the way while Queenie
and Mama Garcia cleaned up. Mama Garcia was the sebaceous
owner of the truck stop who fooled tourists into thinking she was
Spanish even though she spoke with a Bronx accent and had Green-
stein as a surname: but they wanted to believe it because if they
believed it they could think that they were having authentic enchi-
ladas and could write a postcard home about it. Queenie and I left
arm-in-arm. Her uniform was damned short and nearly trans-
parent and as we walked I wanted her very badly. That was the way
it always was with her. But it began to thunder, and Queenie got
scared because she hated thunder, and just as we reached shelter
under the roof of a medical building on the University of New
Mexico campus, it began to rain. The rain came out of the sky in a
solid mass. The wind was blowing, and it was cold, and it was thundering, and Queenie was hiding her head on my shoulder. When it
stopped thundering Queenie wanted to run in the rain. But I hated
the rain. A man exited from the building and said to no one in
particular, "It sure is cold" and then looked at us and said "But you
have your love to keep you warm," and then dashed off into the
rain. And that night I wrote what he said in my little black notebook where I keep addresses of people I have forgotten, and serial
numbers of items lost long ago, and plot lines for stories I never
will write.

And this. We sat in the grass at our high school eating sack
lunches and it was pleasant and warm there in the spring sun, and
I never could eat much because when she sat close to me her hair
exuded a sun-warmed smell of some sort of spice with a trace of
sulfur in it which must have been from her shampoo and which for
me was always the smell of desire. And our friends came to visit us
there sometimes — Gary James, and Zebra the freak, and my best
friend Don Dark. But I did not want them there because I wanted
Queenie alone: but no one would ever let us be alone. One time our
assistant principal caught us kissing and threatened to call our
parents for showing "undue affection." Queenie talked him out of
it, but she always felt guilty about the episode. My favorite teacher
said the assistant principal would practically jump over people for-
nicating on the lawn to chastise a couple holding hands. And she
said one day Queenie would be a beautiful woman.

And much more: Queenie in her short spring dresses, Queenie's body warmly pressed against mine, Queenie and I trying to talk on the phone while our mothers listened, Queenie's letters my first year away at school, her legs deeply tanned the next summer, the tears at leaving again, and wanting her always.

Halfway downtown I stopped running because I was hot and out of breath, even though I had quit smoking for Queenie at Christmas, the last time I had seen her. I walked to the seedy hotel which served as the bus depot, and she was standing there in the lobby with a dilapidated leather suitcase beside her.

"Queenie! God I'm glad you're here!"

"Happy Birthday, Jack!" My birthday was next Friday, and that was one reason she had come to see me.

I kissed her.

"I'm dying of thirst, Jack. Isn't there some place where we can get something to drink? It's so hot and sticky here. Albuquerque was cool and dry when I left."

I kissed her. I kissed her again, and picked up her bag, and set it down and kissed her again, and we went across the street to the Paragon Cafe, where it was not much cooler than outside and where a squadron of flies began a kamikaze attack on our iced teas. She took out a cigarette.

"When did you start smoking?"

"I picked it up at work. A couple months ago. Oh Jack, you don't know how it was. It was awful. All those cowboys coming in and trying to make time with you and you know they're staring at your butt when you bend over. I'm glad I quit that job."

I took a cigarette because I was nervous, impatient to go so I could have her alone for once. I took a long look at Maria Celeste Williams through the smoke and this is what I saw: eyes so clear and so brown that was what you thought of when you thought of brown; and a square chin which was the family trademark; a fine nose which flared a little with passion for life; shoulders which hunched forward like she was trying to protect the breasts she thought too small; her lower lip soft and full, the upper lip thinner, able to change expressions more quickly that Proteus could change shapes; and from her black hair, curled in delicate ringlets, wafted the old smell of desire.

"Let's go."

"Just a minute." I heard again in her voice something I had

never heard before until I had heard her talk about the cowboys, and it was like the querulous timbre of an English horn chaunting in an orchestra. "Can't we stay a little longer? It's so hot outside."

"O.K." I did not want to stay any longer. Finally she was ready, and I picked up her bag and started walking.

"Can't we take a taxi?" sang the English horn.

"I thought we'd walk and you could see part of Southview." I didn't have much money, but I could hardly have her pay for a taxi because she had paid so much to come and see me. We used to walk everywhere together.

The taxi took us to the student union. There my elaborate plan went into action. Olav Haraldsson College was affiliated with the Lutheran Church, and to protect our morals and the money the administration gleaned from aged alumni, the bigwigs had only recently instituted an intervisitation policy which allowed us to entertain guests of the opposite sex in our rooms from twelve noon to twelve midnight. But Queenie would be staying with me all the time, and I did not want anybody to know the truth. So while she stayed at the union, I brought her suitcase to the dorm. If anyone saw it, they would think it was mine. Then I walked her to the dorm.

"This is a nice room."

I shut the door.

"Jack, couldn't we open the door? It's so hot."

"But we're all alone now," and I pulled her to me and tried to kiss her long and deep like the priest had said was wicked but she pulled away in a moment and opened the door and took out a cigarette and smoked. I took a cigarette and we talked. Another thing I noticed: she had picked up some rather shocking language from somewhere; and then she told me how sometimes at the truck stop when she worked the graveyard shift she had taken speed to keep awake, and how she and her girlfriend Tina Sanchez had gone to parties and smoked grass and gotten drunk.

"Queenie, honey, I don't like you doing those things. You never used to before." And the thin part of her lip curled around the cigarette butt made something I thought was a sneer, and she shrugged her shoulders. Then she laughed melodically, and was what I had always known her to be, and she started tickling me and wrinkling her nose at me, and all my desire rose up in me, and my throat was hot and dry and we were on the floor, she still tickling me and I plunging my tongue deep into her mouth, running my hands through her hair and releasing that sulfurous smell of desire, and noticing from her body pressed against mine that she was not wearing a bra. But as my hand crept up inside her loose shirt to explore this new phenomenon further, she rolled away from me and sat up and said she wanted something to eat.

That night she made me close my eyes when she undressed to go to bed, and when I opened them she was in the top bunk wearing a long tie-dyed tee shirt which showed just the bottoms of her panties. I lay down in the bunk underneath her and thought. And mainly I thought about how much I wanted her. And since she had come all the way up here . . .

"Queenie, would you come here a minute?" She got down like a small child coming into dinner late with torn pants and a skinned knee, and lay down on the edge of bunk not touching me. It was a moment of truth, like writers talk about. Then as I reached for her, with one movement she rolled against me and plastered her mouth against mine. But in another second she pulled away, and said, "Jack, it's too hot." So to cool her off I reached for her shirt and pulled it up around her neck, and I raised up on one elbow and we stared at each other like strangers because we had never dared do anything like this before, and then she sighed deeply and with a quick jerk removed her shirt. I put my hand on her smooth breast, and her tongue met mine, and it was good.

Then she turned away again. I pulled her back, and kissed her fiercely, but her mouth was shut against mine and her body was tense.

"Jack, there's something I have to tell you."

And then I knew it in a flash, because I was a hot-shot college kid. I knew what it was that she was going to tell me, and struck by its irony I began to laugh.

"Why are you laughing?"

"I know what you're going to tell me. But before you do, I'd better tell you something. You're going to tell me that you're not a virgin anymore." Her fingernails bit into my arm. "Well, I'm suffering from the same problem." Her hand relaxed, and she laughed a little too.

"Becky?"

"Yeah. And yours?"

"His name was Ed Wills. He's a teaching assistant at the U. Tina used to clean house for him, and one time she couldn't so I did and he was drunk and he kept begging me, he kept begging me, Jack, and he said that he was sterile and he had papers to prove it so I didn't have to worry and he kept begging me, Jack."

"I don't care."

"Now we know the truth about each other, and it doesn't matter, does it, Jack? It doesn't matter."

Then we were nude and she was clutching my body and it was vibrating like a high-voltage cable in a forty-mile-per-hour sand storm.

"Jesus I want you. Let's make love."

"No, Jack. I'm afraid I'll get pregnant."

"Queenie, the second time a girl has intercourse, the chances are infinitesimal she'll get pregnant." See what you learn in college?

She said nothing.

I was on top of her, trying to force things to their conclusion, and she was holding me off with her hands in my crotch, and we struggled for an eternity, and then it was over and she rolled against the wall and moaned, "I think some of it got inside me," and I muttered, "I'm sorry," but I didn't see how any of it could and she got up and went to bed above me without saying another word.

Bitter I lay in bed. How could she withhold from me who loved her something that she had given freely to someone who meant nothing to her? How could she, who before had not been able to kiss me deeply because the priest said it was sinful, make love to another man? It did not make sense. But tomorrow I would not so much as touch her. She would have to come to me first. As I lay in bed and thought about how she smoked grass and cigarettes and did other things which she had never done before, but it did not really matter. I did not really care because then I thought of the good times. I lay there in bed and sweat, and it thundered but did not rain.

Sunday we sneaked through the window of my room to go to Mass. Queenie thought the whole thing was queer. "What difference does it make if anyone sees me coming out the doors of your dorm after hours? You have twelve hours to have a girl in your room legally and you could ball her all you wanted then. Why can't you fight against stupid rules like you did in high school?"

"See, the administration has to pretend that the college is still what it was fifty years ago. They have to shield the truth from the virgin eyes of the alumni. They don't know the truth, they still send in the bucks. So if we were caught breaking intervis, they'd make an example of us for the old boys."

"If you feel guilty about me sleeping here, Jack, I can always find someone else that wants me," and she leered at me and poked me in the ribs and I thought that this would be a fine day.

St. Stephen's Church was packed. Judging from the temperature in the house of God, I was willing to take a chance on Hell. Sweat cascaded down my forehead, and I kept brushing it off with my hand and wiping my hand on my thigh until there was a big wet blotch there. Even Queenie snickered at parts of the service, but when I whispered that Lutherans sang hymns better, she got mad. It did not make sense. The whole service did not make sense. I swear that once I heard the priest chant, "Leaveyourmoneyinthe backofthechurchwheretheplatesare," and then this bell rang, and it was supposed to be the moment of truth, but the wine wasn't blood, and if only the bell had levitated itself into the air and rung of its own volition, I would have believed.

Queenie treated me to a meal at The Big Dipper, the only decent restaurant in town, and smoked innumerable cigarettes and got mad at me when I told about the bell, and then we went shopping for presents for her family as if she were buying an indulgence for lying to them that she was sleeping with a girl I knew instead of with me, and she drove me crazy because she couldn't decide which trinket to buy for her dad.

"Are you ready?"

"Almost. When we're married, Jack, you'll have to put up with a lot of shopping." She was happy when we left.

"Where are you going?"

"I thought we would walk."

"Jack, it's too hot. I'm tired. Let's take a taxi."

"You always used to walk with me."

"I don't want to walk. It's too hot."

"And I don't want you to spend all your money on taxi-fare."

"It doesn't matter."

"It matters to me."

"It's my money. I worked a long time to come here and now I want to have fun."

"OK. OK."

"You're mad, aren't you?"

"No."

"Yes you are. Old Crabbyappleton Jack." And she walked off toward the taxi stand, and we had to wait there for half an hour because the entire fleet of two delapidated jalopies that comprised the taxi service of Southview, Minnesota, was gone. I couldn't help muttering that we could have been there by now if we had walked, and she got mad, and jouncing in the taxi on the way up I thought that we had never gotten mad so much at each other before. It must be the heat.

When we got back I said I had to study and she said she wanted to lie down because it was so hot so I studied and she lay down. But after a few minutes she got up and crouched in front of my chair and put her hands on my knees and looked up into my face. There is something that happens to you when a woman crouches in front of you and puts her hands on your knees, and looks you in the eyes, especially if that woman is Queenie Williams and her eyes are very deep and brown and clear, and she looks up at you like a trusting child.

Then she said, "How's Becky?" and something went off in my head like the first kernels starting to pop in a popcorn popper, and I sat there for a minute while the corn popped and the cooking oil sizzled and then I said, "Why?"

"You love her, don't you?"

"I feel sorry for her."

"I hate this place with all the blond Norwegian Lutheran girls that want you because you are blond, and Norwegian, and Lutheran. And I'm English and Catholic and can't afford a school like this."

"Becky's Episcopalian."

"But you made love to her once."

"Because she seduced me." And I added very quietly to myself that I had made love to Becky many, many more times than once, because the flesh was weak and Becky was crazy. But it did not matter because I loved Queenie.

"But how is she now? I mean, what you told me at Christmas is really heavy."

"I don't know. I mean, it's really hard to tell the truth about the whole thing. The shoplifting thing was true, and she really had some sort of emotional breakdown, and at the very end of the year I found out that she still wasn't totally OK. But ever since her . . .

problems, sometimes I can't believe her. She's very dependent on
. . . people. She doesn't have any sense of self — you know? I mean,
I'm OK, you're OK, and all that. Well, I don't know whether she
thinks she's OK or not. I mean, I haven't seen her since May . . . "

I did not want to talk about it, and I was getting the same feeling
I had when I talked to Becky and it looked like she was trying to
drown herself in my eyes, only this time I was floundering in
Queenie's.

"Does she want to marry you?"

"What Becky wants and what I want are two different things."

Queenie just looked at me. I grabbed her and kissed her, but she
pulled away, and the happy child now looked like I had taken away
her favorite toy.

"Jack."

"Look. Queenie, I love you. I always have. Even when I made
love to Becky I was making love to you. That's the truth."

She said nothing.

"It gets so lonely here without you I tried to write . . . "

"You didn't try very hard, Jack."

"I was busy."

"With Becky?"

"Queenie."

"It doesn't matter. I'm here now. But I felt the same thing, you
know. You've been so far away. And all courses were so heavy, and
I hated the truck stop. I had to have somebody to talk to. You went
out with Becky. Well, I've been going out with some guys too.
Byron Keats, and there were some other guys from the U — wow,
they were too freaky for me, though — and Gary James and Don
Dark. With all your friends back home. They didn't want me just
for sex like the guys at work. They took good care of me. Wow, we
went to some really cool parties. Far out!" Which she said in her
fake Bronx accent, meaning she was happy again.

And I said, "I guess that's fair if we both go out with other
people. I mean, we still love each other. Only I wish you wouldn't
get drunk and smoke dope and stuff like that. You didn't used to."

"You used to."

"I know. But I've pretty much stopped."

"Why did you have to go to summer school?"

"I told you. I'm getting three majors. I needed some extra credits. It gives me the possibility of doing more when I graduate."

"Couldn't you have gotten them at the University of New Mexico?"

"The credits won't transfer."

"You wanted to get away from me. Didn't you?"

"No."

"I'm getting *three* majors. It gives me the *possibility* of doing *more* when I graduate." She mimicked me so cutely that I couldn't get angry. "But I wish you were home and we could get married right now."

And there it ended. We had fun in the afternoon smoking cigarettes and talking about old times, but when I wanted to tell her how much it meant to me that I was going to work on the newspaper next year, and what I wanted to do as orchestra president, she would change the subject, and start talking about old times; and when she started telling me about the parties she had gone to and which kids did which drugs, I would change the subject, and start talking about old times: and so we looked at my high school yearbooks and played "Whatever Happened To?" and "Do You Remember When?" and talked about nothing. We were very chaste, and when I went to bed the sweat pumps started up in my pores, and all I could think about was Queenie smoking and drinking and getting stoned and speeding and how she was a Catholic and I was a Lutheran and how I loved her and how she didn't care about the newspaper or the orchestra and how I loved her and how she got screwed by that dude who was certified 100% sterile by the USDA and why she didn't want me like I wanted her and how I loved her and how I wanted her now.

And those thoughts did not stop all day Monday and Monday night we had another one of our wonderful arguments about birth control. You could never tell how they might start, but in the past we had lived in a Cloud-Cuckoo-Land where we would have a lot of kids, or use the rhythm method, or practice abstinence. Like I was able to practice abstinence with Becky.

This time I talked about Mark Twain and the candlestick and the candleholder and how they were meant to fit together; and how God had created man and woman unlike animals with a continual sex drive, and then said that you couldn't make love when you wanted to, and that wasn't quite cricket; and how it would be cruel to have kids you couldn't afford: and she pulled a little booklet out of her purse entitled "Concerning Human Life," and said that the Pope had spoken *ex cathedra* and condoned only the rhythm method; and how men and women weren't animals after all and had minds and faith and should be able to control their desires: and I pointed out that the rhythm method didn't work, and that yes, men had minds and so had created scientific solutions to the problem so you could have your cake and eat it too: and she said that I never could be a Catholic like I had sworn so many times I would be when we were married: and I said that I could be a Catholic without believing in birth control: and she said that was fine, but that she couldn't, and that all men were alike because all they thought about was sex: and I said that even the Pope would not leave us alone: and she smoked and sneered at me.

My brain was sizzling, and the thoughts that had haunted me all day were jumping madly through my head. So I said it.

"Queenie," I said, "I still love you, but I just don't think things will work out between us. I mean, we've both changed a lot and . . . " And I left the rest unsaid.

Queenie's face was frozen, but the big tears slowly rolled down her cheeks and fell on her blouse.

"I quit my job, and paid all kinds of money to come up here for your birthday, and now you say you don't love me because you love Becky, and I think I'm pregnant."

That started the popcorn popping inside my head, only this time it was in one of those big machines they have inside movie theaters. I felt like I was watching a movie in which Queenie and I were acting. But I never could get involved in movies the way I could get involved in a good novel like *A Farewell To Arms* or *All The King's Men*. When you read a book, the words echo in your head, but when you watch a movie you can always go out in the lobby and get something to eat. So I left Queenie and myself up there on the screen and went out into the lobby to get something to eat. I smoked a cigarette or two sitting on one of those red fake-velvet couches manufactured especially for theater lobbies, but after a while I got up and wandered back into the theater where Queenie was still crying, because I knew there were still a few reels of the picture left.

And I heard my voice say, "Pregnant from me? From Saturday night?"

And her voice said, "Oh Christ. Oh Christ, Jack, don't be such an ass. It was a guy back home. We've been . . . screwing for about two months."

And my voice said, "Anybody I know?"

And her voice said, "It doesn't matter. Nothing matters any more because you don't love me. And now my period's almost a week late." All the time the tears rolled down her cheeks and onto a growing wet blotch on her blouse, and she was rocking slightly back and forth.

I tried to hold her, but she pushed me away. That hurt me, and I started to cry a little, but it was a lie because I felt more sorry for myself than for her. After a very long time while she cried and I sat there, she went up to her bunk and curled up like an unhappy child with her fist to her mouth and slept with a frown on her face. I sat in a chair and chain-smoked far into the night.

I got back from class on Tuesday and she was still curled up in her bunk, with her fist to her mouth, and her face was still frowning.

When she woke up, I said, "I brought you something to eat."

"I don't want it." But after a while she did want it, and when she started to eat, I said, "Queenie, I'm sorry."

"It doesn't matter."

And when she was finished eating, I said again, "Queenie, I'm sorry," and she held out her hands and I buried my face in her lap and was truly sorry.

"There's nothing to be sorry for, Jack. That's the way things are. It doesn't matter."

"You still matter to me. I still love you."

"I still love you too, Jack." And she started to cry again.

"Come on, tell your Uncle Jack what's wrong."

"Oh Jack, you were right. I have changed. I'm so mixed up. I don't want to do the things I do. I can't believe in the Church much any more. No one cares about me." And though I had known that she had changed, when she said it, it left a bitter taste in my mouth.

"I care. And I bet the guys you went out with at home care about you. Especially . . . " Sometimes it feels good to stick the spear in and twist.

"If I tell him I think I'm pregnant, he'll go away and leave me. But it doesn't matter. Nothing matters any more."

That got me scared. "You sound like Becky. You've got to believe in yourself. He'll take care of you."

"The only thing I believed in was you."

"I don't matter. The only thing that matters is you. You've got to believe that."

And while we were talking it began to thunder, and she was very frightened. She held me tightly and buried her face on my shoulder. I held her face in my hands and kissed her. And she gave herself up to me like a condemned criminal and we made love.

And after we were done, it was very still. But then the rain came, came without warning, came without thunder. Queenie saw it and got up to run out of the room. I caught her by the arm.

"Let me go, Jack. It's raining right now and I don't want to miss it." So we ran in the rain, and she lifted up her head to the heavens and let the rain wash away her tears until she looked like a kid playing in a sprinkler on a hot summer day.

"I love the rain, Jack." And she held my face in her hands, and sang demonically gay like the girl I used to know: "My Jackie loves the thunder, my Jackie hates the rain. And Queenie hates the thunder, but Queenie loves the rain." My poor Jackie hated the rain, but he loved Queenie in it.

We went inside and embraced and our thin wet clothes clung to our bodies and we fell into bed. We made love gently and when it was over, I said, "I bet he did it better," because the wound was not bleeding enough.

"No. It feels the best when you do it with someone you really love."

And later she began to caress me. "Does that feel good, Jack?"

"Yeah."

"Let's make love again."

But I did not want to make love again. I did not want to make love to Queenie Williams because things could never happen like they had before because Queenie loved the rain and I loved the thunder.

That did not stop us the next day from making love again, only this time it was just the lust of our young bodies that brought us together and then threw us apart when it was over. It was the lust of a Catholic girl who loved the rain and didn't know what she wanted. And it was the lust of a Lutheran boy who loved the thunder and had a still small voice inside him that whispered that now the act had no consequences. And that was why we both sat away from each other not daring to look at each other after we had done, and smoking cigarettes, and that was why Queenie told me that she was going to leave the next day.

"I don't want you to go."

"Don't lie, Jack. Not after all this. You want to get rid of me because I remind you of what could have been if it had turned out a different way. And you make me think of what I used to be."

"You don't have to go."

"What times are the buses?"

"There's one at twelve-fifteen."

That night we went downtown without using a taxi and had a pizza. Neither of us ate very much of it, and Queenie played some songs on the jukebox: sad songs that had some sort of cryptic meaning for us that I never caught.

So I sat there and looked at her and thought. You judged what happened and it all balanced out. Before it had been wicked even to touch each other and I had wanted her very much and we had loved. To her our love was sacred and pure and nothing on the outside could touch it, and having other lovers did not mean we had betrayed each other. Only after we broke up could we make love. It all balanced out. She had made love, but she would not sin by practicing birth control, because she believed in something. So she got pregnant. At least we knew the truth about each other now. Well, she would go home and her new man would make her happy. It all balanced out.

And as we were walking back I knew. It just figured. I was blind not to have seen it before.

"The father of your supposed child — it was Don Dark, wasn't it?"

She walked a while in silence.

"Yes."

And then:

"I'm sorry, Jack."

"It doesn't matter."

"Don't say it that way, Jack."

"Do you love him?"

"A little. He talked to me. When you didn't write."

"Does he love you?"

"No. He has a girlfriend. She's been away for a while. She'll be back soon. He's going to marry her."

"He was my goddamned best friend."

About halfway up the road to the college there is a park which contains a playground for the local kids. We sat there in silence on a park bench, and smoked some cigarettes. The thunderclouds were building on the horizon, but you could tell in the pit of your stomach that it wouldn't rain. My heart was as heavy as the air, and nothing really mattered any more because the film was over and the crowd had filed out and it was just me and Queenie left there staring as the diaphanous folds of the curtain fell down to the floor and covered the screen. We walked slowly to the dorm and went to bed and I never thought of touching her even when I started to sweat and the disconnected thoughts sizzled in my brain.

Thursday morning after class I met her in the union and when I checked my mailbox I had gotten a package.

"What is it, Jack?"

"I think it's a birthday cake from my mom. She wrote that she was sending one."

We took a taxi to the bus depot. The bus was late, and we sat outside on the steps and smoked.

"Don't be so sad, Jack." She tried to be gay in a somber sort of way because she was trying to cheer me up, but her brown eyes were like puddles of water when a kid stirs them up with a twig.

"I can't help it."

"And you had quit smoking for me."

"It doesn't matter. I probably would have started again anyway. But you will write me and tell me if . . . ?"

"If I'm pregnant? Yes. And Jack, keep writing me. Please. Even if I don't write back. I need something like that now, Jack."

The bus came, and she got on, and the busdriver who was collecting tickets winked at me and said, "Don't worry, pal, I'll take good care of her," and then the bus drove off, and she waved at me, and I waved at her, and then stood there with someone's hand tightening around my stomach. I went across the street, and bought a pack of cigarettes, and then walked as fast as I could to my room so I would not see the playground or have to think. I sat in my room and smoked, and after a while I opened my package and it was a birthday cake, so I went to Leeward's room and Erickson's room and invited them to my early happy birthday party.

They had a second piece of cake while I smoked, and pretty soon I saw in Lief's eyes that he was going to ask what had happened with Queenie and me because he was such a goddamned sensitive Christian, so to distract him I asked, "How do you know that everything in the Bible is the truth?" and Leeward smiled bitterly because he had gotten an engagement broken off and said, "It's hard to know," and I muttered, "What is truth?" and Erickson said, "God's love is truth," and I mumbled "What is love?" and they started to argue about truth and love and I tried not to think.

WARD JUST

Dietz at War

(FROM THE VIRGINIA QUARTERLY)

TWICE OR THREE times a week Dietz wrote his children. They were
informal letters that began Dear Girls and ended Much Love From
Dad. He liked to describe the country and the hotel in which he
lived, and at every opportunity he wrote about the various animals
he saw. Around the corner from the hotel was a crippled vendor
with a monkey and once a month he'd visit the zoo. The zoo's
attractions were a single Bengal tiger and two mangy elephants.
The tiger he called Charlie and the two elephants Ike and Mike. In
his frequent trips to the countryside he'd see water buffaloes and
pigs, and once he'd taken a photograph of a Marine major with an
eighteen-foot anaconda wrapped around his neck. Dietz hated
snakes but his children didn't. He invented wild and improbable
stories about the animals, giving them names and personalities and
droll adventures. From time to time he'd give the girls a glimpse
into his own life, opening the door a crack and then shutting it
again. He thought the letters and his motives for writing them were
straightforward, but his former wife did not. On one of Dietz's
visits home she told him that the letters were interesting, but not
much use to the children. "You're really writing those letters to
me," she said.

Dietz was very serious about the letters; in three years in the war
zone he missed a week just once. He wrote the letters early in the
morning, before he began the day's work. When he expected to be
out of touch for any length of time he'd leave several letters with
the concierge of the hotel, with instructions to mail one every three
days. It was important to him to be part of the lives of his children,

and he considered the letters as valuable and necessary substitutes for personal visits. The letters were as long as they needed to be, and were posted with exotic stamps.

However, he was careful never to disclose too much. Because he lived in a war zone he felt entitled to keep his personal life to himself. He did not want to alarm or upset the children, nor did he want to leave the impression he was enjoying himself. He thought if he phrased the letters with care the girls would understand his obligations to himself and to his work. Dietz never had the slightest feeling of heroism, still less of advancing any national interest. He was a newspaper correspondent and believed in journalism. He believed in his value as an expert witness whose testimony might one day prove valuable. The work was demanding and not to everyone's taste but Dietz found it congenial. Because the war zone was dangerous he felt he had the right to make his own rules and that meant the right to withhold certain information from his children and the others.

There were several love affairs, and many friends both male and female. During the worst part of the war scarcely a week went by without someone he knew, or knew of, being wounded or killed. There was one terrible week when five correspondents were killed and a number of others wounded, but Dietz did not mention this to the children except in an oblique way. In a letter home he told a long and complicated animal story and assigned the names of the dead to various enchanting animals. Dietz felt in that way he commemorated his colleagues.

He worked eighteen-hour days and considered himself at the top of his craft. Everyone he knew had difficult personal problems that obliged them to sail close to the wind, as his friend Puller expressed it. Puller described the war zone as a neurotics' retreat no less than the Elizabeth Arden beauty farm or the Esalen Institute. While recognizing the truth of what Puller said, Dietz did not apply it to his own life. The various personal problems, serious as they might appear to outsiders, were not allowed to interfere with the job he was paid to do.

Therefore, the letters home were not factual but invented. Dietz did not completely understand this until years later, when he chanced upon the correspondence and reread it. Dietz kept carbons of everything he wrote.

Odd — there was not a line in any of the letters about the good times he'd had. It was awkward to talk of good times because people put you down as a war lover, a man who drew pleasure from the suffering of others. And from *this* war, no less. Borrowing a concept from older writers who had covered earlier wars, Dietz told himself that a sense of carelessness and adventure was necessary in order to remain sane. In order not to become permanently depressed. He explained this idea one night to an experienced woman who had witnessed a number of European wars and she laughed in his face, not unkindly. The other wars were sane, she said. This war was insane.

"And?"

"Draw your own conclusions."

Still, in his letters home, there was not a word about casual things — pleasant walks through the damp scented air in the deserted parks early in the morning. Nothing about late night swims in the pool at the old country club, nor afternoons at the rundown race track. Nothing about the long evenings playing bridge, nor the occasional sprees at restaurants in the Chinese quarter. There was nothing at all about the constant noisy laughter as the correspondents drifted down the boulevard to a cafe where there were drinks and hot roasted peanuts in shallow dishes. There were no descriptions or explanations of the many wonderful friendships he'd made.

While there was nothing at all in the letters about the good times, there was nothing about the bad times either.

Having decided to cut himself off from America, Dietz felt it was important and necessary to take an aggressively neutral stance in his attitude toward the war. He felt that the one could only be justified in terms of the other — for he had *fled* the United States, no question about that. This belief was reflected both in the letters and in the articles he wrote. His heaviest gun was irony. Dietz acquired an uncommon ability to turn sentences in such a way that left his readers empty and puzzled and, when he was writing at the top of his form, depressed. The facts he selected implied foreboding, and his descriptions suggested darkness and disease. This was done subtly. He wheeled his irony into position at the end of every story, and gave his readers a salvo. Standing outside events, evenhanded Dietz believed he was uniquely equipped to describe an enterprise that was plainly misconceived: deformed, doomed. He never wrote of anything as crude and obvious as wounded children or wrecked churches. Instead, he devoted a series of articles to the remarkable military hospitals and their talented surgeons, who saved lives and left men vegetables or worse. He became something of a social historian, describing the furious whims and customs of those involved in the war. Dietz developed a theory that there was a still center in the middle of the war, a safe location without vibrations of any kind, and if he could occupy that center he could present the war from a disinterested position. A moral fortress. It would be the more precise and persuasive for being factually impartial because it was evident to him that the public was skeptical of anything that hinted at the lurid or the grotesque. Dietz worked at trimming adjectives from his prose, and was careful to spell everything out with near-mathematical precision.

He wanted to describe the war with the delicacy and restraint of Henry James setting forth the details of a love affair.

His life enlarged and grew in harmony with the war. He was rooted, comfortable and at ease, feeling himself outside the war and inside it at the same time. Dietz refused to learn the history of the country or its language or the origins of the struggle in the belief that the war was necessarily a sentient experience. He brought emotion to his portraiture, but the emotions were solidly based on fact.

He was scrupulous. Aircraft, artillery, small arms, battalions, battlefields — all of them were precisely identified by name, number or location. Dietz's room at the hotel was covered with American military maps, and he'd obtained weapons manuals from a friendly colonel at American military headquarters. Readers understood immediately where they were and what was happening, who was doing the fighting, and with what weaponry, and the name and age of the dead and wounded. These facts, so precise and unassailable, gave Dietz's journalism the stamp of authenticity and therefore of authority. Dietz believed that facts described the truth in the same way that shapes and colors describe a landscape, and in that way journalism resembled art.

One April afternoon he was almost killed.

They'd encouraged him to accompany a long-range patrol. They did not conceal its danger: this was a reconnaissance patrol that would establish beyond any doubt the existence of sanctuaries in the supposedly neutral country to the west. They were frank to say that public knowledge of these sanctuaries would be . . . helpful. Dietz was free to write what he pleased, and of course it was entirely possible that there would be no sanctuaries. But they trusted Dietz to write what he saw.

Dietz was eager, listening to them explain the mission. This was not a patrol that would engage the enemy. It was purely reconnaissance for the purpose of intelligence-gathering. But they did not lie to him about the danger. There was at least an even chance that the patrol would be discovered in some way, and that would mean serious trouble. They would be deep in enemy territory. However, the commander would be the best reconnaissance man in the zone and his team would be hand-picked. It would be an all-volunteer force. A helicopter squadron would monitor their progress and be prepared for immediate action. The mission had the highest priority and Dietz was free to go along without restraint. It was appealing, the story was appealing on a number of levels; Dietz put danger out of his mind.

On the second day the patrol was ambushed and nearly annihilated. The commander and his number two were killed, and Dietz and half a dozen others were wounded. They owed their lives to the quick reaction time of the helicopter force, though for an hour they were obliged to defend themselves without aid of any kind. Of course they found no sanctuaries nor anything else of value, and in that sense the mission was a failure.

Dietz was five days in a field hospital, half-delirious and very weak from loss of blood. They watched him around the clock. As soon as they were able, the authorities moved him to a small private clinic in the capital. Having urged him to undertake the mission, they now felt responsible. They'd make certain he had the best medical attention available in the zone.

In ten days the danger was past, though the effects lingered. Dietz was euphoric.

His friend Puller, looking at him lying in bed, remarked, "You look like hell."

"Feel fine," Dietz said.

"White as a sheet," Puller said.

"Lost all my blood," Dietz said.

"You need a drink. Can you have a drink?"

Dietz laughed and extended his hand, and Puller poured him a gin and tonic.

"Actually you look OK."

The nurse was working on his arm, cutting the steel sutures that bound his wounds. "It's a load off my mind," Dietz said.

"How's that?"

"This can only happen to you once. The odds. I've used up my ticket."

Puller looked at the nurse and asked her in French how Dietz was.

The nurse said, Fine. Recovery was rapid.

How long would Dietz remain in the hospital?

Perhaps a week, the nurse said. But he would have to remain quiet when he got out. He'd sustained shock and was more disoriented than he realized. If Monsieur Dietz were wise, he'd take a long holiday.

Puller observed that his friend seemed in very good spirits.

The nurse nodded, Indeed. A model patient, always cheerful.

Puller turned back to Dietz. "I talked with your office on the telephone today." He smiled. "They wanted to know when to expect the story."

"I'm writing it in my head," Dietz said.

"Well, they said not to worry. They're giving you a month's leave, you can have it whenever you want it. They'd like you to return to the 'States for a couple of weeks. But you can do what you want."

Dietz winced as the nurse washed and dried the large wound on his forearm. "Ask her how long I'll be in here."

"You really don't know any French at all?"

"Only the basics," Dietz said.

Puller smiled, Dietz made no concessions. He was the same wherever he was, the Middle East, Latin America. He didn't know Arabic or Spanish either. He was like a camera, his settings operated in any environment. "She says you'll be out in a week but you'll have to take it easy."

Dietz pointed to a pile of mail on the bureau. There was a foot-high stack of letters and telegrams. "Did you pick up any mail today?"

"None for you," Puller said.

Dietz looked puzzled. "Nothing at all?"

"You're a greedy bastard. Christ, you've heard from everybody
but the Secretary of Defense."

"I love to read expressions of sympathy," Dietz said.

"When are you going to write the story?"

"Well, I told you. I am writing it. In my head."

"I mean for the newspaper."

"I have to write it for the kids first."

"Oh, sure," Puller said.

"I have to get the characters straight. These stories are damned
complicated, and the kids count on them."

"Right."

" . . . got to get the plot worked out."

"Do you want your portable?"

"No, I'm writing it in my head, memorizing it. I'll memorize it
and write it up in longhand. But it's taking a hell of a long time, I'm
only up to the first night." He smiled benignly. "Bivouac."

Puller put two ice cubes and a finger of gin in Dietz's drink,
watching the nurse frown and turn away. He told Dietz that he had
to leave but would look in at dinner time, perhaps bring a few
friends. He moved to go, then looked back at the bed. "What did
you mean a moment ago, that you've used up your ticket. What
does that mean?"

"I'm invulnerable. This can only happen to you once. The odds
are all in my favor. I've done everything now, I'm clean. They've
got nothing on me."

"I'd like to know the name of that oddsmaker. That bastard is
practicing without a license."

Dietz laughed. "It's true!"

"And who hasn't got anything on you?"

"They don't. None of them do." Dietz said, "I've paid my dues."
That was a private joke and they both laughed. "I'm in fat city."

"Jesus Christ," Puller muttered. "I suppose you are, as long as
you're here."

Dietz drained his glass and grinned. "When you come back
tonight, bring me some stationery. The kids are probably worried,
they haven't heard from me in two weeks. Probably don't know
where the hell I am."

Puller nodded, Sure. Then, "Well, they know you got hit."

"No reason for them to."

"But — "

"Listen. It's a long story, so bring plenty of stationery."

"Honest to God, you look in damn good shape," Puller said.

"Feel fine," said Dietz.

In the end Dietz wrote a story for the children and the news-paper, and they were entirely different stories. The story for the children was witty, crammed with incident and populated with strange animal characters in a mythical setting. He set one charac-ter against the others, though all of them were friends. The story began darkly but ended sweetly, it was very exciting and covered twelve sheets of paper. In the act of writing it, Dietz discarded most of the myths and composed a loveable story about animals. The article for the newspaper was deft and straightforward. He wrote the article in one draft from memory and did not consult his note-book at all. Reading it over, he was alarmed to find he'd neglected his facts, save the central incident and one or two names. To his surprise and confusion it was a cruel but cheerful story, and some-how uplifting despite its savage details. He kept himself out of it and most readers did not understand until the final sentences that it was an eyewitness account. But the editors liked it and put it on page one with a box and a picture of Dietz. The picture caption read, "Dietz At War."

He cabled the story, then did a strange thing. He wrote the editor of the newspaper and told him to inform his ex-wife when the article would be published. The editor was to tell the ex-wife to keep the newspaper out of the house that day. Under no circum-stances were the children to see the article Dietz had written about himself.

Dietz went from success to success. He matured with the war, developing a singular style of journalism in order to arrive at the still center of the violence. In the years following the murderous afternoon in April he devoted himself entirely to journalism and to his letters home. He removed himself from the life of the capital and ventured ever farther afield for his stories. He'd spend two weeks among the mountain people, then a week investigating the political structure of an obscure coastal province. His dispatches contained detailed descriptions of the flora and fauna of the country, its landscapes and population. There were many places where the war was not present and he was careful to visit those as well. Often Dietz's stories contained no more than two or three facts — the dateline, the subject, the subject's age. No more, often less.

But his sense of irony, his understanding of awful paradox, was exquisite. He saw the war in delicate balance and reported it as he would report the life and atmosphere of an asylum, or zoo. He adopted various points of view in his reportage, convinced that each moment possessed its own life; he often impersonated a traveler from abroad. Energetic and restless in his inquires, he occasionally published fictitious information. These were the devices he used to move the emotions of his readers. As the dead piled on dead his images became blacker and more melancholy, though he fought for balance. He'd bring himself back into equilibrium by writing a long letter to his children. Every month he spent at least a fortnight with troops on the line, though he always refused to carry a weapon.

During one of the periodic cease-fires (they came as interregnums, pauses between seizures), Dietz's old friend Puller returned from the United States. Puller'd done a year's time in the zone and departed without hesitation. That was two years ago, and now Puller was back for a visit. They spent a long and sour night drinking in Dietz's hotel room.

Puller demanded, "Why are you still here? No one cares any more, what are you doing here?"

"I live here. It's my home."

"It's a forgotten front, I'll tell you that."

"Not by me."

"No one gives a damn any more."

"Well, I do."

"Odds in your favor, is that it?"

"Well, I'm here. In one piece. Healthy. Sound."

"You ought to quit it," Puller said. "There's a limit —"

"It's a rich vein," Dietz said. "Hardly touched."

"A vein of pure crap."

"The rest of you, it's all right. You can watch it from the United States. The point is, you can't *know* this place until you've lived here. You have to *live* here, in it."

Puller looked at him. "It's a place like any other. One more place to get stale in."

"You think I'm stale?"

"The stuff you're writing, a lot of it doesn't make any sense."

"Are you reading it?"

"Well, no. I don't read it much any more."

Dietz smiled. His expression was one of satisfaction. "Well, it's strange. Perhaps true." He smiled warmly, and poured fresh drinks for them both. "You know, because of the cease-fire there's been no dead this week. No killed or wounded. No casualty lists." He shrugged, amused, amazed. The casualty lists had been part of his life for so long that he could not imagine their absence. They and the war were what he lived with. He had not come to terms with parting from either of them, the dead or the war. America seemed to him remote, at an infinite remove; the back of beyond. "None," he said.

"You think you're *part* of this war. You think you can't leave it. You think that if you go away, the war will disappear."

"No man is indispensable." Dietz grinned.

"Paying your dues. You're *paid up!*" Puller glanced around the familiar room, it hadn't changed in two years. The transistor radio, the bottles on the sideboard, the photograph over the typewriter — Dietz in fatigues, fording a nameless river in the jungle. Puller had taken the picture, catching Dietz's winning smile as the water washed over his chest. Dietz hung the picture — why? Perhaps it reminded him of hardship. Whenever he looked up from the typewriter he saw himself in fatigues, fording some nameless river, smiling.

"Yes I am," Dietz agreed.

"Then why —"

Dietz roared, "My God, Puller — how can that compare to *this?*"

Puller left shortly after midnight (they were both drunk, and less friendly than at the beginning), and Dietz prepared another drink and set about securing himself for the night. A hotel room was a world away, a haven in its safety and invisibility; its neutrality. No man's land. Drink in hand, he set the latch and the chain and the bolt, and tucked the deskchair under the doorknob. He checked the tape that criss-crossed the windows that looked out onto the main square of the capital; on advice of army friends, he'd taped the windows to prevent flying glass in the event of an explosion. He locked the windows and carefully removed the pictures from the walls and stacked them under the bed, where they'd be safe. The bottles of gin and whiskey were placed in the closet, next to the carbine and the filled canteens. There was a full clip of ammunition taped to the stock of the carbine; he inspected that to verify that it was clean, and that the breech was oiled and the barrel spotless. His steel pot and knapsack were in their places, on the shelf in the clothes closet. He drew the blinds and covered his typewriter and put the table lamp on the floor next to his desk.

Dietz took a long pull on his drink and looked around the room, satisfied. He undressed slowly, taking small sips every few seconds. He listened for any disturbance in the street but heard nothing. The sentry was still in the square — how did they expect one man to fend off an attack, if it came? The sentry was leaning against a lamppost like some dapper soak in a Peter Arno cartoon; it was useless, he was probably asleep. He was either asleep or working for the other side. The most dangerous time was between midnight and three a.m., he'd learned that much from the military authorities. It was during the early morning hours that the enemy struck without warning, moving anonymously from the shadows, planting satchel charges and mines. A month earlier there'd been a scare in the hotel and half a dozen downtown restaurants were now off limits to American personnel. His drink empty, Dietz flicked on an overhead light and the two lamps next to his bed. The desk lamp on the floor was already burning, as were the lights in the bathroom. He stripped and lay naked on the sheets, listening to the hum of the air conditioner. Then he reached for his pen, and the box of stationery.

Dietz never wearied of writing to his children. Over the years the letters grew prolix, four and five letters a week, some of them five and six hundred words long. Dear Girls, Much Love From Dad. It didn't bother him that his children didn't reply for months at a time, and it did not occur to him at all that one of them was too young to write anything. His former wife, suddenly sympathetic, kept him informed of their progress. He had not been to America in more than three years; his vacations were limited to long weekends at a secure seaside resort. He felt it would be a tragedy to be out of the country the day it "blew," so he kept himself in constant readiness. He invented wonderful stories about the animals in the zoo, and his letters home were entirely concerned with the Bengal tiger, the two elephants, the zebra, the monkey, the antelope, the water buffalo, the snake and the civet cat. These animals were assigned personalities that corresponded to the men who managed the war.

Dietz stayed on in the zone, assembling ever more powerful ironies with which to ravage the consciences of his readers. After five years the management of the newspaper insisted that he come home for good. When he refused, the publisher of the paper sent him a brief note informing him that he would either come home or consider himself fired. Dietz scanned the note and decided there were loopholes, they would not dare to fire him. He'd plead for time, and if necessary take leave and file on a free-lance basis. He knew that in the last analysis they would not fire him; they never fired anybody.

Dietz's critics insisted that he was out of touch with the realities of the war. It was no longer a war but a depradation. The realities had changed but Dietz had not. He was rarely seen at the various important news briefings, preferring instead to investigate the mood of the provinces. In the provinces he found life and therefore hope and from time to time a strange sweetness infused his copy. He had long since given up his love affairs and was an infrequent visitor to the downtown cafes. It was true that his ironic turn of mind no longer puzzled or depressed his readers, as it was true his children found his letters home tedious. However, his readers still thought him authoritative and his children assured him they loved him. He was a majestic figure inside his moral fortress, healthy, astute and entirely free of bias. In that way the war never lost its savor, and Dietz was free of facts forever.

JOHN McCLUSKEY

John Henry's Home

(FROM THE IOWA REVIEW)

IN THE LONGEST moment of his life, John Henry Moore stared down the barrel of a shotgun and reached slowly for the toothpick in the corner of his mouth. The cigarette in his other hand was burning down to the filter and he let his aching fingers drop it, checking any sudden move. He watched the eyes of the man holding the gun and, finding no mercy, looked to the man's screaming wife.

"Don't kill him, Lou! Don't kill him!"

He cursed his luck, his life that flashed by like a doomed comet, and that first weekend after he had returned to the world. He had lied to himself about what was possible at home, lied about how easy things would be. He had looked too long at the reflection of the present and he had called that good. He held his breath, hoping to ease the strain on his kidneys, and looked again at the open lips of the barrel, down its blueblack length to the man's nervous fingers . . .

He had closed the closet door, straightened the full-length mirror hanging against its back, and studied his front. He had dragged on his cigarette and watched the smoke ooze evilly from his nostrils. The pose had dictated some kind of badassed movie detective or mackman. He had pulled his slacks up, then frowned at the tightness through the crotch and thighs. Most other dudes home from the war were underweight. Like Mitchell. John Henry was good sized when he came home and going strong now on his mother's cooking. He had already put on five pounds in his first week home. The added weight didn't look too bad except that women seemed to prefer their men looking like skinny sissies these days. It wasn't that way when he left. Tight pants and shirts and high heel shoes. It isn't how much or how little you have that counts, he knew. It's how you use it. He had grinned at himself, patted his belly, and left.

The barbershop was four blocks away and John Henry, as cool as he wanted to be, took them slowly. After all, there was the brightness of the day to consider. It was early March, though it looked more like October and touch football time for the old-timers and fake high school stars in the park. His second night home, Alice and Jody had thrown a welcome-home party for him and, drunk, he had promised to get together with the fellows for a game. Of course, he knew that the game would be forgotten in the morning. The party had been one of the few events in his life when more than two people in a room seemed happy to see him, listen to him, touch him. He had liked the feeling, despite the war, despite everything. He was not hard enough to shut out everything like Tony, his Army buddy now riding shotgun for a Detroit gangster. Tony had sent a photo of himself posing against a silver-grey Rolls-Royce. Nor was John Henry soft enough to retire like Mitchell at the age of twenty-three. He'd look for himself somewhere in between. Here, back in the world.

He pushed into the barbershop and waved at RoughHouse and Irwin, the barbers. Then he nodded at faces vaguely remembered and at others, younger, he didn't remember at all. Little jitterbugs were shooting up like weeds. Like that Bobbie who was a basketball star now. John Henry had seen him on the street once and had teased him about playing marbles and wearing a Davy Crockett hat. Grabbing an old magazine, John Henry took a seat and pretended to read.

RoughHouse finishing a tale and giving a razor-line at the same time. "Some crackers too dumb to be white. They deserve to catch hell . . ."

Then Rough dragged out stories of hants and fools. John Henry did not look up. He hoped they wouldn't start on him, wouldn't ask about the war and whether he had killed a man, whether it was true the Blacks and whites were shooting at one another and calling such murders accidents. Did the Cong really take it easy on the brothers when they sneaked into camps and cut throats? Did they really seek out the white-only bars as targets for grenades? Huh, was it like that for true? John Henry wanted to be left alone with the memories of his war. His burned arm was reminder enough.

Still the room grew smaller. RoughHouse, dipper in the business of all, cleared his throat. "John Henry, I'm sho glad you here 'cause maybe you can straighten out something I was trying to tell that hardheaded Jew-Don awhile ago. He claim he fought the Japanese in the Second World War. I fought in Korea myself. I was trying to tell him that the Japs were smaller and had bigger heads than the Koreans. He come tellin me that the Japs is the biggest, then the Vietnamese, then the Koreans."

"Well, Rough, I've never seen a Korean," John Henry said. "I saw a few Japanese in California but that wasn't close up." Yellow men among the snows, wave on wave through the jungles. One was a wave, as precise as a scorpion.

They leaned back in their seats when John Henry couldn't deliver the decisive word. RoughHouse started again. "I know one thing, though. They can fight their asses off, can't they? I mean, hell, I was in the Philippines and saw them coming and coming."

"What did you do then, RoughHouse?" some joker asked.

"I kept shooting and praying. Yeah, buddy, that was me all right. Look here, y'all, I cut Mitchell's hair last week and he come talking about they would cool it on brothers over there. You believe that mess? War is war and niggas always get caught in the middle of it and after it's over we get booted out of the army with some funky papers."

Then the war stories were strung together on the knotted thread of memory. Certain that he had to give them something, Roscoe shared a story told him by a buddy. He'd tell it early so they wouldn't keep bothering him. His own story he would tell some other time.

"Yeah, that war things is never always cool. I had to drive a jeep miles down a road that had been closed off for a while because of heavy shelling. So I drove out of camp for about a mile when I met this white boy with a rifle. I told him where I had to go and asked him whether the road up ahead had been opened yet. He said yes that everything was OK, so I took off, and had that old jeep hummin. All I had was a big pistol on my hip, you understand. It was kind of nice that day, about like today but a lot warmer, so I settled back to enjoy the drive. I was weaving around them big holes in the road where the shells had hit, all between the trees and stuff on the road. That drive was the only peaceful time I had all the time I was over there. Anyway, I'm doing it all the way in and when I get near the village there's another sentry, a brother. He looked at me like his eyes were going to pop. 'Where you come from?' he asked me. When I told him he sat down on the ground and started laughing like crazy. 'Man, that road been closed,' he said. 'You coulda had your head blown off. Them Viet Cong must have thought you was one crazy blood driving through there like that and they was probably laughin so hard they let you through.' I almost peed on myself behind that. I started thinkin of that soldier at the other end who let me through so I finished my business in that town and went back down that road. When I got to the other end, I found that cat and whipped him 'til he roped like okra."

The barbers stopped their clippers to rest against their chairs, laughing. When that died down they saw John Henry's stolid expression and started again. A belly-holding, thigh-slapping laughter, a welcome-home laughter that rumbled up from collective pasts. John Henry, never the athlete, never the smartest, slow with the girls, slow with the dozens, was ever swift with the jokes. Could beat One-Eyed Tommie when it came to stories. John Henry, that crazy John Henry, was home.

"What you plan on doing now that you're home, John Henry?" You couldn't beat RoughHouse for directness.

"I don't know yet. Right now I'm just gonna let Uncle Sam's pay support me." Then he pulled up his sleeve and showed the ugly scars of napalm. An accidental drop near his platoon. Fire-jelly from the sky, from one of their own nervous pilots. "Uncle Sam owe me something, don't he?" Waiting customers leaned closer for a better look and frowned at the ugly scars.

"I hear the mill is hiring," Irwin said.

"I ain't in no hurry for the mill, man," he said. He had to watch it: most of the men in the barbershop owed their thin bank accounts, their mortgages, their past bail bonds, doctor bills, and their children's first years in college to the steel mill. "Like I say, I'm still thinking. I'm behind by four years and I ain't gone catch up working for no hillbilly in a mill. You can bet on that."

RoughHouse noticed John Henry's eyes rolling up and the vacant stare. Another world was where he was now. Though the customers agreed within themselves about the mill, they didn't like his saying it. After all, they were beyond choices now. Loans had to be repaid. RoughHouse stropped his razor again, humming in the quiet. It was always a long way home and John Henry wasn't there yet. Might never make it back. Rough knew so many who could never make it back.

"Y'all read the other day about Ali talkin about he could have whipped Joe Louis and Joe Frazier in a telephone booth, blind-folded and with one arm tied around his back . . . ?"

Smoke. A smoke no more harmful to the lungs than the dust-filled smoke at the mill where men like his father and two brothers breathed it and brought it back up with phlegm. Mill men were tough enough to work in the smoke for forty years and accept cheap watches for their struggle, men who would later die cough-ing on front porches or in bed, smoke never ever gone. John Henry dealt in a smoke that would keep the slicker men happy, could have them wrestling the bulls of the universe, could have them riding and leaning on falling stars as easily as they could in big cars. Just a gentle thing, this smoke.

Share it, John Henry. Ease a little pain, man. It started the very next day with a couple of nickel bags as a gift from an ex-soldier in the next town, a gift to John Henry, to the town. Two of his side-kicks, Tucker & Art, would go for it. They've been to the big city, they know what's happening.

"Man, this some righteous shit, John Henry . . . "

Noon was midnight and burning moon caught them in Tucker's car parked in front of the pool hall. They were on the Strip — a pool hall, grocery store, laundromat, bar and an abandoned prin-ter's office — a block that had struggled to life while John Henry was away. Yokel cops cruising by, trying to scowl. Art blew smoke at them. Hip Art with no front teeth and the runny eyes.

"Simple dudes never heard of marijuana, let alone know what it smell like."

Dance strange and funky — butt bumping dances under this moon, town. Come on out, saditty couples living behind venetian blinds and hating the town and what your mirrors throw back. Did you hear what foxy Jeanette said about smoke opening her up and bringing her love down as if strange fingers tripped along the insides of her thighs? She would even buy John Henry a suit behind that pleasure. Come, dance. Not his fault the war-gods have died with the thunder and now the angels of pleasure had slipped on in.

John Henry moved from his home to a small apartment and later went to the mill. A front, though. He saw death there, slow, his. But young workers came to him and begged. At lunch-time he cooled them out with dollar joints, rolled tight as toothpicks. A few of the older, steadier workers drifted toward his corner of the plant. They were used to gin or scotch all night and slightly bored with it. He'd help them make it through the hard nights of their days.

Good news had traveled fast there. He was called into the office of one of the top men. The executive's face was pocked and puffed by alcohol. Grinning, he had pumped John Henry's hand and reached the point quickly. He had heard of John Henry around the plant (tomming spies, everywhere!) and wanted to know whether John Henry could help him. Of course, a small raise and protection would be given in exchange. They had figured the man as he had figured most of the executives at that plant: aging Christians aching to wear dungarees & sandals, to grow a beard, to stroke the behinds of their secretaries. He would be middleman to their heavens, too.

But if smoke could get you moving, the White Horse could get you there extra swift. That was how his soldier friend had described it. John Henry saw himself catching up with high school classmates who owned homes now. He saw the streets of his town paved with twenty dollar bills. Saw money in the faces of the young kids standing on the corners. It would be so easy, so quick. But he hesitated.

"Look, man. This heavy stuff is new for me. You been doing it up here ever since you came back from the war so you know what's what. I mean, for one thing you dealing in a big town. My town so tiny you can hear a fly fart."

"Don't worry, man. I'm just turning you on to something slick, that's all. It's not like a life-time thing. You think I want to spend my life pushing to jive chumps? I'm into bigger stuff. I got a brain, John Henry, and I'm gonna use it for the bigger things, know what I mean? Uncle Sam will be sorry he ever cut this pretty nigga loose with some messed up discharge papers. And I know you, John Henry. I know you didn't suck mud in stupid-assed war for three years just to come home and knock your brains out in a steel mill. Tell me anything, man, but don't tell me that!"

How much heart, John Henry, how much heart you got? Be so bad you roll grass in ten dollar bills. He drove back to town to stay on top of things. To think.

He had run into Mitchell many times, God-fearing Mitchell who had a bad leg from the war. He had tried to share smoke with Mitchell but got nowhere. Mitchell worked in the post office and had married within four weeks after returning home. During John Henry's first month back, they stood one another a round of drinks in Roscoe's Place, early evening before the crowd.

"How's married life, Mitch?" John Henry usually began.

"It's cool with me, John Henry. You know me, man, I never was into a whole lot of running and stuff."

"Yeah, you and Jackie been tight, too, going way way back. Look like the post office ain't hurting you none either."

Mitchell laughed, stroked his goatee. He was shorter than John Henry, neat, always and forever a neat man. John Henry had concluded that Mitchell went to battle pressed clean. "You the one to talk. If I had your hand to play, I wouldn't have a worry in this world."

"Mitch, you seen bighead George Pendergrast? Somebody said he's teaching college in Cincinnati. They say he's got him a nice pad down there."

"No, man, I never see him. He comes home for a minute to see his people then — zoom! — he's back in Cincinnati. That dude ain't got no time for this place. I guess he's doing OK, though. Remember Billie Barnes? He tried out for the Detroit Lions, you know. He didn't make it so they say he kind of drifted out West. He didn't have anything to be ashamed of, if you ask me. Ain't too many from this town ever done much of anything except raise a lot of hell. Well, anyway, he's changed his name to Billy Africa and he's out in Colorado trying to start the revolution. Yeah, they say he's cutting hands off of dope pushers, too."

Mitchell coughed. He did not want that to slip. It had started as a joke, probably.

"Billy always was half-crazy," John Henry said, squirming. "Whatever happened to Daniel White? That cat was always quiet, but he could beat all of us drinking gin."

Mitchell laughed, slapping his chest. "John Henry, Daniel is way out in Los Angeles. I hear he's got a good job, too. They say the last time he was home he was pushing a deuce-and-a-quarter. Which must be a lie because we both know that wasn't his style. I can just see his stiffnecked self trying to be cool."

"You never know, Mitch. You never know how anybody's going to change." He had asked himself how Mitchell could be so blind. All their friends gone, living well, and the two of them sitting in a funky bar. And Mitchell has the nerve to laugh at their new ways. He's probably so confused he doesn't know whether to hate me or love me for what I'm doing.

"Why don't you drop over some time, John Henry?" Mitchell asked. "Bring one of your ladies and we'll play some whist or something."

John Henry nodded, wondering how many things Mitch could have been. College, maybe, a hellified basketball player. Might have made a dynamite lawyer; Mitchell always was smart. But he said he didn't want that now. Maybe he wasn't up to the strain of getting it. Maybe the war left him with only one ambition: to rest in peace. But John Henry would never go out that way. After making up lost ground, he'd start a business in another town and push on to the top. They'd remember him in this town. He'd visit home once a year and prowl the streets in a new car. Yes, they'd remember.

"What about you, John Henry? You thinking of staying here for awhile?"

"Not if I can help it. I'll be out of here before it turns warm again. Watch. You know I never was too crazy about this place, even though it is home."

Mitchell smiled and they finished their beers. They'd get together again, soon. They were as serious with that promise as buddies growing apart could ever be. John Henry had decided to do what he knew he would do all along. At the end of the summer he paraded the White Horse through town. At home they found this creature beautiful. They quietly lost their minds at the sight of it, taking turns to mount. They wanted its flesh, wanted to suck its veins, wanted its power. Instant friends offered their services now, wanted to walk in the shadow of John Henry. He paused on street corners to show off weird greens or way-out red outfits. But all the folk he touched, even the one or two who might have loved him, turned to stone.

That summer Bobbie played basketball in the shadow of the

Horse. In the fall he would be a junior in high school and would start for the varsity. Knew he would start, though he had quit the junior varsity last winter because he couldn't get along with that team's coach. The coach had pronounced the sentence and benched him many times: Bobbie Powers is not a team player, Bobbie Powers has a bad attitude. A new year and a few new moves like the spinning jump shot and he'd be back out front again. No one worried. The coach needed a winning team to keep his job. He was no fool.

So Bobbie sharpened his moves that summer and when not playing he hung out with Chico, Cool Chico, his only real buddy. But one buddy is enough to turn you around. He shot up with Chico on a simple dare. Bobbie would try anything once, or twice.

On a hot afternoon in August, Bobbie fell out of a car at a highway rest stop twenty miles north of Cincinnati. Turning grey and dying. The needle was an ugly exclamation point to the vein. Chico vomited, cried and beat his fists on the hood of the car, while the sleepy-eyed truck drivers at the stop kept their distance. Miles away a few boys were playing ball on the hot court. The weaker players, minds steamed by dreams of superstardom, stood in the shade and waited their turn, making the myth of Bad Bobbie.

As Bobbie lay dying, John Henry and Tucker were making connections in New York. It was Tucker who had given Chico the phone number of the Cincinnati pusher. Nose running, Chico had been impatient and did not want to wait until they would get back from New York.

When John Henry and Tucker returned to town, they went directly to John Henry's apartment. A few minutes later Jeanette burst in to bring breathless news of Bobbie's death.

"A couple cops were around yesterday, asking questions," she said. "But I don't think they found out anything. Still they must know something on you, John Henry. Somebody must have told them something!"

Tucker was standing, shaking his head. "I told that stupid-assed Chico to hold off, but he kept pushing and pushing for the address. Did the boy O.D. or what, Jeanette?"

"I don't know, I don't know," she said. "O.D., poison, whatever. All I know is that he's dead."

In the silence they watched John Henry. He felt their eyes, knew

their questions, and looked off. They had nothing to do with Bobbie's death. Directly, at least. It's too bad the boy died like that, a
helluva shame, but they were clean. Then he lit a cigarette and
announced, "Let's go to the park. Jeanette, we'll drop you off at
your place, OK?"

By the time he and Tucker reached the park, John Henry had
decided that the sale of the new batch would be his last at home.
He'd leave, maybe go in with his friend in Dayton. Yes, he'd leave.

"I come back from the war to make money, not to go to jail," he
said as they parked.

Tucker nodded. "But big money and risking jail go together."

They headed for the basketball court and John Henry watched
the players for awhile. They were clowning around, all of them.
None of them could ever be as smooth as Bobbie with the ball. John
Henry told the players that they were sloppy, but they ignored him.

When a few more fellows showed up, Tucker got a nickel tonk
game going. They were gathered on a picnic table in the shade.
John Henry was grinning over his hand when he saw a car swerve
to a stop across the street. A short squat man in work clothes
rushed from the car. The basketball players saw the shotgun first
and scattered. The card players froze. They were older and knew
the danger of sudden movement. It was in the man's eyes, that
danger. The man walked slowly to John Henry and aimed the gun
at his chest. They had watched one another for long seconds before
John Henry heard his breath slowly coming out . . .

"You chickenshit bastard! You're the one who killed my son."

And from behind the man the wife screamed and screamed
again, reaching out to him, and John Henry's life in the town was
no longer something bright and definite as a path leading upward,
but as futile as aimless steps across a desert. He saw sand quaking,
saw only his hand above it to show the world that someone had
gone down slow. He controlled so little anymore.

"I was out of town when it happened. I just heard about it a few
minutes ago. I've never sold your son anything."

"Don't lie to me or I'll blow your ass to Kingdom Come! You
didn't have to sell it and I'll get that Chico and that punk in Cincinnati. But you the one brought the dope in this town. Because of you
my son will be buried tomorrow. Before you came there wasn't no
shit like this. They never should have let you out. You should have
died in the war!"

The man was shaking his head wildly, one of his fingers tapping beneath the barrel now. The rush of fear was ebbing now, leaving John Henry weak. The toothpick was splintering in his mouth.

Junior Cooper, sitting across from John Henry, eased away and tried to speak. "It was really a dude in Cincinnati, Mr. Powers. Not John Henry, sir . . . " He looked into the man's eyes and stopped.

"Don't, Lou . . ." The woman's voice was pleading. Another man, an uncle of Bobbie's whom John Henry recognized, walked slowly up to his brother.

"Don't go to jail behind this no-good boy, Lou." He stood next to Lou Powers, then reached slowly for the gun. John Henry knew that if he were to die today it would have to come in that instant as the man's hand came closer and closer to the barrel. The hand of Bobbie's uncle gripped the barrel and firmly pulled it from Powers. Then he threw an arm around his brother's shoulder and pulled him away.

The man turned to John Henry. "You lucky to be sittin there. You better get the hell away while you can."

The card players had stood up and a few started moving off, not too quickly because now they could afford swagger in the face of the boys with the basketball.

"Damn man's crazy," John Henry said, lighting a cigarette. "Always was crazy as long as I known him." He wanted to pee, his bladder was still strained. He wanted to go someplace and think. If he had died that afternoon, they'd forget him in less than a year and only remember that before he went off to war he was something of a clown and not even a good one. And someone new and slicker would come along to claim the Horse. They'd forget.

A week later as summer chilled toward another fall, John Henry packed two bags. He lied to his mother, telling her he was on his way to a Detroit assembly line. He knew she had heard about Bobbie. He timed his visit to miss his father who was at work and who had cursed him the last time they talked. John Henry had only tried to make a little money to catch up with his tired friends, most of whom were working two jobs. The Horse would have come to his hometown anyway. Someone would have brought it, yes. He turned on the radio as he picked up the expressway outside of town. A bigger town with better contacts might do wonders for his luck.

STEPHEN MINOT

Grubbing for Roots

(FROM THE NORTH AMERICAN REVIEW)

ERIK WOKE, sat up abruptly. The iron springs squealed under the
weight of his bulk. From downstairs Sal's voice — the sound that
had jolted him awake — continued:

"I said stop it now before. . . . Oh, *no!*" Then, her voice weary,
"God, your father will be furious. Honestly, Michael, you must be
psychotic."

Well, it was done. No use worrying — particularly on his day off.
So Michael had gouged the kitchen table with his wood-block carving or broken a window or . . . No, it was something father-owned.
Erik frowned, concentrating. Had he left his axe out? The chain
saw? The possibilities were limitless. Michael, seven, was the
dreamer, the reader. Only last Christmas he had been left to watch
on the cookstove a batch of inkberry brew — a dye they used for
decorations — and with his head in a book he had let it boil right
down to a stinking scum. The house had smelled for a week.

With Michael it was always daydreaming carelessness. But with
Timmy, two years younger, it was cheerful rebellion. Once Timmy
had dismantled the family typewriter in less than an hour.

On such occasions Erik bellowed, spanked, roared protests, had
everyone in tears. But he held no grudges. For the first time in his
life he owned land, plenty of it, and that gave them room for error.
No upstairs tenants to complain about the noise. Not even neighbors. This was a place where he and his family could work out their
problems directly. For all the destruction that went on, their life
there was far less damaging than the tightlipped, dour, and oppressive world he had endured as a boy back in St. Louis.

He threw off the covers and shivered. It was April and still raw.

Spring comes slowly in upstate Maine, and this was still the mud season. He swung his feet onto the floor, each one striking the cold boards like a slab of beef. The windows rattled.

From where he sat he could look down on the shingled wood-shed roof still white with frost but now beginning to steam from the warmth of the sun. Beyond was the barn, swaybacked and wave-sided in the swirls of old window-glass. He thought of all the calcu-lations that had once gone into that barn — careful measurements to the inch, ridgepole made to match the horizon of the sea with a spirit level, uprights aimed directly at the center of the earth with a plumb bob; all that planning, yet it looked far better to him through this old glass, no two lines parallel or even straight.

His neighbors, country bred, probably wouldn't see it that way. But Erik's childhood had been straight-edged, straight-backed, with plumb lines drawn right to the heart of the lower middle class. He wanted no more of that. Neither he nor Sal wanted any more of that.

"He won't take you with him," Timmy was chanting to his older brother. "He won't take you. He won't take you."

"He will too."

"Won't!"

"Hush up, both of you. Try being quiet. Just try."

"We'll be quiet as . . . mice," Michael said, pleased with the simile.

"No," Timmy said. "Quiet as ghosts."

"There aren't any ghosts."

"There are."

"*Silence!*" And she was granted it.

But of course there were ghosts. For Erik that was a good part of the farm. The Skolfields, for example — distant relatives of Sal's. Generations of them had bred cattle in the barn where Erik now kept his Jeep and four Nubian goats. Skolfields had bred Skolfields on the creaking, squealing bed he slept in. And when they died, they didn't go far. Down behind the barn, just barely within view of that upstairs bedroom, was the family cemetery, stones half hid-den in the untended grass. There were generations lying there, though he hadn't had time yet to sort them all out.

There had come a time when the cities began to seduce the survivors — Sal's branch moving south to Kittery. It was the same pull which had drawn Erik's family off the Missouri farm into St. Louis and the servitude of a retail business. The Maine farm went on the market and was eventually bought by a wealthy out-of-stater who was generally regarded as crazy. His goal in life was to save the arctic musk ox from extinction. Maine, apparently, had the right combination of fodder and isolation. They didn't mind the cold and they needed space for grazing. Some he brought down from the Aleutian Islands at great cost; others he wheedled from zoos where they were prone to be sickly and irascible. The neighbors, tolerant yet highly conservative in their husbandry, predicted disaster.

Erik had heard from them grim tales of bulls that gored their young and cows gone sterile. A pack of troubles, they said. But for all this the herd did grow. There was a time when those hillside pastures were dotted with the shaggy and foreign-looking beasts. The juniper bushes through which they wandered were adorned with long wisps of fur finer than cashmere.

So the experiment was a success. But no one cared, possibly because there was no real money in it. The story was that he needed more land and moved further north — to New Brunswick or perhaps Newfoundland.

As soon as the farm was on the market a second time, a distant cousin wrote Sal's aunt, wondering if someone in that great extended family would buy the place back. They had a high regard for continuity.

The decison to move to Maine was too big for them to have done it with logic and planning. Chance put the pieces together. As lovers they had shared an aching dislike for the college they were both attending and for the city in which it was located. Even in winter they would seek out deserted beaches along the Rhode Island coast and walk for miles, their silent pleasure a kind of communication.

For him, college was an entrapment. He had been lured there by parents who saw it as financial security; and when they told him how much they had sacrificed to keep him there, it was like locking the gate of a cage. How could he leave?

He could never tell them how he spent his hours in class imagining himself smashing every window in the room with his fist. Or that he had dreams of knocking down walls. The only person he could confess that to was Sal.

They both wanted to break out, but the escape route was unclear. Where would they go? Both of them had grandparents who had farmed, but everyone knew that you couldn't do that any more — not without making a business out of it. And neither Erik nor Sal was drawn to communes. So they remained in captivity and graduated with honors.

Freed, they stepped right into another trap. They tried teaching in an urban school. It was the Right Thing to be doing, but horrible. Then, in a single week, their apartment was robbed, they were served with an eviction notice from the Highway Department, and they received the news about the farm in Maine. Never mind that the place was without telephone, electricity, and running water; even without seeing it they had made the decision.

Voices drifted up again. They were arguing about boots. That meant breakfast was over and he had wasted more time than he should even for a Sunday. He planned to put in four hours at the boat yard that day, extra work to make up for the long, jobless winter.

"But there's no snow," Michael was saying.

"There's mud," she said. "The road is a veritable quagmire."

"What's 'veritable?' " That from Timmy.

"To you, kiddo, 'irresistible.' Now get those boots on."

"But they're so heavy," Michael said.

"Builds leg muscles."

"And make us strong?" As the youngest, Timmy was on a strength kick.

"Incredibly strong."

"As strong as Daddy?"

"Almost."

"When I'm grown up . . . "

"Get that damn boot on."

"When I'm grown up . . . "

"The boot."

"But when I'm grown up will I be as big as Daddy?"

"At least. Hold still now, I'll do it."

"And I'll have a car. And be tall."

"Sure you will."

"And have a big wee-wee like . . . "

"Right. Now stamp on that boot."

"A giant has a wee-wee as big as my arm."

"There aren't any giants. Now the other boot."

"But if there were?"

"As big as your arm. At least."

"Wow! Hey Michael, did you hear that? Mom says . . . "

"Knock it off, kids. Get those damn boots zipped." Her voice was brusque. "O.K., out, both of you." The door slammed and there was silence. Erik grinned and began dressing.

When Erik came down the stairs, the house shook. He liked the sensation. When the boys were there, he would thunder out "Fee, Fi, Fo, Fum," one syllable for each step. But this time there was only Sal and he couldn't be sure what her mood would be. Three months pregnant, she was having a hard time with mornings.

And then too, there was the matter of his working weekends and evenings at the boat yard. She could see the sense of it — for the length of a bitter winter he had not worked more than two days a week. It was half a day here helping to plaster the church basement and a day there shoveling crap out of a four-story chicken barn. What few lobstermen went out didn't need help and the boat yard lay silent and unheated. Now at last he was offered work seven days a week if he could stand it, and he could damn well stand it. It would be two months before all the lobster boats and the few pleasure-craft were scraped, painted, and hauled out of that sagging, leaking old boathouse and launched. And for the rest of the summer he would be kept busy as hired hand on lobster boats and tending his goats and his garden.

Right now he had to earn some cash and she knew it. But she was also feeling dependent. He wasn't used to that.

As he came into the kitchen she was at the soapstone sink, scraping the breakfast dishes into the triangular slop-sieve and rinsing them, working the pump handle with an easy regularity, two dogs at her feet and a cat on the counter all waiting to be fed.

"Click!" he said. His two hands were raised, forming a rectangle with fingers and thumbs. "Country girl at pump. Pretty as a picture. . . . "

She turned around and he stopped grinning. Her face was white and there were circles under her eyes.

"You feel as bad as you look?"

She shrugged. "Planning to work today?"

"I was thinking of it."

"I figured you might."

Her tone was neutral, but there was something else hanging in the air. He couldn't quite place it.

"Have a bad night?"

"Good beginning," she said with a ghostly little smile. They had agreed to abstain during her first three months, but they hadn't been able to stick to it. "So now the stomach's acting up. Retribution."

"I can get my own eggs."

"Relax." She poured his coffee from the kettle which simmered at the back of the old wood-burning range. He sipped it while she put eggs in the frypan. The room was as quiet as it ever was — just the sound of the wood fire, the sizzle of hot fat in the pan, the scratching of a dog, the rustling of the guinea pigs in their cage next to the stove.

"Something's eating you," he said.

"Huh."

"Something's knotted up in there. What's the trouble?"

A weary little smile and then she lifted the egg off the hot iron, flipping it over. "Can't a girl have any privacy?"

"Like that blister?"

When they were in college they had taken a four-day hike in the wilds of Baxter State Park. She had come down from the peak of Mt. Katahdin without complaining about a blister which had already become infected. Later, she almost lost the toe.

"Erik, how about staying home today?"

He set his mug down hard. "Stay home? When I've been sitting on my butt all winter? Aren't you tired of looking at my ugly face day after day?"

He was grinning, but he didn't feel it. Did she think he went down there and froze his hands scraping and painting in an unheated boat yard just for fun?

She scraped the eggs out of the pan and slid them onto a plate without blotting the oil off with a paper towel the way she usually did. Her face and the tired carelessness of her movement startled him.

"Look," he said, "how about this? How about if I take the kids?"

"To the yard?"

"To the yard. I'll put them to work."

"Yuh. O.K."

No protest. Not even thanks. She went back to the sink and he ate in silence. The eggs were leathery.

The trip to the boat yard was surprisingly quiet. The boys had worn themselves out feeding and currying the four goats and they were impressed at being hired as helpers at the yard.

"Will they pay us?" Michael asked.

"*I* will."

"How much?"

"Twenty cents an hour for you and ten for Timmy."

"That doesn't seem like very much." This from Timmy.

"You're just starting out. Life's hard when you're just starting out."

And there it rested. The boys really didn't have any choice. They rode in silence, three men going to work.

The route was mostly by back roads. It took them through small clusters of weathered and tar-papered shacks surrounded by rusting auto bodies, broken lobster traps, spare lumber, battered dories, baby carriages filled with kindling — nothing expendable in this harsh land.

"What's that?" Timmy asked. There was something quite bloody in the road ahead.

"Probably a fox," Michael said from the back seat with the annoying assurance of an older brother. He had been curled up in fetal comfort in a clutter of brown-stained drop cloths. Now he leaned forward with interest.

"Tail's not big enough," Erik said. Its head had been mashed, but the rest of it looked rather like a woodchuck. He slowed up, partly to swing clear of it and partly to see it better.

"Poor little fox," Timmy said. His tone was one he reserved for dead mice, dead flies, and even ants. Erik found this vaguely disturbing. Shouldn't the boy be out trapping and skinning animals at his age? It was hard to know; he had no measure with which to judge what a country boy should be doing.

"Save your pity," he said. "He had to go sometime. That way's as good as another."

"Yuch!" Michael said.

"What do you mean, 'yuch'?"

"Well, *I* wouldn't want to go that way — just like a thing."

"You wouldn't know what hit you."

They drove on in silence for a few moments. Erik gripped the wheel, angry at himself for reasons he couldn't place. There were times when he said things to the boys he didn't really believe and that didn't make any sense to him. It was as if they drove him to it.

"Daddy," Timmy said, "couldn't we go back and give it a funeral?"

"It's a dead goddamned *thing* in the road. What's the matter with you?"

That killed the conversation. They drove the rest of the way in silence.

By the time they reached the boat yard, the incident had been forgotten. As soon as they turned onto the old, pitted, dirt road, the boys started jumping in their seats, exaggerating the bumps in the road and laughing. Erik swerved unnecessarily on the curves, joining the joke.

When he caught sight of the old gray sheds and the cold shimmer of the bay beyond, he found himself looking for other cars. There were none. Most of the men avoided Sunday work. He felt a twinge of regret. For an instant he had imagined arriving with two lanky adolescents, shaggy haired, slouching, and good-natured. Erik and his boys, all members of that kindly, shabby group who spent their days scraping and caulking and painting.

But the illusion was broken by their shrieks of delight at those bumps in the road. He pulled to a stop by the main shed with more abruptness than was necessary. His sons had altogether too much exuberance. And they were too verbal. He wished they were more like the boys who went lobstering — low keyed, given to wry comments delivered straight-faced. *They* never jumped in their seats or shrieked like that, not even at five. They had been hardened in a way his own had not — in a way *he* had not.

"O.K. now," he said sharply as soon as they were in the chill twilight of the main shed, "if you're old enough to work, you're old enough to remember a few basic rules." Both boys looked at him soberly. "You stick to your own work, right? If you take a break, just let me know and then rest. No wandering off and climbing on other boats. And a couple of other things. No teasing, no complaining. Keep your eyes on your work. And don't keep chattering away. You boys talk too much."

The boys nodded solemnly, and they began opening and mixing paints. It was an old lobster boat they were working on — a large,

scruffy vessel but proudly equipped with a converted Chrysler engine, eight cylinders, and over $6,000 worth of electronic gear.

Erik felt a reverence for such boats. Each one represented a life-
time of work. Most of the lobstermen had started with open dories
powered by outboards and year by year worked toward something
they could take pride in. Erik's starting point was land based, the
Nubian goats. Four so far and one pregnant. He had land for grazing and new markets for the fur, the milk — used in yogurt — and
the animals themselves as pets. All it would take was an agony of
work.

For a while, the boys worked quietly and steadily. Erik stayed
above them, painting the decks a utility gray. The boys remained
on the ground below, assigned to the red-copper bottom paint.
There was a good margin for error there; and Timmy, too young
for real work, could pretend to be doing his part. Erik could finish
that side later.

It was just as well that the other workers were not down that day.
Theirs was an easy, close fraternity of men who had gone to school
together. Erik was still the outsider. They respected his strength
and his willingness to work, but they were uneasy about a man who
raised goats and sold yogurt to summer people. "How's things on
the Musk Ox Farm?" they would ask as if Erik and his family were
themselves some slightly odd herd. His boys, not yet fully broken to
work, would not have been appreciated.

At the end of the second hour, the complaints began to mount.
What time was it? How much longer would it take? How come the
paint was so drippy? He held his temper, but he wondered how
long it would be before they would stay with a job.

"Lunch break," he said, and there were exaggerated groans of
relief. "Come on now, you've only put in two hours." He climbed
down the ladder to help Timmy wrap his brush in newspaper. He
watched Michael out of the corner of his eyes, pleased that his
eldest was willing to imitate the ritual without being instructed.

He would have preferred to eat down by the shore — the sun
made it warmer outside than in. But the boys wanted to eat in the
cockpit and they needed some reward.

Erik opened his can of beer and leaned against a pile of life
preservers, ropes, and tarpaulins stained red with bottom paint. He
drew his knees up under his chin to rest his back. Looking aft he
could see a kind of trail in the dirt floor where the skids under the

cradle had been dragged last fall. Soon — the next day, perhaps — they would move the cradle back again along that same path, easing it with cables, prying it this way and that with crowbars, old Skolfield cursing without anger, nudging it until it was on the tracks which led from the door down to the sea. This was the part that Erik liked — sweating under the directions of the old master, a distant relative by marriage, responding to terse directions — "Ease her an inch thisaway . . . . I didn't mean no inch-and-a-quarter." Up from the sea in the fall, down again in the spring. The yard had been built in the Civil War and that rhythm — a six-month tide — had been repeated for over a hundred years.

"Well," he said, coming back to the task at hand, "lunch time is over. Back to work."

"So soon?" Michael asked.

"So soon," he said. "Let's get this over with quickly. Your mother doesn't like being left home all alone on a Sunday. Neither would you."

"But I'm not a grownup."

"Grownups don't change *that* much. Think you can finish with that bottom paint in an hour or so?"

"Jees." Michael's enthusiasm was flagging; Timmy's was gone.

"This isn't any fun," he said.

"So who promised fun? Do you think *I* come down here for fun? Listen," he said, again on the edge of rage, "this has to be done. Are you old enough for it or not?"

They all went back to work in silence. There was no way of telling how they felt about it. He didn't really want to know. Besides, he had given them a choice, hadn't he?

He threw himself into brute effort. Mindless, he moved the brush as rapidly as it would go without splattering. His arm and back ached, but it would all be worth it. If he was going to be known as the grubber, he might as well earn the title.

There had been times when he had been put down for that, of course. Like the previous week when he was varnishing masts outside, moving fast, and old Skolfield gave him hell. "No sense to that. Stop and look up." The sky was purple-black with rain clouds. "Any fool could see it's going to rain and ruin everything you've done there. You work like a grubber, you do. A man's got to look up once in a while."

Well, that was an exception. Most of the time it paid to get the job

done. Right now he had finished the deck and moved down into
the cockpit. If he could complete that before the end of the day,
they could launch her at high tide the following noon, a day before promised. There would be satisfaction in that.

When the squall hit, he was caught by surprise.

"Damn it to hell!" Timmy's voice from outside. And then
"thunk!" like a brush being slapped against the hull. Again,
"thunk!"

Erik scrambled up out of the cockpit and jumped to the ground
without even touching the ladder. "Watch it," he shouted. "No
paint slinging in this yard. What's going on?"

"It keeps *drip*ping," he wailed and deliberately whacked the wet
paint again.

Erik's temper snapped with that third slap of the brush. It was a
goddamned tantrum, that's what it was. He charged at his son,
head lowered like a bull. "Didn't I just tell you . . ."

The boy was eye-wide terrified, but he held his ground. His face
was streaked with dirt, tears, and red paint; he was a tiny savage in
bloody war paint.

Erik stopped, put his hands on his hips, stared down at Timmy,
and laughed.

"Hail, Timothy," he said, "King of the Pigmies."

The boy's paintbrush struck him hard on the left cheek, an inch
below his eye.

In the nightmare which followed there were no clear pictures.
Somehow he had got the boy jammed down over his knees to spank
his rear, and over the howling there was another child yelling and
beating him about the shoulders and neck like a mother bird. And
at some point the other child got his thrashing too, cries echoing as
if in a cave, sending a flock of outraged pigeons wheeling out from
the rafters.

The trip home was as silent as a funeral. It was perfect idiocy, he
decided, trying to shape them in the image he wanted for himself.
His own father had been a distant figure, working at the hardware
store all day and caring for the books evenings and even some
weekends. He was hard on himself and others. Once in a long while,
the old man would loosen up enough to talk. Usually it was about
his childhood, his life on the farm which in retrospect he made
sound ideal. All the good values were back there. But these were

such rare moments — how could Erik learn from those how to be a father? These boys made him feel brutish, clumsy, and irascible.

On the way home he stopped at a general store and bought a Popsicle for each of the boys. They muttered thanks and he started the Jeep and continued on their way.

"Aren't you having any?" Michael asked.

"I don't feel like eating."

Michael held out his Popsicle stick. "Here," he said. "Have a bite."

Erik took a bite for the ritual of it. Then Timmy, with a nudge from his brother, made his offering. Erik accepted that too.

When at last they drove down their own muddy road, past the family cemetery, and around the barn, they were talking about the goats and what the billy did to get the nanny pregnant, and how they would market the fur, and how the place would one day support them all without his having to find outside work, how they would share it, and, yes, how there would be a time when the boys would be running it themselves. It was marvelous how often they could listen to all that when they were in the mood.

Pulling to a stop by the house, he noticed that the wind had shifted to the north, coming in hard and cold. He also saw fabric draped over the juniper bushes. It reminded him of the wisps of musk ox hair they used to find when they first moved there. But no, it was clothing. The laundry — she hadn't bothered to use clothespins, hadn't even finished the rest of the load. Shirts, sheets, and pillowcases were scattered in the tall grass. What he had first seen in the juniper was a pair of her panties. Incredibly careless.

"Damn her," he said aloud. If he was willing to care for children for a whole afternoon, couldn't she finish a simple job?

"You play outside," he said to the boys. He went inside, slamming the door behind him. She was not in the kitchen or the livingroom. "Sal," he called.

"Upstairs."

He charged up, shaking the house. He found her in bed, listening to music from the portable radio, the cat curled up beside her. In bed in the middle of the day? Her maternal privilege, perhaps, but not his image of her.

"The laundry's all over the yard," he said.

"I've had it," she said.

"*You've* had it! Wait till I tell you about *my* goddamned day."

"I mean the baby."

He took a deep breath. "Here? Alone?"

She nodded, pointing to the floor beside the bed without looking down. There, surrounded by dark-stained towels and torn sheeting, was the chamber pot. And in it, curled and bloody, was his child. It was about as long as his own thumb. He knelt down.

She was saying something. Repeating it. "Erik, is it a boy or a girl?"

"Never mind that. What about you? Are you bleeding?"

"I'm all right, I guess. It's stopped. But the laundry's blowing all over the hillside. I had to leave it."

"To hell with the laundry." How could she be thinking about that when her whole being should have been filled with rage against what had happened. No, rage against *him*. He had left her alone — no car and no phone. And there had been signs. "Any fool could see it." Skolfield's words. Crazy for work, he'd gone and ruined everything. Spending his day midwifing a goddamned boat! Was he blind as well as brutal?

"My fault," he muttered, laying his head on the edge of the bed. "The whole idea." He meant coming to live there in the first place. Trying to make the land work for them. He had made a brute of himself. Even the boys had more sensitivity than he, wanting to bury that miserable thing in the road. No wonder men had abandoned the farms, blunted by the agony of effort. Brutalized.

"A killing place. It's turned into a killing place."

His eyes filled with tears for the first time since childhood. He had hold of her arm. He had led her into this and now he would have to lead her out again. They would have to start looking for a new life all over again.

"*Not* a killing place," she said.

"I killed it."

"Don't be stupid. Listen, we shouldn't be saying 'it,' we should find a name which could be either." He looked at her, amazed, but she went on. "Like Robin, maybe. It's a spring name. And I've been thinking — could we bury him or her in the cemetery? With a little stone? Some kind of marker."

"O.K.," he said gently, "but you hush up now. Get some rest." He wasn't following her. It sounded morbid to him. It wasn't good to be talking like that.

"I've *been* hushed up all afternoon," she said gently. "I've had time to think. That's our cemetery too, now. I was thinking, maybe we could fix up the other stones. Set them up. Fence it. And let the goats crop the plot. Keep it trim. I like that, having the goats keeping it trim. And . . . hey, don't look at me as if I'm sick. I'll be O.K. tomorrow. Can you do my chores this afternoon?"

He nodded. "Stupid question."

"Don't forget the laundry."

"Laundry first. Then milking the goats."

"Yes, the goats. And feeding the dogs."

"There's a fish head for the cat."

"Hamburger for the four of us?"

"Hamburgers, and we still have three jars of our own beets. You know, we did all right last winter. Three jars left and it's spring already."

In a great flooding of gratitude he laid his shaggy head on her stomach. Instinctively she winced, but there was no need to; he rested it there with a new gentleness, weightless with compassion. Touching her there, he felt in the same instant a remorse for the dead and a new, trembling love for the living.

KENT NELSON

Looking into Nothing

(FROM THE TRANSATLANTIC REVIEW)

THE TRUCK brought up dust as it bounced over the roadless flat
land. It pulled up near where two men were already standing by
the edge of a deep canyon. Barry watched the west-falling sun turn
the dust red in the air. The motor died and Turner got out.

"Where's he at?" Turner asked, coming up to the two men.

Barry turned away.

The other man, John, the oldest of the three, answered. "Down
there," he said, pointing toward the draw.

Turner walked to the edge. He was a graying man, short and
deeply tanned. He had the air of an investigator. "What's he
doing?"

"Barry said he heard him crying. I didn't hear anything."

"You hear him?" Turner asked the younger man.

Barry took off his cowboy hat, smoothed out his long brown hair,
and snugged the hat back on his head. It was a nervous gesture he
made sometimes around people. "Yes, I heard him." He said the
words as though his honesty were doubted.

"Where is he exactly?" Turner was used to the tone of his men.

Barry faced around. He directed Turner's gaze to the stand of
aspens in the bottom of the draw. "About in the trees there," he
said.

Turner shielded his eyes from the low sun. John, too, heavy and
slow, stepped to the edge and raised his hand against the sun. The
draw was steep-sloped, hollowed out of the flat-topped mesquite
land by centuries of storm water rushing through. Below them the
aspens and the grassy bottom were already in heavy shadow.

"He go down at the end?" Turner asked.

"Not really any other way. I wouldn't have known he was down there except that I heard him."

"Maybe you heard something else," John said.

Barry shook his head. "Sounded like crying."

Turner stepped away from the edge. "How long has he been gone?"

John looked at his watch. "Hour, two hours since I told him."

"That why he's down there?"

" 'Course that's why," Barry said roughly. "John shouldn't have said anything."

"I just told him what everybody says. Even Turner." John looked at Turner.

"You shouldn't have told him the way you did," Barry said.

Turner tried to break in. "Well, he never knew the boy was going to do this."

"It's his own fault," John added, turning away from the edge, too.

Barry stayed out near the edge of the cliff overlooking the draw.

"What are you going to do?" he asked, looking back toward Turner and John.

"I'm not going to do anything," Turner said.

"You just can't talk to him like that," Barry said more quietly.

John eased his stance, but it made him look more defensive. "I tell you I didn't know the boy was going to run off." John spoke more to Turner. "It was just plain language, same as any other."

"Not to a man like Rail."

Turner looked from one to the other. "It's done," he said. "It wasn't anybody's fault."

The men stood waiting. The sun slipped beyond the horizon and the flatland was suddenly all gray light, the same as the light in the bottom of the draw. Without the sun the air started to cool.

"What do you suggest?" Turner asked, coming over once again to the edge.

"I think we ought to get him out."

They all knew it would not be easy to get down into the draw. The upper end was the only way, and it was a steep pitch of rocks and loose dirt. The sides were impossible without a rope.

"Maybe he's already gone down," John said. "We couldn't have seen him if he had."

"If he's gone down, we'd never find him," Turner said.

They meant that it was possible for Rail to have gone down the length of the draw four or five miles to where the draw opened out onto the river.

"Anyway, the boy knows the way home," John said.

John's words hung in the air. There was no need for anyone to say that Rail wouldn't come back home alone.

"Call down to him," Turner said to Barry. "See if he's down there."

Turner backed off. Barry stood out on the very edge and cupped his hands around his mouth.

"Rail! Hey, Rail! It's Barry. You down there?"

The voice echoed from the other side of the draw. Barry waited for the voice to dissipate.

"Rail, listen, we want you to come out. We'll help you."

The echo died.

"You down there? Come on, answer up!"

"He's not down there," John said.

Barry looked down. The sound of his voice had stopped. He could see the leaves of the aspens shaking white and then dark in the last light, like the changing sparkles of sun upon moving water. The aspens made a slight sound.

"Rail, we want to do something. John's sorry. We want to help you get out." There was a halfhearted quality in Barry's voice which belied his feeling. He turned around.

"He's down there," Barry said.

"Listen, I'm not sorry. I didn't do anything." John's voice was loud and angry and brought an echo.

"Shut up," Barry said.

The two men looked at one another. John's heavy frame seemed to make his gray eyes small and pouched. Barry felt the heat rise into his face. He took his hat and smoothed his hair again. He saw himself, for a moment, as though outside himself, looking at his own gaunt features and dark eyes.

They had worked too long together to feel hatred, but neither of them was above fighting when angered.

Turner stepped in. "If he's down there," Turner said, "he's not going to answer."

For a moment they all stood there, not knowing what to do. The sky was an even, darkening blue-gray, without a cloud. From the top of the rim it stretched across the mesquite land for miles around.

"We might as well go on," Turner said at last.

"And leave him?" Barry asked.

"There's nothing wrong with spending a chilly night once in a while," Turner said evenly. "Won't hurt him."

"I'm not worried about the night," Barry said. "I'm worried about Rail."

"What's there to worry about? He can come home," Turner said.

"I'm worried about what he's thinking."

"What can he be thinking?" John asked. It was the first thing he'd said since Barry had told him to shut up.

For a long moment Barry didn't answer. He just stood and looked at them. His anger had gone. He couldn't help it. "You two go on back," he said at last. "I'll stay out here for a while and talk to him."

Turner sighed. "Okay," he said.

The two of them turned to go back to the truck. Barry watched them go. Then he called out, "John?"

"Yeah?" John stopped.

"Maybe you'd better wonder what he's thinking down there. If you don't know, it might help you."

John stood for a moment. Barry could see his graying form against the sky. Finally, without saying anything, John turned and walked to the truck. Turner had already started the motor and turned on the lights.

Somewhere below, in the dark stand of trees, Rail was sitting. Barry imagined the young man sitting and not walking. He imagined the difference between the broad sky which he could see from the rim of the draw and the black-bordered sky which Rail could see from the bottom.

Barry tried to listen for Rail's crying. He had heard it so clearly before, when he and John had first come to look for Rail. John had gone up the mountain, while he had come down to the edge of the draw. There had been no breeze. The aspens had been limp. It was a low moaning sound he had heard, brought up short with breaths. Barry had called out once, softly, "Rail?" and the low moaning had stopped.

The night seemed to hang over the draw. The shapes of the trees below merged with the ground, and Barry could distinguish only a vague outline of the rocks bordering. The draw seemed to flow downward, as though filled with a dark water.

He sat down on the edge of the rock and took out a cigarette. The air had cooled, but it was not yet cold. Barry knew the early morning would be the coldest time, around four or so when the dew would fall. He lit the cigarette, wondering whether Rail could see the light from the match where he sat.

He did not know why he was so certain that Rail had not gone down the draw toward the river. Rail knew the draw and knew where it went, even if he'd never walked the whole length of it. It was true that Rail was slight, and not as strong as most men. A hundred and thirty pounds. Barry smiled, thinking of Rail's thinness. Skinny as a rail. But Rail was more than that. Barry had seen him determined, and if Rail wanted to make it down, he would have done it.

Barry stared down into the blackness. "Rail?" The voice, disembodied, came back.

"It's all right, Rail, you don't have to answer. Just listen to me. I'll talk slowly or play a little, and you can listen."

Barry took a harmonica from his shirt pocket, dusted it, and then played for a minute. He carried the harp with him everywhere and often, when he had a moment alone, he would take it out for his own pleasure. He stopped the fast tune he had been playing, and then started in on "Shenandoah." When he finished, he spoke out into the darkness.

"Now you listen" he said in a steady voice. "I'm going to sit out here with you for a while. Maybe I'll play a little and maybe I'll talk, but I'll be here."

He played "Oh, Susannah." The notes slid into the stillness and kept coming back. As he played, he looked down into the draw and then at the sky. The stars were out by the thousands. He played another refrain and then stopped. The silence seemed welcome.

"You know, when I was a kid," he said in the same steady voice, "I did some pretty funny things. Not things to laugh at, but strange things. I never knew where I was going the way you do. You do know, Rail. Sure, you run into people like John. Even Turner to some extent. But they aren't holding you back. You won't be here forever. You know what you want."

From across the draw and far beyond, the howl of a coyote went up. It yapped as if wounded.

"Sounds almost better than me on my harp," Barry said. He paused to listen again to the hollow whine. "You know, that's what I was like when I was younger. I was like one of those damn coyotes. Couldn't do anything by myself. I was always too scared. I'd howl when I was alone, though. It isn't necessary to sing to the stars. I wasn't practising for anything."

Barry paused another moment. The coyote had stopped. Looking at the stars, he absently picked out the Dipper and traced a line with the cup stars to the north. "Stars are something, huh? Never see them often enough."

He didn't know whether Rail was listening, but he did not stop. He had a certain faith that he was, and that was all he needed.

"I had a boy once." The voice was strong. "No one else at the ranch knows that I had a boy. It's one of those things that you keep hidden from the people you're around every day. Sort of like a secret only much more severe. Like a dream, too, only more real. The boy's mother doesn't even know that I know about my own son. I read it in the newspaper when he was born." Barry laughed and then was silent for a moment, thinking. "Maybe you'd think she was an ugly bitch to go with someone like me. But she wasn't ugly. I met her when I was still living in the city. She was a beautiful woman. I know you'll ask why she went with me."

He waited, as though expecting the question to come of itself from the draw.

"I can't answer why. I met her in a bar where she didn't belong. I was sitting at a table and she came up to me. She could have had anybody else, I tell you. She just came up to me. At first she didn't say anything. She just came up pretty close and stared at me. I've never seen a look like that anywhere else."

Barry caught himself. He sensed that his voice was getting too loud, and he calmed himself down. "You know me, Rail. Nothing too pretty to look at. My mouth's too big and thick, and my face is too long. I could use some weight just like you, and my hair's never combed down. But she picked me. If I'd have been in my right mind, I might have wondered why at the time."

For a long time Barry was silent. He looked at the pelting of the sky. He could remember having often seen the stars as thick as they were that night. But never before had he understood the great

depth of the blackness behind the stars. It was like looking into
nothing. Neither air nor color, but nothing. It hurt him to look at
the sky like that.

He started out again in an uneven voice. "Sometimes you go, too.
I mean, you, Rail. Sometimes your feeling is all gone. I've seen that
in you before. Like that evening when Lavern came down." Barry
laughed strangely in the night. "Remember? Lavern said she was
going to see to you. You believed her. And then she didn't so much
as look at you. Well, that's just what happened to me here as I was
looking at the sky. It's as though you understand once and for all
what you're all about." He laughed again. " 'Course the next morning you've forgotten it again. And that's lucky."

He stopped looking at the night sky and took out his harmonica
again. He played a fast tune, sliding up and down the scale, letting
the sound out with his hand. He stopped suddenly in the middle.

"I know you didn't forget Lavern. I know it got to you, and I
know you did something about it. That's the way you are."

He played a train on the harp, starting slowly in the distance,
speeding up and getting louder, and ending with a whistle.

"Hey, how was that?"

He expected an answer. The draw remained as dark and as silent
as the blackness behind the stars.

"Rail?"

" 'Rail?' "

"You down there, Rail?"

" 'You down there, Rail?' "

"All right."

" 'All right.' "

Barry took out another cigarette. A breeze blew out the first
match, but the second stuck.

"I'll stay out here with you all night, Rail," he said, back again in
his even voice. "Wish I knew that you were all right, though. Wish I
knew that you wanted me to. Night isn't so long that I can't stay out
here."

A breeze came up again. Barry looked around him to see
whether anything was with it. Nothing. Neither a cloud nor a
moon. He stood up and buttoned his jacket. Then he sat down
again with his back toward the breeze.

"She took me," he said, a little louder against the sound of the
wind. He could hear the rustle of aspen leaves down in the draw.

"She took me right out of my seat with my beer not even half drunk. That's the way my boy was begun. A night like that. I found out later what she was. Do you know?" He laughed again, nervously. "Not what you're thinking."

He shook his head. "She was a doctor's wife. A smart girl who lived in a big house on the hill. She had my boy."

Then a thought struck.

"Rail?"

" 'Rail?' "

"Listen, tell me if you don't want me here."

" '. . . don't want me here.' "

Barry wondered whether he was keeping Rail from starting a fire, from keeping warm. Maybe Rail didn't want to be talked at and didn't want to be seen, and all the nonsense of words was keeping Rail from being a little more comfortable. Barry stood up. "I'm going on home now, Rail," he said. "Let you be alone if you want to. Just speak up now if you want me to stay."

The silence bore down. The breeze had stopped for a moment, but the clouds had started in the north. Barry moved away from the edge, out of the line of sight from the bottom of the draw. Then he sat back down.

Maybe Rail had gone back to the house after all. There'd be only John there, and maybe Nolan. Turner would be working on the ledger. No one would come out to get him if Rail were back. They'd let him sit out the whole night.

But if Rail hadn't gone back, if Rail had to sit out, within himself, then Barry knew he could, too.

He waited half an hour. Seemed like two hours. The sky kept coming down from the north. He knew that somehow there were pictures in the stars, but the only one he knew was the Dipper. He watched the clouds blow fast across it.

He stood up. There was no fire in the draw. Was Rail being cautious? Or didn't he have any matches? It occurred to him that when Rail had run off, he'd only had his jacket on, the jean one, and tennis shoes. Not even boots on. He wouldn't have had any matches.

Barry walked over to the edge once again. "Rail? I know you don't have anything, Rail. Listen, I never went away, I've been here, waiting for you to start a fire or make some sign. but it's all right to stay quiet. I'll be here."

Barry looked down the black flow of the draw. The breeze had come up stronger, and there was the scent of rain. He settled down again on the rock.

"That was fourteen years ago," Barry said. "I was twenty. Just a year older than you. Was never married to the woman, see? As soon as she knew, well, she came to me and said . . . you want to know what she said?"

The scene flashed through his mind. She had come to him in the evening in late fall. It was already dark. She had no time to wait. She was on her way from somewhere to somewhere and had to be home to the doctor. She didn't knock on the door, but rather burst in. He had been lying on the bed in his washed-out room, reading a magazine. She came across the room flying. He had thought she was going to strike him, but she stopped at the edge of the bed and looked down at him. He had not moved, except to lay the magazine on his chest.

"I'm going to have your baby," she said.

He stared. He said it aloud to Rail. "She said, 'I'm going to have your baby.' "

The words seemed to float out into the draw. The breeze destroyed any echo.

"I thought after that she would ask what I was going to do about it. I thought she would hit me. I was to blame. But she said, 'I want to leave my husband and come with you.' "

It had turned colder. The flat mesquite land was darker under the clouds. The wet smell of sage was in the air.

The rain started with a few drops. A desert storm blew quickly across the land. Barry turned his back to it. On the rim of the draw there was no protection. He thought of Rail among the trees. There was always the danger of flash flood in the draw, but below him, he knew it was wide enough that it was a simple matter to be safe. He tried to see Rail's movement.

The rain washed through quickly without thunder or lightning, leaving again the stars in its wake. Barry was soaked and cold and sat on the ledge shivering. It had lasted only ten minutes at most. The sage smell was strong and the rock glistening wet as the moon started up over the mountain.

He had said nothing to Rail during the storm, knowing that words could not have penetrated the sound of the rain. It seemed brighter now in the draw, as though the rain had lightened the canyon walls.

"She never appeared more beautiful to me than at that moment. I guess she'd resolved everything in her own mind. But I couldn't do it. Oh, at first, when she told me and said what she wanted, I was happy. But when she left to go home, I looked back at my room and at what I was, and I saw it was impossible. We didn't belong to the same world. We could never have been happy." Barry stopped. "So I know a little bit, too, about growing up and admitting to myself. You don't have to worry about anything, Rail."

Barry took out the harp again. The moon had passed the crest of the mountain and bathed the wet land. With shaking hands he put the metal to his mouth and blew on the harp the long wailing notes of his saddest song.

The buildings of the ranch spread out through the trees. On the far end, just where the trees ended, was the bunkhouse where Barry, John, Nolan, and Rail lived. Barry walked onto the porch at six-thirty.

He stood for a long moment, shivering, looking out at the sun. It burned his tired eyes.

John came out. "Find him?" John asked.

"No." Barry looked at the older man. "Didn't he come back here?"

"Not last night."

"Then he must still be down in the draw," Barry said. "I talked to him all last night."

"What'd he say?"

"Lots of things you wouldn't understand."

The two men stood in silence. Nolan came out. He was a small, ferret-like man with dark eyes and hair. He had a toothpick in his mouth.

"Where you been?" Nolan asked.

"Up on the rim of the draw," Barry said.

"Looking for Rail," John explained.

"Any luck?"

"Nope."

From across the way, Turner came out of his house into the sun. He walked toward the three of them with easy strides. Every morning he gave them their work assignments for the day. John and Nolan went out to meet him halfway.

Barry watched them standing out in the sun. He couldn't hear their voices, but he knew they were talking about the day's work. When Nolan and John had started off toward the barn, Turner came over to where Barry stood on the porch.

"How do you feel?" Turner asked.

"All right."

"Stay up there all night?"

Barry nodded.

"Just got a call," Turner said. "He's all right."

"Where is he?"

"In Aylard. The sheriff called. They've got him locked up."

"What do you mean locked up?"

"Rail was drunk last night in town. I guess he was bragging he'd put it to one of the girls. Somebody got mad. Rail's pretty feisty when he's drunk."

"Want me to go in and get him?"

Turner nodded. "I told the sheriff somebody'd be in. He said you'd need thirty dollars."

"I've got it," Barry said.

"Okay. Let me know when you get back. I'll be down in the meadow."

Turner turned away and walked across toward the barn where John and Nolan had gone. Barry stayed on the porch. Finally, he went inside to change clothes. There wasn't any hurry to get to town. Rail could wait a little longer.

CYNTHIA OZICK

A Mercenary

(FROM THE AMERICAN REVIEW)

> Today we are all expressionists — men who want to make the world outside themselves take the form of their life within themselves.
> — JOSEPH GOEBBELS

STANISLAV LUSHINSKI, a Pole and a diplomat, was not a Polish diplomat. People joked that he was a mercenary, and would sell his tongue to any nation that bargained for it. In certain offices of the glass rectangle in New York he was known as "the P.M." — which meant not so much that they considered him easily as influential as the Prime Minister of his country (itself a joke: his country was a speck, no more frightening than a small wart on the western — or perhaps it was the eastern — flank of Africa, but stood, rather, for Paid Mouthpiece.

His country. Altogether he had lived in it, not counting certain lengthy official and confidential visits, for something over 14 consecutive months, at the age of 19 — that was 27 years ago — en route to America. But though it was true that he was not a native, it was a lie that he was not a patriot. Something in that place had entered him, he could not shake out of his nostrils the musky dreamy fragrance of nights in the capital — the capital was, as it happened, the third-largest city, though it had the most sophisticated populace. There, his colleagues claimed, the men wore trousers and the women covered their teats.

The thick night-blossoms excited him. Born to a flagstoned Warsaw garden, Lushinski did not know the names of flowers beyond the most staid dooryard sprigs, daisies and roses, and was hardly conscious that these heaps of petals, meat-white, a red as dark and boiling as an animal's maw, fevered oranges and mauves, the lobe-leafed mallows, all hanging downward like dyed hairy hanged heads from tall bushes at dusk, were less than animal. It was as if he disbelieved in botany, although he believed gravely enough in jungle. He felt himself native to these mammalian perfumes, to the dense sweetness of so many roundnesses, those round burnt hills at the edge of the capital, the little round brown mounds of the girls he pressed down under the trees — he, fresh out of the roil of Europe; they, secret to the ground, grown out of the brown ground, on which he threw himself, with his tongue on their black-brown nipples, learning their language.

He spoke it not like a native — though he was master of that tangled clot of extraordinary inflections scraped on the palate, nasal whistles, beetle-clicks — but like a preacher. The language had no written literature. A century ago a band of missionaries had lent it the Roman alphabet and transcribed in it queer versions of the Psalms, so that

thou satest in the throne judging right

came out in argot:

god squat-on-earth-mound tells who owns accidentally-decapitated-by-fallen-tree-trunk deer,

and it was from this Bible, curiously like a moralizing hunting manual, the young Lushinski received his lessons in syntax. Except for when he lay under a cave of foliage with a brown girl, he studied alone, and afterward (he was still only approaching 20) translated much of Jonah, which the exhausted missionaries had left unfinished. But the story of the big fish seemed simpleminded in that rich deep tongue, which had 54 words describing the various parts and positions of a single rear fin. And for "prow" many more: "nose-of-boat-facing-brightest-star," or star of middle dimness, or dimmest of all; "nose-of-boat-fully-invisible-in-rain-fog"; half visible; quarter visible; and so on. It was an observant, measuring, meticulous language.

His English was less given to sermonizing. It was diplomat's English: which does not mean that it was deceitful, but that it was innocent before passion, and minutely truthful about the order of paragraphs in all previous documentation.

He lived, in New York, with a mistress: a great rosy woman, buxom, tall and talkative. To him she was submissive.

In Geneva — no one could prove this — he lived on occasion with a strenuous young Italian, a coppersmith, a boy of 24, red-haired and lean and not at all submissive.

His colleagues discovered with surprise that Lushinski was no bore. It astounded them. They resented him for it, because the comedy had been theirs, and he the object of it. A white man, he spoke for a black country: this made a place for him on television. At first he came as a sober financial attaché, droning economic complaints (the recently-expelled colonial power had exploited the soil by excessive plantings; not an acre was left fallow; the chief crop — jute? cocoa? rye? Lushinski was too publicly fastidious ever to call it by its name — was thereby severely diminished; there was famine in the south). And then it was noticed that he was, if one listened with care, inclined to obliqueness — to, in fact, irony.

It became plain that he could make people laugh. Not that he told jokes, not even that he was a wit — but he began to recount incidents out of his own life. Sometimes he was believed; often not.

In his office he was ambitious but gregarious. His assistant, Morris Ngambe, held an Oxford degree in political science. He was a fat-cheeked, flirtatious young man with a glossy bronze forehead, perfectly rounded, like a goblet. He was exactly half Lushinski's age, and sometimes, awash in papers after midnight, their ties thrown off and their collars undone, they would send out for sandwiches and root beer (Lushinski lusted after everything American and sugared); in this atmosphere almost of equals they would compare boyhoods.

Ngambe's grandfather was the brother of a chief; his father had gone into trade, aided by the colonial governor himself. The history and politics of all this was murky; nevertheless, Ngambe's father became rich. He owned a kind of assembly line consisting of many huts. Painted gourds stood in the doorways like monitory dwarfs; these were to assure prosperity. His house grew larger and larger; he built a wing for each wife. Morris was the eldest son of the favorite wife, a woman of intellect and religious attachment. She stuck, Morris said, to the old faith. A friend of Morris's childhood — a boy raised in the missionary school, who had grown up

into a model bookkeeper and dedicated Christian — accused her
of scandal: instead of the Trinity, he shouted to her husband (his
employer), she worshipped plural gods; instead of caring for the
Holy Spirit, she adhered to animism. Society was progressing, and
she represented nothing but regression: a backslider into primitiv-
ism. The village could not tolerate it, even in a female. Since it was
fundamental propriety to ignore wives, it was clear that the fellow
was crazy to raise a fuss over what one of a man's females thought
or did. But it was also fundamental propriety to ignore an insane
man (in argot the word for "insane" was, in fact, "becoming-
childbearer," or, alternatively, "bottom-hole-mouth"), so everyone
politely turned away, except Morris's mother, who followed a pre-
cept of her religion: a female who has a man (in elevated argot,
"lord") for her enemy must offer him her loins in reconciliation.
Morris's mother came naked at night to her accuser's hut and
parted her legs for him on the floor. Earlier he had been sharpening pencils; he took the knife from his pencil-pot (a gourd hol-
lowed-out and painted, one of Morris's father's most successful
export items) and stabbed her breasts. Since she had recently given
birth (Morris was 20 years older than his youngest brother), she
bled both blood and milk, and died howling, smeared pink. But
because in her religion the goddess Tanake declares before 500
lords that she herself became divine through having been cooked
in her own milk, Morris's mother, with her last cry, pleaded for
similar immortality; and so his father, who was less pious but who
had loved her profoundly, made a feast. While the governor
looked the other way, the murderer was murdered; Morris was
unwilling to describe the execution. It was, he said in his resplendent Oxonian voice, "very clean." His mother was ceremonially
eaten; this accomplished her transfiguration. Her husband and
eldest son were obliged to share the principal sacrament, the nose,
"emanator-of-wind-of-birth." The six other wives — Morris called
each of them Auntie — divided among them a leg steamed in
goat's milk. And everyone who ate at that festival, despite the
plague of gnats that attended the day, became lucky ever after.
Morris was admitted to Oxford; his grandfather's brother died at a
very great age and his father replaced him as chief; the factory
acquired brick buildings and chimneys and began manufacturing
vases both of ceramic and glass; the colonial power was thrown out;
Morris's mother was turned into a goddess, and her picture sold in
the villages. Her name had been Tuka. Now she was Tanake-Tuka,

and could perform miracles for devout women, and sometimes for men.

Some of Ngambe's tales Lushinski passed off as his own observations of what he always referred to on television as "bush life." In the privacy of his office he chided Morris for having read too many Tarzan books. "I have only seen the movies," Ngambe protested. He recalled how in London on Sunday afternoons there was almost nothing else to do. But he believed his mother had been transformed into a divinity. He said he often prayed to her. The taste of her flesh had bestowed on him simplicity and geniality.

From those tedious interviews by political analysts, Lushinski moved at length to false living rooms with false "hosts" contriving false conversation. He felt himself recognized, a foreign celebrity. He took up the habit of looking caressingly into the very camera with the red light alive on it, signaling it was sensitive to his nostrils, his eyebrows, his teeth, and his ears. And under all that lucid theatrical blaze, joyful captive on an easy chair between an imbecile film reviewer and a cretinous actress, he began to weave out a life.

Sometimes he wished he could write out of imagination: he fancied a small memoir, as crowded with desires as with black leafy woods, or else sharp and deathly as a blizzard; and at the same time very brief and chaste, though full of horror. But he was too intelligent to be a writer. His intelligence was a version of cynicism. He rolled irony like an extra liquid in his mouth. He could taste it exactly the way Morris tasted his mother's nose. It gave him powers.

He pretended to educate. The host asked him why he, a white man, represented a black nation. He replied that Disraeli too had been of another race, though he led Britain. The host asked him whether his fondness for his adopted country induced him to patronize its inhabitants. This he did not answer; instead he hawked up into the actress's handkerchief — leaning right over to pluck it from her décolletage where she had tucked it — and gave the host a shocked stare. The audience laughed — he seemed one of those gruff angry comedians they relished.

Then he said: "You can only patronize if you are a customer. In my country we have no brothels."

Louisa — his mistress — did not appear on the programs with him. She worried about his stomach. "Stasek has such a very small stomach," she said. She herself had oversized eyes, rubbed blue over the lids, a large fine nose, a mouth both large and nervous. She mothered him and made him eat. If he ate corn she would slice the kernels off the cob and warn him about his stomach. "It is very hard for Stasek to eat, with his little stomach. It shrank when he was a boy. You know he was thrown into the forest when he was only six."

Then she would say: "Stasek is generous to Jews but he doesn't like the pious ones."

They spoke of her as a German countess — her last name was preceded by a "von" — but she seemed altogether American, though her accent had a fake melody either Irish or Swedish. She claimed she had once run a famous chemical corporation in California, and truly she seemed as worldly as that, an executive, with her sudden jagged gestures, her large hands all alertness, her curious attentiveness to her own voice, her lips painted orange as fire. But with Lushinski she could be very quiet. If they sat at some party on opposite sides of the room, and if he lifted one eyebrow, or less, if he twitched a corner of his mouth or a piece of eyelid, she understood and came to him at once. People gaped; but she was proud. "I gave up everything for Stanislav. Once I had three hundred and sixty people under me. I had two women who were my private secretaries, one for general work, one exclusively for dictation and correspondence. I wasn't always the way you see me now. When Stasek tells me to come, I come. When he tells me to stay, I stay."

She confessed all this aloofly, and with the panache of royalty. On official business he went everywhere without her. It was true his stomach was very flat. He was like one of those playing-card soldiers in *Alice in Wonderland*: his shoulders a pair of neat thin corners, everything else cut along straight lines. The part in his hair (so sleekly black it looked painted on) was a clean line exactly above the terrifying pupil of his left eye. This pupil measured and divided, the lid was as cold and precise as the blade of a knife. Even his nose was a rod of machined steel there under the live skin — separated from his face, it could have sliced anything. Still, he was handsome, or almost so, and when he spoke it was necessary to attend. It was as if everything he said was like the magic pipe in the folktale, the sound of which casts a spell on its hearers' feet and makes the whole town dance madly, willy-nilly. His colleagues only remembered to be scornful when they were not face to face with him; otherwise, like everybody else, they were held by his mobile powerful eyes, as if controlled by silent secret wheels behind, and his small smile that was not a smile, rather a contemptuous little mock-curtsy of those narrow cheeks, and for the moment they believed anything he told them, they believed that his country was larger than it seemed and was deserving of rapt respect.

In New York Morris Ngambe had certain urban difficulties typical of the times. He was snubbed and sent to the service entrance (despite the grandeur of his tie) by a Puerto Rican elevator man in an apartment house on Riverside Drive, he was knocked down and robbed not in Central Park but a block away by a gang of seven young men in windbreakers reading "AFRICA FIRST, HARLEM NOWHERE"; a yellow-gold cap covering his right front incisor fell off, and was aesthetically replaced by a Dr. Korngelb of East 49th Street, who substituted a fine white up-to-date acrylic jacket. Also he was set upon by a big horrible dog, a rusty-furred female chow, who, rising from a squat, having defecated in the middle of the sidewalk, inexplicably flew up and bit deep into Morris's arm. Poor Morris had to go to Bellevue Outclinic for rabies injections in his stomach. For days afterward he groaned with the pain. "This city, this city!" he wailed to Lushinski. "London is boring but at least civilized. New York is just what they say of it — a wilderness, a jungle." He prayed to his mother's picture, and forgot that his own village at home was enveloped by a rubbery skein of gray forest with all its sucking, whistling, croaking, gnawing, perilously breathing beasts and their fearful eyes luminous with moonlight.

But at other times he did not forget, and he and Lushinski would compare the forests of their boyhoods. That sort of conversation always made Morris happy: he had been gifted with an ecstatic childhood, racing with other boys over fallen berries, feeling the squush of warm juice under his swift toes, stopping to try the bitter taste of one or two; and once they swallowed sour flies, for fun, and on a dare. But mostly there were games — so clever and elaborate he wondered at them even now, who had invented them, and in what inspired age long ago: concealing games, with complicated clue-songs attached, and quiet games with twigs of different sizes from different kinds of bark, requiring as much concentration as chess; and acrobatic games, boys suspended upside down from branches to stretch the muscles of the neck, around which, one day, the great width of the initiation-band would be fitted; and sneaking-up games, mimicking the silence of certain deer-faced little rodents with tender flanks who streaked by so quickly they could be perceived only as a silver blur. And best of all, strolling home after a whole dusty day in the bright swarm of the glade, insects jigging in the slotted sunbeams and underfoot the fleshlike fever-pad of the forest floor; and then, nearing the huts, the hazy smell of dusk beginning and all the aunties' indulgent giggles; then their hearts swelled: the aunties called them "lord"; they were nearly men. Morris — in those days he was Mdulgo-kt'dulgo ("prime-soul-born-of-prime-soul") — licked the last bit of luscious goat-fat from his banana leaf and knew he would one day weigh in the world.

Lushinski told little of his own forest. But for a moment its savagery wandered up and down the brutal bone of his nose.

"Wolves?" Morris asked; in his forest ran sleek red jackals with black swathes down their backs, difficult to trap but not dangerous if handled intelligently, their heads as red as some of these female redheads one saw taking big immodest strides in the streets of London and New York. But wolves are northern terrors, Slavic emanations, spun out of snow and legends of the Baba Yaga.

"Human wolves," Lushinski answered, and said nothing after that. Sometimes he grew sullen all at once, or else a spurt of fury would boil up in him; and then Morris would think of the chow. It had never been determined whether the chow was rabid or not. Morris had endured all that wretchedness for nothing, probably. Lulu (this was Louisa: a name that privately disturbed Morris — he was ashamed to contemplate what these two horrid syllables denoted in argot, and prayed to his mother to help him blot out the pictures that came into his thoughts whenever Lushinski called her on the telephone and began with — O Tanake-Tuka! — "Lulu?") — Lulu also was sometimes bewildered by these storms which broke out in him: then he would reach out a long hard hand and chop at her with it, and she would remember that once he had killed a man. He had killed; she saw in him the power to kill.

On television he confessed to murder:

Once upon a time, long ago in a snowy region of the world called Poland, there lived a man and his wife in the city of Warsaw. The man ruled over a certain palace — it was a bank — and the woman ruled over another palace, very comfortable and rambling, with hundreds of delightful storybooks behind glass doors in mahogany cases and secret niches to hide toy soldiers in and caves under chairs and closets that mysteriously connected with one another through dark and enticing passageways — it was a rich fine mansion on one of the best streets in Warsaw. This noble and blessed couple had a little son, whom they loved more than their very lives, and whom they named Stanislav. He was unusually bright, and learned everything more rapidly than he could be taught, and was soon so accomplished that they rejoiced in his genius and could not get over their good luck in having given life to so splendid a little man. The cook used to bring him jigsaw puzzles consisting of one thousand pieces all seemingly of the same shape and color, just for the marvel of watching him make a picture out of them in no time at all. His father's chauffeur once came half an hour early, just to challenge the boy at chess; he was then not yet five, and the maneuvers he invented for his toy soldiers were amusingly in imitation of the witty pursuits of the chessboard. He was already joyously reading about insects, stars, and trolley cars. His father had brought home for him one evening a little violin, and his mother had engaged a teacher of celebrated reputation. Almost immediately he began to play with finesse and ease.

In Stanislav there was only one defect — at least they thought it a defect — that grieved his parents. The father and mother were both fair, like a Polish prince and a Polish princess; the mother kept her golden hair plaited in a snail-like bun over each pink ear, the father wore a sober gray waistcoat under his satiny pink chin. The father was ruddy, the mother rosy, and when they looked into one another's eyes, the father's as gray as the buttery gray cloth of his vest, the mother's as clamorously blue as the blue chips of glass in her son's kaleidoscope, they felt themselves graced by God with such an extraordinary child, indeed a prodigy (he was obsessed by an interest in algebra) — but, pink and ruddy and golden and rosy as they were, the boy, it seemed, was a gypsy. His hair was black with a slick will of its own, like a gypsy's, his eyes were brilliant but disappointingly black, like gypsy eyes, and even the skin of his clever small hands had a dusky glow, like gypsy skin. His mother grew angry when the servants called him by a degrading nickname — Ziggi, short for *Zigeuner,* the German word for gypsy. But when she forbade it, she did not let slip to them that it was the darkness she reviled, she pretended it was only the German word itself; she would not allow German to be uttered in that house — German, the language of the barbarian invaders, enemies of all good Polish people.

All the same, she heard them whisper under the stairs, or in the kitchen: *Zigeuner;* and the next day the Germans came, in helmets, in boots, tanks grinding up even the most fashionable streets, and the life of the Warsaw palaces, the fair father in his bank, the fair mother under her rose-trellis, came to an end. The fair father and the fair mother sewed *zloty* in their underclothes and took the dark child far off into a peasant village at the edge of the forest and left him, together with the money to pay for it, in the care of a rough but kindhearted farmer until the world should right itself again. And the fair blessed couple fled East, hoping to escape to Russia: but on the way, despite fair hair and pale eyes and aristocratic manners and the cultivated Polish speech of city people with a literary bent, they were perceived to be non-Aryan and were roped to a silver birch at the other end of the woods and shot.

All this happened on the very day Stanislav had his sixth birthday. And what devisings, months and months ahead of time, there had been for that birthday! Pony rides, and a clown in a silken suit, and his father promising to start him on Euclid . . . And here instead was this horrid dirty squat-necked man with a bald head and a fat nose and such terrible fingers with thick horny blackened nails like angle irons, and a dreadful witchlike woman standing there with her face on fire, and four children in filthy smocks peering out of a crack in a door tied shut with a rubber strap.

"He's too black," said the witch. "I didn't know he'd be a black one. You couldn't tell from the looks of *them*. He'll expose us, there's danger in it for us."

"They paid," the man said.

"Too black. Get rid of him."

"All right," said the man, and that night he put the boy out in the forest . . .

But now the host interrupted, and the glass mouth of the television filled up with a song about grimy shirt collars and a soap that could clean them properly. "Ring around the collar," the television sang, and then the host asked, "Was that the man you killed?"

"No," Lushinski said. "It was somebody else."

"And you were only six?"

"No," Lushinski said, "by then I was older."

"And you lived on your own in the forest — a little child, imagine! — all that time?"

"In the forest. On my own."

"But how? How? You were only a child!"

"Cunning," Lushinski said. It was all mockery and parody. And somehow — because he mocked and parodied, sitting under the

cameras absurdly smiling and replete with contradictions, the man
telling about the boy, Pole putting himself out as African, candor
offering cunning — an uneasy blossom of laughter opened in his
listeners, the laughter convinced: he was making himself up. He
had made himself over, and now he was making himself up, like
one of those comedians who tell uproarious anecdotes about their
preposterous relatives. "You see," Lushinski said, "by then the peasants wanted to catch me. They thought if they caught me and gave
me to the Germans there would be advantage in it for them — the
Germans might go easy on the village, not come in and cart away all
the grain without paying and steal the milk — oh, I was proper
prey. And then I heard the slaver of a dog: a big sick bulldog, I
knew him, his name was Andor and he had chewed-up genitals and
vomit on his lower jaw. He belonged to the sexton's helper who
lived in a shed behind the parish house, a brute he was, old but a
brute, so I took a stick when Andor came near and stuck it right in
his eye, as deep as I could push it. And Andor comes rolling and
yowling like a demon, and the sexton's helper lunges after him,
and I grab Andor — heavy as a log, heavy as a boulder, believe me
— I grab him and lift him and smash him right down against the
sexton's helper, and he's knocked over on his back, by now Andor
is crazy, Andor is screeching and sticky with a river of blood spilling out of his eye, and he digs his smelly teeth like spades, like
spikes, like daggers, into the old brute's neck — "
    All this was comedy: Marx Brothers, Keystone Cops, the au-
dience is elated by its own disbelief. The bulldog is a dragon, the
sexton's helper an ogre, Lushinski is only a storyteller, and the host
asks, "Then that's the man you killed?"
    "Oh no, Jan's Andor killed Jan."
    "Is it true?" Morris wanted to know — he sat in the front row and
laughed with the rest — and began at once to tell about the horrid
chow on East 90th Street; but Lulu never asked this. She saw how
true. Often enough she shook him out of nightmares, tears falling
from his nostrils, his tongue curling after air with hideous sucking
noises. Then she brought him hot milk, and combed down his nape
with a wet hand, and reminded him he was out of it all, Poland a
figment, Europe a fancy, he now a great man, a figure the world
took notice of.
    He told no one who the man was — the man he killed: not even
Lulu. And so she did not know whether he had killed in the Polish
forest, or in the camp afterward when they caught him, or in Mos-

cow where they took him, or perhaps long afterward, in Africa. And she did not know whether the man he killed was a gypsy, or a Pole, or a German, or a Russian, or a Jew, or one of those short brown warriors from his own country, from whom the political caste was drawn. And she did not know whether he had killed with his hands, or with a weapon, or through some device or ruse. Sometimes she was frightened to think she was the mistress of a murderer; and sometimes it gladdened her, and made her life seem different from all other lives, adventurous and poignant; she could pity and admire herself all at once.

He took Morris with him to Washington to visit the Secretary of State. The Secretary was worried about the threatened renewal of the northern tribal wars: certain corporate interests, he explained in that vapid dialect he used on purpose to hide the name of the one furious man whose fear he was making known, who had yielded his anxiety to the Secretary over a lunch of avocado salad, fish in some paradisal sauce, wine-and-mushroom-scented roast, a dessert of sweetened asparagus in peppered apricot liqueur, surrounded by a peony-pattern of almond cakes — certain corporate interests, said the Secretary (he still meant his friend), were concerned about the steadiness of shipments of the single raw material vital to the manufacture of their indispensable product; the last outbreak of tribal hostility had brought the cutting in the plantations to a dead halt; the shippers had nothing to send, and instead hauled some rotted stuff out of last year's discarded cuttings in the storehouses; it wouldn't do, an entire American industry depended on peace in that important region; but when he said "an entire American industry," he still meant the one furious man, his friend, whose young third wife had been at the luncheon too, a poor girl who carried herself now like a poor girl's idea of a queen, with hair expensively turned stiff as straw, but worth looking at all the same. And so again he said "that important region."

"You know last time with the famine up there," the Secretary continued, "I remember twenty years or so ago, before your time, I was out in the Cameroon, and they were at each other's throats over God knows what."

Morris said, "It was the linguistic issue. Don't think of 'tribes,' sir; think of nations, and you will comprehend better the question of linguistic pride."

"It's not a matter of comprehension, it's a matter of money. They wouldn't go to the plantations to cut, you see."

"They were at war. There was the famine."

"Mr. Ngambe, you weren't born then. If they had cut something, there wouldn't have been famine."

"Oh, that crop's not edible, sir," Morris protested: "it's like eating rope!"

The Secretary did not know what to do with such obtuseness; he was not at all worried about a hunger so far away which, full of lunch, he could not credit. His own stomach seemed a bit acid to him, he hid a modest belch. "God knows," he said, "what those fellows eat — "

"Sir," said Lushinski, "you have received our documents on the famine in the south. The pressure on our northern stocks — believe me, sir, they are dwindling — can be alleviated by a simple release of Number Three grain deposits, for which you recall we made an appeal last week — "

"I haven't gotten to the Number Threes, Mr. Lushinski. I'll look them over this weekend, I give you my word. I'll put my staff right on it. But the fact is if there's an outbreak — "

"Of cholera?" said Morris. "We've had word of some slight cholera in the south already."

"I'm talking about war. It's a pity about the cholera, but that's strictly internal. We can't do anything about it, unless the Red Cross . . . Now look here, we can't have that sort of interference again with cutting and with shipments. We can't have it. There has got to be a way — "

"Negotiations have begun between the Dt' and the Rundabi," Morris said; he always understood when Lushinski wished him to speak, but he felt confused, because he could feel also that the Secretary did not wish him to speak and was in fact annoyed with him, and looked to Lushinski only. All at once bitterness ran in him, as when the Puerto Rican elevator man sent him to the service entrance: but then it ebbed, and he admonished himself that Lushinski was his superior in rank and in years, a man the Prime Minister said had a heart like a root of a tree in his own back yard. This was a saying derived from the Dt' proverb: the man whose heart is rooted in his own garden will betray your garden, but the man whose heart is rooted in your garden will take care of it as if it were his own. (In the beautiful compressed idiom of the Prime Minister's middle-region argot: *bl'kt pk'ralwa, bl'kt duwam pk'ralwi*.)

And so instead of allowing himself to cultivate the hard little knob of jealousy that lived inside his neck, in the very spot where

he swallowed food and drink, Morris reminded himself of his patri-
otism — his dear little country, still more a concept than a real
nation, a confederacy of vast and enviously competitive families,
his own prestigious tribe the most prominent, its females renowned
for having the sleekest skin, even grandmothers' flesh smooth and
tight as the flesh of panthers. He considered how inventiveness and
adaptability marked his father and all his father's brothers, how on
the tribe-god's day all the other families had to bring his great-
uncle baskets of bean-flour and garlic buds, how on that day his
great-uncle took out the tall tribe-god from its locked hut, and
wreathed a garland of mallows on its *lulu,* and the females were
shut into the tribe-god's stockade, and how at the first star of night
the songs from the females behind the wall heated the sky and
every boy of 14 had his new bronze collar hitched on, and then
how, wearing his collar, Morris led out of the god's stockade and
into the shuddering forest his first female of his own, one of the
aunties' young cousins, a pliant little girl of 11 . . .

In New York there were many dangerous houses, it was necessary to be married to be respectable, not to acquire a disease, in
New York it was not possible for an important young man to have a
female of his own who was not his wife; in London it was rather
more possible, he had gone often to the bedsitter of Isabel Oxenham, a cheerful, bony, homely young woman who explained that
being a Cockney meant you were born within the sound of Bow
Bells and therefore she was a Cockney, but in New York there was
prejudice, it was more difficult, in this Lushinski could not be his
model . . . now he was almost listening to the Secretary, and oh, he
had conquered jealousy, he was proud that his country, so tender,
so wise, so full of feeling, could claim a mind like Lushinski's to
represent it! It was not a foreign mind, it was a mind like his own,
elevated and polished. He heard the Secretary say "universal," and
it occurred to him that the conversation had turned philosophical.
Instantly he made a contribution to it; he was certain that philosophy and poetry were his only real interests: his strengths.

"At bottom," Morris said, "there is no contradiction between the
tribal and the universal. Remember William Blake, sir: 'To see a
world in a grain of sand' — "

The Secretary had white hair and an old, creased face; Morris
loathed the slender purple veins that made flower patterns along
the sides of his nose. The ugliness, the defectiveness, of some

human beings! God must have had a plan for them if He created them, but since one could not understand the plan, one could not withhold one's loathing. It was not a moral loathing, it was only aesthetic. "Nationalism," Morris said, "in the West is so very recent: a nineteenth-century development. But in Africa we have never had that sort of thing. Our notion of nationhood is different, it has nothing political attached to it: it is for the dear land itself, the customs, the rites, the cousins, the sense of family. A sense of family gives one a more sublime concept: one is readier to think of the Human Family," but he thanked his mother that he was not related to this old, carmine-colored, creased, and ugly man.

On the way back to New York in the shuttle plane, Lushinski spoke to him like a teacher — avoiding English, so as not to be overheard. "That man is a peasant," he told Morris. "It is never necessary to make conversation with peasants. They are like their own dogs or pigs or donkeys. They only know if it rains. They look out only for their own corner. He will make us starve if we let him." And he said, using the middle-region argot of the Prime Minister, "Let him eat air," which was, in that place, a dark curse, but one that always brought laughter. In spite of this, and in spite of the funny way he pronounced *hl'tk,* "starve," aspirating it (*hlt'k*) instead of churning it in his throat, so that it came out a sort of half-pun for "take-away-the-virginity-of," Morris noticed again that whenever Lushinski said the word "peasant," he looked afraid.

The war, of course, happened. For a week the cables flew. Lushinski flew too, to consult with the Prime Minister; he had letters from the Secretary, which he took with him to burn in the Prime Minister's ashtray. Morris remained in New York. One evening Lulu telephoned, to invite him to supper. He heard in her voice that she was obeying her lover, so he declined.

The war was more than 50 miles north of the capital. The Prime Minister's bungalow was beaten by rain; after the rain, blasts of hot wind shook the shutters. The leaves, which had been turned into cups and wells, dried instantly. Evaporation everywhere sent up steam and threads of rainbows. The air-conditioners rattled like tin pans. One by one Lushinski tore up the Secretary's letters, kindling them in the Prime Minister's ashtray with the Prime Minister's cigarette lighter — it was in the shape of the Leaning Tower of Pisa. Then he stoked them in the Prime Minister's ashtray with the Prime Minister's Japanese-made fountain pen. Even indoors, even with the air-conditioners grinding away, the sunlight was dense with scents unknown in New York: rubber mingled with straw and tar and monkey-droppings and always the drifting smell of the mimosas. The Prime Minister's wife (he pretended to be monogamous, though he had left off using this one long ago) — rather, the female who had the status of the Prime Minister's wife went on her knees to Lushinski and presented him with a sacerdotal bean-flour cake.

The war lasted a second week; when the Prime Minister signed the cease-fire, Lushinski stood at his side, wearing no expression at all. From the Secretary came a congratulatory cable; Lushinski read it under those perfumed trees, heavy as cabbage-heads, smoking and smoking — he was addicted to the local tobacco. His flesh drank the sun. The hills, rounder and greener than any other on the planet, made his chest blaze. From the airplane — now he was leaving Africa again — he imagined he saw the tarred roofs of the guerrilla camps in the shadows of the hills; or perhaps those were only the dark nests of vultures. They ascended, and through the window he fixed on the huge silver horn on the jet, and under it the white cloud-meadows.

In New York the Secretary praised him and called him a peace-maker. Privately Lushinski did not so much as twitch, but he watched Morris smile. They had given the Secretary air to eat! A month after the "war" — the quotation marks were visible in Lushinski's enunciation: what was it but a combination of village riots and semistrikes? only 200 or so people killed, one of them unfortunately the Dt' poet L'duy — the price of the indispensable cuttings rose 60 percent, increasing gross national income by two-thirds. The land was like a mother whose breasts overflow. This was Morris's image: but Lushinski said, "She has expensive nipples, our mother." And then Morris understood that Lushinski had made the war the way a man in his sleep makes a genital dream, and that the Prime Minister had transfigured the dream into wet blood.

The Prime Minister ordered a bronze monument to commemorate the dead poet. Along the base were the lines, both in argot and in English,

> The deer intends,   *Kt'ratalwo*
> The lion fulfills.   *Mnep g'trpa*

Man the hunter   *Kt'bl ngaya wiba*
Only chooses sides.   *Gagl gagl mrpa.*

The translation into English was Lushinski's. Morris said worshipfully, "Ah, there is no one like you," and Lulu said, "How terrible to make a war just to raise prices," and Lushinski said, "For this there are many precedents."

To Morris he explained: "The war would have come in any case. It was necessary to adjust the timing. The adjustment saved lives" — here he set forth the preemptive strategy of the Rundabi, and how it was foiled: his mouth looked sly, he loved tricks — "and simultaneously it accomplished our needs. Remember this for when you are Ambassador. Don't try to ram against the inevitable. Instead, tinker with the timing." Though it was after midnight and they were alone in Morris's office — Lushinski's was too grand for unofficial conversation — they spoke in argot. Lushinski was thirstily downing a can of Coca-Cola and Morris was eating salted crackers spread with apple butter. "Will I be Ambassador?" Morris asked. "One day," Lushinski said, "the mother will throw me out." Morris did not understand. "The motherland? Never!" "The mother," Lushinski corrected, "Tanake-Tuka." "Oh, never!" cried Morris, "you bring her luck." "I am not a totem," Lushinski said. But Morris pondered. "We civilized men," he said (using for "men" the formal term "lords," so that his thought ascended, he turned eloquent), "we do not comprehend what the more passionate primitive means when he says 'totem.'" "I am not afraid of words," Lushinski said. "You are," Morris said.

Lulu, like Morris, had also noticed a word which made Lushinski afraid. But she distinguished intelligently between bad memories and bad moods. He told her he was the century's one free man. She scoffed at such foolery. "Well, not the only one," he conceded. "But more free than most. Every survivor is free. Everything that can happen to a human being has already happened inside the survivor. The future can invent nothing worse. What he owns now is recklessness without fear."

This was his diplomat's English. Lulu hated it. "You didn't die," she said. "Don't be pompous about being alive. If you were dead like the others, you would have something to be pompous about. People call them martyrs, and they were only ordinary. If you were a martyr, you could preen about it."

"Do you think me ordinary?" he asked. He looked just then like a crazy man burning with a secret will; but this was nothing, he could make himself look any way he pleased. "If I were ordinary I would be dead."

She could not deny this. A child strung of sticks, he survived the peasants who baited and blistered and beat and hunted him. One of them had hanged him from the rafter of a shed, by the wrists. He was four sticks hanging. And his stomach shrank and shrank, and now it was inelastic, still the size of a boy's stomach, and he could not eat. She brought him a bowl of warm farina, and watched him push the spoon several times into the straight line of his mouth, then he put away the spoon; then she took his head down into her lap, as if it were the head of a doll, and needed her own thoughts to give it heat.

He offered her books.

"Why should I read all this? I'm not curious about history, only about you."

"One and the same," he said.

"Pompous," she told him again. He allowed her only this one subject. "Death," she said. "Death, death, death. What do you care? *You* came out alive." "I care about the record," he insisted. There were easy books and there were hard books. The easier ones were stories; these she brought home herself. But they made him angry. "No stories, no tales," he said. "Sources. Documents only. Politics. This is what led to my profession. Accretion of data. There are no holy men of stories," he said, "there are only holy men of data. Remember this before you fall at the feet of anyone who makes romances out of what really happened. If you want something liturgical, say to yourself: *what really happened.*" He crashed down on the bed beside her an enormous volume: it was called *The Destruction.* She opened it and saw tables and figures and asterisks; she saw train-schedules. It was all dry, dry. "Do you know that writer?" she asked; she was accustomed to his being acquainted with everyone. "Yes," he said, "do you want to have dinner with him?" "No," she said.

She read the stories and wept. She wept over the camps. She read a book called *Night;* she wept. "But I can't separate all that," she pleaded, "the stories and the sources."

"Imagination is romance. Romance blurs. Instead count the numbers of freight trains."

She read a little in the enormous book. The title irritated her. It was a lie. "It isn't as if the whole *world* was wiped out. It wasn't like the Flood. It wasn't *mankind,* after all, it was only one population. The Jews aren't the whole world, they aren't mankind, are they?"

She caught in his face a prolonged strangeness: he was new to her, like someone she had never looked at before. "What's the matter, Stasek?" But all at once she saw: she had said he was not mankind.

"Whenever people remember mankind," he said, "they don't fail to omit the Jews."

"An epigram!" she threw out. "What's the good of an epigram! Self-conscious! In public you make jokes, but at home —"

"At home I make water," and went into the bathroom.

"Stasek?" she said through the door.

"You'd better go read."

"Why do you want me to know all that?"

"To show you what you're living with."

"I know who I'm living with!"

"I didn't say *who,* I said *what.*"

The shower water began.

She shouted, "You always want a bath whenever I say that word!"

"Baptism," he called. "Which word? Mankind?"

"Stasek!" She shook the knob; he had turned the lock. "Listen, Stasek, I want to tell you something. Stasek! I want to say something *important.*"

He opened the door. He was naked. "Do you know what's important?" he asked her.

She fixed on his member; it was swollen. She announced, "I want to tell you what I hate."

"I hope it's not what you're staring at," he said.

"History," she said. "History's what I hate."

"Poor Lulu, some of it got stuck on you and it won't come off — "

"Stasek!"

"Come wash it away, we'll have a tandem baptism."

"I know what *you* hate," she accused. "You hate being part of the Jews. You hate that."

"I am not part of the Jews. I am part of mankind. You're not going to say they're the same thing?"

She stood and reflected. She was sick of his satire. She felt vacuous and ignorant. "Practically nobody knows you're a Jew," she said. "*I* never think of it. You always make me think of it. If I forget it for a while you give me a book, you make me read history, three wars ago, as remote as Attila the Hun. And then I say that word" — she breathed, she made an effort — "I say *Jew,* and you run the water, you get afraid. And then when you get afraid you *attack,* it all comes back on you, you attack like an animal —"

Out of the darkness came the illusion of his smile: oh, a sun! She saw him beautifully beaming. "If not for history," he said, "think! You'd still be in the *Schloss,* you wouldn't have become a little American girl, you wouldn't have grown up to the lipstick factory —"

"Did you leave the drain closed?" she said suddenly. "Stasek, with the shower going, how stupid, now look, the tub's almost ready to overflow —"

He smiled and smiled: "Practically nobody knows you're a princess."

"I'm *not.* It's my great-aunt — oh for God's sake, there it goes, over the side." She peeled off her shoes and went barefoot into the flood and reached to shut off the water. Her feet streamed, her two hands streamed. Then she faced him. "Princess! I know what it is with you! The more you mock, the more you mean it, but I know what it is! You want little stories, deep gossip, you want to pump me and pump me, you have a dream of royalty, and you know perfectly well, you've known it from the first *minute,* I've told and told how I spent the whole of the war in school in England! And then you say nonsense like 'little American girl' because you want that too, you want a princess and you want America and you want Europe and you want Africa —"

But he intervened. "I don't want Europe," he said.

"Pompous! Mockery! You want everything you're not, *that's* what it's about! Because of what you are!" She let herself laugh; she fell into laughter like one of his audiences. "An African! An African!"

"Louisa" — he had a different emphasis now: "I am an African," and in such a voice, all the sinister gaming out of it, the voice of a believer. Did he in truth believe in Africa? He did not take her there. Pictures swam in her of what it might be — herons, plumage, a red stalk of bird-leg in an unmoving pool, mahogany nakedness and golden collars, drums, black bodies, the women with their hooped lips, loinstrings, yellow fur stalking, dappled, striped . . . the fear, the fear.

He pushed his nakedness against her. Her hand was wet. Always he was cold to Jews. He never went among them. In the Assembly he turned his back on the ambassador from Israel; she was in the reserved seats, she saw it herself; she heard the gallery gasp. All New York Jews in the gallery. She knew the word he was afraid of. He pressed her, he made himself her master, she read what he gave her, she, once securely her own mistress, who now followed when he instructed and stayed when he ordered it, she knew when to make him afraid.

"You Jew," she said.

Without words he had told her when to say those words; she was obedient and restored him to fear.

Morris, despite his classical education, had no taste for Europe. No matter that he had studied "political science" — he turned it all into poetry, or at the least, psychology; better yet, gossip. He might read a biography but he did not care about the consequences of any life. He remembered the names of Princess Margaret's dogs and it seemed to him that Hitler, though unluckily mad, was a genius, because he saw how to make a whole people search for ecstasy. Morris did not understand Europe. Nevertheless he knew he was superior to Europe, as people who are accustomed to a stable temperature are always superior to those who must live with the zaniness of the seasons. His reveries were attuned to a steady climate — summer, summer. In his marrow the crickets were always rioting, the mantises always flashing: sometimes a mantis stood on a leaf and put its two front legs one over the other, like a good child.

Luchinski seemed to him invincibly European: Africa was all light, all fine scent, sweet deep rain and again light, brilliance, the cleansing heat of shining. And Europe by contrast a coal, hellish and horrible, even the snows dark because humped and shadowy, caves, paw-prints of wolves, shoe-troughs of fleeing. In Africa you ran for joy, the joyous thighs begged for fleetness, you ran into veld and bush and green. In Europe you fled, it was flight, you ran like prey into shadows: Europe the Dark Continent.

Under klieg lights Lushinski grew more and more polished; he was becoming a comic artist, he learned when to stop for water, when to keep the tail of a phrase in abeyance. Because of television he was invited to talk everywhere. His stories were grotesque, but he told them so plausibly that he outraged everyone into nervous howls. People liked him to describe his student days in Moscow, after the Russian soldiers had liberated him; they liked him to tell about his suitcase, about his uniform.

He gave very little. He was always very brief. But they laughed.

"In Moscow," he said, "we lived five in one room. It had once been the servant's room of a large elegant house. Twenty-seven persons, male and female, shared the toilet; but we in our room were lucky because we had a balcony. One day I went out on the balcony to build a bookcase for the room. I had some boards for shelves and a tin of nails and a hammer and a saw, and I began banging away. And suddenly one of the other students came flying out onto the balcony: 'People at the door! People at the door!' There were mobs of callers out there, ringing, knocking, yelling. That afternoon I received forty-six orders in three hours, for a table, a credenza, endless bookshelves, a bed, a desk, a portable commode. They thought I was an illegal carpenter working out in the open that way to advertise: you had to wait months for a State carpenter. One of the orders — it was for the commode — was from an informer. I explained that I was only a student and not in business, but they locked me up for hooliganism because I had drawn a crowd. Five days in a cell with drunkards. They said I had organized a demonstration against the regime.

"A little while afterward, the plumbing of our communal toilet became defective — I will not say just how. The solid refuse had to be gathered in buckets. It was unbearable, worse than any stable. And again I saw my opportunity as a carpenter. I constructed a commode and delivered it to the informer — and oh, it was full, it was full. Twenty-seven Soviet citizens paid tribute."

Such a story made Morris uncomfortable. His underwear felt too tight, he perspired. He wondered why everyone laughed. The story seemed to him European, uncivilized. It was something that could have happened but probably did not happen. He did not know what he ought to believe.

The suitcase, on the other hand, he knew well. It was always reliably present, leaning against Lushinski's foot, or propped up against the bottom of his desk, or the door of his official car. Lushinski was willing enough to explain its contents: "Several complete sets of false papers," he said with satisfaction, looking the opposite of sly. One day he displayed them. There were passports for various identities — English, French, Brazilian, Norwegian, Dutch, Australian — and a number of diplomas in different languages. "The two Russian ones," he boasted, "aren't forgeries," putting everything back among new shirts still in their wrappers.

"But why, why?" Morris said.

"A maxim. Always have your bags packed."

"But why?"

"To get away."

"Why?"

"Sometimes it's better where you aren't than where you are."

Morris wished the Prime Minister had heard this; surely he would have trusted Lushinski less. But Lushinski guessed his thought. "Only the traitors stay home," he said. "In times of trouble only the patriots have false papers."

"But now the whole world knows," Morris said reasonably. "You've told the whole world on television."

"That will make it easier to get away. They will recognize a patriot and defer."

He became a dervish of travel: he was mad about America and went to Detroit and to Tampa, to Cincinnati and to Biloxi. They asked him how he managed to keep up with his diplomatic duties; he referred them to Morris, whom he called his "conscientious blackamoor." Letters came to the consulate in New York accusing him of being a colonialist and a racist. Lushinski remarked that he was not so much that as a cyclist, and immediately — to prove his solidarity with cyclists of every color — bought Morris a gleaming ten-speed two-wheeler. Morris had learned to ride at Oxford, and was overjoyed once again to pedal into a rush of wind. He rode south on Second Avenue; he circled the whole Lower East Side. But in only two days his bike was stolen by a gang of what the police designated as "teenage black male perpetrators." Morris liked America less and less.

Lushinski liked it more and more. He went to civic clubs, clubs with animal names, clubs with Indian names; societies internationalist and jingoist; veterans, pacifists, vegetarians, feminists, vivisectionists; he would agree to speak anywhere. No Jews invited him; he had turned his back on the Israeli ambassador. Meanwhile the Secretary of State withdrew a little, and omitted Lushinski from his dinner list; he was repelled by a man who would want to go to Cincinnati, a place the Secretary had left forever. But the Prime Minister was delighted and cabled Lushinski to "get to know the proletariat" — nowadays the Prime Minister often used such language: he said "dialectic," "collective," and "Third World." Occasionally he said "peoples," as in "peoples' republic." In a place called Oneonta, New York, Lushinski told about the uniform: in Paris he

had gone to a tailor and asked him to make up the costume of an
officer. "Of which nationality, sir?" "Oh, no particular one." "What
rank, sir?" "High. As high as you can imagine." The coat was long,
had epaulets, several golden bands on the sleeves, and metal buttons engraved with the head of a dead monarch. From a toy store
Lushinski bought ribbons and medals to hang on its breast. The
cap was tall and fearsomely military, with a strong bill ringed by a
scarlet cord. Wearing this concoction, Lushinski journeyed to the
Rhineland. In hotels they gave him the ducal suite and charged
nothing, in restaurants he swept past everyone to the most devoted
service, at airports he was served drinks in carpeted sitting rooms
and ushered on board, with a guard, into a curtained parlor.

"Your own position commands all that," Morris said gravely.
Again he was puzzled. All around him they rattled with hilarity.
Lushinski's straight mouth remained straight; Morris brooded
about impersonation. It was no joke (but this was years and years
ago, in the company of Isabel Oxenham) that he sought out Tarzan
movies: Africa in the Mind of the West. It could have been his
thesis, but it was not. He was too inward for such a generality: it was
his own mind he meant to observe. Was he no better than that lout
Tarzan, investing himself with a chatter not his own? How long
could the ingested, the invented foreignness endure? He felt himself — himself, Mdulgo-kt'dulgo, called Morris, dressed in suit and
tie, his academic gown thrown down on a chair 20 miles north of
this cinema — he felt himself to be self-duped, an impersonator.
The film passed (jungle, vines, apes, the famous leap and screech
and fisted thump, natives each with his rubber spear and extra's
face — janitors and barmen), it was a confusion, a mist. His thumb
climbed Isabel's vertebrae: such a nice even row, up and down like
a stair. The children's matinee was done, the evening film commenced. It was in Italian, and he never forgot it, a comedy about an
unwilling impostor, a common criminal mistaken for a heroic soldier: General della Rovere.

The movie made Isabel's tears fall onto Morris's left wrist.

The criminal, an ordinary thug, is jailed; the real General's political enemies want the General put away. The real General is a
remarkable man, a saint, a hero. And, little by little, the criminal
acquires the General's qualities, he becomes selfless, he becomes
courageous, glorious. At the end of the movie he has a chance to
reveal that he is not the real General della Rovere. Nobly, he
chooses instead to be executed in the General's place, he atones for

his past life, a voluntary sacrifice. Morris explained to Isabel that the ferocious natives encountered by Tarzan are in the same moral situation as the false General della Rovere: they accommodate, they adapt to what is expected. Asked to howl like men who inhabit no culture, they howl. "But they have souls, once they were advanced beings. If you jump into someone else's skin," he asked, "doesn't it begin to fit you?"

"Oi wouldn now, oi hev now ejucytion," Isabel said.

Morris himself did not know.

All the same, he did not believe that Lushinski was this sort of impersonator. A Tarzan perhaps, not a della Rovere. The problem of sincerity disturbed and engrossed him. He boldly asked Lushinski his views.

"People who deal in diplomacy attach too much importance to being believed," Lushinski declaimed. "Sincerity is only a maneuver, like any other. A quantity of lies is a much more sensible method — it gives the effect of greater choice. Sincerity offers only one course. But if you select among a great variety of insincerities, you're bound to strike a better course."

He said all this because it was exactly what Morris wanted to hear from him.

The Prime Minister had no interest in questions of identity. "He is not a false African," the Prime Minister said in a parliamentary speech defending his appointment, "he is a true advocate." Though vainglorious, this seemed plausible enough; but for Morris, Lushinski was not an African at all. "It isn't enough to be *politically* African," Morris argued one night; "politically you can assume the culture. No one can assume the cult." Then he remembered the little bones of Isabel Oxenham's back. "Morris, Morris," Lushinski said, "you're not beginning to preach Negritude?" "No," said Morris; he wanted to speak of religion, of his mother; but just then he could not — the telephone broke in, though it was two in the morning and not the official number, rather his own private one, used by Louisa. She spoke of returning to her profession; she was too often alone. "Where are you going tomorrow?" she asked Lushinski. Morris could hear the little electric voice in the receiver. "You say you do it for public relations," she said, "but why really? What do they need to know about Africa in Shaker Heights that they don't know already?" The little electric voice forked and fragmented, tiny lightnings in her lover's ear.

The next day a terrorist from the hills shot the Prime Minister's

wife at a State ceremony with many Westerners present; he had
intended to shoot the Prime Minister. The Prime Minister, it was
noted, appeared to grieve, and ordered a bubble-top for his car
and a bulletproof vest to wear under his shirt. In a cable he instructed Lushinski to cease his circulation among the American
proletariat. Lulu was pleased. Lushinski began to refuse invita-
tions, his American career was over. In the Assembly he spoke —
"with supernal," Morris acknowledged, "eloquence" — against ter-
rorism; though their countries had no diplomatic relations, and in
spite of Lushinski's public snub, the Israeli ambassador applauded,
with liquid eyes. But Lushinski missed something. To address an
international body representing every nation on the planet seemed
less than before; seemed limiting; he missed the laughter of Oneonta, New York. The American provinces moved him — how gull-
ible they were, how little they knew, or would ever know, of
cruelty's breadth! A country of babies. His half-year among all
those cities had elated him: a visit to an innocent star: no sarcasm,
cynicism, innuendo grew there; such nice church ladies; a benevo-
lent passiveness which his tales,with their wily spikes, could rouse to
nervous pleasure.

Behind Lushinski's ears threads of white hairs sprang; he worried about the Prime Minister's stability in the aftermath of the
attack. While the representative from Uganda "exercised," Lushinski sneered, "his right of reply" — "The distinguished representative from our sister-country to the north fabricates dangerous
adventures for make-believe pirates who exist only in his fantasies,
and we all know how colorfully, how excessively, he is given to
whimsy" — Lushinski drew on his pad a self-portrait: the head of a
cormorant, with a sack under its beak. Though there was no overt
resemblance, it could pass nevertheless for a self-portrait.

In October he returned to his capital. The Prime Minister had a
new public wife. He had replenished his ebullience, and no longer
wore the bulletproof vest. The new wife kneeled before Lushinski
with a bean-flour cake. The Prime Minister was sanguine: the cap-
tured terrorist had informed on his colleagues, entire nests of them
had been cleaned out of four nearby villages. The Prime Minister
begged Lushinski to allow him to lend him one of his younger
females. Lushinski examined her and accepted. He took also one of
Morris's sisters, and with these two went to live for a month alone in
a white villa on the blue coast.

Every day the Prime Minister sent a courier with documents and newspapers; also the consular pouch from New York.

Morris in New York: Morris in a city of Jews. He walked. He crossed a bridge. He walked. He was attentive to their houses, their neighborhoods. Their religious schools. Their synagagues. Their multitudinous societies. Announcements of debates, ice-cream, speeches, rallies, delicatessens, violins, felafel, books. Ah, the avalanche of their books!

Where their streets ended, the streets of the blacks began. Mdulgo-kt'dulgo in exile among the kidnapped — cargo-Africans, victims with African faces, lost to language and faith; impostors sunk in barbarism, primitives, impersonators. Emptied-out creatures, with their hidden knives, their swift silver guns, their poisoned red eyes, christianized, made not new but neuter, fabricated: oh, only restore them to their inmost selves, to the serenity of orthodoxy, redemption of the true gods who speak in them without voice!

Morris Ngambe in New York. Alone, treading among traps, in jeopardy of ambush, with no female.

And in Africa, in a white villa on the blue coast: the Prime Minister's gaudy pet, on a blue sofa before an open window, smoking and smoking, under the breath of the scented trees, under the sleek palms of a pair of young females, smoking and caressing — snug in Africa, Lushinski.

In his last week in the villa, the pouch from New York held a letter from Morris.

The letter:

A curious note concerning the terrorist personality. I have just read of an incident which took place in a Jerusalem prison. A captive terrorist, a Japanese who had murdered twenty-nine pilgrims at the Tel Aviv airport, was permitted to keep in his cell, besides reading matter, a comb, a hairbrush, a nailbrush, and a fingernail clippers. A dapper chap, apparently. One morning he was found to have partially circumcised himself. His instrument was the clippers. He lost consciousness and the job was completed in the prison hospital. The doctor questioned him. It turned out he had begun to read intensively in the Jewish religion. He had a Bible and a text for learning the Hebrew language. He had begun to grow a beard and earlocks. Perhaps you will understand better than I the spiritual side of this matter.

You recall my remarks on culture and cult. Here is a man who wishes to annihilate a society and its culture, but he is captivated by its cult. For its cult he will bleed himself.

Captivity leading to captivation: an interesting notion.

It may be that every man at length becomes what he wishes to victimize.

It may be that every man needs to impersonate what he first must kill.

Lushinski recognized in Morris's musings a lumpy parroting of *Reading Gaol* mixed with — what? Fanon? Genet? No; only Oscar Wilde, sentimentally epigrammatic. Oscar Wilde in Jerusalem! As unlikely as the remorse of Gemorrah. Like everyone the British had once blessed with Empire, Morris was a Victorian. He was a gentleman. He believed in civilizing influences; even more in civility. He was besotted by style. If he thought of knives, it was for buttering scones.

But Lushinski, a man with the nose and mouth of a knife, and the body of a knife, understood this letter as a blade between them. It meant a severing. Morris saw him as an impersonator. Morris uncovered him; then stabbed. Morris had called him a transmuted, a transfigured, African. A man in love with his cell. A traitor. Perfidious. A fake.

Morris had called him Jew.

— Morris in New York, alone, treading among traps, in jeopardy of ambush, with no female. He knew his ascendancy. Victory of that bird-bright forest, glistening with the bodies of boys, over the old terror in the Polish woods.

Morris prayed. He prayed to his mother: down, take him down, bring him something evil. The divine mother answers sincere believers: O Tanake-Tuka!

And in Africa, in a white villa on the blue coast, the Prime Minister's gaudy pet, on a blue sofa before an open window, smoking and smoking, under the breath of the scented trees, under the shadow of the bluish snow, under the blue-black pillars of the Polish woods, under the breath of Andor, under the merciless palms of peasants and fists of peasants, under the rafters, under the stone-white hanging stars of Poland — Lushinski.

Against the stones and under the snow.

REYNOLDS PRICE

Broad Day

(FROM SHENANDOAH)

JUNE 1944

They had slept four hours when the dream began, ran its slow course, and woke them — Rob, then Min. Rob woke in fact well before the end, to stop it. Naked on his back on the soaked narrow mattress, he had managed to refuse to endure the end again and he opened his eyes. But he didn't touch Min or turn in the dark to find her. He lay flat, waiting for the fan's next swing, and watched the low ceiling while she saw it through beside him eight inches away, suffering little yips and moans toward the end as she struggled to surface and took the first breath of consciousness, hot for early June. Then they both lay quiet, still separate though bare, testing in the rate and depth of breath how ready each was to speak, start a day.

Finally Min said "Have you been asleep?"

"Long as you, two minutes less."

"What got you?" she said.

He said "You know."

"But tell me." She turned — in place, no nearer — and saw him by the streetlight filtered through shades: the line of his features like a map for the road of the rest of her life (she saw it that way, had seen it for years despite his refusal).

Rob understood both her turn and what she saw; and neither from cruelty nor fear, he turned away — the need to focus on the story he'd seen and learn its demands. Then he put one finger longway between his teeth — a bridle should he need one — and said, "I was a boy. Fourteen, fifteen. We lived in the country and a war was on, around us but not near us. We were in the foothills, unharmed and green; and I had a sickness — my chest, my breath — though I felt well and safe and ready for my life. My father walked with me to the nearest town; and the doctor said — smiling, everybody was smiling, clear beautiful day — 'T.B., very grave' and that, owing to the war, I must walk on up in the mountains to the springs. The good air, the waters. I left from there, not even going home — Father just vanished, no kiss, no wave — and I walked west for days through emptiness. Little towns in the distance, churches, trains; but not a living soul and I wasn't lonesome or hungry either. I just had the clothes on my back — a blue poplin shirt with the collar gone, big brown pants, old brogans — and a silver dollar to pay for my treatments at the end of the line. But I never ate a mouthful on the whole long trip, never felt the need. I was happy. All the way, every step of the way — all steep uphill — I was smiling to myself, needing nothing but me. Oh I touched a deer and saw most other kinds of harmless creatures; and every now and then I would hear the war, guns behind me muttering away. All the men were there, I guess; but old folks and children — where had they gone? And I never slept once. It was that far to go; and I wanted it that bad — the place, the springs, and not just my health but something beneath it, better than health: a magnet in the ground." Rob waited, the finger still in his teeth, still turned away.

Min said, "Are you telling me all that is true?"

He began to answer but only exhaled.

"Are you saying that happened?"

"It seemed to be," he said.

"But not to you."

"Maybe not," he said. "I'd have to think back."

"Think forward," she said. "Tell on to the end."

"I didn't let it end." Both their voices were as clear and clean as if they had never slept in their lives but had watched at doors steadily for arrivals.

"Tell as far as you want." Min watched him still, just the side of his head. He was beautiful and seemed calm now, which was why she urged him on — to learn all she could in the spaces of calm.

"The final night of the trip, all night, I walked through a storm like Hell on the rise. Night bright as day with lightning, trees crashing, rocks big as sheds falling at my feet — tame as dogs, sparing me."

"You were scared though."

"Was I? I don't remember."

"Yes."

"But I didn't stop, did I? That wasn't what it meant anyhow, the storm. It was not for me. I just went on — one foot, then the other, steeper up — into calm and morning which came together. And the first sight of people in all those days. I had come round a curve near the top of the mountain; and the road stretched before me, half a mile. At the far end were people all turned toward me — they'd been turned when I came into sight; they were waiting — so I went on toward them and knew I was there, my destination. Still I asked the first man — tall, old as my father — 'Is this the springs?' He said, 'It was and it was mine.' Everybody else nodded — men and women, all grown but a girl a little younger than me; all sad but not hard. I said to him '*Was?* I've walked days to drink. I'm dying, mister.' And he said, 'Well, die. The springs is gone.' I looked round at everybody there, all nodding, and said to them 'Help!' "

"You were scared."

"I remember — and honest, in earnest. Not a human moved. So I said it again; and the one girl stepped forward, just beyond being a child, a month or two beyond. And she said, 'Listen. We had the storm too, and it flooded our river and buried our springs.' I said 'Under what?' She said 'Six feet of dirt'; and I said, 'Hell, I'm dying. Let's *dig*.' The girl said 'Yes' but the first man said, 'How much do you cost?' I said, 'I'm free if you'll save my life.' The girl said 'No.' I said, 'You want me to die?' She said, 'No, not that. But nothing's free. I just meant that — don't give away anything except for *return*.' So I said, 'Fair enough. I'll take you then'; and knew I was cured — healed down to the sockets, and the springs still buried. The man didn't like it, frowned a lot; but all the rest grinned, and the girl led the way toward a little springhouse, white lattice work that was half under mud. And we dug forever. Days. Weeks more nearly. Every man but that one, who was my girl's father; and the women would cook us things and stand round and hum."

"This is much too pretty," Min said. "You're lying."

"I said it was a dream."

"— That you said was true."

"True the way dreams are, good stories that could happen."

Min waited. "My dreams have been literally true for thirty-nine years."

"I was coming to the true part next."

"That you were healed? That's never been the truth."

"— That I thought I was, felt truly that I was. Hell, I *was* then and there. The sight of that one girl had made me feel it, her voice saying 'Don't give except for return' — Hell, sight and sound, just plain human words, have cured old lepers and lighted the blind. Who was I to fail? I was just weak-chested."

"In the dream," Min said. "Weak-chested in the dream. What would that be in life?"

Rob said, "I thought you were volunteering help. I can find mean bitches in any bus station."

She touched him, her left hand firmly on his belly.

He took it and moved it to her own side gently. "That's another thing available at every streetlight."

"Mine was free," Min said. She smiled toward his turned face.

He answered it fully as if smiles were as easy in his life as they'd been in the years she first knew him. "Nothing's free," he said, "like the young lady said."

"What else did she say?"

"She didn't speak again through all that digging. Not to me anyhow. I'd see her at a distance tell her father to smile; it was him we were saving more than me. I could read it on her lips. But all she'd do to me was grin and feed me and listen to my chest when we'd quit at night. I'd ask her 'What do you hear?' — meaning *death?* or *what?* (I could still hear the war every day or so, no nearer but there) — and she wouldn't say so much as 'Hush' but just smile. I knew she was right, though I'd never told her I was sound as a dollar from the hour I met her — *because* I'd met her — and that all my digging in mud for a spring was just work for her, to earn my gift. She wouldn't have known a lung from a kidney anyhow; she was real in the dream, no magic girl. Real and waiting. So was I."

"For what?" Min said.

"Ma'm?"

"Waiting for what?"

"I told you once; this is nothing but a dream. Don't press it so hard. Just a story I made to pass one night."

Min waited. "But you know what you wanted from her."

"I do," Rob said, "— to love her, the girl."

"— For her to love *you*."

"I might have hoped for that in time; but no, the way I said it — I wanted her to stand there and bear my love."

"To sleep inside her?"

He thought it out as slowly as if it still mattered (it was still dark enough to take the question gravely). "I don't think I knew people entered each other or wanted to, even."

"Didn't know in the dream or in actual life?"

"They're the same, I told you. I was fourteen, fifteen; I lived in the country surrounded by animals. I still didn't know human beings needed that — to rub little tits of themselves on each other. But I knew there was something called love in the world. Most children do; it is God's main gift, once he's given blood and breath. It may be his last if you don't take and work it. I *knew* as I say not from hearing folks praise it or do it in my sight but from parts of my heart that had always been with me. A loving heart."

Min had waited for that; but she didn't try to touch him again, didn't smile.

Rob smiled and looked toward her quickly, then back.

"So you loved her," she said.

"Not yet, not at once. I'd made a deal. Her father stood there to keep me to it if I'd wanted to quit. So days, weeks later I found the first spring, a little ring round it of white flint rock. Everybody clapped but her father, and then we stood quiet till the water ran clean. I offered it to him, the first pure drink; and he came forward to me still frowning and said 'It's yours' so I drank. He said 'It's all yours' and showed with his hand the whole place — the people, the spring, the girl. It was his to give. I said 'Yes' and stopped."

"Stopped the dream?" Min said.

"Yes."

"You could stop it that easy?"

"By waking up, yes. I was happy enough."

Min said, "Mine lasted. Mine went on from there."

"I knew it would." Rob lay on silent through the pass of the fan, then silent in its absence.

"Ask me how," she said. "Ask me what I dreamt."

He said "All right."

"— That I was the one smiling girl — and you killed me."

He turned to her slowly, to within four inches of her breathing face; then rose to his elbow, then to his knees, straddled her flanks, studied her face still dim and vague, then struck her in the mouth.

She gave no sound, never flinched or turned, never broke her own stare at his dim face above her.

He rode on another minute, bearing her look; then dismantled himself and lay down again, flat on his back.

No sound from Min. No move of response once her face had settled.

They both lay prostrate, staring up through the minutes till dawn — summer dawn, early. Then when daylight had clearly begun to replace the lamp outside and the dead-heavy weight of heat above them gave the first signs of new life, active pressure, Min turned to her side and faced Rob again. After half a minute, he accepted the gaze; and she said very quietly, "Listen to this. Please listen to this. I haven't ever dreamt it; but it's all I know, a story that could not only happen but did. I have used you in every way I could, every way you'd let me since I got old enough to have needs other than food and a roof and a few kind words. I have always known it was second-best — God, *fourteenth*-best. I've stood, don't forget, and watched you sucking on the ones you needed; that fed your craving. I could have turned and left. Well, no I *couldn't;* maybe even shouldn't — where would we be, either one, right now if I'd kept my pride?" She paused, not specifically waiting for an answer.

But Rob said, "Dead. I at least would be dead. You'd be far better off — a real home, some rest."

"I might be," she said. Then helpless she smiled —"I also might be Eleanor Roosevelt and saving the world. I might be a high-yellow girl in heels at a Saturday dance in some shaky hall with my bosoms on fire and my razor fresh-honed —"

"You might have been some people's decent wife and mother."

"— Not a whore pushing forty with a poor drunk friend, school-teaching by day?" She had not intended to strike so soon or with so blunt a sledge. She hadn't intended to strike at all but to state the true past and plead one last time to have a true future, honest lives.

"*You* said that," he said. "But if that's what you think, if that's all it's been, I would still say thank you."

There was more to the story she'd meant to tell — the demand she had meant to make at the end: that at last Rob take her or leave her completely — but now he had stopped her with guileless thanks. She knew or had always chosen to believe that what she had loved and served in him through years of disorder, refusal, and shame was that one piece of the heart of the world — the precious meaning of life and pain, both cause and reward — which had been held toward her very early in her life (a small quiet life), the one chance for service and meaning and use which life had extended her. She half-rose now on her right elbow and looked all down him. Softened as he was, encased in his years, even a little rank from the heat, it was still buried in him — a perfect core which she'd once seen clearly in both their youths and reachable now in one last try. She knew of no other way to reach it but this — she silently climbed to the posture he'd taken: straddled him, kneeling but lower down, her knees at his calves. She rose there above him a long silent moment, her own surrenders to wear and gravity honestly shown; then her face sank toward him, and she brushed back her short hair with both hands carefully as if it were long and would hinder them.

He didn't touch her but he said "Please don't."

She shook her head No and loosened a forelock that hid her eyes. Then she used him as if he were nourishment; as if feeding on him would not exhaust any store he possessed but would honor, replenish.

So he didn't withhold but when she had roused him (his body which had never been all of him), he set both hands on the crown of her head and let them ride out her long careful act (too tired to ask was she giving or taking, healing or harming) till he'd given himself — again not all but a little hot clot that cut its way out more like death than pleasure.

Her face still hid, Min said her own thanks and rolled — never rising to his face — and slowly lay beside him, asking nothing more.

Rob waited to be sure, even offered her his own large hand to use any way she needed.

But she only pressed his fingers once more in thanks, then half-turned away and shut her eyes calmly as if headed for sleep.

Rob knew they mustn't rest; light was well underway. In another half hour he would hear his landlady cough herself out of bed, and then he and Min would be trapped here till eight when she might take her old scottie out for his walk. He must get Min out now and back to her place, get himself finally on the road he had planned and dreaded all spring.

He sat up quietly and propped himself to look round and let the room reel him up the last few fathoms into day and duty — a good-sized room, fifteen by twenty; all he had here at least, twelve dollars a month from a widow so lonely she made him feel lucky. But the room was still hers despite his long presence, going on nine years. One deep breath proved her ownership. It was drowned in the smell of her life not his, not to mention poor Min's — the dense dry smell of her dead kin, vanished children, as if in his absence at school or at meals she'd slip in to clean and, helpless, would grease every inch of floor and wall with glandular musk from the depths of her body. Even his clothes — two suits in a wardrobe, four shirts in a drawer — his worn hairbrushes, his pocketknife, gold watch, each day's small change: all conquered by her, it seemed to him now. Maybe even the pictures, unframed and curling by the dresser mirror. He stood and went to them and bent to see.

A girl fifteen, not smiling, long curls, staring fearless at the camera as if it might save her. A boy not twelve yet, still safe in childhood, brown-haired, smiling freely out from ample stores, the eyes a little crouched. The one of the boy was newer by years, raw and glossy, a school picture — Hutch his one child. The girl's was precious, though bare and unprotected — his picture of Rachel, the only one she'd ever given him, the only one he knew. Rob reached for them both; put them face to face and held them at his side, not studying them. They were still his at least. He looked to the bed.

Min lay jackknifed on her side; but her hair was well back, and half her face showed. The eyes were still shut; and the good full line of her leg, hip, side was pulled overhill by her calm loose belly —"the abandoned melon," Min called it when he cupped her unawares at night.

Rob smiled and thought, "At my mercy. Offered. Unprotected, ruin or take." Then he went to the wardrobe and took out an old black Gladstone bag which had been his father's. He carefully laid the two pictures in the bottom; then covered them with two suits of underwear, black socks, two shirts. Then he dressed himself in his summer suit and shoes, tied his tie, combed his hair, drank a glass of stale water from the china pitcher. Then he went to his side of the bed and stood, trusting the force of his wait to wake her. In a minute it hadn't — out the open window a cardinal burst on its bossy song. Rob said "Time's up" pleasantly.

She turned at once; she had not been asleep but waiting for this.

When she saw him all dressed, shielded against her, she knew she could say it after twenty-three years. She covered her breasts with folded arms, raised her knees toward her waist to hide her slit, nodded slowly and said "It is. Sure is."

Rob also nodded. "Let me take you home — a working girl."

"Working woman," Min said. "Where are you going then?"

He still could smile. "To the moon, thereabouts."

"You don't understand what I just said, do you?"

"I thought I did, yes ma'm. I — "

She shook her head. "The *time* part, the part about time being up."

He didn't speak but sat, straight and neat, to listen.

"My waiting-time," she said "I cannot wait on. You have got to find out soon and let me know. In words I can hear and understand — final words, Rob, soon."

"It's a bad time," he said "Let me go see the boy; I've promised him a trip. Let me get some things settled. I plan to see the principal in Fontaine tomorrow; Mother thinks he may hire me. Let me check the old house; I doubt you could stand it."

"I'm too old," she said.

"It's dry," he said. "I could halfway heat it if it's not too ruined."

She shook her head again. "Not the house Rob," she said. "I could live in the tomb of Cheops tomorrow. I am what's too old."

"For what?" Rob said.

"For waiting on you one extra week." She reached down and hauled the crushed sheet to her chin. "If you can't tell me Yes by a week from today, don't ever speak again, not to me. I'll be gone."

"Next Monday," he said. "I may well be in Richmond or James-town even."

"They have telephones and wires. Send me one cheap wire — *Minnie Tharrington, Raleigh. I accept. Come on.* Signed *Robinson, always.*" She had counted the words on her fingers as she spoke. "Nine words," she said. "A whole word to spare. You could even say *love.*"

Rob sat still awhile. Then he said "You mean that?"

"I do. I'm sorry. I know it's a bad time for you — no job and all your scattered families — but what you haven't seen is, it's gotten bad for me. Too bad to keep bearing."

"You told me you were strong. I asked you that — remember? — when we started this at all."

"I still am," she said. "I think I still am. But I'm also older and I want to be kind to me and to you. Another round of this and we'll both be worse, much worse by the minute. All the tides are going out."

Rob nodded. "Right now. I'm bad off now." He held out his right hand halfway toward her.

Min didn't take it but watched as he intended.

It shuddered in the air with a movement as delicate, as hard to see, as a struck bell's rigor or a bird's not breathing and as hard to stop.

"Meaning what?" she said.

"Meaning *help*, I guess." He dropped it to the sheet.

She sat up, no effort to keep the sheet on her. "Rob," she said, "try to comprehend this. I am saying one thing and very little else — Min has not got any help left to give. Not in this situation. Not another day of this."

He let it all land, arrive deep in him; she meant it at least. He'd outlasted worse, he'd maybe last this, he could not think how — except for the boy. He thought of his son, who seemed a real goal. "I've got to go," he said. "Please get up now."

"You've not shaved," she said.

"You've seen beard before."

"For your trip, I mean."

He thumbed toward his landlady's room downstairs. "If we draw water now, we'll have her up, the damn dog howling. I'll take you and come back. I need to see her anyhow, explain about the rent. I need to write a letter. I'll leave by ten maybe."

Min nodded and wiped at her eyes with dry hands. Then she stood up and, not glancing once at the mirror, she quickly dressed. Then she took up her own handbag and went toward him, stopping two feet away so he could choose — precede her out the door or wish her goodbye.

Rob wished it but he said it; he could no longer touch her. "I think I'll be back. I think you can believe me. Let me just see Hutch and Mother and some others; I'll try to get us right. Believe that; believe *me*. And still try to help."

Min faced him clearly, calm in the knowledge that settled heavy on her — he must take or leave — but she lied again to save him a few days longer. "I'll try," she said. "I'll hunt for ways, no promise though to find them."

"I know that," he said. "I won't expect much. I just said it anyhow for old time's sake." He felt a smile and showed it; it spread up his throat and across his stale face like a slow show of broad firm wings from his youth, opened to morning. "I won't sink now. Men forty years old don't sink in broad day with the waters calm beneath them just because they've lost a job through a little weak whisky; just because they can't make up their mind to have a life, take the people who are present, and ignore the poor dead." The smile had survived. "They seldom sink, do they?"

"Every day," Min said. "Every day on every street." But she also smiled.

For the moment they stood there as willing mirrors, they seemed themselves again, their early selves, savable. Rob led her out quietly and safely down the stairs.

MICHAEL ROTHSCHILD

Wondermonger

(FROM ANTAEUS)

I

LONG AGO, when Sunbury Town was a particle of sugar on the rim
of black and plotless wilderness, there lived a woodsman named
Mordecai Rime who was, until his fortieth year, the most ascetic
and profligate man in the north country.

Late in the fall of every year a coldness formed inside Mordecai
Rime and before snowfall he left Sunbury Town and journeyed for
days to reach some opening in the forest where the camp and low
hovel stood, and roads were swamped from stands of pine to the
landings along riverbanks and upon the frozen lakes. There, he
bedded the winter long with fifteen or twenty woodsmen — other
choppers, swampers, barkers, the ox teamster, and a boss — and
with them, in monkish silence, ate beans, salt pork and drank the
pitch-black tea. Before each sunrise he tramped over crust to his
chance and, from December until the mud or rotten ice of March,
felled the old pines and bull saplings, with scarfs smooth as the
cheeks of women he tried not to think on before the freshet came.

Then the sun hesitated longer at the top of the sky, moist winds
blew, the river rose, and when the drive started every man knew
that death, which only now and again visited winter camp, lived on
the river. Crushed while breaking a landing or jam, drowned, dead
men were wrapped in bark and buried without fanfare. While
water mounted no drive could hold back, so there was little time for
the soul which, according to the oldest loggers, hastily trans-
migrated into meat-birds, gray jays, moose-birds, or whatever else
the brash thieves chanced to be called. Besides, as Mordecai Rime

once remarked carving a late friend's initials in a tree below the man's hanging calked boots, the toes slit so rainwater could drain out, "Death don't have much character."

And after a winter's work in grimmest seclusion no amount of fatigue or fear was enough to sweat out a winter's accumulation of lust. The spring of his fortieth year, when the meltwater rose high and the rollways were broken at last, Mordecai Rime felt as blister-hot as his red flannel shirt. Steel-calked boots on his feet, cant-dog in his fists, a whopping desire and a bit of money in his poke, he was riding the thaw on the big logs to the brothels of Sunbury Town.

All the people of Sunbury Town gathered at the riverfront when they heard the distant grind and grumble of log upon log chafing downriver to the mills of the town; for the townspeople, too, had endured a dull, cold time of winter. And so they gathered: merchants with raucous racks of suits, jewellers, barbers with scented fingers, smiling saloonkeepers and ministers, widows, farmers, husbands closeby their curious wives, whores and especially school-children were all variously eager to rejoice in the brawling prodigality, the tales of death and skill and love; in sum, to warm themselves by the hot squander about to burst upon Sunbury Town. And more than any other name, the name Rime was in the minds of wives standing on their toes and shading their eyes to see over the calliope of crowded heads. The bright lips of whores whispered and laughed, "Rime," and "Mordecai Rime" squealed from the shining tongues of children as they surged along the riverbank to catch sight of him first.

"Once I seen'm jig on a log."

"I saw Rime break a jam by himself."

"Liar!"

"So didn't I."

"I heard'm sing."

"Rime! Look out there! Rime! I see'm!"

"Which one?"

"I see'm to. Look!"

And indeed, there in the middle of the heaving corduroy river, a red-shirted, red-sashed man was prancing as if those careening froth-beating logs were flat and steady as a stage. Short of body, thick of neck, skin waffled by calk-booted foes, teeth of a size and number that only his own outsized mouth could hold, and eyes

small and bright as a bird's, Mordecai Rime was in no wise a handsome man. Taken one piece at a time, there was not a lovely piece
to be found in all of him; and yet, whatever held those pieces
together was of a stuff so grand and innocent and rare that the
children who beheld his capers atop the death he seemed to ignore
were astonished to silence, and Rime, on spotting those bands of
children, waved his cant-dog, jabbed it into the log he was riding,
and of all things, walked the length of that slick, battered log on his
hands.

Some children covered their eyes and dared peek only through
fingerchinks, some started to bawl or howled with terror and won-
derment, but every cheering one of them scurried back toward
Sunbury Town to keep pace with that fantastical man on the water.

Hopping here and hopping there, a dozen bright figures were
sighted far upriver, small as blood-filled fleas. A united whoop
roared from the gathered townspeople. And above the groans of
the clotted river the faint, answering whoop of a lone throat was
heard; and each passing moment it grew louder and wilder, until
the blue-faced whooper himself hurdled from a log, dug his spikes
into the muddy bank and bellowed for all that merry but speechless
assembly: "Pickin' time's come sure as I'm Mordecai Rime an' a
man, the fruit's red, ripe an' near rotten. So let's get an' pick 'til it's
gotten!"

No sooner had the Mayor of Sunbury Town, in official greeting,
tipped his beaver-felt top hat to the riverman than the hat was gone
and like a king and fool in one, Mordecai Rime marched up the
bank amidst a festive court of children, a painted queen on each
arm and a glorious new top hat cocked upon his head.

The whole red-shirted brigade of bachelors followed suit, and
before long, other crews landed, each with its distinctive brand in
the scarf of its logs. Wooden sidewalks were quickly pocked by all
their boots, black with tobacco spit and wet with rum. The dizzy
screech of fiddling and jubilation commenced; mothers hunted for
their children; hustlers' their marks; husbands' their wives; and but
one thing was certain — Sunbury Town was topsy-turvy.

By nightfall, however, a different note, less playful and charming than before, intruded upon the screeking logs and the strains
of merrymaking. Most townspeople understood at once, disappeared from the streets and in their places, bolted themselves in.
"Put the boots to 'im," a man yelled past midnight. The sharp,

frantic note of hunger and energy was unmistakable now, and all over town open-eyed husbands lay beside their wives in the dark and, not without pleasure, listened to the carnival break into menace.

The fierce night wore on, the revels wore down, and at dawn they ceased, as though first daylight had chased the wood demons back to the wilderness and restored a gloss of sweetness to Sunbury Town. Everyone knew this lull of early morning was a respite, that the satyr was catching his wind and so long as money held out, misrule was in town to stay. And so while broken glass was swept up, windows were replaced and blood and urine were mopped off the sidewalks below the snoring brothels where men and their ladies mended and charged themselves for the coming night, Sunbury Town readied for business proper.

Now, among those up and about at this hour was the young schoolmistress, Lucille Triller, and it was evident that neither her high-necked shoe-shining dun dress nor the hard bun she had rolled at the back of her neck could conceal the juice and bloom of her face. At the edge of the schoolyard Miss Triller spied a ring of excited children and drawing nearer to them she paused a pause which, however ordinary it may then have seemed, led to the transformation — if not the transmigration — of Mordecai Rime's soul.

She had hesitated because in ring-center one of her pupils had struck a heroic posture. A wooden staff held high in his tiny fist, he erupted all in one high-pitched, hurried exhalation, "Show me a hole'n I'll fill't, hole ain't there'n I'll drill't." As when the hawk bolts upon the chicken-yard and in dust and din hooks a self-concentrating bantam, so Lucille Triller broke that ring of children, got hold of one scalding ear and in a trice twisted a bawling apology from the youngster, and the name "Rime."

That restless morning — counting the desks of truants, confiscating lewd doodles, ever demanding attention — the schoolmistress discovered that the disorder which visited Sunbury Town had, in particular, subverted its children. And once school was out she marched toward the river district, resolved, in behalf of her pupils, to search out and upbraid this Rime, the sound of whose name alone incited children to deplorable antics, and herself to such ferocious ill will.

"Where might I locate Rime, Sir?" she inquired of a grandfatherly man pipe-smoking on a stoop. He shook his head, fondly puckered his eyes and lips to say, "Git'n line, Honey, he's the king log," and spat by his boot.

A smile so vulgar and presumptive answered each query that she began to fancy an image of Rime, Lord of Boors, and stalked it with such intensity that the old woman who finally directed her to an establishment known as "Pink Chimney" thought certain she had been wronged by her man and was about to get even.

When the schoolmistress stood beneath Pink Chimney itself, and gazing upwards, saw that the mortar between the pink-painted brick of its prodigious stack had been painted vein-blue, she lost hold, and shuddering, tripped inside. Her eyes smarted from the gray and yellow bands of smoke. She inhaled the exhaust of to-bacco-sweat-rum-perfume, choked, and as if blinded in a house afire, reeled in panic while the floor bounced to the jagged fiddle and the rowdy, rhythmic clap of hands and stomp of feet. Bit by bit, colored shapes revealed themselves through the hot murk of the barroom; but though her eyes cleared, her muddle worsened. She knew it was daytime in the civilized town of Sunbury where she lived and taught school, and yet here was neither day nor civiliza-tion, but the sort of woolly land she had toured only when, unable to sleep, she read her Shakespeare and was afterwards tossed in wicked dreams of cannibals and the Anthropophagi.

Tree-necked men and bare-backed women thronged to view one stocky man atop a table. In wads of smoke, this man's head was thrown back, motionless and soaking. His enormous mouth was locked in such an immense smile and his teeth were so big, he looked ready to bite a chunk from the hewn beam high above him. Both his arms were crooked rigid at his chest. Indeed, for half an hour not a muscle moved above his red-sashed waist. But no one was looking there. Every admiring eye watched his legs and feet going like crazy, on and on in time to the hoarse wail of a fiddle.

He leaped off that tiny stage and crossed his legs in the air; he twirled; he pigeon-winged and whirled; he pawed heel and toe; the fiddling speeded fast, and faster, and at its peak the fiddler's bow blurred, the Jigger jumped up, twice crossed his legs before land-ing and then, to each sharp, separate squeal of the finale he stamped, hopped, stamped again, and his feet came to rest as the fiddle, which seemed to make the feet move, fell silent.

In the stillness a bare braceleted arm lifted up a ladle, the pant-ing Jigger kissed the arm, drank down the rum, grinned, took in a deep breath and roared, "By the chimin' blue balls o' Jesus an' sure as my muscle be long, hard, an' not so straight as a steeple, I can jump higher — squat lower — hump longer — jig better — bite harder — drink deeper — piss further — sing sweeter — fart louder — an' talk quicker'n any man made in the slipp'ry knot o' love tied 'tween a woman an' the creature she's found fit to tie with — whether she trapped it in woods or pulled it from sky or grow'd it in 'er garden — an' if a body doubts me I'll swear to it by the sweetest blue milk I ever sucked from the flowin' teats o'my good mother to start growin' into who stands before you now, Mordecai Rime, an' a man." And with that he spread a large scarlet handkerchief over his head and jumped with three heel snaps to the floor of Pink Chimney, rocking in cheer and cockalarity.

Drenched from his jig, Rime was on his way to cool himself out of doors when his eyes snagged upon the single partridge in that roomful of brash-colored parrots. Beside the entrance, her bun unrolled and dangling over her hands, the school mistress stood. Without a noise but with the entire confused might of her body, she was weeping.

Mordecai Rime stopped dead. He pulled the wet handkerchief off his stiff hair, wrung his sweat onto the sawdusted floor, and gently commenced to sponge her scarlet forehead. She opened her eyes to his great-toothed smile, started, let out a faint, surprised sound, went slack, and was waltzed into the fresh air and down to the riverbank by the partner of her choice.

"Where d'you hurt, Ma'am?" Rime soberly asked, and paused, and continued, "Ma'am, suff'rin' aches an' pains, are you?" adding nervously, "Now y'ain't dyin' now, are you?" to which she managed after a time to say, "I am the schoolmistress Lucille Triller, and I am lost," an answer that frightened Mordecai Rime into trying to cajole her to a sensible calm, and so he said, "Up in the woods we call twin-boled trees, those crotched ones with their legs stuck fast, well, Lucy, we call'm school-marms," and he made a chuckle before she made more tears, so many, in fact, they infected the good-hearted Rime who joined in with his own awful, big tears until, mysteriously, one of them laughed and, before long, there they were, sitting together in the mud of the river bank hugging, kissing, and the both of them laughing mad.

Every man and woman was hushed, huddled outside of Pink Chimney. They saw the couple pass through the thick, black

shadow of the chimney which slanted far up the road; and afterwards they waited, watching the shadow be sucked down into the
gray dirt road and be gone. All at once, jewellery jangled up the
Madam's plump wrist. "Ain't no wake," she cracked, and jostling
her way first inside, yelling "Free round!!" she ducked behind the
pine bar.

II

Along a dead, flat stretch of river in a solitary intervale far to the
northwest of Sunbury Town, a trapper and timber cruiser's stop-
over had lately grown into Tantrattle, a farming settlement so small
it was said that when one of its women gave child, all the rest came
to their milk. And upon a narrow rise of meadow not half a mile
downriver from Tantrattle, the rantipole logger who had always
made mock of the husbandmen's staid plight (who had branded
"farmer" any woodsman slow of foot, hand, or tongue), himself
planted pumpkins, corn, potatoes and peas on a burn, and built a
low two-room house modeled on the hovels he had wintered in
since becoming a man.

Although the husbandmen of Tantrattle were hospitable enough
whenever Mordecai Rime entered the settlement for supplies or
asked their advice on some practical matter, he returned to his
homestead sadder than he set out. There was an awful design to
the way these farmers settled one spot with one woman under one
God and from a lifelong scrutiny of soil and sky, lived guardedly
and wasted nothing. They answered Rime as if each word moved
death one day closer. The foolishness native to man had been
burned out of them through constant, necessary prudence. And so
that summer Mordecai Rime visited Tantrattle only when he had
reason. There were no diversions, and he had much to do.

From late in May when he chose the site, he lived alone except
for a black hound puppy, and labored as long as there was light to
labor by. The first time in his life he washed regularly, after dark in
the river, and for the first time, however weary he was, he could not
sleep. Half the nights he strolled through the cherry and fireweed
speckling the charred meadow with the puppy tripping alongside
him; or he sat by the river and listened to the last songbirds sing
like wet fingers on glass. He lay in the damp sedge, hour after hour
following the dark concert of sounds until it appeared that each

song was mated to another and no note was left unanswered. Above the river, love bellows of bullfrogs fanned the heavy air and from behind his half-built cabin began the incessant heave of whip-poorwills. But when the exultations of woodcocks fell breathless from the skytops, when it seemed Concord was come to earth, then miserable Mordecai Rime thought up songs about his woman in Sunbury Town, and as he made them up he sang them out loud, along with all the rest of the nightsongs, and felt better for it. . . .

> *I dreamed up a woman*
> *Skin red everywhere*
> *I kissed her heart gentle*
> *Afraid it'd tear.*
> *Go away summer*
> *Hurry up fall*
> *Sleepin' alone*
> *Ain't sleepin' a'tall,*
> *'Cause I dreamed o' that woman*
> *An' such was 'er fright*
> *When flat on my bed*
> *She turn'd frosty white*
> *But I kiss'd her womb gentle*
> *She open'd so wide*
> *We held on for dear life*
> *We took such a ride*
> *She planted my seed*
> *An' I took me a bride.*
> *So go away summer*
> *Hurry here fall*
> *Sleepin' without her*
> *Ain't sleepin' a'tall.*

If his lids closed, late night rains sometimes jarred him from half-sleep in the sedge, or he woke before dawn in a chill shroud of dew that the spidery swallows, glancing in and out of the fog on the river, appeared to have wound him in.

Relieved and busy with the start of day, Mordecai Rime toiled so for the completion of his task that no progress seemed to be made. He imagined he would never be done; he would never return to fetch her in Sunbury Town. Often he wondered if she existed at all.

The air had already turned clear and bright on the afternoon he realized in a daze how high the cob-laid chimney had grown above the bark roof. Two small windows were oil-papered, and around the farm cabin, stacks of wood bled and seasoned. Beans were busheled in the root cellar and cornsilks darkened above the weeds. With a start, Mordecai Rime stumbled into the jungle of garden to investigate the golden-orange blossoms which overnight had burst, bugle-like, along the pumpkin vines. He squatted over the first cluster he reached, bent his head, lifted one large, fuzzy blossom and intently cupped it to his nostrils.

How long a while he knelt there, Mordecai Rime never knew or, indeed, if he did kneel or hover, even, mid-air. For the hound began to yelp, a shadow fell over him and his shoulders were squeezed hard. More bear than man, he turned on his knees, clasped her skirt and bawling as a bear bawls slashing a honey-trunk apart, he tore at her skirt and there in the garden beneath the pumpkin blossoms that had powdered his nose dull orange, beneath the prancing paws and prying snout of the hound, Mordecai Rime held his wife Lucy Rime and she fast onto him.

Upon waking, he blushed as bright as the ruby burns she displayed on the insides of her thighs, and straightway shaved his cocklebur lips and chin and swore to keep them barbered ever after. Honeymoon continued the rest of August and on in festive earnest through September, October, and still it went on. Summertime, however, which had dallied like a snake upon a sun-hot rock before her arrival, now, as if started at her coming, slickered by. Mordecai Rime began to pray that the air would never cease its hum or the haze fall away. He prayed for Indian Summer without end, so he might never return to the wifeless forests of winter. He loved Lucy Rime as if each of the women he ever had held during all the spring nights in Sunbury Town had been pressed into a single, vivid body; and more than that, he loved her as he loved himself, for her belly and her breasts showed traces of his child.

They swam at dawn, harvested the days and, at twilight, washed in the cool river. Lucy wove a rug for the rough, chill floor and stitched a crazy-quilt for their bed. From the village they toted sacks of goosedown, stuffed a mattress plump, and promptly buried themselves in it. She often read aloud from books he could not fathom in a voice which nonetheless made sense of everything. Of the rapidly changing season, however, neither spoke. The earnings she had saved as a schoolmistress were nearly gone and both sickened to consider winter, separation, the birth of their child.

Lucy Rime tried and largely succeeded in keeping her terror concealed. Only once, on a picnic by a beaver pond where she went wading and afterwards tweezed a tiny leech from between her toes and scraped it off on a stone, did she suddenly begin to cry.

Mordecai Rime was a different matter. The leaves had fallen by the start of November, and with a husband's eye he gazed upon the bleached rushes, coarsened to knives along the black river. Never before when winter began to lock the ground had fears of loss and schemes to protect against that loss so locked up his mind. But this November he dwelt within a different law and smiled bitterly to see stalks lose their bend and the brittle stems let go. When pods split and emptied, he tagged a morbid dream to every seed cast on the sharpening wind. And while he sat, his wide, scaly hands cupped on his knees, he figured what was the matter with him:

> *My eyes look'd in*
> *Beneath my skin*
> *To see what I could find.*
>
> *Old Sin, new Dread*
> *Was newly wed*
> *An' kiss'd inside my mind.*

The ground crackled as Lucy advanced down the path with a quiltful of laundry. "Why so grim, Farmer Rime?" she asked, but he remained stooped in gloom, and she settled beside him.

"True, a farmer an' scar'd somethin' awful," Mordecai Rime abruptly said. "I love you so, Lucy. Why I seen five toes settin' by themselves like beans on the snow, an' I seen men froze stiff an' drownd'd, burn'd an' squash'd, but nothin' of 't scar'd me 'till now I'm shakin' like ev'ry other fart-fill'd sheep-toppin' farmer in Tantrattle. What's to happen t' you and the child, Wife? What're we t'do?"

Lucy Rime felt panic rise in her chest and she stopped it up. "I've lived alone before," she said giddily. "See here," she added, tapping her belly with a smile, "I've stored plenty of fat to live on and feed a cub besides. I'll just sleep until thaw when you come back to us." Wind lashed hair across her freckled, ruddy nose and Mordecai Rime watched her tongue flicker a glisten on her dry lips while her eyes wandered over the cold water.

"Know somethin', you're so pretty I'm pain'd and jealous." He had on a face she hadn't seen before. His mouth teetered between a smirk and a grimace of contempt, and there was a mean, dull suspicion in his eyes. "I swear it, Wife, you're pretty enough for killin'."

Afterwards, when he had set out to arrange for the services of Midwife Cawkins in Tantrattle and Lucy was scrubbing the quilt clean in the river, she remembered the strange spite which had warped his face. With difficulty she tugged the quilt onto the bank to squeeze out the frigid water. "Pretty enough for killin'," she repeated, and abstractedly scanned upriver. On the last skirt of bank before the river curled behind woodlands toward the settlement, Lucy glimpsed him standing out among the black cattails.

Mordecai Rime, meanwhile, crunched along a hardened mud path through the ice-scarred willows and poplar of the flood plain, and kept to the burnished dirt road that passed over the crib-work bridge and cleaved the village. At last a natty blue and red sparrow-hawk sighted him, drawing too near its prospect atop a maple. Rime heard its scream and followed the skating flight down the field of dun stubble, above long rows of stumps and a small graveyard. Tilting crazily before the Cawkins' farmhouse, it was gone.

Rime went striding down the bouldered field, pausing to scoop a fat yellow apple from the fresh chippings around an apple-tree butt. Perplexed, he bit into the apple and regarded the hundreds of other stumps that had recently been an orchard. The apple tasted so good he concentrated upon eating it until stopped short by a neat, marble row of head-stones. Although he had helped bury a dozen corpses in the acid mold of the wilderness floor, Mordecai Rime was a stranger to such a civilized cemetery as this, with a winter vault on its river side. A marble lamb reposed there upon a body's face, and there, the pearly index of a sculpted hand pointed straight up to the low-covered sky. Mechanically he tore off a mouthful of apple, glanced at the line of five, same-sized slabs at his feet, and unable to chew or swallow, gaped.

Vilda A.	Freedom A.	Arletta A.	Sampel A.	Letitia A.
Dau. of	Son of	Dau. of	Son of	Dau. of
Freedom and	Freedom and	Freedom and	Freedom and	Freedom and
Solemna Air	Solemna Air	Solemna Air	Solemna Air	Solemna Air
Ae. 10m. 16d.	Ae. 2yrs.	Ae. 1yr. 7d.	Ae. 9m. 23d.	Ae. 1m. 2d.
	8m. 19d.			
Our Bud	Our Bud	Our Bud	Our Bud	Our Bud
is	is	is	is	is
blooming	blooming	blooming	blooming	blooming
on high	on high	on high	on high	on high

"Must be one Christly bloom up there!"

"It is indeed," replied a creased, shawled woman.

"An' one witchery o' marriage down here, I'll wager, Ma'am," twinkled Rime, the plug of apple in his cheek.

"T'was I delivered the little ones into this world and the Reverend Cawkins, he. . . ."

"Life is hard, Sir," pronounced a sturdy sunburned farmer with an authoritative snowdrift of hair piled on his head. "Your business?"

Mordecai Rime stared into the healthy red and white face of the old man in consternation. "I'm 'bout ready to pack off for winter an' Lucy's goin' to be needin' a midwife come Feb'yary. She's my wife, see, an' she's with child."

The Midwife Cawkins pinched a fold of throat and smiled, "Why then, you must be the woodsman settling downriver?"

"Mordecai Rime, Missus."

"Keep to home," counseled the Reverend Cawkins. "Lumbering and farming don't mix. Build a stout fence about your garden and keep to home." The Reverend fell silent when he noticed the woodsman's eyes drift to a stop alongside the meeting house where the apple orchard was stacked horizontal, and barrels of ash caught rainwater to leach their lye.

"Fine tastin' apples," Rime remarked, beginning to chew again. "What ailed your trees?"

"No price for cider," the Midwife said, and her husband added, "Serves the enemy. If there be a way to serve, Man will find it. Do you pray, Rime?"

"Only that you an' your missus don't lay hold o' my wife an' child," he answered, and with a low bow to them, started up the rise. He hurdled every apple-butt along his way, skipping queerly up the knoll toward the bare maple, never once looking behind.

Later on that cold, still evening Lucy Rime was darning one of his wool mittens when a terrible thought visited Mordecai Rime, and he let it stay and nursed it while the fire played on her hair and buffed her brow orange. Before long the thought had lodged inside him as a certainty, and he winced at her as if he had freed something fierce that someday would kill him. "How many before, Wife?"

"Many?" She asked drowsily.

"Men. Other men. Before me."

"There are *real* things to worry us. Don't be a fool."

"Real things? Fool?" Rime grinned ear to ear. "Cause you're so friggin' book'd up you look down your lyin' snout at me."

"What is it, say," she begged, setting the mitten in her lap. There were no more words, however, and Lucy Rime was awakened in the night by a dream she was to dream and wake from on many another night of the coming winter. She called and called for Mordecai to come help her, but the windows were shuttered and the door was bolted against the snow-carving wind. She screamed for his help, she screamed for help, but she was alone, she knew, and this night she clasped Mordecai Rime's throat and soaked him with her sweat. Throttled from sleep, his daytime malice forgotten, he pressed his mouth into her scalding hair and hummed tunes, rocking her jumping eyelids together to the rhythmic groans of the quilt stiffening on the line outside their door.

The last cricket straggled in from shocks of weed to get warm, an ice-skin thickened at the river's edge and as green lights unlashed and lashed the night sky, frost sank deeper in. First snow soon crusted the weeds, ice and metal-hard sod and then, their final night passed by. He looked her hard in the face and before he turned said only, "You'd best be true, Lucy Rime, or you'll make a meat-bird o' me."

She watched him enter the tangle of cherry, birch and poplar on a once-burned hillside northeast of Tantrattle, and she waited there while the snow slowly blurred, dimpled and effaced his nearest boot track.

Mordecai Rime drove himself dumb for three days, through damp tracts of cedar where little snow gathered and half-frozen earth puckered around boulders, across boglands of spruce and naked tamarack, pushing for an exhaustion so great he might sleep some of the nights.

The fourth morning he was buffeted over the frozen surface of a long, thin lake. He recognized it from a decade before when he had lumbered its margin and seen the shafts of many thousands of pines crowded upon its ice to be girdled in a boom. Several old pines, those with hollow heart, had been left to topple of themselves; yet here and there, rising high above a glittering desolation of decaying slash, they remained, and more massive in their isolation than he had remembered them.

He paced the flat stretch of lake hour after hour, and before twilight climbed the steep, slick eastern shore and camped without sleep in the ruins of the hovel where he had lived that earlier winter.

Not two days from his destination, at dawn, he tunneled into the constant half-night of a spruce and fir wilderness and walked the frozen pathway of the Quick River. Small as a mite that burrows under the shag of some huge beast and works its methodical way down to the beast's tail, Mordecai Rime picked along the barren floor where he had lived to make himself Mordecai Rime and a man, and he sensed his death might be hidden behind any black needle of the trees above him, and he feared he was a woodsman no longer.

III

Amidst scattered hardwoods, hemlock, fir and spruce, the lumber camp and hovel had been built at the foot of a ridge where old white pines clustered around the expanse of Lower, or Little Mooselip Lake whose outlet, the Quick River, flowed beneath the softwood wilds and fed the Sunbury River sixty miles northwest of Sunbury Town. It was here before each December dawn that Mordecai Rime and the chopping crews meandered down blue crystal corridors of snow on the packed branch roads. Sled runners smoked and squealed beneath mammoth pine boles and Clarence Smiles cursed his three yoke of oxen to and from the landing until not enough day was left to see those hazards that might be seen. The crew straggled to the warm camp, ate, and under a communal spread of cotton batting, slept in a row on hemlock boughs.

Every man on that operation had heard the large tales and claims made for and by Mordecai Rime. Those who had worked other winters or blown into Sunbury Town with him were now particularly baffled to find such a man resigned, separate, stingy with melancholy. Rime's chopper and barker, old John Gorges, privately ascribed the transformation to some bodily disease like hollow heart, at work inside of Rime; one swamper speculated that he had burned himself out and suffered horrors from the fierce way his first forty years on earth had been lived; and asquat on the frozen manure of the hovel floor to rub bean grease on his oxen's puffed legs, Clarence Smiles confided to his beast that, "On'y a woman could'a broke a back hard as Rime's."

Theories abounded, but no one asked Rime for reasons. Many avoided his murky black eyes, others swapped pitying or ironic glances. Nevertheless, the crew stayed respectfully aloof and tried to pretend he was still the same man; all, that is, but one young newcomer, a vain, well-muscled chopper by the name of Rudolph Sarsen.

From the very night Rime arrived and tucked himself in his own crazy-quilt apart from the crew, Sarsen let it be known that he slaved for more than a winter's wage. "Seems our lice's too ugly for the gent," he announced while he sat on the deacon seat and brushed out his orange, shoulder-length hair. Rime offered no rejoinder; and cheated, Sarsen was put in a sullen rage. Presently, as became his custom each night, Sarsen heated a bucket, stripped down before the flabbergasted crew, and whistling a melody, poured the steaming water down his huge orange-haired body.

"Ain't no human bean," Mordecai Rime said sleepily. "Holy Jesus, I seen one o'them things in a picture book. 'Xact same size an' same red hair all over. I do believe we're hovel'd with a Rang-tang."

"Get outta your friggin' quilt, Rime, an' I'll kick your ass-hole so hard your eyes'll bleed," screamed naked Sarsen, but the jeers and laughter drowned out his threat, and Rime rolled over.

From then on, Sarsen was known in camp as "Rang-tang" Sarsen; and from then on the camp understood that his business was not so much to fell pine as to contest, win, and absorb the skill and the courage and the energy accorded everywhere to the name Mordecai Rime so that he, Rudolph Sarsen, might ride the swollen spring rivers and reach Sunbury Town, resplendent in Rime's place.

Boss Urban Burlock made certain that Sarsen and Rime worked chances that were far apart. He had seen the preservative framework of game and insult come apart, and the sole prevention he knew was work. The second week in January a cold snap hit, stayed on a week, another, and Burlock refused to let up. Warm breath turned beards bone-white and the laboring oxen drooled icicles. Men complained of how their brittle axe-heads broke or bounced queerly off icy trunks, and frequently pine fell with unpredictable jumps and twists. Numb fingertips started to crack open the second week of prolonged cold, and they were sewed up like socks. Already, the pine closest to shore had been twitched onto the ice, and each day the crews ranged farther, to skin the exposed clumps of pine rolling and crackling higher up the ridge.

Early on the severest morning of the cold snap Mordecai Rime was circling an ancient ivory shaft of pine halfway up the ridge when there appeared a throng of gray jays, diving and squawking around Rime's toque and mackinaw. Instead of notching the pine, he clamped his axe under his arm, made fists inside his mittens and settled on a nearby butt. "Them meat-birds's tellin' us t'ain't safe," he told his chopping-mate Gorges.

"A bitch," John Gorges mumbled and tamping his pipe, huddled beside Rime on the wide stump. Neither of them turned towards the scrape-scrape of snowshoes side-stepping down the ridge behind them until Boss Burlock asked, "What's holdin' up, Rime?"

"Too mean a mornin' to cut I should say, Urban."

"That so?" shrugged the Boss, "Is't really so?" He glanced at his stiff bindings and briefly searched Rime's face which squinted after the sooty jays, hollering away in the dead, indigo air. "Never know'd a freeze an'a coupla birds to spook Mordecai Rime," whispered Burlock, hesitating to let the ring of axes working elsewhere speak for him. "Do what you see fit," he said, and shuffled off to traverse the ridge and reach the next chance.

Rather than hazard a word, John Gorges sneaked a sideways look and decided, from Rime's passive attitude, to light his pipe when up Rime bolted, hastily paced a line parallel the skidroad and shouted, "Bed 'er here."

Gorges nodded and began to cut young spruce and fir along the designated pathway. Of the many axemen Gorges had observed, he considered Rime best and smartest. He had seen a thousand pines felled by the careful, redundant ease of Rime's musical stroke. No shock drove up Rime's arms and neck when his blade half-vanished into a tree and magically sprang back with a flat orange chip the size of a head. Long ago, mystified Gorges had asked Rime how he managed to throw his axe at the wood with no effort and yet such devastating results. "T'ain't me," Rime had claimed, "I but squeeze the helve. 'Tis the thinkin' head o' my axe does the job."

But now, all the while he spread evergreen saplings to cushion the falling pine, Gorges fixed a disturbed eye upon Mordecai Rime and shuddered in his chest. In the clearing the monster pine grew seventy straight feet before a first horizontal limb stretched out beneath another shelf of limb, itself overhung by a higher tier, and still another that lidded the surrounding birch and spruce forest. Tapering upward, the pine tree rose to a single, fluent lead shoot one hundred and fifty feet above the spot where Mordecai Rime had got his footing and slashed his poleaxe into the gray-plated trunk as though he meant less to fell that tree than murder it.

"Quit't now, hey Rime, quit," yelled John Gorges once the sparking bit glanced off a frozen fiber and Rime skidded to one knee. But Rime would not stop. He grunted onto his feet and with blue vapor rolling over his pinched white lips, with fingers bleeding from his barked knuckles, hacked at the tree and could stop for nothing.

Near to an hour passed, marked by an incessant thump of cleaver on bone, the hard, dull, uneven, urgent pound of Rime's axe as it opened a cleft and drove home to the heart of the pine. Gorges was first to sight a tremor in the pine-top. He shouted warning and scrambled up a rise, out of reach, and looked on.

Rime pushed his pole against the truck and heaved; from the top-most shaft a spasm reverberated, down to the spur roots; the ponderous bole nodded slightly as if to fall, then, despite its all but severed base, remained suspended perfectly erect and motionless.

Rime contemptuously hurled aside the pole and shouldered the trunk. "Clear out!" Gorges screamed in alarm. Rime half-circled the yawning girth and leveled a mad flurry of axe-blows into the back-cut. Nothing remained now to keep the pine upright, but there it stood and did not budge.

Twice, Rime butted the tree. His boots kicked and fists smashed and tore on the bark. Smoldering from sweat and cold, he staggered backwards, stretched out on the snowcrust, and John Gorges heard but could not believe a human throat able to make the laugh Mordecai Rime laughed then.

Gorges maintained afterwards it was the laughter itself which gave the final prod — for no sooner had it commenced than slowly, the pine leaned and, clawing and wrenching loose everything within reach, tumbled with a horrendous crackling and with a quake and hollow boom, bounced as Rime had indicated it would, atop the evergreen bedding.

Black twigs, chafings and ice rained down in the wake of the pine and Gorges lost sight of Rime until the destruction in the air settled. Then, there he was, still flat on his back beneath a skim of debris.

Inspecting the hole ripped in the forest roof, Gorges rushed fast as he could down to Rime and reached out his hand. Rime pulled himself up, chattered the same ugly, braying laugh as before, and as suddenly stopped and gave a hearty slap on the back of Gorges' mackinaw.

"Limb that stubbo'n mother," Rime said, "Skin 'er extra sung." He set his jaw hard but his black pupils were so dilated and glossy that Gorges felt ashamed staring into them. "Meat-birds wanted to carry me off with'm somethin' wicked," Rime said quietly.

He fetched his poleaxe and returned, chuckling. "Didn't. Miss'd. Miss'd me." And with that he dragged himself through the marsh grass and manure strewn over the glassy skidboard to brake the ox-sled, and staggered towards the lumber camp.

"Man's goddam good an' lucky," scowled John Gorges. He fidgeted for his cold-stemmed pipe and crouched beside the toppled pine to use it for windbreak. "Haywire," he said. "Haywire as hell."

IV

On the day her husband departed for camp above Little Mooselip Lake, Lucy Rime had returned home in a warm fall of thick, gentle-dropping snow, despising the flakes which alighted on her cape as though curses fell from the sky. Wind now and again rattled canes and seeds in the hollowed pods that poked above snow level beside her path. She wrapped the cape snugly about her and watched the footprintless trail, not lifting her head before she heard the hound yelp. Tethered beside the threshold of her cabin, he was half-strangled in his eagerness to greet her, be fed, and stretch before the fire.

The milky afternoon air darkened and further dimmed the two rooms where she banked the fire, bolted shut the door, gazed at the musket, the hooded hemlock cradle, and knelt to stroke the hound's winter fur and quiet the scrabble of his dream. Mice chirping, the hiss and collapse of logs and the snap of walls contracting in the colder evening air: house-sounds, like spruce at the rim of a vacant snowfield, struck her now with remarkable and unpleasant sharpness. But the keenest and the strangest of the sounds she heard was the noise of herself, movements in an empty house, her terrible intimacy with the fetus burrowing, relentlessly scooping its way out of her.

Through a chink in the wall some snowflakes seeped and sifted over Lucy Rime crouched by the hearthstone, her eyes pinched and dry. Back and forth she rocked with one palm upon her flat breastbone. Her chest seemed ready to burst from the tread of tiny feet on her heart. Slowly, as if to rock away the anguish, she swayed before the fire and her mind journeyed back to the genial bustle of Sunbury Town, her schoolhouse, the uncanny ease with which her reasonable life had come unravelled that spring twilight on the bank of the Sunbury River. She remembered the strange, beguiling tales he told her of sullen and holy Indians, and a crew snow-cribbed in a burning hovel; of handling a bateau over treacherous falls, fingers clutching a log in a black eddy, a human skull on a gravel bar; the many dozens of cleat marks in his chest and belly and finally, the bashful revelation of the entire coded map of his skin which they deciphered, greedily hunting like children after a treasure they discovered anew each night.

Fire-red with sweat, Lucy Rime spied the hemlock cradle from the corner of her eye and a shrill desire seized her to cast it upon the fire and see it burn. Her head shook from side to side. She began to cry. For a long time she wailed out hatred for her husband and for his child who fed upon the marrow of her bones. Weariness at last dulled her heart and silenced her mind, and her first night alone in their cabin she slept beside the querulous hound who now and again rolled his tongue along her thin wrist.

Miserable, and bewildered to find herself at the edge of the hearthstone, she awakened, breathing gray vapor into the dark chill of the room. At once she scraped aside the ashes, blew and blew on the dull embers until the kindling ignited, and considering the prospect of a winterlong marriage to this fire, she crossed the gloomy cabin and let out the whimpering hound.

The flash of yellow sky and blue snow made her recoil. While the hound pecked mouthfuls of fresh flakes and like a needle threaded in and out of the soft drifts, Lucy Rime gradually adjusted to the abstract brilliance which left so little for the eye to grapple with and insinuated its glare upon the mind.

Winter fostered neighborliness among the denned-up settlers of Tantrattle. Just as deer, to survive the depth of snow and boreal winds, yard beneath a sheltering stand of cedar and paw after browse within the steep-walled confines of their maze, so the scattered families tunneled out from storm upon December storm to call upon friends or, with new fervor and frequency, congregated, Sunday morning and Wednesday evenings, at the Reverend Cawkins' meeting house.

And so it was that before December, the eighth month of her pregnancy had gone by, Lucy Rime, despite her increasing fatigue, began to give weekday morning lessons to a small group of children, receiving in return a loaf of bread, pale green candles, half a jug of milk, and the grace of occupied morning hours. As the shrinking days deepened isolation and sharpened need, she was particularly grateful to hear the shrieks of children when they leapt from a sledge and skittered atop the snow to her door, to hear their laughter whenever the same crust caved beneath a parent's weight.

Once the children had gone, however, her mind would be filled with morbid confusion about the childbirth she knew so little about and which the several farmwives who did pay visits spoke of as they might of damnation, Indians and woodsmen, in whispers. Then one afternoon she heard sled bells and opened her door to see a shaggy horse in traces, and to be greeted by the Reverend Cawkins himself. Behind him stood Midwife Cawkins, a basket filled with eggs and a bar of soap crooked on her arm.

During this brief interview the Reverend Cawkins stood by the inglenook and kept his austere gaze directly upon Lucy while the midwife asked how the children got on with their schooling and proceeded to ramble on about old Culverwell's death, and the storage of his coffin in their winter vault. Ice had to be broken up in the christening bowl and the Rabbow infant never once complained. As soon as the Reverend walked to the door the midwife fell silent, patted the back of Lucy's hand saying "In due time," and they took their leave.

Left alone, Lucy Rime grew irked and puzzled at why, when she suffered grotesque fancies of childbirth, she had never interrupted the midwife's gossip with questions and proposals. Something in the reserve of the Reverend Cawkins had unnerved her. Even now his mute condescension lingered and disquieted her mind. She dismissed him as the darkness settled in, but however much she worked to beat down her thoughts, they disobeyed.

A confirmation of her disquietude arrived later that evening when there was a soft knock on her bolted door. She opened it and drew back, frightened to see the Reverend Cawkins planted at her threshold like a monstrous snowman. That stern, censorious Reverend who had visited earlier bore scant resemblance to this simpering gentleman who hesitantly presented her with a sack of precious salt, tottered between cavernous drifts and faded behind the scrim of continuous snowfall.

And two nights later, carrying a small block of butter, appeared the Reverend Cawkins. This time, a large red fist poised upon each knee, he remained long enough to speak of how winter seclusion compounded the dreadful loneliness brought on by the winter of a man's life. Indignant at his sad duplicity and humiliated by her acceptance of his offerings, Lucy Rime could not touch the butter.

The second week of January, on the eve of the cold snap, the Reverend Cawkins paid his final, and for Lucy Rime, most destructive visit. Standing, he spoke of his prospering estate: the grist- and sawmills he planned to build; tanning, potash, the land already purchased. He set an earthen crock of honey on the table and pacing the room, halted at the hooded cradle and started to whine — uttering now a hoarse confession of reverence for Lucy, now bellowing brutal abuse upon his long-barren wife.

"Get out!" ordered Lucy Rime, a trembling edge to her voice. Aghast, the Reverend Cawkins flinched as if she intended to strike him with the crock she shoved into his chest.

When not a single child arrived for lessons the next morning, she attributed it to the extraordinary cold. But then, no one came the following day. Nor the next. And at last, Lucy Rime comprehended what had happened and for days afterwards, seated on the pallet bed pushed close to the hearth, she plotted and hoped for little else than Cawkins' death.

So long as half a dozen children had scribbled on their slates or, when the mornings were warm, had clambered out of doors to roll great snowballs into figures and forts, Lucy had secured some respite from herself. Abruptly now, the brittle cohesion of busyness, distraction, was gone.

And now the meager extent of her intercourse with the settlement of Tantrattle had shrunken to the torrid perimeter of light shed by her fire. Pain, like a fierce night animal, stole out from her heart and chewed at her mind. These were the hours when her love and desire for Mordecai Rime summoned the image of his countenance and received vague and gruesome distortions: the peevish head of the Reverend Cawkins grafted upon her husband's bull neck and shoulders. Invariably, when she willed her perverse creations to be gone they came nearer, became more vivid, so that Cawkins might grimace and gravely exhibit to her the reach of his tongue. The moment she scoffed, aware of and disgusted with herself, her composite man vanished. Despite the numbing cold she often prowled her two small rooms as if entranced by the quick drum of her pulse. She employed one of a thousand devices to balk at the bridge to unreality, a plank across a brook, and keep sane. She might open a book and chatter its words aloud; once, when the neglected hound rolled onto his back, his legs crooked, she abstractedly dug her nails along his belly, causing him to squeal and skulk off. As the final month of pregnancy began, she crossed over that bridge more readily and took asylum in the bright ambitious time before her marriage. And if each passing day aggravated fierce yearning for Mordecai Rime's return, the frozen nights inspired a parade of suitors, half-seen and unknown men who often amused her and tantalized her. Increasingly too, she looked upon this or that man's attentions favorably and thereby stimulated such burdensome self-despisal that she was overwhelmed with sorrow for herself and furiously despised the spectral marshal of every parade, the wondermonger who had entrapped and stranded her on this margin of nothing and nowhere. She began to fathom a profound justice in her creation of a man having the body of Mordecai Rime and the head of the Reverend Cawkins; the pathetic old farmer who sneakily reviled his childless wife, and the infantile woodsman able to do nothing but abandon her to an isolation so abysmal that it seemed she had fathered and carried and would surely deliver her child, alone. Indeed, were not the righteous farmer and the nomadic woodsman but different phases of the selfsame illness? She bitterly recollected Rime's parting threat — "You'd best be true, Lucy Rime, or you'll make a meat-bird o' me" — and wondered how she had restrained from cursing, jeering, spitting in the face of his cruel egoism.

Week after week, these were the characteristic rounds of that night animal whenever it got loose from her heart and turned her mind in its sharp jaws.

V

> *Red Hot holes*
> *Hot as coals*
> *Step right up*
> *Mad Molly said.*
> *Sup an' sup*
> *'Fore you're dead,*
> *T'ain't no sin —*
> *Shove't in!*
> *Moll rides a cock to heaven.*

Whoooo-oo-eee, tongues clacked, fingers drummed the deacon seat and the wiry young swamper, flushed with his election, went another round:

> *Red hot holes*
> *Hot as coals*
> *Step right up*
> *Mad Molly said.*
> *My knee's spread*
> *My hole's as red*
> *As the day I wed*
> *Moll rides a cock to heaven.*

There ensued then a debate concerning the various merits, breadths and depths of vaginas to be met with in the natural world. Sheep, as ever, found a champion, as did women, goats, bears, deer, and dogs. Continually teased about the length and frequency of his visits to the hovel, the teamster Clarence Smiles confessed a preference for the oxen's company to their own, as he considered the ox the more sensible beast.

Above catcalls and hoots, Smiles yelled, "You bullshit ba'stads do all your screwin' here in camp an' all your lumb'rin in Sunb'ry Town," and bundling up, he plunged scowling into a chest-deep drift outside the entrance.

John Gorges folded his arms on his anxious chest and scanned the grimy fume-filled heads which cramped the room. In particular, he scrutinized Mordecai Rime who for days had kept to his corner berth carving a chunk of yellow wood. Since the crew had become snowbound Gorges regretted having talked of Rime's lunatic bout with the pine tree; and the more so the night Rang-tang Sarsen snapped his red galluses off his yoke-sized shoulders and jeered, "Whittlin' out a tree beatin' club?" Sarsen drew the tin dipper to his humid, orange lips, his eyes narrowed upon Rime.

"Nope," answered Mordecai Rime without lifting his eyes, "a doll."

Uproarious Sarsen tried to stem the tea snorting out his nostrils. "Doll!" he gasped. "Feelin' need o' somethin' to sleep nights with? Myself, I'd hafta start off with a bigger slab so's the hole'd accommodate me."

Snickerings broke out in the close camp. They were not in sympathy with Mordecai Rime and so, with a derisive huff, Sarsen let be. Whipping back his bushy mane Sarsen began, "Know'd this Witch Woman," staring up at the cupola as if the woman in question were hung there, "An' Christ a'mighty, did she have a way with wild things. Seen 'er walk straight up to a bull moose an' rub on his lip whiskers."

Sarsen waited to make certain the ears of the camp were his. "Happen'd I was trappin' late that fall an' doin' poorly, so's when I hear talk o' the Witch Woman I get this idea in my head. Witch Woman lived in the middle o' nowhere an' my ass was froze to get there but when I get there I seen grown wolves, cat'mounts, bears, wildcats, foxes, an' all manner o' 'coons an' weasels, and they was all circlin' her dooryard.

"Not a one o' 'em was quarrelin'. Too busy, what with their moanin', howlin', pissin', pawin' an' scratchin', an' I warn't five minutes inside with the Witch Woman an' I know'd the reason why."

Sarsen's head tilted back, he tousled his shaggy red eyebrows and whistling appreciation and disbelief, he jumped up. Holding apart his hands nearly a foot he whispered, "Yay wide," nodding to confirm the distance.

"Like a chuck hole, an' so slipp'ry t'was, so wet an' slipp'ry, the miracle of 't 'was no toadstools grow'd along her walls. No problem soakin' both hands at a time clear to the elbows, an' I rubb'd her cracklin's on my lips an' nose 'cause they was chapped an' by next mornin', they was healed up.

"But the real gift o' the Witch Woman, what had them beasts moonin' an' wastin' themselves so, was the smell o' her. Trappin', I know somethin' about smells. I musta mixed every stink there is: eel oil, beeswax, al'chol, them blue an' green an' yellow asshole sacs, junks o' meat — but there never was no rut-musk an' never no bait like that o' the Witch Woman.

"T'was a smell to craze.

"I'd only to slip outdoors, pick the handsomest beast, stun it, skin it, and flesh'm out. I tell ya, if that woman's juice'd been bottl'd, her man 'ould been richer'n any man in the north country."

"Where's this Witch Woman live anyways?" asked the pop-eyed swamper.

Sprawled on the field bed, another man crooned, "Big as a chuck hole," and fell silent.

"Slipp'ry wet too," said his bunk-mate.

"Rang-tang, jus' why ain't you wed to that Witch Woman?" challenged the riled sled-tender when Sarsen, beginning to undress, appeared done.

Cross-legged, listless at the far corner of the camp, Mordecai Rime felt mud slug through his veins. He marked Sarsen standing amidst the blue and yellow coils of smoke, how he stretched in full pride above the tiers of mute, blurry heads and, like a handkerchief, dropped the words: "She's dead," and how the squabbling crew cried: "How? Dead? When?" to try and pick up that handkerchief first.

The exasperating Rang-tang heated a bucket of water and tossed a pitch knot on the camboose. "Busted in 'er door," he revealed at last. "Gang'd er. Bull moose, bears, wolves, cats, weasels — the whole lot of 'em claw'd an' slash'd an' mobb'd her an' all the while she was able she pump'd back an' sung out songs, right up the time that Witch Woman was prong'd to death."

White and orange in the flare of the pitch knot, Sarsen snorted a period to the end of his tale and commenced his shower.

When Mordecai Rime perceived the awe on the crew's faces, he could not determine whether Sarsen had created those faces or they Sarsen. Together they made an inseparable unit. There was no question as to why this crew had fallen out with him. He had cheated on all of them: The master passion of his former life, of woods life — the passion among men — he had betrayed; its cardinal law — that women be the meeting place of men — he had broken.

These men in the thick steam and fumes appeared utterly contented. It was this contentment which disgusted and angered Mordecai Rime. Bereft of fight and language, he gazed upon the men and they were alien as the Reverend Cawkins had appeared alien to him. They watched Sarsen, entranced, while Sarsen stood wailing out an old ballad with a cruel, new edge:

> *To the woods he will go*
> *With his heart full up with woe*
> *And he w-a-nders from tree to tree*
> *'Till six months are gone and past, he forgets it all at last.*
>
> *It is time he should have another spree*
> *It is time he should have another spree.*
>
> *When old age does him alarm*
> *He will settle on a farm*
> *An' he'll find some young girl to be his wife;*
> *But to his sad mistake, she* Mock *love to him will make.*
>
> *And kind death will cut the tender threads of life*
> *And kind death will cut the tender threads of life.*

Stroking himself daintily dry, Sarsen minced, "Sung that special for Deacon Rime."

"Wonder why 'tis dogs chew hardest on the dog that's hurtin'?" said John Gorges.

Sarsen bent his soaked chestnut body near to Gorges, clutched his woolen shirt, and easily hoisted him into the air. "Old man, hope you ain't callin' Rudolph Sarsen a dog?"

"Nope," Gorges promptly answered, adroitly mouthing the pipe-stem, "I was jus' wond'rin' why. You'd 'spose the sound 'o pain so scares 'em, they try an' eat the pain up."

Sarsen glared at the grizzled vacancy of Gorges' face and kept him harnessed. The crew watched, absorbed by how the strained buttons unravelled on the red shirt and squirted one by one between Sarsen's clenched, ruddy paws, and spun to the ground.

No one noticed that Rime quit his place in the remote corner of the camp and no one heard him stalk along the log wall. With the dry scrunch of a boot in frozen snow he ordered — "Set the man down!" — and every head swung around to see Mordecai Rime, his upper lip lifted on his wry, dark-yellow face, crouched twenty steps from Rang-tang Sarsen.

There was a stone-still moment: the crew gaped; Rime bunched in a ball; Gorges dangled; Sarsen smiled, fascinated, abstracted but for the plum-colored splotches exploding on his throat and brow. His gray eyes grew larger, shinier, rounder, and green veins inside his arms and on the sides of his neck and forehead swelled and twanged.

Then, all at once Sarsen giggled, hugged Gorges to his bare chest and like a moody child, cross of a sudden with its doll, he hurled Gorges into the live coals and ash that buried the bean-hole.

Although Sarsen wheeled instantly about and planted his feet, he was not among the swift-eyed few to glimpse Mordecai Rime rear from a crouch and shoot headlong across the room. Rime's neck recoiled into his shoulders, his skull battered Sarsen's abdomen, and Sarsen, a benign sheen to his eyes, bellowed what sounded like a life's-breath, jack-knifed backwards through the air, straightened, half-somersaulted, and cracked his head on the packed earth where he came to a crumpled halt, his superb naked bulk unconscious and an expression of astonishment upon his face.

Mordecai Rime had forgotten what it was that had incited him. He was oblivious to the crew whose respect and devotion he had so vigorously reclaimed and which awaited now his victor's gloat, some cock-a-doodling.

A pallor washed over Rime's sallow, impassive countenance. Transfixed, he hunched over the body as if it were a tree-trunk, some thready russet-barked cedar tree which, but a moment ago, had wind-toppled across his path.

Filmy eyes starting from their sockets, Adam's apple seething,

Sarsen's rosy head was flung back, glistening in the unsteady fire-glow. His long, brick-colored shock of hair spread, fan-like, upon the dirt.

It happened so swiftly, or else so appalled the already agitated crew — Rime's seizing of the heavy broadaxe off the wall and con-centratedly wielding its curved helve, as if to hew a log, at Sarsen's upturned face — that no man stirred to grab hold of Rime before that fire-bright broadaxe had bitten off a sheaf of auburn hair and riven the earth not half an inch from Rang-tang Sarsen's deaf ear.

A relieved thunderous laughter broke the stillness and its roar kept up all the while Mordecai Rime lifted and heaved down the broadaxe to score an outline around Sarsen's tight-cropped head.

Rime cast the broadaxe aside. He had won no gratification; there was no gratification to be won. Fury continued to gather and crowd his chest and he could not yet be done with the flesh inert at his feet. He swayed above the body and searched it that it might dis-close, and he inflict, that humiliation potent enough to expel the terror at large inside him.

The smug fashion in which Sarsen's languid tongue licked along the tufted edge of his mouth struck Rime as so hideous that he desired only to make a corpse of him.

Rime knelt beside Sarsen and frantically scooped the severed locks into one red wad. Underhanded, he chucked it onto the fire and slapped clean his palms while the burning wad came apart, snapped, writhed and stank.

That instant the flame bent, riffled, the door thudded open and down the snow dune slid Clarence Smiles. "Easin' up outside," he reported, "Warmin'," and he frisked patches of snow off his rump. The teamster perceived the bewildered stillness in the camp, and Mordecai Rime, and then the prostrate Sarsen, shorn and stomach-up, blinking in groggy disbelief at the splint roof. "Hey . . . what's," was all Smiles had stammered when pell-mell, Rime snatched Sar-sen's wrist, jolted him to a sit and crooking an arm around his neck, gripped a thigh, jerked the dormant hulk across his shoulders, toted it to the door, and dumped it like a skinned carcass atop the snowdrift.

Rime latched the door. He crossed the room and sagged in his corner berth — wrists propped on his knees, head on the log wall, eyes slitted, steadfast upon the latch. In open-mouthed silence the crew listened, and they too eagerly eyed the latch. After a most protracted moment the bar lifted from its strike. The halting shove which opened the door loosed such riot indoors as to blast with insult the abject and scalded man who reeled, doubled up, in the doorway. One hand clawing his shorn hair, the other cupping his genitals, he plunged into the noise.

Some few men guffawed and badgered him as he tripped towards the fire and his clothes, but the din had broken off. Everything brazen appeared to have been smelted from Sarsen's aspect. He pulled a red toque on his head, rushed into all his four layers of scarlet underwear, his stockings, stagged trousers, and moccasin boots. Then, padded in a stout mackinaw, he hunched shivering above the fire. His lips pulsed, parted imperceptibly and released "Boss" in a whisper. He never looked at Urban Burlock when he asked for and was given his pay from the chamois pouch hung on Burlock's chest. And he never spoke or raised his eyes the while he packed his gear. He sulked to the entrance, reached for the latch, and stopped. Though his head kept depressed and did not turn, his throat raved as only an animal badly shot or at the peak of rut can rave: "YOU'RE GONNA DIE, RIME."

As the door cracked shut, Mordecai Rime had tried to rejoin, "Never thought diff'rent," but nothing had come out.

Some of the crew loitered, more crawled beneath the single cotton batting spread. "One helluva haircut!" exclaimed the swamper.

"Holy Shit'n Heaven!" agreed the sled-tender.

"Serves the whorin' ape," said proud John Gorges, pondering his blistered fingertips and tapping empty his pipe-bowl on the deacon seat.

Mortified, the crazy-quilt drawn to his chin, Mordecai Rime watched and listened, and was watching and listening still many hours afterwards, blood pumping so fast inside his head that the room jigged up and down with each heartbeat and the crew, wriggling and rolling in the mellow light, resembled one enormous centipede. He wished then to scream as Sarsen had — one steady, throat-cleaving noise to last the night long — but again, he found his throat horror-clogged. At last, sitting against the wall, he fell asleep and, deadly cold, directly awakened from a dream. There had been an infant in his dream, a bare girl infant, plump-jointed, his daughter. He tickled her along the arch of her ribcage and she grunted with glee and pedaled her arms and legs and displayed her tongue, gums, the patterned roof of her mouth. He spread his thick fingers apart and raised his arm. Of themselves those fingers made a fist, and he witnessed but could not halt the fist from driving her pliant belly right down, flush to her spine.

Mordecai Rime squeezed his ears to muffle the loud chatter of his teeth for he remembered finally how his baby's limbs had flapped and how she stopped, went limp and lay back whiter than paraffin, blank as the whitest snow.

VI

The days of static dead cold were succeeded by a week of blizzard and wind, but when finally at the end of January a false thaw did come, Lucy Rime stayed sealed in, sleepily fingered her painful belly and mused upon the seductive lethargy which would let her mind burn down and go out. Then one afternoon on the verge of nightfall, there came a hollow thud outside the entrance. Had the noise not provoked a string of barks and growls from the hound, she would have considered it snow tumbling off the roof and ignored it altogether.

Immediately, hard poundings shook her bolted door and swept the vindictive face of the Reverend Cawkins across her mind. A voice shouted, the hound barked, and the hammering continued while Lucy Rime carefully inspected the muzzle-loader, ramrod, powder, balls, and vainly tried to recall how a charge was loaded. After a flustered moment, the question made no difference. Steeled by the queer calm which only the severest hostility can produce, and holding the unloaded weapon, she unbolted the door and stepped back, her thumb on the fire-lock.

From atop the crest of snow-wall that had drifted against the threshold, there peered and immediately vanished an unfamiliar bearded face. Concealed behind the edge of the bank he nervously asked, "This the Rime place?"

No reply came forth besides the wild barking of the hound.

"Crew'd with Mordecai Rime. You his Missus?"

"What is it?" said Lucy anxiously, hearing the harsh quaver in her throat.

"Name's Sarsen, Missus Rime, Rudolph Sarsen. Would you set down that rifle? I come a long ways to get here an' I'm wet through." His head rose warily over the pitted ridge of snow and he glanced down into the room.

Every waking second of his tramp through the melting wilderness to Tantrattle, Rudolph Sarsen had been craving to play havoc with the place where Mordecai Rime lived. Humiliation had fabricated his scheme. Rage, indifferent to the leaden snow clinging to the stitches of his snowshoes, had lifted his screaming legs and staggered him onward. He lowered himself woodenly to the cabin floor.

Narrowing his attention to the hound, he scooped out tiny wads of snow caught inside his boot-tops and uttered the words: "I come straight down from camp on Mooselip to tell you Mordecai Rime's dead!"

A feeling of desolation, an unaccountable sadness overcame Sarsen once his hoax was accomplished. Suddenly he wanted to retract his words and like a child listening for his father's angry tread, be elsewhere.

"I mean you no harm," he said, and forced himself to look full into Lucy Rime's face. "I mean you no harm," repeated his dreadful voice. Although opened unnaturally wide, her eyes gazed as the suspended eyes of a caught animal gaze dumbly about the advancing trapper.

Forgetful of the anguish of soaked boots and trousers in a hardening night wind, Sarsen thought to run outside and keep running. She turned and moved away. While she hung the musket on the crotched brackets Sarsen noticed her fine, bony profile, her slender wrists, and for the first time, the frightful low-slung jutting between her hips. She sat on the pallet bed and nestled beneath a heap of woolen stuffs, blankets, and a goose-down coverlet, entirely out of sight.

Sarsen waited and stared and listened intently, but not a noise or a movement could he detect in the mound on the pallet. Fearing she had crawled underneath the pile and died, he pulled off a sopping mitten and gently pressed his red fingers to the coverlet, feeling the faint rise and fall his eye had missed.

He took a deep breath and, shivering, collapsed into the chair at the foot of the bed by the hearth corner. As though burdocks were matted in his hair, Sarsen tenderly fingered his scalp. He would show her exactly what Rime had done to him. He would explain, apologize, and leave. Strangely, once Rudolph Sarsen determined to remain only until she awakened, the oppressive cabin and the horrible wrongness of his presence in it ceased to rack his mind. He followed the aimless play of shadows on the bark ceiling, touched the hound curled in a knot to one side of him, glimpsed the huddled woman concealed on his other side, and before long, suffused with an almost domestic well-being, slumped towards the blazing warmth and was fast asleep until dawn.

Still tired from the long journey and his uneasy dreams and hunger, he shifted in the rude chair and drowsily looked at the curled tongue of the yawning hound. The fire at his feet had burned low. Sarsen also yawned, stood, and stretched.

Then, he caught sight of Lucy Rime. Although she took no notice of him, that single look convinced him that her mind had broken overnight. Seated on her heels in the crumpled bedding at the edge of the pallet, she seemed to scan the cabin corner to corner, as from a great height. Her rigid eye flashed upon Sarsen and kept turning. Suddenly pain screwed up her remote and haggard face. She rolled onto her back with quivering legs akimbo and made soft rapid noises. After several moments the noises subsided.

"Fits!" Sarsen mumbled. Spellbound, he watched her strain up and perch motionless as a hawk on the rim of a nest.

Time and again paralyzed Rudolph Sarsen saw her throw back her disheveled head, arch her spine and shake her fists all about. Twice, unmindful of Sarsen's existence, she shuffled the length of the room, squatted over a clay bowl in the dark corner, urinated, and wavered to the pallet bed. For an hour, for two hours and longer Sarsen beheld elaborate and enigmatic sleep-walking procedures so alien to common humanness that he deemed her possessed.

And the whole time Sarsen stood planted in horror and did nothing but witness what he believed to be some potently unholy mechanism, Lucy Rime had felt her insides tugged downward, wave upon harsher wave, as if the moon had fallen out of the sky and buried itself under those very floorplanks. Not until the downward pull had become so great within her that all her muscles rolled in unison and fastened her to the hot stone hearth where she yanked her skirt and soaking layers of underskirt above her knees and groped between her thighs to ease herself — not until that moment did panicky Rudolph Sarsen comprehend the nature of the event taking place before his eyes. Hastily, he fetched a bucket of icy water, hung another to heat, and began to wipe sweat from her neck and brow.

Dazedly nodding, she clasped his stout wrist and guided it with uncanny strength between her shaking legs. The wet cloth dropped from his fingers, his hand shied and she let go gasping as a stronger wave crested with a pale spurt, and Sarsen saw the purple cone of head splay out her shining red flesh and be towed, the wave spent, back inside her. His trepidation sloughed off him. He fell to his knees and systematically wrung out rags, cleaned her vagina, swabbed down her thighs, his breathing quickening to coincide with hers.

Then the strongest wave of all mounted, pinned her fast, down, apart; her lips opened, jaw gaped at its widest, and grasping Sarsen's neck she hoisted herself into a squat just as there rode on the wave's brutal edge an astonishing and dented blue head.

Sarsen squealed a falsetto laugh which restrained him from hauling out the rest of the baby at once. He elbowed away the hound's snout and crouched, cupping together his trembling hands as if to catch the head which revolved to show him its impassive profile. The spot above Sarsen's stomach clinched hard as stone and allowed no breath until piecemeal, a shoulder, slippery chest, flailing blue fists and everything else had slithered into his grip, whereupon the impassive features of the infant girl inflamed and convulsed with an absolute purity of rage.

In the close, sallow cabin Sarsen gawked with awe and aversion at the sleek-ribbed infant he held clamped, ankles and nape. What with her wailing, sneezing, bending, and scraping her nails along her matted black temple; with her streaked coating, like frog eggs and curdled milk, and the thick smell of just-gutted animal rising up from her, the baby girl so dumfounded Sarsen he nearly overlooked the cord spiraling down into Lucy Rime.

Between his curved knifeblade and thumb he severed the blue cord. Blood spilled over his fingers. Scrupulously, he washed the baby's head with warm water, and the chalky creases of her body. Lucy Rime never turned sideways when he arranged the baby in blanketing below her white arm. Eyelids slightly apart, Lucy twisted silently and left an enormous slab of bright meat draped over the inside of her thigh.

Once again Sarsen tried to bathe her and shift bedding as best he could. The whole room seemed to him one pudding of sweat, flesh, wood-smoke and blood, in which everyone bogged and swam about. Stupefied, he sloshed the heavy cross-hatched afterbirth in a bucket of pink water and tottered out of doors, beneath icicles hanging, thick as legs, from the eaves of the cabin.

At each step toward the hooded river Sarsen sank, the hound plunging avidly at his heels. He quit halfway down the soft pitch, kicked a hole in the slush, emptied out the bucket and wearily buried its steaming contents. Once he had struggled a dozen steps back up the slope he felt dizzy and dropped onto his back for a rest. He was sucking a mouthful of snow and pressing another handful to his forehead, hoping to clear his brain, when he heard the whining. He sat up to see the hound shoveling away the snow he had packed into the hole. He scolded and hurled two snowballs, but the hound's forelegs dug on.

The faint, long-drawn yowl of the baby sounded through the gray air. Sarsen smiled and planted the back of his head in the rotting snow. Soon the hound, afterbirth adangle in his straining jaws, glided past Sarsen and secreted himself behind the cabin for a feast. Sarsen was unconcerned. Shallowly imbedded in the snow, he abandoned himself to a most joyful, gratified, even triumphant smile. Rudolph Sarsen, with his two red hands, had delivered a child!

And now, inside, Lucy Rime briefly surfaced, pulled back blanketing to discover its hapless enlarged sex, and wanly tracing her baby's clasping mouth with the yellow-crusted tip of her breast, she was again submerged in a dream-swamp.

One drizzling day and night of sleet after the next Lucy Rime floundered in this swamp of reverie and fever with scarcely a word or gesture for Rudolph Sarsen. Fitfully, she rose from the heavy bedfolds and moved about, despite his scrutiny, like something in the damp privacy of a den.

Sarsen woke humiliated and regretful each day, determined anew to rescind his lie; a resolve he shrank from each evening when her listless dejection gave way to chills and night sweat. Lodged thus, with a tormented somnambulant woman and her wretched child, Sarsen at the start worked solely to rid them of infection and the interminable nightmare he had precipitated. To this end he cooked and fed porridges, gruels, made tea, tended fire; he hunted partridge near by, and snowshoe hare; and in the blunt, suspicious settlement of Tantrattle he exchanged his pay for eggs and clean cloths and goat's milk. Less and less frequently he thought to escape; and soon, all consideration of admitting his deceit had vanished.

It was singular, perhaps, that while he diligently nursed Lucy Rime and attended her infant, nothing disquieted him more than the very prospect of her recovery. Into the nights, seated on the floor beside the pallet bed, he sponged cold water over Lucy's white neck and lips while his knee rolled the hooded cradle. That Lucy Rime kept silent, insensible of his doings, captivated and encouraged Sarsen, and also relieved him of his characteristic bashfulness with females — a conceit so extreme and precarious that outside of brothels, he heard censure in a woman's laugh. When her fever had risen one evening, Sarsen was able to hazard an initial small tenderness: stroking back hair glued to her wet jaw he leaned down, tentatively, nuzzled a place over her ear, and drew back.

Fortified by the acquiesence of her delirium that night, Sarsen's confidence built until the extent of his audacity unnerved him. And after long restless hours, at the break of day, he first tasted the sweet leakage from her nipple and looked about, rattled by the calm eyes of the hound. Sarsen turned then, to find himself the object of Lucy Rime's wideawake and apprehensive watch. There seemed no blood in her head. She looked wasted and held up her head unsteadily, but the traces of fever and daze were gone. She wet her lips with pasty saliva, reached for Sarsen's hand and covered it.

"You've been awfully good . . . Mr. . . ." and because she did not know the name she smiled gruesomely and dropped back, closing her eyes.

"Rudolph," and standing, he said "Rudolph Sarsen."

Lucy Rime wadded half the coverlet behind her shoulder-blades and looked down her chin at one large, knotted breast sticking through her kersey dress. She winced and regarded the knife sheathed on Sarsen's hip. Then, without concealing the breast she glanced into the cradle. "You have kept us clean, I see," she said.

Over her bed he stood, baffled. More swiftly than any crisp silence or hair-and-heart-rending lamentation, the powerfully controlled immodesty of Lucy Rime had disabled him.

"How long ago did it happen?" she asked, shifting upon an elbow to examine Sarsen's bright thick-bearded face.

"The little baby, Missus?"

"His death."

"I . . . lose track," he stammered, and subdued and nettled, edged into the chair.

"He warned it would happen."

Sarsen had broken into hectic sweat. " 'Twasn't you," he whispered, eyes averted. "Was a birchtop. I seen't hit his neck. You ain't got nothin' t' do with the matter."

Following this unexpected and belated mutual introduction, unhappy Sarsen could not make her out. He resented her for having risen and thereby having summarily excluded him from the former intimacy of his office. Watching her now, he fell to pitying himself. "Rather I'd be off?"

The manner in which she lay back, smiled at the blackened bark ceiling and carefully pronounced "Ru-dolph" completed his sullen relapse into timidity and mistrustfulness.

He went out and rambled over the slick, pocked crust, but try as he might, he could not bring himself to leave the vicinity of Tantrattle. By dark he had circled to a stop at the cabin door. He slept where he spent every night of the following weeks, uneasily crumpled on his mackinaw at the hot foot of her pallet bed.

The false thaw returned to winter without his noticing. The snow fell, shut them in, and kept falling. Sarsen noticed nothing besides Lucy Rime. He watched her sponge herself and suckle the snorting baby and gobble food and sleep badly and change her dress. What small distance might be kept in the cramped space before the hearth, Lucy Rime ignored.

Daily, the damage which Mordecai Rime had administered to Sarsen's physical vanity was delivered in subtle miniature by his nerveless wife. Close within his reach Lucy Rime held herself aloof, alert, secluded in herself. If she were a man, thought Sarsen, he would beat her outright. As it was, powerless to disengage himself, he bided in idleness and figured how to equalize things between them. Her health gained rapidly, together with this independence which Sarsen variously construed as hostility, fear, grief, desire, and whatever else, surely a deviant want of the decorum befitting of widow, mother, and woman.

And before long, she excited such a ferocious churn of energy inside him that he shovelled needless paths, split extra wood. Yet despite any number of brutal exertions, he throbbed and mulled away the nights. Warming his feet on the hearthstone one evening while the baby loudly grubbed out its supper, Rudolph Sarsen realized that he must be in love.

With a thick lip-smack the infant jerked sideways and distracted Sarsen by siphoning a powerful, fine strand of milk into the air. Lucy watched the spray a moment and capped it with the tip of her finger, "Lilah!" she burst out abruptly, "Lilah Rime. Do you like it?" She glanced across the pallet bed and caught Sarsen's eye. "Well?" she asked calmly.

Rapidly stroking whiskers along his upper lip Sarsen turned away in frustration and sulked with such conviction that Lucy Rime wondered what she had done to so offend him. She realized how unbearably exposed and abused he considered himself and it irritated her. "I'm certain you know my body better than I," she said.

Sarsen's brow and nose changed to the same bright orange as his beard and he glowered down at his heavy fists.

"What is it you want?" said Lucy Rime. "You want to sleep here, in my bed?"

Scarlet, he jumped to his feet, threw on his mackinaw, toque, and bolted into the soft blackness outside with so radiant and astonishing a display of outrage that Lucy Rime broke into a fit of silly laughter which he tried not to hear. He felt an intense sympathy for Mordecai Rime who had disgraced him, and who now was sure to try and kill him.

If Sarsen's terror and outlandish indignation had set off Lucy Rime's laughter, what kept it going was the sight of her daughter, smiling asleep in the hooded cradle; thoughts of men Miss Lilah Rime might some day meet. The hound groaned and cocked his head, as if the sound pained his ears. She laughed and she was empty. Her eyelids could no longer be held apart, and she could not prevent her emptiness from filling up with a landscape which even in dream she recognized from a day at the end of the past October. Once again, above the edge of the beaver pond where Mordecai Rime had led her for their picnic, the same chilly sun shone on the incandescent colors of decay when she unfurled the quilt beside a log tiered with fungus the shade of a red-winged blackbird's shoulder. Nothing had altered except that this time she sat by herself. The spank of a beaver's tail summoned her to a closer look, down among the crisp, rank grasses encircling the pond. Dozens of frogs spurted into the silt at her rustling footfalls while she strolled along and leaped troughs of bronze water. Clacking his red teeth, the beaver hooked up his hind legs, his paddle, and jabbed them into the water, diving with a surly whack. Happy for the company of the beaver's noisy surveillance, she smiled each time the beaver surfaced, farther from his wattled house, circling the dead cedars which stuck white and jagged above the water. The pondwater was warmer than the air and since she found herself naked, she entered the shallow, coppery water, waded, and settled down into the black leaves, in the thick sediment. Why the pond grew oppressive, suddenly darkening, she could not at first understand. Beneath the water her legs were spread and they seemed ugly to her, orange and stunted. Disturbed, she got to her feet and her long strides agitated the muck as she made her way towards the reedy shore. There, with a squeal of horror, she saw them — leeches, hundreds upon hundreds of tiny leeches hitched along the length of her legs, battening. Unable to move, her rigid mouth open, she watched the one parent leech among the hideous gray swarm, a single black muscle cartwheeling, end over end across her knee-cap. Now and again it paused, waggled one of its tapered ends into the air as if to fix its course and slowly climbed on. Rigid mouth open, she screamed a plea for husband's help; screamed so hard that amidst the gnawed willows and alders she heard a miraculous crack of twigs and there beside her knelt Mordecai Rime, his small shiny eyes concentrated on his blunt thumb and forefinger which gently tweezed leech after tiny leech from her ankles and calves. An outsized tooth-chocked grin, a delighted chuckle and shake of his bristled head beguiled away her terror and he eased her down, his hands at work moving up her thighs until finally, the pudgy black leech was plucked from a red welt on her skin and her shock of wet hair had engulfed half his hand. His whole weight rushed upon her then, and with stunning immediacy Lucy Rime was wrenched from dream and sleep, at once to feel milk soaking her from neck to belly beneath his smothering heat; against her forehead scratched a beard, and in the quivering firelight she glimpsed his red-haired shoulder, and with all the stark might of her fury she threw herself open to greet Rudolph Sarsen.

VII

Nothing could be seen, and the squabble of crows scavenging the melting crust echoed in the grim air that closed upon Tantrattle at winter's end. Sunken, discolored drifts withdrew from three trunks, the heat of dwellings, compost and piled excrement. First signs of spring were everywhere. Even the Rime hound, on sniffing the scented, wet air blowing from the settlement, had pranced into the fog and days later drooped back haggard, an ear torn. Nevertheless, Lucy Rime treated Rudolph Sarsen with the same sharp-eyed, even-handed disinterest which also informed her dealings with her daughter and hound.

The contradiction between this remote, ironical workaday Lucy Rime and the amorous and anonymous woman of their nights confounded and entranced Sarsen before the beginnings of the thaw led him to the realization that winter camp on Little Mooselip had broken up; that if the majority of loggers stayed for the ice-out and drive into Sunbury Town, others had doubtless left already.

The transformation in him was apparent overnight. For hours he reclined indoors, torpid, and for impassioned hours he exhorted Lucy Rime to leave the intolerable north country and with him make a pitch somewhere to the benign west; recklessly he hobbled about the steaming thaw or lay waiting above the path into Tantrattle; but most markedly, the change showed in the nights clasped alongside her praying down Mordecai Rime and wishing, as winter came apart, for cold and snow everlasting.

The dreamy thickness of the days was but a shade paler than the nights, and the air, concealing or misshaping the contour, depth and sound of the land, seemed not to move. With so little to help an eye gauge the passage of time, distorted time haunted Sarsen worst of all.

Upon tugging open the swollen door one morning, Sarsen stood peering into the lusterless space. And before the stagnant draft caused Lucy Rime to take notice of the open doorway Sarsen was already off, once again planting his boots in the harder, narrow surface of the path leading above the river to the settlement.

Any day the path would be impassable. Edgeless drifts, although some ten feet high in places, and the overall two or three foot cover, had rotted, and Sarsen now heard snow puckering and oozing as cell by cell it dropped from canopies over the river below him and dissolved in the rising amber water.

A shaft of sunlight penetrated the mist before him, illuminating a bush of willows and glancing off a towering slab of air. Then Sarsen heard a peculiar noise. Convinced that it was a human voice, he hid behind the bowed willows on the embankment. Chest flush to the snow, he watched the vertical band of light smear and dissolve until, unable to see, straining to catch a footstep, a voice, he heard several drops spatter from catkins of the willows overhead.

He had calmed enough to consider himself fooled by a nervous ear, when there resounded, as from the bottom of a well, the words: "I done the most haulin'."

"Shit, you did," said a second voice.

"So you do the talkin'."

"Nope."

"Well I ain't go'n'ta."

With a heartbeat so tumultuous it seemed a partridge was drumming on his neck, Sarsen hugged fast to the dripping embankment. At the next moment, for an unbearable succession of moments, he expected men to halt beside the loudly drumming willows, and seize him. His uplifted eyes darted this way and that when the scraping, trudging, and laboring snorts appeared to shift directions in the vapor.

"Sona-abitch's boggin' down" was muttered, as if confidentially into Sarsen's ear, and then a silhouette cut through the fog, boots sank within range to kick his eyes, sled-runners churned, and then another, far larger silhouette plodded out of the mildew, passed, and nothing was left of the procession but murmurs and the faint splash of snow.

Rudolph Sarsen lay on his taut, drenched stomach beneath the pussy-willows, his whiskers lodged up to the lower lip in snow and his eyes locked straight ahead until his mind was made up to leave Tantrattle at once and forever. Cautiously, he quit his hiding place and crouched to examine the footprints and the soft, deep ruts left by the sled. He started to recall the fog-warped conversation and the fleeting outlines. To his positive astonishment, he realized that neither of the bickering voices and neither silhouette could have belonged to Mordecai Rime.

And when he remembered one of the travellers had said, "You do the talkin'," he whooped out a snicker at himself, cried, "Peddlers by Jesus!" and recklessly lunged in pursuit.

At the end of the track of parallel ruts Sarsen came upon the handsled, laden with a wet flour or molasses cask, its runners wedged in the remnant drift in front of the cabin. He shouldered in the door and his eyes strayed from the black pipestem clamped in the miserable smirk of John Gorges to black-bearded Teamster Smiles, the hound snuffling the teamster's woolens, and on, to settle upon the gracefully carved, wooden doll held by Lucy Rime.

"They've brought the body," Lucy said in a flat, diminished voice.

Sarsen cast half a glance behind him, toward the black-staved cask, and went rigid as a pelt on a stretching board.

No one gestured and no one spoke until the bluff teamster winced at John Gorges and stammered, "Don't figure how she could'a know'da . . . the accident . . . 'cause how could'a Sarsen. . . ."

"Figures perfect," interrupted Gorges, ogling Lucy Rime's vexed, heat-burned features. "Figures perfect when you figure her an' him's in cahoots!"

Clarence Smiles fidgeted out of doors. The hound followed and commenced circling the cask, baying as if he had treed something. John Gorges lingered a moment beside Sarsen. "You was lyin', Rang-tang," he mumbled, "Witch Woman ain't been kill't," and he jammed shut the door.

"C'mon, lit's get," urged the spooked teamster.

"We ain't leavin'm," Gorges said, slapping a mitten on the cask-head. He wrestled the sled handles up and down, but the runners would not unstick.

"I want nothin' t'do with the ba'steds. C'mon."

"Take off," snarled Gorges, landing a boot on the ribs of the hound and also, to no effect, resuming his struggle with the impacted runners. He was roundly upbraided for his willful foolishness by the stalwart teamster who yielded in the end, wrested loose the runners and vehemently sledged the difficult way back to Tantrattle, from where they were directed yonder, to a homestead where the entire party — the unnerving hound, teamster Smiles, Old John Gorges and the unwieldy cask — stopped while Gorges beat and hammered until, risen from his early sleep, the Reverend Cawkins glared petulantly through the narrowly opened door.

"A barrel?" reproached Cawkins once Smiles had indicated the cask. "Savages do better by their dead."

"Weren't nothin' else," Gorges explained. "This man Rime was a. . . ." and at once, the Reverend's door opened wide.

"Rime, you say? Mordecai Rime's in that barrel?"

"Curl'd up like a baby," declared Gorges.

Cawkins took measure of John Gorges: "A proper burying costs time and money. Gold money."

"Gold money," repeated Gorges.

"I'll be out," declared Cawkins, closing the door on them.

"Friggin' ol' Christer," growled the teamster.

Carrying a seething pitch pine torch, the Reverend Cawkins emerged in a black greatcoat and waded stiffly around the cemetery. Torchlight shone on the tops of the slate headstones and the hound bayed without stop. "What's into the creature?" shouted Cawkins, swishing the torch to scare the hound off. The reluctant Smiles helped John Gorges trundle the cask over the Reverend's foot-holes, below the cemetery and down to the winter vault.

"Plague winter," uttered Cawkins as he knocked the cedar braces from the tomb's double door. Once the cask was set upright inside the vault, the woodsmen pulled back.

The long melt had begun to thaw the corpses and neither would follow when Cawkins stooped deeper inside the putrid cavern. Cobwebs crisped from the flame like hairs and the torch glowed upon frozen mud, caked spades, a stone boat, and stacked to the low ceiling, caskets of all sizes.

"Greater than forty years," said Cawkins, nodding his torch at one short and slender casket, "the good Midwife here shared my bed. And there, Rideout. Culverwell. Keen, Highstone, Gentle. These, the Rabbow children. Here, in my vault, one third our settlement."

"Plague o' what?" queried John Gorges.

Reverend Cawkins had barely directed himself toward the dark entrance when the black hound sprang hallooing into the winter vault. Cawkins jabbed and lunged again, his torch clubbing the hound's back. One lunge singed the muzzle, driving the hound against the bottom of the piled wall of coffins; another caught the glistening black nose — and the yelping hound slipped under the sparking cudgel and rushed into the outside darkness.

Winded almost to faintness Cawkins grabbed hold of the bank of coffins and wheezed, "No natural dog!" He tilted the spitting torch to light up the woodsmen, but they had gone, and he addressed himself to nothing besides the frigid glint of coins strewn atop the head of the cask.

VIII

May, especially in the environs of Tantrattle, proved severely backward, a month of freezing nights which retarded the long thaw of

April until the snow, full of trapped water, packed and broke into turquoise bits of ice. Seeping between snow and frozen ground, daytime rivulets of meltwater made shallow green ponds of every intervale depression and drained into the widening river. Indeed, such a multitude of jagged floes crammed the river by the end of May that a squeeze occurred in a narrow crook not far downriver from the Rime cabin, ice-boulders fused and before long amassed into one prodigious upheaval of ice. Catastrophe lacked only the rains which the first night of June delivered in abundance.

A sudden, tumultuous overflow of hillside ravines and gulleys and brooks and flooding streams descended upon Tantrattle that night with rush and roar enough to drive the Reverend Cawkins and a goodly proportion of the diminished settlement from their beds onto their knees. Loosing sheets of snow, ice and topsoil, the night torrent deafened the knock of stones and splintering wood and the bleats and bellows of the panicky stock. Incredulous farmers watched the black rains tumble from eaves and drill moats in the snowbanks outside their thresholds. Below their homesteads the shallow riverbanks were mauled and gave way; swelling the floodplains, the boiling ice-freshet rose, to chase half-dressed farmers and their wives after herds of pallid, bawling children, cows, horses, and tormented sheep — all groping through the splashing dark for higher ground. The stone crib-work bridge in the midst of Tantrattle was filliped by the surging, thick current and swept downriver, towards the ice-dam. No one witnessed the thundering convergence of freshet and dam, but when the rain ceased and at daybreak, winds began to blow, the outcome — a foaming trough-like reservoir flooding the intervale — was surveyed by the hapless survivors upon the hillsides.

Beneath a mud surface the frozen ground held the brown, scumfilled lake for days afterwards. Families built shelters and salvaged what they could before the morning when the floodwaters began gradually to subside and an inventory of ruin was commenced.

Everything, everywhere had suffered the derangements of this freshet, and certainly not least was the Reverend Cawkins. That his entire meeting house had vanished, he had known days before this unhappy morning when he slumped in despair over the broken and missing headstones of the five infants, a marble hand in the silt, and whatever else was left of his ransacked cemetery. Not even the Reverend's capacity for gloom however could withstand the surfeit of havoc awaiting him at the winter vault: cedar braces and one door ripped from the entrance; the remaining door buried awry in the dimpled mud; the center of the vault's earth roof fallen in.

While he viewed this harrowing debris, an explanation for it dimly lit Cawkins' mind. Scarcely a moment had passed when the explanation blazed forth with conviction. This man, deprived of a large portion of his wealth, his meeting house, his winter vault and his wife, began at once to trudge up the guttered knoll flinging about his arms and cursing. And all along his upland route to the settlement he grew ever more profane and embattled as he inspected the drowned landscape. He discovered a heifer, forked high in the alders of the floodplain; in the orange willows two chickens roosted, and a broken loom; and like an ark outside Tantrattle proper foundered the skeleton of his meeting house.

He soon met the forlorn group of nine settlers assembled upon the mound overlooking the former sites of the Airs' farm and bridge: Neither the farm and the bridge nor Freedom and Solemna his wife had been accounted for.

"Terrible, Rev'rend."

"You seen the jam?"

"Was your place spared, Rev'rend?"

But Reverend Cawkins, squelching through the mud with long, patriarchal strides, marched on.

"Visionings," whispered one farmer.

"Wrath, you see the wrath and fever in those eyes!"

"Awful eyes," it was agreed. Smitten with wonder they followed him at a cautious distance. They no sooner had arrived at the wooded prospect outside the settlement than three of the party deserted. There, upon the washed-out slope, the Reverend Cawkins recoiled from an onrushing figure of a man, a large and fire-colored man galloping over the muck, tripping onto all fours, sliding, glancing behind, and again scrambling his savage way in poor Cawkins' direction.

The creature swerved before laying hands on the swooning Reverend, clambered uphill, and lurched into the green poplars. Footprints near the scene of the ruffle were examined while Cawkins revived. It was clear that one of the man's feet had been bootless and that in all likelihood he had intended to escape rather than assault something.

Bedraggled and panting the Reverend Cawkins arose and proceeded to head the daunted group. When chimney smoke came
into view, and the intact Rime cabin, Cawkins faltered. In the distance beyond the cabin the ice-dam mouldered like a giant wall of
butter and Cawkins' aplomb was so visibly enfeebled that two more
farmers lagged behind.

Cawkins mustered himself, and perceiving the door ajar, made
for the cabin entrance. The hearth was ablaze and on the floor of
the musty room the baby Lilah, knees tucked to her chin, screamed
as if poisoned. While Cawkins investigated the otherwise empty
dwelling, one of his dwindled band noticed a moccasin boot lodged
in the soft mud. Slurred tracks below the boot led them to such an
appalling conclusion that when the Reverend Cawkins stormed
from the cabin he spied those last four of his followers stampeding
through the mud above the plain.

Crestfallen, he too saw footprints, only these had barely filled
with cloudy brown water and they were, unmistakably, a woman's.
Cawkins trailed them down the slippery rise, past the lone moccasin boot to the border of the receding floodwaters, whereupon the
very mire reared up in the form of the black hound. The hound
crouched, as terrified of the Reverend as the Reverend was over-
awed by the snapping hound and the wild woman cradling the blue
head of the corpse. Cawkins' skin began to crawl. He staggered
backwards and fled Lucy Rime and the spoiled flesh doubled up in
the tattered crazy-quilt.

Sentinels kept vigil that night on the perimeter of the encamp-
ment where all Tantrattle huddled around a single fire on the slope
above their demolished settlement. However worn-out and belea-
guered by the ice-freshet and its gruesome aftermath, none but
children and livestock was able to sleep. At midnight, in the laven-
der smoke pouring up from the bubbling heap of wet twigs and
branches, the Reverend Cawkins got to his feet, broke his silence,
and set them shivering in their greatcoats and blankets. The
previous January, had he not apprised them of the cunning solici-
tations of the Rime whore, his rebukes and sharp refusals, his immediate loss of the Midwife Cawkins? The swirling glare of steam
and fire aggravated the contortion of Cawkins' ivory-yellow face
and lent dismal authority to his description of the black spy-dog he
had beaten from the now decimated vault, the ice-jam behind the
Rime place, and the dead woodsman Mordecai Rime run aground

at the threshold of his dwelling. "Winter plague . . . whoredom . . . hell dogs . . . flood . . . returning corpses . . . you behold Pestilence," exalted the hoarse, portentous voice of the Reverend Cawkins. "Pestilence infesting the north . . . spreading westward . . . Pestilence thriving, for thrive it will until that golden . . ." and hesitating with an implacable scowl, he was interrupted by the ringing alarm of a sentinel.

Every smarting eye fixed upon the speck of orange flame pulsing beyond the poplars on the bluff downriver. Cawkins sat through the night hours hugging his knees and nodding at the confirmative spectacle of enlarging flame until the black smoke-column rising from the Rime cabin scored the dawn. And later that day, from an abundance of hieroglyphs made in the morass before the cabin (a groove running from the spot where the corpse had been stranded, up to the roofless and gutted dwelling), and the charred infant, preserved in a dug-out cradle beneath the bones and rubble of the pyre, the hellish fate of the Rime family was confirmed by several bold residents of Tantrattle.

All Tantrattle, however, had reason to consider the fireside prophecy of the Reverend Cawkins before that summer was out; for whether those direful forebodings had issued from a body ungratified to the verge of distemper or from a bonafide seer, there assuredly did come to pass hardships of such an inordinate nature that the succeeding months were to be remembered as the Ice Summer. Late frosts withered the buds of orchards throughout the northlands and early crops were blasted in the freak blizzard at the start of July. Birds' eggs hatched only to have nestlings frozen as solid as the ice which formed an inch thick upon the streams. When the sleet of that weird season lashed down the first corn-shoots and cold fever wasted entire households overnight, thousands of mystified, half-starved families surrendered, pulled stakes, and escaped before October snows had sealed the afflicted north country.

IX

In the wake of the ice-freshet, the fire and calamitous summer, Tantrattle virtually disbanded. Settlers departing Tantrattle never talked about bad luck or happenstance as did emigrants from other stricken regions of the north. Hastening through Sunbury Town on their ways south and westward, those who had stayed in Tantrattle the longest, sowing and grimly sowing again, encountered woodsmen already heading north to set up winter quarters. These forthright husbandmen — possessed of little tolerance of ambiguity or fabrication — gave the superstitious woodsmen outlandish explanations for why the Ice Summer had befallen them. That fall, it was the talk of lumber camps.

While there was light on the shores of Upper, or Big Mooselip Lake, Boss Urban Burlock made certain that no one in his skeleton crew had leisure to brood and gossip and rail. Once the camp was established and the ox hovel built, Burlock tailored the operation to the run of the freezing water (which pinched through narrows and tumbled down a ravine, Quick Falls, into Little Mooselip), and its surrounding terrain. Burlock personally directed half the crew in damming the narrows and constructing a sluice for easing logs over Quick Falls; John Gorges supervised the clearance of windfalls, boulders and roots from the brook-beds and gulleys; skidpoles trestled ravines; rises were sheared; and as premature snows covered the frozen shores, a criss-cross of branch roads was swamped in and out of every stand of pine, and each branch road connected with the main road alongside Big Mooselip Lake and ended at the landing upon the ice.

Each day woodsmen trickled into camp and then, with the arrival of teamster Clarence Smiles and his oxen, hauling a long sled packed with goods and additional recruits, winter camp was sufficiently filled out to begin operations at dawn. None of the crew retired to the field bed after supper that night. They straddled the deacon seat, greased boots, and oilstoned axes, stared into the fire and listened to the sizzle of their brown spit. A knot of three or four men hunched over a bedraggled deck of cards, and several others, while they stood watching the game, traded lies and plans for the faraway spring before the usual nightly fare of hunting and river-driving and rum-drinking stories was supplanted by accounts of the bizarre summer, Mordecai Rime, tales of marriage and death.

Straightway the teamster Clarence Smiles joined his cattle and John Gorges sucked a pipe and kept silent. Rumors were reviewed and savored until someone mentioned the all too recognizable man with the fluttering orange hair had charged into the wilderness as if the King of Terrors were saddled on his back. Indeed, the destiny of this wild man had excited so many fabulous surmises that when the boy who toted nose-bags into the swamp to feed the crew next day swore Rang-tang himself was arrived in camp, the poor young-ster was scouted down by every man on that operation. Pranks ceased after the crew ducked inside and milled around the swing-ing crane and bean-hole. Every amazed soul tried in vain to dis-regard Rudolph Sarsen as he combed out his auburn beard and then his hair with long insolent strokes. His tight-jawed leer singled out John Gorges and Clarence Smiles.

"Locks's grow'd back nicely, Rang-tang," said John Gorges. Sar-sen nodded. Smoke, rising from the open fire to the log cupola, was blasted back upon them by winds shaving the cedar-splint roof. Coughing, spitting and rubbing red-rimmed eyes, the intimidated crew passed the dipper of tea and hastily couched for the night, fully dressed, upon the boughs of the field bed.

If Sarsen apprehended the fact that there would be no room for him beneath the crew's single bedspread that winter, it was evident in nothing so much as the way he deliberately performed — and performed with flagrant bravado — the ritual shower before he dressed and wrapped himself in a coverlet to stretch in a corner at the edge of the field bed.

Chopping crews were scattered out at daybreak, felling pines along the marble floor. The binding ice of Big Mooselip Lake thun-derclapped in the hard bitter air. Throughout a November of such cold it scorched nostrils and made brains dance, all the choppers but Rudolph Sarsen cut in pairs. He had no choice but to work alone. And after a day's labor, when crews trod the complicated night-blue shadows to camp, every man on the operation refused to eat so long as Rudolph Sarsen stood by the camboose wolfing down great heaps of beans and salt pork. Icy air clung to them while they clapped and stamped on the dirt floor to get their limbs working, and their bitterness grew by the day.

Had the unreasonable amounts of lumber felled and twitched from Sarsen's allotted areas not surpassed the output of any chop-ping team in camp, Boss Urban Burlock would never have permit-ted the dissension aroused by Sarsen's antics. The boy who carried grub into the woods told how the meat-birds always thronging about him chattering for food drove Sarsen to such states of frenzy that he held his head, took cover, or swung his axe as if to cleave the birds in mid-air. And Clarence Smiles, whose team snaked wood from Sarsen's chance to the landing, thought it strange that

Sarsen was never once at work when he arrived, but leaning against a tree, grinning and watching.

The belief made its rounds that Sarsen napped or sat upon a stump while the day long his uncanny poleaxe chopped by itself. And since Sarsen conversed with nobody, showed no signs of needing to, and furthermore, slept, ate, and worked apart from the crew, he was quickly considered something more or less than an ordinary man. Smiles said he was jinxed and treacherous. Another claimed he "didn't get all that skill for nothin'." He had signed away the gift of speech to cut such quantities of pine.

Level-headed John Gorges repeatedly took his stand on the phrase, "Fear's th' on'y devil can drive'n axe like that," and stood firm, until the night came when he no longer could believe his words, or, for that matter, his eyes.

It began, at first with the relief that the wicked freeze of November showed signs of breaking. The gusts, which had filed Big Mooselip Lake and jiggled loose moss chinking the camp walls, slackened and died down when a low cloud blocked off the pure, cold sky. All night huge flakes of moist snow filtered under the log cupola and melted above the fire. Without wind the soggy snow mounted, and hours before dawn, when Clarence Smiles opened the door on his way to provender his oxen, snow had piled up groin-deep. By noon storm winds drove an icy snow sideways and the crew dozed, moodily bided time, and kept watch of Rudolph Sarsen who paced with an ugly expectant look in his eyes while the storm outside rose to a full blizzard.

Whenever Sarsen unlatched the entrance and held the door slightly ajar to check outside, he grimaced and kneed it shut upon the white snake of drift that squeezed in and along the earth floor. Again that night, and the following day, gray land was welded seamless to the gray sky, banking such energy indoors by the second evening that Boss Urban Burlock worried that his men would not stay pent another day.

A dozen grumbling woodsmen were sprawled in tedium on the field bed and a dozen more men ripped their shares of salt pork, sopped fat from the common kettle, and sat vacantly upon the deacon seat drinking tea — molasses-sweetened that night by Burlock's order — smoking, and glancing about, when Sarsen jerked open the door and stuck out his shaggy head. This time, to the alarm of everyone but Sarsen, the winds chanced to tumble past Sarsen's leg one ruffled and woozy gray jay.

Rudolph Sarsen practically jumped to the spot where, plumped against the opposite wall, black beak ajar, the stunned jay tilted its head.

Sarsen had dropped to his knees. As he greedily began to inspect the bird someone jeered, "Some beans's left in the hole, Rang-tang."

"Never know who it might'a been."

"Shows good sense. Comin' in t' warm up."

"Let't be," pleaded John Gorges when Sarsen snatched up the gray jay. Disquietude shot through the room and drew the men into a subdued cluster. " 'Tis unlucky to harm a meat-bird, Sarsen. Toss't out or let't stay the night, but let the soul be!"

Wind made a dirge of roof shakes and joints while Sarsen, turning the bird before his nose, moved slowly to his corner and settled against the unpeeled spruce wall. And presently, for the first time that winter, Sarsen was heard to speak, his red whiskered lips inches from the gray jay's sharp beak: "Old man warns o' bad luck if Rudolph Sarsen don't treat you good," he whispered tenderly. "But the old fart's spoutin' out his ass-hole, 'cause this world don't have a grief that ain't been tried on Rudolph Sarsen." His red fist suddenly closed tighter around the jay's belly and he said, "You seen to't, ain't you Mister, you're the one won't let *me* be." The jay squirmed, gagged out the single protest in the room, and leveled a formal series of pecks at Sarsen's thumb and bristly fingers. "Your comin' here's a bad mistake," he told the bobbing, straining head inside his knuckles. " 'Cause I guess'd you was comin', an' what with your pretty little eyes an' black hair an' cocky ways there's no mistakin' 'twas you chopped off my hair when you was a livin' man." Sarsen relaxed his grip so as to bare the jay's breast, and twisting his fingers, pinched out a mass of pale feathers. The bird wriggled without a squawk and pedaled its dark purple legs. "Dyin', you fool'd me good," admitted Sarsen while the passive crew, watching him pluck the last feathers around the slender pink throat, made faces as though each blood-filled quick of feather screamed as it was yanked out. When he had done with its breast, Sarsen flopped the shrunken jay in his palm, and exclaiming, "Some wicked, mean trick, sneakin' back through the mud when you was long dead," he commenced to strip the charcoal shoulders and back. " 'Twas so clever it spook'd me from the baby girl I pull'd out'a the only woman I ever loved." Sarsen held the jay trembling up to his inflamed, gray eyes. " 'Fore your friggin' feather'd soul came 'round to cause me pains, you should'a know'd there ain't a sufferin' left can pain me." With that, Sarsen got to his feet and pinning each wing-tip, unfolded the alive and naked meat-bird like a paper doll he had finished cutting out. "There's nothin' now can overcome Rudolph Sarsen," he declared, and rushing to the door, he flung the gray jay into the riled snow.

The twenty-five woodsmen voiced no objection and made no gesture. They kept staring at the man who closed the door and took a breath as though he had just earned the largest fulfillment of his life. In no rush to let such satisfaction go, he unlaced his boots and peeled down his stagged trousers. Whistling a catch, unbuttoning his layers of red underwear, ruffing up his briary chest, letting the coverlet drop from his nakedness and stretching for the bucket of heated water on the swinging crane, he prepared for that shower and acknowledged no one. And the shower itself was the more pleasurable because he never responded to the gazes he knew were trained upon him and upon the water splashing down the contours of his orange skin to the cold floor. Ebulliently, he tousled his sopping hair.

But suddenly a queer whimper issued from that pillar of dispersing steam. Masses of hair were coming loose from Rudolph Sarsen's scalp. Hair clung to his arms and between his fingers.

He stood ankle-deep in hair rich and rusty as shed pine needles.

His fingers circled and scrambled over his utterly bald head. He touched and rubbed his beardless cheeks. He lifted his arms and saw his white armpits; peering down the goose-flesh of his pale chest at his white penis and hairless thighs, he started to tremble, weep and giggle.

Not a single strand of hair was left on his body. On his toes, the small of his back, in his nostrils and ears, his eye-lashes — nothing. He was stripped bare as the figure of a man made from snow.

There was an awful interlude of dumbness before the confusion broke. Like an irate squirrel, one woodsman stuttered and gnashed his teeth; another coiled on the floor shielding his head while John Gorges leveled curse upon curse at Sarsen's whoredam and hell-sire. Clarence Smiles barreled into the storm winds to the refuge of his oxen and hovel, and Urban Burlock managed but shakily to brace the head of the youngster who retched loud as sobs and babblings stirred those cramped quarters into bedlam.

And senseless as a man made from snow, Sarsen never cowered, indeed, never seemed to apprehend that the eyes closing upon him were crazy with terror and hatred. Slap-dash, with neither his compliance nor his resistance, Sarsen's hairless legs were rammed into his trousers, his arms stuffed rudely into sleeves and mackinaw, an axe was put in his hand and he was half-hauled and half-driven from winter camp into such whirligigs of snow that no trace of him was to be found the next morning when, notwithstanding the night-long winds which had the entire ground scoured, doubting John Gorges concluded, "Devil don't leave no tracks."

X

From the beginning he had plowed through the black drifts with no destination save a place to hide his gruesome baldness and be done. He floundered in terror before he collapsed finally, lame and shivering in the orange break of day, upon a half-uprooted clump of white maple. Sweat had frozen the collar of his mackinaw and his woolen trousers were stiff with urine. Lacking the strength to lift his eyes and the courage to survey the brilliant landscape, he pried the axe-handle from his numb grip and hung his head.

Beneath the wall of snow and tangled maple roots, a glistening caught his eye. He tumbled down the wall, briefly held an ear to the frosted opening, sniffed, and hectically chipped ice and then plugs of grass and sod from the edge of the hole.

No sooner was the entrance enlarged to the breadth of his shoulders than he squeezed inside and shoving the axe ahead, crawled down the narrow tunnel toward the reeking, dark cavity. Shortly the axe touched softness, provoking a pother of grunts and sneezes. He squatted high as the verge of the cavity let him and held back the pole-axe in readiness. The moment his eyes adapted to the blackness, the instant he marked a snout paler than a brow, the axe-blade was driven into the bear's skull, the helve was wrenched from his fists and he was clubbed on the ear when the blind bear hollered and wheeled against the den-sides.

Many hours later, after tugging the fat bear up through the tunnel, he emerged. Underneath the leaning maples he rubbed the handsome, long fur, removing every bit of matt and burr and mud he found, while the dead bear, its turned-in legs flexed in the air, lay steaming in the new snow.

He stuck his knife between its hind legs, circled its vent and straddled the belly while he slit between hide and flesh, halving the white splotch on its chest and proceeding neatly up the heavily clotted neck to the tip of its lower jaw. Once he had opened each leg to the toes, he gently ripped web after silvery web of membrane, working loose skin from the hips, spine, sloping shoulders until the fine pelt was entirely free of its blue-white tendons, purple muscle and plates of buttery fat.

Despite the oncoming dusk he cleared no ground for fire, set up no wind-break and left the meat as it had rolled, unbled and undressed. The bearskin alone claimed his interest. Secure beneath the snow and frozen ground, at nightfall he smoothed the floor of the choking den, spread the bearskin, fur-down, and in darkness scraped flesh and gobs of fat off the skin with an edged stone. When he had finished, he removed his mackinaw and used it to brush away loose particles and mop up grease. Reclining then on his mackinaw, he covered himself with the raw skin and dozed, his fingers locked in the thick fur upon his chest.

Mistrustful on awakening, even in the perfect darkness of the underground cavity, he tried to be still before he stripped to the waist and knelt, undersleeves hanging down the seat of his trousers. He despised the feel of his bare ribs against the insides of his arms as he nervously cut into the heavy circle of pelt. Halfway through it he stopped, and mantled himself in its cold, wet skin.

By cinching the fur about his throat, he fashioned a snug cone. Careful slashes were made for his arms, and when the whole was tautly wrapped about his shoulders and chest, the one skin was flush to the other. He tucked the bottom margin of fur into his underpants and trousers, and forced the crimson undershirts to stretch over his new and shaggy black torso. Only then did he begin creeping to the surface.

Slow-flapping ravens lifted themselves to the trees and the red fox looked over his shimmering tail to see what was issuing from the mouth of the opening. The horde of gray jays, however, continued to gorge upon and stipple the bright carcass with droppings. The jays scattered in a dither when the fox trotted back to the carcass after the intruder's flight.

Fear drove him due north, schooling his tense eye to pick out the smallest incongruity in a monotonous field; he had always to look between rather than at the landscapes of his chaotic rambles beyond the stripped maple and birch forests, seeking that secluded and empty land of ledge-hard slopes where ice winds crippled even the design of balsam and spruce, and the human face would never gaze upon him.

Rest multiplied his fear swifter than hunger and fatigue; make-shift shelters were abandoned as soon as built; and if the craving to join the life of other men took hold of him, he ventured higher into the north country.

By the heart of winter it was less a man than a state of lookout and loneliness that ranged the territory, checking cubbies and snares, sampling the freshness of every mound of black pellets, and the spoor that crossed his path; ignoring the larger prospect of ridge and hill-line for the single bough shuddering on a windless day or in a snowy thicket, the bronze iris of a snowshoe hare.

From the outset when he had stumbled upon the bear's den, an uncanny luck seemed to watch over him. No snare set in a funnel of withes failed to yield a strangled rabbit, marten or fox; and the first deadfall he contrived fell squarely upon the skull of a wolverine.

Months went by, months lived in such brutal estrangement from human kind that he came to believe that something powerful was bent on keeping him alive. Survival became his assumption, and his pride. Not infrequently, while trying to sleep in some cache of pelt bales, he wondered if he would ever die.

And with the completion of his outfit, it scarcely appeared a mortal or earthly being that weaved among the prostrate spruce at the timberline. Long, black-tasseled lynx ears pronged his brow. Gray ruff of lynx bearded his chin. His chest was bearskin, his girdle yellow-striped wolverine, and he wore a mosaic of skins for breeches. And no matter now where he turned or what he heard, there, pressing ever closer to an eternal reckoning, was Mordecai Rime — albeit this Rime grew with each vigilant day and listening night; and grew, finally to overshadow the last grand pines, his footfalls shelling hoar from pine needles, until grown to the extent of Sarsen's brain, he was north winter itself.

BARRY TARGAN

Surviving Adverse Seasons

(FROM SALMAGUNDI)

The Universe is either a chaos of involution and dispersion, or a unity of order and providence. If the first be truth, why should I desire to linger in the midst of chance, conglomeration, and confusion?

— MARCUS AURELIUS ANTONINUS

Britannia est insula.

So it began, again, for Abel Harnack. Another beginning in a life, lengthening, of many beginnings. And now a few endings. One at least.

Britannia est magna insula.

"And now, so that you will learn to hear as well as see the language, so that you will *feel* the beauty of it in the mouth, will you please read aloud? Will you," she glanced down at her class list, "Mr. Harnack, begin for us."

He read clearly and accurately the two lines and then the two lines following it to the end of the paragraph. *Britannia non est patria nostra, sed Britannia est terra pulchra.*

It had taken him a year to get here, this far. Monday evening. Page one. *Britannia est insula.* But even that morning he had not been certain that he would do it. He had not felt compelled into it as, in the past, he always had been — urgent, hungry, charging into endeavor, racing after accomplishment. Now he did not feel that way at all.

"Go on," his daughter had said to him at breakfast. "Do it." He did not live with Vivian, but after her husband Charles had driven off to his work and the two children had left for school, he would come often to eat a later breakfast with her. Unless she had something else to do that took her away. Then he would walk on past her house and into the city and into whatever vagaries his life just then, that day, would tilt him towards.

He might conclude upon a group of workmen breaking a street apart to fix a sewage pipe. He would drift down the street to them like a heavy log in a slow stream and go aground upon them, caught in their activity, the shattered air, the blasting of the pummeling jackhammer, the sputtering of the blue arcwelder, the revving up and down of the gasoline engine generator.

They would all subside at lunch time and he would drift on, free. Perhaps to spiral through department stores, sometimes to visit factories and small machinist shops he had once known well. Through the summer past he had watched young men play baseball in all the city's parks. And in the evening he would walk home, past his daughter's house (though at least once a week to supper there) to his house and to his evening in which he would do whatever occurred to him, unless nothing did.

At twelve or a little before, he would drink a small glass of scotch whiskey and then go to a thorough sleep, unprovoked by fears or passions or expectations. And at six he would awake.

"Go on," his daughter Vivian said to him at breakfast. "Do it. Go on and do it. It will do you good."

"Good? Good for what?" he asked her.

"Oh come on, Dad," she said, turning from the sink and their dishes. She said no more. That was as far as they ever got upon that point any longer.

"Very good, Mr. Harnack," Sylvia Warren said to him. "Thank you. Now Mrs.? . . . Miss Green, will you take it from there?" Miss Green took it from there, from Britannia through Europa to Sardinia, to Italia, some being insula, some not, some being magna, some parva.

At the end of the two hours, at the end of the first and second conjugations and the first declension and warnings about the ablative case, Abel Harnack decided not to return the coming Monday.

"*Vale,*" Sylvia Warren said to them as they all gathered up their books.

"*Vale,*" they answered back.

Outside, in the parking lot behind the high school, the group of them broke off to their own cars, except Abel Harnack, who would walk.

"Do you want a ride?" she called to him when she saw him, alone, crossing the asphalt parking lot to Wilson Street.

"Is that your car?" he asked, walking back to her, although it clearly was her car, the small door to it already opened, her briefcase already dropped into the catch-all area behind the seat.

"Yes. My joy." The car was an earlier model MG, the classic squarish roadster with narrow, wire-spoked wheels and headlights separated from the fenders, with a windshield that folded down, a walnut steering wheel, leather upholstery, the car a gleamingly waxed deep green. It was not the car he would have imagined her to drive.

But she was thin, lithe, enough for it, her motions strong and quick. Nimble, he thought. And although she was gray, she wore her hair modishly straight and long, out like a helmet, square across her forehead and to an inch above her shoulders. And she smiled like the young, easily and without complication and at everything. Perhaps her car suited her after all, even if she must be, Abel Harnack guessed, fifty-five or more.

"That's a fine looking car." They both waited beside it. "OK," he said. "But I don't live far. Only down Wilson Street about a half a mile." He went to the other side of the car. "How do I get in?"

"Like this. You sit in first and then swing your legs in." She did it. He opened his door and followed her example. "Fine. You did that just fine."

"I learn things quickly."

"I noticed that in class." The car burst to life. She backed up and then drove across and out of the lot, turning left on Wilson Street at his direction. She drove gracefully, snapping the gearshift through its pattern, pushing the car a little quickly, but well-controlled. She drove with pleasure, Abel Harnack thought.

In two minutes she stopped before his house, where he had pointed it out, the motor running. He swung himself out of the car.

"Thanks."

"It's nothing." She shifted and started off slowly. "See you next Monday." Between gears she waved her free hand. "*Vale*," she shouted back over her exhaust.

"*Vale*," he said softly.

Latona est irata quod agricolae sunt in aqua.

"Now here, you see," she said, "*quod agricolae sunt in aqua* is the dependent clause. It depends upon *irata* for its full meaning."

He had come back.

After the first class, at breakfast Tuesday, he had told Vivian that he probably would not go to the Latin classes again, but when she asked him why he could not say except to say that he was not so interested in Latin as he thought he might have been and that, after all, it was not something he had been strongly decided for in the first place. He had gone and he had seen and that was that.

Vivian, sitting across from him, shrugged. After a year of trying, of anxiety and duty, she would have to go along now with him as he was. He was sixty, voluntarily retired for a year now, ever since his wife Estelle had died, in one week, in a wretched spasm of sudden dying for which you cannot prepare, and from which kind of dying you cannot recover.

Abel Harnack buried his wife and then stopped. That was the only word for it, as if to permit himself to do anything at all again would be to accept again the world — his life, the possibility of life — as it had been. And that he would not do. He had too much decency for that, and besides, he learned things quickly. And what he had learned — quickly, in a week — was that all the assumptions of his life had been unquestioned, had simply been assumed the way a child assumes the universe: *post hos, proctor hoc*. But what he had learned was that nothing did or *did not* follow from anything at all. Not the seasons, not the tides, and least of all even the smallest aspirations of man.

So for a year now he had sat out, finally neither in anger nor in contemplation. He would not get caught by the old — by any — assumptions again.

"And for next week I want you to review all we've learned about first and second declension nouns and to study the declension of *bonus* in all its genders. And I want you to read and translate the first three stories in appendix a, which begins on page 280. Write out your translations, and remember, think of the principles involved."

After class, in the parking lot, he told her he would not be coming back to class.

"But why? You do so well. I'm surprised. You seemed to be enjoying yourself."

"*Bonus, bona, bonum?*" he asked her. "*Midas in magna regia habitabat?* I already know the story of King Midas."

"But this is just the start, just the beginning. Surely you understand that Latin isn't declensions. It's Vergil and Horace and Ovid. It's Catullus.

> *Vivamus, mea Lesbia, atque amemus,*
> *rumoresque senum seueriorum*
> *omnes uninus aestimemus assis.*
> *Soles occidere et redire possunt:*
> *nobis cum semel occidit breuis lux,*
> *nox est perpetua una dormienda.*

Do you know what that says?

> *Come, Lesbia, let us live and love,*
> *nor give a damn what sour old men say.*
> *The sun that sets may rise again*
> *but when our light has sunk into the earth,*
> *it is gone forever.*

Oh, no, Mr. Harnack. Declensions and exercises are just the beginning, the end is poetry."

Beginnings again.

It was the first week of October but summery yet. The lights defining the parking lot flickered through the still heavy pulsing screen of attracted insects like candles wavering in a slight breeze. The sound of Catullus lingered as if reverberating back from the night around them. Had she spoken, declaimed, so loudly? Were neighbors sitting now on darkened porches across Wilson Street listening to this woman cast Latin poetry at him, themselves listening to it hovering in the evening air? But of beginnings he had had enough.

"It's too far between King Midas and . . . and what you recited."

"Too far?"

"Too long. For me. I haven't time. I'm not so young a man."

"Perhaps you do. Perhaps you unconsciously remember much in your past that you think you've forgotten. It's all there, you know. The past."

He said nothing.

"Well, come on. Let me give you a ride home." She walked away from where they were standing and to her car. He did not follow.

"It's a nice night, thank you. I think I'll walk," he called over to her softly. He did not like this openness. Catullus blatant in the wide night, the talk of endings, of pasts and possibilities for all, for the air itself, to know.

"Oh come on, Mr. Harnack. I've lost students before. I don't take it personally. Don't you. Latin's not for everyone. Come on." She got into the car and waited. He came over quickly and got in. To be gone and done.

In front of his house she stopped and he got out.

"Thank you," he said.

"I hope you'll reconsider," Sylvia Warren said and waved and drove off.

He continued with Latin although he did not reconsider. It was his determination now, after a year, not to reconsider anything. He returned on the following Monday, his lessons prepared, his exercises neatly typed. He returned as if the effort of halting the small momentum of going on, slight as it was, would require of him energies he did not wish to ever use again. Now, after a year, he had started something about which he could not care, something about which there could be no purpose, no meaning or accountability. Above all, he would — must — avoid the traps of purpose. Latin was what he had come up with, an act too remote from him to count at all; an act that could not, would never, matter to him in the years, perhaps the decades, left. He did not particularly enjoy the Latin, but he would do it and he would not think about doing it again.

During the class the raining that had gone on all day thickened, drove down like a summer storm improbably late even for the warm October they had been having.

"*Cadens imber mari similis est*: The rain falls like the sea," she had stopped the class to say, gesturing at the windows. The rain came now in sheets so dense that the wind slapped them against the building, shaking it. At the end of class she called for him to come to her desk.

"I'm glad you decided to come back. Your work is really superlative." And then. "You'll certainly need a ride home on a night like this."

"I brought my car. Thank you."

She nodded and smiled and gathered up her books and papers into her briefcase and they walked out of the room together as the janitor came in to turn out the lights after them. From the doorway to the parking lot the rain made the darkness palpable.

"It's a bad night to drive in." Abel Harnack said.

"It can't rain this hard for long," she said. "It'll taper off." The class had gathered into a tight knot at the door wedged between the two darknesses.

"Well, here goes," Sylvia Warren said. She hunched herself over, her briefcase tight to her chest, and tucked her chin and sprinted to her car. They watched her, students now to her daring, but in ten feet they could not see her, the light from the lamps around the parking lot squeezed by the viscous rain back into the quavering globes. Then the others followed, four to one car, three to another, several to another, and Abel Harnack to his.

The cars started up and eased out slowly into Wilson Street. In the instant before he drove out, through a gap in the rain he saw her car, low and dead. He circled back into the lot and drove up next to her. Then he saw that she was out of the car with the right side of the hood up. She was bent into the engine with a flashlight. Her rain hat slipped back. He got out and walked around to her side.

"Damn thing," she said to him. The rain eased off for a moment, and then a moment more. "It's water somewhere. I'm getting short-ed out, but I can't tell where. Inside the distributor probably."

"Try and start it," he told her.. "I'll take a look."

After a minute or two he waved her out. "I think it's here." He pointed to an element fixed into the line leading to the coil. "This is a radio static suppressor."

"Yes, I know. I put it in."

"They're a bad business, I think." He pulled the plug apart and removed the suppressor and reconnected the heavy wires. "Try it now."

The car started at once.

"Thank you," she shouted out to him. She raced the engine, securing it, herself. "I'm sorry you got so wet. You'll have to explain it to me next week. Please, hurry in out of the rain." She pulled the door closed and turned on her driving lights. He opened the door before she could drive off.

"Wait," he said. "That connection is still too open. You might get it wet again in this weather before you got home. Stop at my house and I'll fix it right for you." He held his coat tight about his throat but he was already wet through.

"OK."

He drove slowly, keeping her watery headlights in his mirror. He turned into his driveway and pressed a button on his dash that opened the door to the large garage. She drove in after him into the space on the left and got out of the car and shook herself like a retriever.

"Well," she said looking about "This is certainly more than just a place to put a car."

Abel Harnack's garage was a workshop equipped to rebuild or mend whatever was. Or to create what was not. A large metal lathe with various milling heads, drill presses, band saws and bench saws, sanding drums, levering and bending devices, compression tools, testing equipment, oxy-acetylene and electric arc welders, racks and cabinets of wrenches, tap and die pieces, hammers, chisels, hydraulic jacks, lubrication guns and nozzles, a motorized hoist that ran on an overhead metal beam. In a corner, stacked up nearly to the roof, were dozens of small drawers like those in the oldest hardware stores where one of the objects in the drawer was tacked to the front: springs, nuts, bolts, shims, washers, wires, rods and stock until the mind could not comprehend the variety of pieces demanded by the mechanisms of manufactured life. From an overhead rack, belts and hoses and rubber and plastic fittings draped down like stalactites.

And everything in perfect array, spectacular as much for that lucidity, for the enormous accomplishment of arrangement, as for the objective demonstration that there existed so many things from which to make so many things.

"Mr. Harnack, whatever do you *do*?"

He had already lifted the hood and was at work sealing the connection, remaking it, in fact. In less than five minutes he was done.

"There," he said, pointing to it. "Better than new. You won't get stuck from that again. Your next trouble is going to come from here." He pointed to the gaskets beneath the double carburetors. He could have told her more about her car, everything perhaps. But he thought that he had gone too far already. He closed the hood and looked for her. She was still turning about in the marvel of the shop.

"I've never seen anything like it. Not even pictures or anything." She was wet and shivering but did not notice, still warmed by her discovery. Her hair was shining and flattened against her head, the ridges and notches of her bone structure clear and pronounced as the cold drew her skin tight to her skull.

"Would you like a cup of coffee?"

"Yes," she said turning to him now. "Thank you. That would be wonderful." She walked with him across the workshop to the doorway to the house. Instead of a doorknob or handle there was a square metal plate, brushed steel. She watched him run his finger in a design over the surface of the plate. The door opened. They walked into the warmer house.

"What are you, Mr. Harnack?" she asked as she followed him into the kitchen. "What magic is this?" She laughed in delight as children do at wonder, thrilled and unnerved at sorcery all at once. He had not heard her laughter before.

"Nothing," he said. "Retired." He said nothing more until he placed the coffee before her. Until then she looked about quietly at what she could see of the house from the kitchen through its two doors and over its counter into the dining room and living room. The house was as neat and clean as ice, like water poured into a mold and frozen and then left.

"My wife died about a year ago. A year last August."

"I'm sorry," Sylvia Warren said. And then there was nothing more to say, nothing more that she *could* say. She understood boundaries. She bent to her coffee.

But it was not such a boundary that Abel Harnack wanted to exist within. He wanted to erect no special defense because there are no such defenses, and he wanted nothing to defend, only to avoid, like the bitterness that had at first consumed him. In the staggering weeks after Estelle's death, after drowning and drowning, he had struck up into the thin air of life again. In a second life, only this time to be lived carefully balanced upon the interstices between events and attitudes, cautiously in the shifting spaces between the molecules of human concern. So he would talk to her in order *not* to care.

"I was an inventor of sorts. And a salesman."

"An inventor?" She put down her coffee cup.

"Yes. More a tinkerer, you might say. I understood how things worked and I figured out ways to make them work better. You'd be surprised. Sometimes just the slightest thickness of the metal in a gear or the gauge of a wire in a motor can make a big difference."

"I've never met an inventor before. I'm genuinely impressed. Whenever I think of an inventor I think of Thomas Edison." She raised her cup to him.

Her eyes were very young, sharp and quick, the whites blue with vigor. He did not want to look at them.

"I'm hardly an Edison," he said. "More a Mr. Fix-it. That's how I began, as a kid. By the time I started college I had a good business going, a real one. I was making enough to pay my way and then some. And it's what I came back to. Fixing things. And then small manufacturing. And then I got a little larger. And then larger. The usual story. I guess. After a while I had become a businessman instead of a mechanic, so I sold out so I could get back to things themselves. I took a job as a special kind of salesman. I'd go into highly technical production problems and help the engineers figure out what equipment and materials they needed and where they could get it. It was a great job for me. A little bit of everything going on, but deep too, if you see what I mean. And it left me with enough time for my own projects." He told her more about the work he had done for the industries and companies great and small and of the shape that his advice had helped to give to our material lives. He hadn't spoken so much to someone for a long time, excepting Vivian.

Sylvia Warren got up and went to the stove to make herself another cup of coffee. As she began to pour the hot water into the cup, she stopped. "I'm sorry," she said. "How presumptuous of me. You made me feel too comfortable."

"Oh please, help yourself. Go on, go on," he motioned to her to help herself.

But it was true. He had spoken more than he had thought to. He had intended a cup of coffee's worth of civility. Now she had bound him to a cup more. A slight tremor of refusal tickled through his legs, a memory from his more recent history of agony and rage when his body crashed about inside itself out of all control, his organs ripping themselves apart as directed by the hormones and enzymes of grief and confusion. But that had ended. When everything else had ended except the simplest activities of the life process itself, his body had come back to itself. Only sometimes, such as now, an old forgotten neuron would synapse, but it would soon subside, for there was no energy of special hope for it to subsist upon, for it to generate a potential for action: nothing got you nothing *either way*. In the dark night of his soul he had learned that, and it had saved him.

"Go on," he said to her. He was not a victim any longer.

She poured her coffee and came back to her seat, drier, softer, her color returning.

"How do you invent something? How do you do it? How do you think of what to invent? It seems so . . . so *mystical*."

"Not so mystical," he said. "All you do is think about something that somebody needs. Then you figure out how to make it."

"For instance?"

"Well, take a door lock, like the one you saw. People are always buying them, more now than ever. So there is your need. Then I figured out how to make one better than the others."

"Tell me. Tell me about the lock. How does it work?"

He took some paper from a drawer in the kitchen counter and drew diagrams to explain.

"You see, the metal plate is really quite flexible even if you can't see it is. And here, in back of the plate, are thousand of tubes. By putting fluid into some of the tubes you make a design. That's the key. When you trace the same design on the metal plate you put pressure on the harder tubes which then push down here." He indicated where on the diagram. "And from then on it works like a conventional lock with tumblers that shoot a bolt."

"That's marvelous," she said. "I'll bet you make a fortune with it."

"No," he said. "The psychology of it is wrong. People want a key they can hold in their hand, even for all the trouble it gives them. And there are other problems, like in a large family with little children who couldn't learn the design. Or suppose you wanted a friend or neighbor to come in while you were away, to water the plants or feed the fish? Instead of leaving the key under the doormat, you'd have to leave a drawing of the design." They laughed together.

"Oh my," Sylvia Warren said. "How disappointing. Did you think of all that when you invented the lock?"

"Oh yes," he said. "I've had a lot of experience with that sort of thing. But I wanted to do it. It interested me. And I did get a patent out of part of it, so I might make a little money from that."

Then he told her more about inventing. About the complicated process of a patent search and other legalities and about the cost, which surprised her ("Between one or two thousand, depending upon the complexity of the thing.") and about all the ways an inventor could go about trying to make while failing to make money. Then he told her about some of his successes, the little artifacts of his skill and imagination and knowledge of the world that had added up to a small place in the spectrum of invention, and to an income that had made it possible for him to stop.

"What next?" she asked at last, her own enthusiasms for such power over things taking over for him. But she had gone too far now for a certainty and could tell, though *how* she could tell, she could not tell, only that for Abel Harnack, his past did not predict his future. No longer. "Sorry," she said, faithful at least to her intuitions.

"What next?" He would answer her. *"Pericula belli non sunt* and the Future Indicative. What else?" Again they both laughed. She rose.

"You've been just splendid," she said. "About everything. The car, the coffee, everything." She slipped quickly, agile and firm, into her still damp coat. "An inventor," she said, flipping her hair over her collar. "I've never met one."

"I've never met a Latin teacher," he said.

"No comparison," she said, her mouth making a pretty gesture. "No comparison at all."

He almost said something.

She stood before the locked kitchen door.

"Open Sesame," she said to it and flung wide her arms and waited. "I guess I didn't say it right," she said to him.

"No, you didn't. Here." He reached to the side of the door and turned a switch and stepped back about six feet. "Open Sesame, or whatever your name is." The door snapped open. Sylvia Warren gave a little shriek. "It's a sound lock. Convenient in a kitchen when your hands are full."

Sylvia Warren awoke to the day bright and scoured by the cold front that had moved quickly through in the night. Autumn was firmly here now, and even some of earliest winter, though there would be weeks left to tramp about in the woods and fields. She got

out of bed and showered, made her small breakfast and, over her
second cup of coffee, opened her ledger to write in it and to consult the architecture of her day of her life.

Tuesday.

She would spend most of that morning correcting and comment-
ing on the papers from her Latin class and then preparing for the
following Monday. In the time left in the morning she would answer letters to friends, pay bills, make plans and lists. Tuesday. She
would go to the Books-Sandwiched-In program at the local library,
noon to one, and then on to the Triverton Nature Preserve where
she and Mildred Latham would beat through the late fields with
their nets and jars for insects to bring to the Biology Club meeting
later that evening. At six o'clock she would eat supper with Mildred
Latham as on Tuesday she always had. But before Tuesday quite
began officially, she wrote about the day and the night before.

She wrote quickly and exactly, more a record than an exam-
ination of events, something like a progress report, the way building contractors complete a day with an accumulation of data about
bricks laid and tons of cement poured and steel girders locked into
place, or as ship captains make log entries about wind and tides and
weather encountered, as if reality were only where we have been
and not where we might go, or want or intend to go. When she
arrived at Abel Harnack in her day, she wrote:

> *Abel Harnack, late 50's (?), widower, good health, extremely knowl-*
> *edgeable and intelligent, fixed my car in a driving rainstorm and then*
> *later at his house. An* inventor. *His workshop a cave of magic. He is*
> *restrained? Shy? Perhaps the death of his wife only a year ago?? What*
> *does he do with himself now that he is retired? How can a man who was*
> *an inventor retire? More to be explored here.*

She shut her ledger, dressed, and settled down at her desk, the
exploration of the *terra incognito* of Abel Harnack put aside for
now. She worked at the Latin exercises briskly. Besides pointing
out what was simply incorrect in a student's work, she explained
why in the margins and between the lines with little sharp indica-
tors, her comments, as much encouragement and exhortation as
corrective.

Sylvia Warren had taught Latin (and some French and a little
Spanish) for twenty-three years at the regional high school with

spirit and affection enough to have made the subject palatable and, finally, even attractive to those dwindling few who worked on past the grinding first year of declensions and conjugations into Caesar's *Commentaries* in the second and, ultimately, in the third years, into the sublimity of Cicero and the Poets and the difficult, silvery Tacitus. It was an odd, an anachronistic, thing to do, she would herself at times consider, this teaching of smooth old Latin in a world spikey and clattering about in the exciting newness of gleaming technology and movement in space and swift-breeding opportunity. She did not defend the Latin itself — for what defense could beauty have or need? But she was not about to accept uncritically the old banners under which the Association of Classical Language Teachers marched each year in thinning ranks at the annual convention: Latin is the Language of History, or, The Study of Latin is the Best Preparation for the Study of English.

No. She could not accept that, and never had. Latin wasn't a tool. Had it been, it might have survived. Latin was its own reward, but what it could promise in that way was no longer worth enough to the young. And she could understand that. Latin was, had become, irrelevant. And Sylvia Warren along with it. Her job, not her person.

She had taught long enough to retire if she chose, though she could have stayed on at the school teaching some French and taking up other chores such as an extra study hall or two. She was fifty-three then. Her pension would be smaller than if she had taught to the end of her possibilities, and she was years away from her social security income, but she had saved enough to balance things out nicely. She could afford to leave if she wanted.

But she did not want to, not exactly. She had come to the high school when she was twenty-nine and within a year she had clicked into place like a well-hung door closing evenly. Within a year she had found the friends and interests and functions that had not changed even to this moment, that had grown larger and deeper instead, rich as wine that ages well. If satisfaction was *in itself* one of life's true joys, then in her wide contentment she was there, and shared the sentiment with Horace in the *Epistles:*

Whatever prosperous hour Providence bestows upon you, receive it with a thankful hand: and defer not the enjoyment of the comforts of life.

So there were no sudden pleasures expected or gained, no longed for excursions to exotic places or into acts that would come to her once free of her daily work. In or out of the structures of the last twenty-three years, little would change.

But she did leave the job even so, as if that step, small as it was, altering her life as little as it would, would make up the difference that she had wondered at in the smallest degrees, in the quietest of ways from the beginning: that nothing more had come about in her life than what had.

It was a curiosity to her, this lost dimension, but not a sorrow, that all her life energy and intelligence, her capacity for experience, had carried her into one experience and then another and to the fluttery and imprecise edge of each into the penumbra where an experience bordered on the verge of becoming something else, something more that the experience, fulfilling as it was, did at last become. As with her painting.

Throughout her large apartment watercolors in double-matted, deep, silver-colored frames determined nearly every wall, every room: barns, seashore villages, fishermen from river banks, countrysides in all their seasons. The competency of each, of the whole, burst forth in a wave of illumination that promised to come, which did not come, and the pictures fell from the near pinnacle of vision down to the flat plains of skill. This was her own estimation, staunchly held through the wind of sweeping praise her friends blew upon her at her yearly show. She did not know how to paint the explosion that she felt in herself when she would work in the rapid light, racing the sun, the shadows surely coming. But she knew enough about what she could not do to accept no man's praise as though she had.

On one wall were her photographs, compositions as logical and controlled as if she had set a huge outdoor stage with perfect sets and actors. Light and dark knew what they were doing to the people moving through their lives before her lens. But then the pictures, dried and mounted, failed to alarm the viewer to the implicit dangers and predicaments of the human transactions they fixed, and instead of perception they became a glance. And Sylvia Warren would look at them and know that. And think that however firm were her trills in the Mozart piano sonatas that she played, the music fluttered into flight but never soared. How in tennis she could never trust her second serve, as certain as it was likely to be good. Nothing, nothing at all, ever went as far as it might have. As it should.

And she had not married. Nor known a man at all. And that had puzzled her more than everything else in her life. But it was not simple longing that she sat with, rarely, through a night. It was the waking urgency to truly know about those processes of life that sometimes inexplicably fail. She had always been attractive to men and was still. And if she had not courted them, neither had she built skittish barricades. At first, younger, she sought for reasons in herself, for the little alienating characteristics like talking too much or being too enthusiastic that she had read and heard and been warned about as a girl. But there were no reasons like that, nor any others. There were no reasons at all. Sometimes people to whom something is bound by every likelihood to happen are simply missed, like the one survivor in a massive air crash or the millionth customer who stops just before he enters the store to tie his shoe and falls from Grace.

So there was nothing to reason about. She had begun as she was and nothing came along to change it. Or end it. No one, she had corrected herself. Yes, she had thought, that's right. Maybe.

She was not afraid to think about herself directly, to examine and explore the crags and crevices of herself. She had lived alone with her good mind long enough to respect it, to not be frightened of it when it was insistent. It was in *not* thinking that there was danger. That was the trouble with old maids, old maid school teachers, she would point out to Mildred Latham. They were afraid to think and so they acted badly, especially with men, about whom they wished to think least, tripping themselves into the safety of the dreary old flighty stereotype or bristling with hearty self-sufficiency.

She had left her job in the school because she thought then that, allowing her energies to be completely loose, perhaps they would meld together, concentrate into a creative juggernaught that would storm the battlements and. . . . But nothing like that had happened. Only the old pleasures that filled her nearly to the brim.

Tuesday morning was concluded. Before she left the apartment she packed a small knapsack with the rough clothes and her field boots that she would change into in the afternoon.

"Do you know how long I've looked for this, for *Vendalia tarda*," Mildred Latham said, shaking one of the five cotton-stoppered test tubes at Sylvia Warren. "And now to find it, in *October* of all times. In plentitudes. Eggs as well." A short, heavy but soft woman, she bounced about in her kitchen like a semi-inflated beach ball, bounding off in unpredictable directions. "Just listen to this," she came back to the table. She read from a copy of *The Entemological Review* splayed across the kitchen table, supper gone awry.

Vendalia tarda, although not considered a truly rare species within the Coleoptera, is yet uncommon even within its natural range, which, in the United States, is mainly southern. V. tarda is seldom found above the thirty-second parallel in the eastern states, the thirty-third parallel west of the Appalachians to the Rockies. It is not yet discovered in the western coastal region.

The uncommonness of V. tarda in its own range and its only seldom and accidental appearance north of its range are accounted for by the insect's highly selective necessity for light and temperature, specific conditions to occur not only once, but twice for the insect's passage from egg to larva to pupa to adult. This condition of quadruple diapause in V. tarda is nearly unique among insects. Apparently the quadruple diapause condition is continuous throughout the life cycle, and it is not unusual for four or five years to pass between the laying of the egg to the development of an adult insect able to lay another egg. And longer periods have been recorded (Bornstein).

Mildred read to her more from the article and explained. "You see, the creature has to pass up through and then down through the same light/temperature ration for each of the four stages — egg, larva, pupa, adult. It has got to be, say, thirty degrees on a twelve hours of light day as the egg goes into winter and then the same after winter as the egg moves into spring and hatches. And listen to this." She read on.

It is unfortunate that this apparently disadvantageous life cycle limits the numerical size of the species, for V. tarda is extremely destructive of not one but five prey insects, all pests. The range of V. tarda's appetite seems clearly to be a consequence of its necessity to develop in such specific stages, thus making certain that food will be available to the insect at widely divergent times within the more normal and limited insect "year."

She read on. About the difficulty of raising the insects in the laboratory because of the complex double cycles involved in the four stages.

The length of time that would be required to work out the possible light temperature permutations would exceed the endurance (and resources) of even the most dedicated entemologist. The very few recorded successes in the raising of V. tarda *have been accounted for more by chance than by knowledge.*

Mildred slapped her hand down on the journal page. "It's just wonderful," she said. *"Vendalia tarda."*

"Slow to live," Sylvia Warren translated.

"Yes, 'slow to live.'" Mildred Latham stood up from the table. "I've killed and pinned six of them for tonight's meeting. A special event, you might say. And I'm taking about a dozen to Dr. Alberts at the University tomorrow. I'll drive down in the morning. Do you want to come?" She rushed on. "I'm keeping the others to see what I can do with them. And I'll check what's going on at Triverton until I can't find them any longer."

"What can you do with them?" Sylvia Warren asked. "What do you mean?"

"Breed them. Try to raise them. Take my shot at it. After all, I've never had these critters to work on. Let it be my turn to fail. Come on now, eat up. We don't want to be late for the meeting."

"Eat up what?" Sylvia Warren asked. Within the scattered paraphernalia of their afternoon — killing jars, bottles and vials, magnifiers, aspirators, nets — here and there poked up lumps of cheese, curls of torn bread, a can of sardines, an onion started and forgotten, cups of tea gone cold.

"Yes," Mildred Lathan said. "I see. I'll tell you what, old Warren. I'll buy you a hamburger later."

In the car on the way to the meeting she explained to Sylvia Warren more about the problems of breeding *Vendalia tarda,* the elaborate devices she would have to imagine and build, the special habitats she must create and control, the exact regulators. "I haven't got a chance," she gaily granted. "Even if I knew just exactly what to do, I couldn't manage it for sure. I was always a field person, never good with complicated lab arrangements, and such. I've bred plenty of insects, but this is going to be something different, more exploring than doing. But what the hell." They drove on.

By the first traffic light, Sylvia Warren had decided that maybe Abel Harnack *could* manage it for sure.

Wednesday.

Wednesday was the luxury of a morning uncommitted, neither to nothing nor to something, the half day of rest in her week, the pause for breath before the rush into the heightening weekend. She was free until one o'clock when she would go to the Y for an afternoon of yoga and swimming and the steam room and the dry sauna; free before Wednesday evening when she would play piano in a trio of old friends. But at eight-thirty she called Abel Harnack and explained as best she could.

"So you see," she concluded, "what she needs is some way to make . . . to make time equal light and . . . and both to equal temperature. Sort of. But look, I'm doing a terrible job of explaining this diapause thing, and the experiment. Perhaps if you could meet Mildred Latham and have her explain the problem, I'm sure it would all be clearer than it is now."

But he said no.

Sylvia Warren recovered and apologized and said goodbye.

In the basement of Abel Harnack's house, in nearly half of it, rested a cat's cradle of various sized wires, knitted and woven, spliced and soldered together into an intricacy too complicated for the eye to comprehend, only that at the moment it all might blur into a meaningless tangle, it did not; it held, instead, taut as sculpture, which it might have been. But it was a machine. An attempt that Abel Harnack had worked upon for years in time he tucked in between his job and his family and his more practical devices. What he wanted to do with this machine was to take an electrical charge and by amplifying it and modulating it in exquisitely calculated increments, make the charge go on endlessly, inexhaustibly under its own power.

"It's what inventors come to sooner or later"; he tried to describe to Estelle what he was doing. "But you see," he had told her, "energy is what we are all about. From the sun to a can opener. It's what we are always working with." Estelle would nod and go on cooking. She did not understand the details of what her husband did. All she understood was him. Which had been enough for both. Still, he would tell her at length the history of the search for the grail of perpetual motion: who had tried what and why it always failed. The mistake of the past was to use materials, which would wear out, which friction would destroy, to use gears and levers that took as much energy to move as the energy that they would try to continue to produce. But he would not use material that way. He would use the electron's energy itself to continue to produce itself.

A year ago he had come to where he could keep a small charge alive within his mechanism for twelve hours before his meters read out for him the slow and then quickening dissolution. On his way home from work that day he knew what he could do to gain two hours more. Even before supper he could make the modification that he had figured in and out of all through that afternoon. But when he opened his door, Estelle was gone. Vivian was there instead.

"Dad," she said. "I tried to reach you." And told him.

He had come home from work one day prepared to gain a centimeter against the universe. He found Estelle gone. She had dropped into the hospital and he had never seen her, as Estelle, again. And there was nothing he could do to help her, nor himself, not even the smallest thing: his voice beside her, the pressure of his hand. There was nothing he could do to help her. And if he could do nothing about that, then he would do nothing at all, ever again. He had raised his fists against the colossal outrage of the vulgarity of her dying that stripped her of the basest dignity and crushed her, smeared her like a swatted fly against a window pane. He shrieked against the badly designed and uncorrectable device called life. And then held still, free now forever from the obscenity of creation.

In class Sylvia Warren said, "But enough of the difficulties of the Imperfect Indicative. Let's spend our remaining time with some poetry." For over an hour and a half she had gone over last week's exercises, through the new lessons, and then had prepared them for the work they would do in the week coming. "Now just sit back and listen to this. Don't worry if you understand it. You probably won't understand it except for a word or a phrase here or there. Just try it get the sound into your head. Each week we'll do a little more of this and you'll be surprised how much it will help you. And what pleasure it will come to be." She read to them from the *Aeneid* and then translated.

"And now, *molliter cubes*. Good night," she said to them.

"Good night. *Vale*," the class said back. Then rose and, piece by piece, left.

"Mr. Harnack," she said to him as he passed her desk. He stopped and turned to her. "I'm sorry about the other morning.

That was presumptuous of me. *Mea culpa*," she smiled, open, clean. "I certainly must appear to be a presumptuous person to you, though I am not. I really respect . . . boundaries." It wasn't the word she wanted, but it was all that came to her. "Anyway, I'm sorry." She held out her hand to shake on it. He took her hand.

"No need for that," he said. "I wasn't offended." They let go of each other. He walked to the door. And then he turned. He did not need to tell her more, but he did not want to make a point of that either. "I just don't get involved in projects," he said.

"Could I ask you for some information, then?" she said.

"Sure," he said and walked back to the desk.

"Could you tell us where we could find someone to design the equipment my friend needs?

"Tell me again what she is doing."

When she had finished telling him, he took a piece of paper from his notebook and made a series of sketches, precise as drafting, sharply defining the problem.

"What she wants to do is this." He explained the drawings to Sylvia Warren pointing to diagrammatic objects where she had given him Mildred Latham's ideas. "And this is a list of what she'll need." He made some quick calculations and then wrote. With small numbers in circles, he coded each item in the list to its place in the drawings. On the bottom of the page he wrote an address of a New York City firm. "Tell your friend to say in her order that I asked she get a professional discount."

"This is marvelous of you," Sylvia Warren said. "You've made it so . . . so *tangible*. We really can't thank you enough. Mildred will be boundless in her thanks. Just wait till you meet. . . ." But she stopped. "Sorry. Thank you. I mean thank you very much."

"You're welcome," he said. "I'm glad I could help. I used to do this for a living. Well, *molliter cubes.*"

What he had rejected when she had telephoned him was his own old assumption that he would do something because he could do it. But even more he had rejected her passionate investment in Mildred Latham's scheme, the implicit invitation for him to join, for he knew well the sound of endeavor and the enticement to contend for form, and of such investments he would have no part. If it was an odd job that she wanted done, that was OK; she was a decent sort; he would help her out. Fix a car, learn Latin, rig up some thermocouples to a few clockwork gears and timers — there was no danger in that. He drove home, the nights cold enough now for him not to want to walk in them.

The following week she spoke to him after class about a problem in the wiring. She described what she and Mildred Latham had done during the week. Too anxious to wait, Mildred Latham had driven down to New York and back the same day. They had built as closely as they could to his plan, and when at last they turned on the lamps, after about five minutes the meter reading would go up continually to dangerously high levels. Everything else seemed to work. Only the light and heat lamps seemed out of control. They could not work out the problem.

"Are you sure you've got a resistor here?" He pointed to where.

"Yes. Definitely. We double checked. We figured that somewhere we must be making a circuit around that resistor. And yet there must be some resistance somewhere. That's why it takes five minutes before it starts to climb. The current is building. We thought we might be shorting through this little chassis here with the switches on it. But that's as far as we could go."

"I'm impressed," he said. "You know about electrical circuits."

"Not much. Only a little. Mildred's worked with lab equipment somewhat. And me, oh I've tried practically everything."

"Well, I'm still impressed that you know as much as you do."

She waited.

"Will you help us out?"

"Yes," he said. "I'm obliged to now. If what you say is right, then the fault is my design, and I can't leave you hanging on that kind of problem. There would be no way for you to fix it. When do you want me to look at it?"

"What's good for you?"

"I'm a free man. The sooner the better I'd guess if you're doing an experiment with living things. Tomorrow morning? Eight-thirty? I know you're up by eight-thirty."

"Tuesday?"

"Is that not good?" He had heard her patterns speak sooner than she did herself, but she heard them too.

"Tuesday will be just fine," she said firmly. "Eight-thirty. Here's the address." She bent to the desk to write it. "We'll throw in breakfast. How's that?"

"I'll have eaten by then," he said. "But thank you."

He came exactly at eight-thirty and started to work at once. He

set up his testing meter and traced through the entire circuit, probing delicately from connection to connection, sometimes stopping
to write numbers down. The two women watched him silently.
After twenty minutes he said, "Here's the problem." He touched
the glass encased recording thermometer. "The safety fuse in here
is larger than I figured. It's pushing current back across here." He
ran his finger along the wire to where. "I'll have it fixed in no time."
He opened the square black case he had carried in and took from it
a soldering gun, some additional tools, and a different resistor and
made the repair. In two minutes he was finished. "Try it now."

Mildred Latham turned the switch, the lamps came on, the meter
needle rose and held. For five and then ten minutes he continued
to test the circuitry.

"You're in business," he said, turning to look at them at last. The
women gave a little cheer.

"May I offer you a cup of coffee, Mr. Harnack?" Mildred Latham said. "At the very least."

"Why yes, Miss Latham. I think I would like a cup of coffee
now."

They sat in the parlor of Mildred Latham's house drinking their
coffee. She placed a dish of fine, thin cookies near him, but he ate
none.

"It's not unlike being a doctor," Sylvia Warren said. "You've even
got the little black bag for it. An electronic stethescope. A thermometer. Instruments. Medicine called resistors and capacitors and
what not. It's a good analogy. Dr. Harnack, you just made a house
call and the patient is doing fine."

Abel Harnack looked down into his coffee, examining it so that
he would not have to look up at her. The women looked across at
each other blankly.

"I think you'd be very interested in insects, Mr. Harnack," Mildred Latham said. Whatever they had suddenly accidentally gone
into for whatever reasons, Mildred Latham knew to try to take
them somewhere else. "They're a lot like machines, like mechanisms," she pushed at him. "No personality. There's nothing you
can love in an insect, only think about." Her voice rose a pitch.
What had happened? "Their attractiveness is abstract, if you see
what I mean, not like with mammals or even birds. It's too easy to
slip into *liking* mammals and birds, too easy to start caring about
what happens to them. Not so with insects." She looked quickly at

Sylvia Warren, stricken. "Insects are fascinating not because of
what they might do, they're too perfectly predictable for that, but
because of how they work, like beautiful chess games, I suppose, or
more like elegant watches."

Abel Harnack looked down deeper into his cup. They were all
sliding down. Mildred Latham, bewildered, struggling to pull them
out, knocked them further in.

"Yes," she went on, "I'd think they would appeal to someone with
your analytical skills and interests. Do you know why some insects
can move their wings so quickly?" She started to explain. "There's
what amounts to a spring in. . . ."

"I'm too busy," Abel Harnack said sharply, looking up, like waking up, interrupting her. Then, quietly, "My head is too full of
Latin these days." He stood. "I'll check the circuits." He walked
quickly away from them through the house to the rear room where
the experiment had been established. Five minutes later the
women followed him. He was working.

"I'm making some changes," he said. "Nothing much. I'll be
through soon." In fifteen minutes more he packed up and said
goodbye and left.

*Diapause is a means for surviving adverse seasons. It is a method in
which the insect enters a state of dormancy, in which all growth changes
cease and metabolism falls to a very low ebb, only just sufficient to keep
the body alive, so that any reserves of food that are available may last for
an extremely long time. This dormant state, or 'diapause,' may supervene
at any stage in the life history of an insect: in the egg, in the young or in
the full-grown larva, in the pupa, and even in the adult — where the
arrest of growth means the cessation of reproduction. It is not uncommon
for diapause to persist for more than one season, and for a pupa to lie
over two or three years before it completes its development and emerges.
But the record is probably held by* Stiodiplosis mosellana, *one of the
wheat blossom gall midges (Cecidomidae), which passes the winter as a
full-grown larva in a cocoon in the soil. In this midge dormancy has
persisted for as long as eighteen years, and yet in the end the larva has
been able to pupate and emerge.*

". . . and yet, in the end the larva has been able to pupate and
emerge." He reread the line. He could hardly believe it.

Halfway home from Mildred Latham's he had turned and driven

back the other way to the library. She had spoken of the perfect predictability of insects, used those exact words. Was it just an expression or did she mean exactly that? She was knowledgeable about these things certainly, but could she have meant precisely what she said, the "perfect predictability" of insects? Now he wanted to find out. He had not felt this importance to know something for a long time. For Abel Harnack *a long time* had come to mean *since before*.

In the library he began with the Encyclopedia Britannica for general information and then had moved on to more complete texts. He browsed about in them and then settled on *The Life of Insects*. He read the first two chapters and then turned to the index to find "diapause." That was what she was experimenting with. Incredible. He shut the book and rose from the table to take it and the two others to the checkout desk. And then they were there again, the two women together as he had left them that morning.

"Why, Mr. Harnack," Sylvia Warren said. "How soon our paths cross." And then she wanted to take it back, to unsay the playfulness; he was not a playful man and she forced him and that was no good. Mildred Latham stood by and examined his books.

"Insects," he said to them, holding the books up. "You made me curious about some things about them."

"Wonderful," she said. "Let me help you learn about them whenever you need help." He nodded.

"We're here for the Books-Sandwiched-In Program. Every Tuesday at noon," Sylvia Warren said. Absurdly, she wanted him to know that he wasn't being followed.

"Have a nice time," he said and nodded again and walked past them to the checkout desk. He did not care why they were in the library. He had taken a leap he could not have imagined three hours before. Now his mind was elsewhere, closing in. Closing down.

And the winter came on.

Through it Abel Harnack stayed diligently at work upon his Latin, moving comfortably from the ablative absolute through the passive periphrastic to the declension of comparatives to such esoteric elements as the conjugation of *Eo* and the constructions of place and time. His vocabulary grew. The system of the language pleased him. And little by little, through what they studied, through what Sylvia Warren would read to them and explain, he came to a feeling of the Latin tone and style of mind, the stoical and heroic or vicious and yet always urban Latin of the Golden Age and beyond. And, so far as he would ever go into such things, he came to a feeling, limited and tentative, for the vast and tumultuous whirligig of ambitions and acts that the Latin language had shaped and was shaped by. Cicero on the nature of Friendship, Horace longing for the simple country life on his Sabine farm, what Pliny thought of the races, Vergil creating a history.

From the greatest to the smallest concerns of the nation or of all humanity, from the most angry denunciations to the most outrageous flattery and groveling, a profound decorum permeated it all, a sensibility to order that resonated in the culture even when there was no order, only the persisting, fading dream of it, the pretense to it, to order that contained the violence of the heart.

For Abel Harnack the ordering of insects was altogether different but more fascinating and better understood. The more he read about them, the more he came to be convinced that the life of insects had achieved the perpetuation of energy in the only way it could ever be achieved. He had been on the right track with his wire net of a machine down in the basement after all, the idea that energy could only be endlessly preserved at its most fundamental and therefore efficient level, but his machine, as simple as it was, was still material first and last, and even if it took a million years, the copper and the tin and the silver would oxidize away back into primary electrons.

Only the insects were perfect, going on in an unending transmogrification of material at whatever pace was possible, like passionless molecules in a chemical formula, the elements of the insects unalterably attached into larger structures as precisely fixed as ions in a bond, as atoms of oxygen in a carbon ring. And even the parts were not necessary to watch each other, so ants could work without abdomens and mantises conspire without heads. Blinded, limbless, the insects could go on. And insects could freeze into crystals and thaw and be insects again.

Abel Harnack saw that the insects, incapable of comprehension or choice, were uninvolved in their fate and thereby had no fate, only function. And he thrilled to see such perfection in the universe, to see that what was prevented to humankind was not prevented in itself, that the dream of endless motion was possible, was already possible, though the price was everything else. And most thrilling of all to him was the diapause, where the insect lost even its own necessity and became an extension, a bloom, of the sun itself.

He read deeply about the insects through the winter but he did not talk much about them to Mildred Latham on the occasions when they met. He listened to her, and he asked questions. But he did not offer. There was an important crossing point that he did not want to have to meet with her or with anyone. She had meant that the insects were machine-*like*. He meant that they were machines. They did not even always need sex to reproduce.

The winter went on. He continued in his new ways but in his old ways as well. The same hours, the same patterns. Many days he would visit Vivian in the morning unless the weather was too fierce to battle. Once a week he would eat with her family. She was pleased that he was active again.

"You're looking good," Vivian said to him.

"My health is fine. I walk a lot most every day if I can. I get enough sleep. I'm fine."

"That Latin must agree with you," she said. Charles was in the t.v. room watching the news. The children thudded about upstairs. Vivian sat with her father in the kitchen, the dinner dishes stacked, the counter and stove already clean and ready for tomorrow.

"It's OK," he said. "I'm learning it."

"And the teacher? What's her name?"

"Miss Warren. Sylvia Warren."

"Yes. What about her?"

"What do you mean?"

"How are you getting on with her?" Vivian looked at him.

"What are you thinking?" her father asked.

"You know what I'm thinking."

"Well, don't," he said. "We're hardly acquainted, hardly even friendly."

"I've seen her. She's not bad looking."

"Stop it, Vivian."

"It's nothing so terrible, you know," she pushed on past him, her voice rising with old impatience and new hope. "You're not an old man." She waited for him, prepared to duel, to fight him *for* him. The past was buried; he had a lot of future to think about. But he said nothing. "She's not an old woman." He would not answer her. At last she stood up from the table and walked around the kitchen picking at it, nervous and irritable at his refusal.

"You think you know so much about life," he said to her. "But all you really know about is man and woman, husband and wife."

"Maybe," she agreed. "Maybe that *is* all I know about life. And maybe that's *all* there is."

"*Less,*" he said, sudden, startlingly, and stood up quickly, stretched to his full height, as if his truth had pulled him up. "*Less,*" he shouted. Then he stooped and kissed her on the forehead. He went through the house and said goodbye to the children and to Charles and went home, above vicissitudes.

The winter deepened. The earth froze and then the sky froze, landscapes and people hunched up, tight and limited, compressed.

About every two weeks he would get a telephone call or a letter beckoning him back to work. Even after a year the offers and the requests continued. His skills had been special, even rare, and so he had continued to be remembered. Sometimes, now, he would give a day or two to the technical problems of old friends, but he knew what limits were, and stayed within them.

In January he signed up for the second semester of the Latin course. The original class of eleven had shrunk to eight by the end of the first semester and now, only five, including himself, had signed up to go on. Five was the minimum. With fewer than five students, the course could not be offered in the extension college curriculum. But he did not sign up as a favor to her. Latin had come to serve him in a way that he had wanted, and if there had been no greater reason to begin than that, then there was now no greater reason to stop.

He won a judgment against General Electric in a patent infringement suit that he had begun five years before. He put the sizeable settlement into a common savings account and left it alone.

The storms turned February thick, the snow wet and heavy. Once when a major transmission line went down, he battered his way to Mildred Latham's with a small, powerful generator and hooked it into her house system so that the light and the heat for *Vendalia tarda* would not go out.

He went on. His days — decorous, predictable — filled up. He had come so very far from a year ago to this sublime calm that he could dare to test himself against memory. Cautiously he would open the door to his empty house that day, to Estelle gone, and would wait for the wave that once had tumbled and suffocated him in the bitter surf of chaos to burst against the clever bulwark he had devised. He would feel the power of the wave on the other side strain and shudder and subside, die and recede. If in his life any longer there was such a thing as pleasure, *that* was pleasure.

At the very end of February after class, before leaving the building, he stopped at the "Boys" room. The sign was still the first one, blue lettering on white porcelain, mounted on the door when the school had been built forty years earlier. Vivian had gone to this school. His grandchildren went here now. Outside the wind blew across the parking lot not quickly nor strongly but with steady pressure, weakening slowly what it pushed against rather than knocking it down. The snow had melted and frozen and melted and frozen into a moon terrain, ripped, pocked, sharp-ridged and uneroded. Nearly to his car, he saw dimly Sylvia Warren on her knees by hers. Her arms were extended forward, her hands flat against the rough ice, her forehead resting against her car door.

He labored through the wind to her.

"Miss Warren," he shouted. She looked up.

"I must have fallen. The footing is treacherous." She looked to him as if she were resting, her eyes quiet. He waited for her to get up, but she stayed.

"Let me help you." He bent to her and took her under her arms.

"Yes," she said, "Please. I'm having trouble." Then she was standing. She had cut her knees.

"Are you all right?"

"A little shaken." She opened the car door and he helped her in.

"Are you sure? Do you want me to drive you home? You could get your car tomorrow."

"No," she said. "It was just a fall."

"He's a very nice man," Mildred Latham said. "He's certainly intelligent. He's quiet, but he's got keen insight. And he's gentle. That's always a good sign."

"A good sign of what?" Sylvia Warren asked her. They were in her apartment. Barely audible Bach floated about, the volume of the sound inappropriate for the size of the music. "For a proper husband? Do you mean, Mildred, that you're still thinking about getting married?"

"Me?" Mildred Latham actually shouted. "Me? *You.*" But Sylvia Warren was laughing; of course she understood that Mildred Latham had meant her then and had meant her for nearly twenty-five years.

"You're still trying to get me married."

"It's not that, really. We've talked about that. It's just that I can still never understand why you never did. You're so attractive." She trailed off into the Bach.

"I'm not about to change my life, Mildred. Or have it changed. It works pretty well as it is. And don't you do anything to make Abel Harnack nervous. He doesn't want involvements. I told you about him. He's a specially nice person to be with. Just leave it at that."

"I wasn't going to *do* anything, Sylvia. I'm not a fool or a child."

But the subject was closed. Sylvia Warren got up to make them both some tea. Once she had tried in an act of disciplined imagining to picture her life differently, but what would it mean to be a wife? A wife to Abel Harnack? The idea was vacant, empty. The vision of it impossible to form, the thought itself wrong, a disvaluing of themselves as they were. They were, all three, becoming good friends. Even if — *if* — life could have offered more, it did not *require* more. And she would not relinquish herself into new passions, whether offered or not. She enjoyed Abel Harnack's interestingness; she enjoyed the civility of their union. It was enough. Another pleasure.

By the beginning of April the experiment with *Vendalia tarda* had failed. The eggs had not hatched; they had not been brought out of diapause.

"But the eggs are still alive, aren't they?" Abel Harnack said. "Maybe they are going to skip a year or even two."

"Then what do you propose, that we just let the experiment go on?" Mildred Latham walked slowly about the caged eggs, still shining ticks of matter, inert but glowing, undetermined yet. "For another year. Or another and another. Then leave the whole contraption to the university after we're all gone?" She flung her hand over the apparatus wiping it out, her disappointment blurring it like a damp rag.

"Yes," Abel Harnack said.

He had come to supper with them. Again. The suppers they had begun to share had gone well, the talk always about Latin and about insects, photography and travel and about the measurable nature of things — how an electron microscope worked, why plastic took its shape, the use that windmills could have, the distance to stars.

"Our own Royal Society," Sylvia Warren had called them, even just that evening, even with the failure of *V. tarda*. Now, supper complete, coffee finished, they stood in the back room of Mildred Latham's house.

"I haven't the heart for it," she said. "Nor the patience. And Spring is here. Nearly." She put her arm across Sylvia Warren's shoulders. "Me and Warren here have to get out in the field where we belong. I want to see what *is* hatching from the eggs, not keep on looking at what isn't."

"What will we do with them?" he asked.

"Put them back where I found them, if you like. Would you like that? Come along with us next Tuesday to Triverton and we'll show you."

He agreed.

The natural world of Triverton, the varying terrain of streams and bogs, upland meadows and woods blending from pines to hardwoods, was as unknown to Abel Harnack as an automobile engine might be to most others. One knew *about* meadows and bogs as one knew *about* engines, which was not the same as knowing a thing in itself, the way Abel Harnack could picture actual steel-hot valves opening and closing and the oily black rocker arms compressing and releasing; or the way Mildred Latham would vision the translucent apical cells at the root tip of the skunk cabbage dividing and expanding down into the grainy earth. But here, where the life of things was objectifying fact, where the network, not the element, was the reality, he had never been. Now, late, he had come to a new boundary.

Bloodroot, hepatica, fiddleheads, the lance-sharp buds of beech, the crusted egg cases of the mantises, fungi fruiting under the powdery bark of rotten trees, tiny mosses greening up, a kestrel darting through the trees, a rare shrew, water-striders already dimpling the quieter waters. But it was too late for him to know this world as they did, like an elixir, like a potion. He watched them as they ranged widely ahead of him, tracking wonder; the older, heavy woman, the younger woman firm, lithe, and effective. From where he watched them, she looked like a young girl, prancy and excited. Both of them did, that day, the place transfiguring them.

"Mr. Harnack," Sylvia Warren called back to him. "Come and see this." Mildred Latham was bent down into the grass. As he approached she stood up with a small snake in her hand. She grasped it behind the head and with her other hand held it by the tail and extended it.

"*Thamnophis ordinatus*," she announced. "The common garter snake. Are you familiar with this?"

"No, I'm afraid not. This is out of my world."

"It's a beautiful thing, a snake. So you see here on the belly, where the single scales stop and the double scales begin? That's the start of the tail." She told him more about snakes, about the musk gland under the anal scale, about the Jacobson glands in the head that sensed heat, that most snakes were born from eggs, but that *Thamnophis ordinatus* was born live like man. She dropped the snake gently and it disappeared with a soft snap into the grasses. For a moment they all three looked at one another. The sun intensified, the slight breeze rustling the still winter-dry fields. Crows called distantly. The scent of the loosening earth rose all around them like a fume. "I am deeply moved by all of this," Mildred Latham said. Her eyes glistened. Sylvia Warren took her arm and moved off with her.

The day darkened quickly as only April can, going from a bright blue glory to a dirty squall gray. The first light mist of rain caught them far from where they had parked the car, and far from each other. The women waved him to them. When he got to them they hurried him into the woods to an enormous green-black spruce. They lifted the lower branches up from the ground like lifting the hem of a floor-length dress.

"Go in," Mildred Latham said to him. He got to his knees and crawled in and they followed. Inside the heavy smell of the spruce was dazing at first, then liquidy, like breathing under water. Inside it was dark, but light enough came through the infinite hatchwork of the needles. The rain increased, but they were dry. Years of soft brown spruce needles cushioned them.

"It was time to eat anyway," Mildred Latham said. She took from her knapsack a thermos of coffee and a package of thick ham sandwiches on dark bread. "I'm glad for the rain. I love this, getting under this tree, eating here safe from the weather, safe from everything. But you need the rain to make it count, so to speak." She passed around the sandwiches and the cupful of coffee. They

ate and spoke a little about their day so far: the extremely early
wood duck they had seen, the witch hazel scrub tree that had not
cast its seed before the winter, the wild ginger already well started.
The year was coming quickly.

"Well, Mr. Harnack, what do you think?" Sylvia Warren asked
him.

"It's all very pleasant, Miss Warren. And quite a new experience
for me."

"It's always going on," Mildred Latham said. "Winter, spring,
summer, fall." She finished the cup of coffee and poured another
and handed it to him. And then she said. "I could stay here. On
days like this. And other days. I feel like I could stay here forever.
Just set up under this spruce and go on until I died here."

"Yes," Sylvia Warren said. "I've had that feeling. Here. But other
places too. And sometimes, when I'm painting. Or playing music.
Or reading Vergil." She laughed. He was startled. Her laughter,
always so soft and easy, echoed in his head now, sharply, like a
volley of sound shot into him. It was as if he had been told a great
and shocking intimate secret, as though what she had told him was
safe with him, would not matter though told to a man whom nothing would ever matter to again.

He did not know what to say or that he could say anything. He
understood what the women meant but there was nothing in his
own life he could gauge it by — except Estelle, shook through him,
and that he would not do.

He raised the thermos cup of coffee to his mouth and then, like
an attack, he jerked and the coffee spilled. Time sagged. The
spilled coffee fell as slow as life itself, a languid cascading moment,
time enough to think of everything before the liquid hit his knee.
Time to understand that he had built his life again upon defense
after all, but that there were gigantic subterranean waves of memory too strong for any barrier. He had betrayed himself. In the
sudden discovery that the fortifications are breeched, the enemy
streaming through the jagged rent, the mind twangs between panic
or act, and the decision made in the moment is the decision, clearly
understood or not, from which all the decisions ever after must
come.

So too had he once shared in the profound, harrowing, and
wordless condition of love, the boundless and shapeless, measure-
less condition which is not chaos though it cannot be formed. In

which he too would have chosen to stay forever and had, unlike
these women, thought he would stay.

Why had he come here with them? What had they had to lose, or
not to lose? He should not have come here with them into this place
of contagion in which there was no safety at all, only the dangerous
belief that there was.

"Oh," Sylvia Warren said as the coffee hit his knee. It quickly
soaked through to his skin but the heat was out of it. His spasm had
passed. He handed her the cup. She drank from it. They finished
eating and the weather changed back as Mildred Latham predicted. Following the women, he crawled out of the spruce shelter
into the cleared, April blue day with all his old vulnerabilities once
again intact.

"As you know," she said to the class, "I do not give a final exam.
Your grade will be based upon the work you have done through
the semester." She went quickly on. "This has been a very pleasant
year for me and I hope as pleasant for you. We have gotten to
know each other rather well through this school year, and we've
gotten to know a lot of Latin. I'm really proud of you. You've done
splendidly." She went on with the small valedictory. "I wish that
you would continue. Do not stop now, here at the beginning of this
great adventure. Perhaps over the summer or next year you will
find a means to go further."

He sat forward. She was saying something more than the words.

"I conclude with this from Marcus Aurelius." She gave them the
Latin as usual, and then translated: "Then depart at peace with all
men, for he who bids thee go is at peace with thee."

"*Vale*," she said and left before more than that could be said.

He had at first promised wildly that he would sever himself from
the women and from Triverton. He would see them no more and
he would not come back. But he did neither.

To refuse to meet with them upon the terms they had established
was pointless. He was interested in their knowledge and in their
friendship, in their companionship. They were fine people. They
had taught him much. He could not allow himself to flee from
goodness. For if he started to run, he would never stop and the old
terror would return and this time there could be nothing that
would stop it. He would go on about his life as he had come to live it

since Estelle's death, only now the anger that had been reborn under the great sheltering spruce he would accommodate. The truce he had arranged was his mistake. There could be no truce while the battle still raged and wounded. He would continue to see Sylvia Warren and Mildred Latham as the occasions arose.

And he did go back to Triverton. They had taught him that. He returned often. Sometimes with them, sometimes with the nature study groups that were conducted there in the summer. And sometimes alone. As now.

He could see them down in the glade of the hill he was sitting on. Mildred Latham was beating through the weeds and grasses with the heavier net in a general sweeping for anything that would tumble her way. Sylvia Warren worked with the lighter net flicking after butterflies or other insects she might spot in flight. They moved slowly through the large field. Even from where he sat he could tell that they were talking to each other, laughing and touching, giggling like animated school girls, transfiguring gaiety turning them childlike.

Her blouse was as yellow as the thick golden rod and the heavy late daisies. Her gray hair had lightened through the summer in the sun, white and mirror-like. He watched their progress, the rhythmic beating of Mildred Latham's net, the short jabbing, staccato swing of Sylvia's. Every ten feet they would stop and deposit their catch in the jars and vials they carried in their knapsacks. Sometimes Mildred Latham would stop longer and set her camera with its close-up attachments and take pictures. And then they would move on. Sometimes Sylvia would run in a small circle about Mildred Latham, raising and lowering her arms like a butterfly herself. Once, even, Mildred Latham ran after her to try and catch her in her net.

Sylvia came to a tree stump wide enough to stand on. She jumped up on it and, flinging wide her arms, her net still in one hand, declaimed to the multitudinous sea of wildflowers and weeds, to the far hill, to the wide sky. Abel Harnack looked up to where she must be looking and smiled to think how she must think that she was so alone. He guessed that it would be Horace that she would be telling the world. When he looked down she was gone. Mildred Latham was running, trying to run, to the tree stump. He stood up quickly and hurried down the side of the hill to them.

She was lying flat out when he got to her. Her forehead, her cheekbones, the bridge of her nose were bright scarlet, as if she had been struck by a wide brush across the top of her face. Mildred Latham was by her side weeping softly.

"What is it?" he said. The women did not show if they were surprised that he should appear, as if they did not separate this day from others that they had shared. "What is it, Miss Warren?"

"I don't know, Mr. Harnack," she said up to him. "I don't know. I don't know. I don't know."

But she did, and as he swooped down to her and lifted her up in his arms, light as a molted shell, so did he.

At the hospital the doctor said to them, "Are you her family?"

"No," Mildred Latham said. "There is no family. We're her friends. We're very close friends." She was trying to tell the doctor what that meant, but he understood, or perhaps he did not care to know; family or friends it did not matter to what he would say, would have to tell them. They were sitting in a small office down the hall from the emergency room. They had waited four hours.

"I'm sorry you had to wait so long. We didn't want to tell you nothing, and we didn't want to tell you anything until we were reasonably sure. We don't have many of the tests back yet, but it looks like a form of *lupus. Lupus erythematosus.*"

"Oh," Mildred Latham said, and could say no more.

"What is it?" Abel Harnack asked. The doctor explained: it was a rheumatoid disease related to arthritis or rheumatic fever, but much more serious; it was a blood disease where the body formed antibodies to its own tissues; it was a wasting disease, attacking mostly the connective tissues, but the vital organs as well, so that in time it crippled; so that in time it killed.

"How much time?" Abel Harnack asked.

"It's not predictable," the doctor said. "The disease is character-ized by sudden periods of remission and then equally sudden at-tacks. There are too many variables, too many complications that can develop. We've already started with injections of a corticoste-roid hormone. For the inflammation and the pain there's aspirin."

"Aspirin?" Abel Harnack said. It seemed too trivial to be pos-sible. The doctor nodded.

"In the morning she'll go down state to the University Medical Center. We'll need to run more tests and to do more examinations. Dr. Felner will be there. He's a rheumatoid specialist. We just can't say, we just can't even guess at what the chances are yet." Then he added, "With *lupus* you never can." They all sat quietly for as long as a minute. "I'm sorry," the doctor said. "I wish there was an easier way to tell you this, but there isn't." He pressed a button on the desk and a nurse came into the small room. The doctor left. The nurse told them where they were going to take Sylvia Warren and when they could see her and what they should bring for her while she would be in the hospital and other things that Mildred Latham did not hear. But Abel Harnack did and wrote them down.

He did not sleep well. He awoke at four in the morning and dressed and ate a small breakfast and then drove off down to the university three hours away. He drove through the gray morning lightening and thought of *lupus erythematosus. Lupus.* The wolf. How terrible a name for a disease! To call it what it was, the disease that devoured like a ravening animal. But why not? And who was not ill? He did not think back to Estelle or forward to Sylvia Warren or beyond that to himself. He was through with all of that, now. At peace at last.

At the university he went to the library, which would not open for two more hours. He walked about the quiet campus as the sun rose higher and hot as yesterday. He walked to the woods edging the campus, but he did not enter them just as a year before, had he been here, at this place, he would not have entered them, although, two days ago, he would have gone in to see what he might see. Not now. Now he knew that there was nothing to see any more. The quickening heat burned off the slight wisps of steamy dew until, at nine, the day was at the clearest it would be.

He had decided to be beaten no longer. He had come here to the library to do what he had once always done, which was what he could only do — mend, fix what was broken, make better, improve. To try.

He took his little Latin and swung it like an axe, chopping rough, splintered pieces out of a thousand years of words, hewing for her as best he could a gift that should say in language better than his own what he would have her know. But there was no better language.

In the great glass cube of the university library he found his material, mostly from PA 6164 to PA 6296 on the third floor, the quiet east wing. Knowing too little to manage it, he set about piecing together a statement. Through collections, anthologies, and book after book of the Loeb Classical Library series of Latin faced by a page of English translation, he scrambled like a man on a canted, rock-strewn plain, no two steps certain. He would claw through pages of the English and, finding a passage, he would transcribe the Latin across from it.

> *And indeed in my opinion, no man can be an orator complete in all points of merit, who has not attained a knowledge of all important subjects and arts.*

Thus Cicero mocked him but he wrote it down:

> *Ac, mea quidem sententia, nomo poterit esse omni laude cumulatus orator, nisi erit omnium rerum magnarum atque artium scientiam sonsecutus.*

His notes piled up. Some appeared before him that he could not account for:

> *Nigro multa mari dicunt portanta nature, monstra repentinis terrentia saepe figuris, cum subito emersere furenti corpora ponto.*

But what could he do with that?

> *Many fearsome things, they say, swim in the black sea — monsters that ofttimes terrify with forms unlooked for, when suddenly they have reared their bodies from the raging deeps.*

Could her infinite Vergil offer him no better? Frequently his eye alone drew him onward, as if directed and compelled by a spirit in him:

> *Just when the farmer wished to reap his yellow*
> *Fields, and thresh his grain,*
> *I have often seen all the winds make war,*
> *Flattening the stout crops from the very roots;*
> *And in the black whirlwind*
> *Carrying off the ears and the light straw.*

He plucked at the golden fruit where he could, often reaching for it and missing it and lurching on.

> *I am minded to sing of bodies to new forms changing;*
> *Begin, O you gods (for you these changes have made),*
> *Breathe on my spirit and lead my continuous song.*

But it was too late for evocations.

He struggled on, Tibullus, Ovid, Propertius, Lucan, and the names of those he had no knowledge of at all, poets who clung to Being by the fragment of a stanza. He willed himself on.

Lucretius:

> *Like children trembling in the blinded dark*
> *and fearing every noise, we sit and dread*
> *the face of light, and all our fears are vain*
> *like things the child has fancied in the dark.*

Horace:

> *Thaw follows frost; hard on the heels of Spring*
> *Treads Summer sure to die, for hard on hers*
> *Comes Autumn, with his apples scattering;*
> *Then back to winter tide, when nothing stirs.*

Catullus, her beloved Catullus:

> *If a wished-for thing and a thing past hoping for*
> *should come to a man, will be welcome it not the more?*
> *Therefore to me more welcome it is than gold*
> *That Lesbia brings back my desire of old*
> *My desire past hoping for, her own self, back.*
> *O mark the day with white in the almanac!*
> *What happier man is alive, or what can bring*
> *To a man, whoever he be, a more wished-for thing?*

From his storm of notes he hammered together a document, banging on it, adding and arranging until the pen at last stumbled from his hand. He pushed back from the books and considered what he had made. He read it, the Latin, which he could not understand, breaking in his teeth. The morning had past. He picked up his pen and, winning and losing with every stroke, wrote to her for himself in his own voice:

> *which is to say we are all as susceptible to death as are the insects. Death is as absolute for humans as for midges. When metabolism ceases, autolysis begins, in* Homo sapiens *or in* Vendalia tarda. *If there is comfort anywhere, it is in truth, whatever the truth, and in this, the act of these words.*

Then he got up and took his paper and walked out leaving everything there just as it was.

Mildred Latham was with her when he came into her room. She looked well enough, though still marked by the red ensignia. It looked like a birthmark. She had been told. He handed her the paper. She read it and wept and then dried her eyes and smiled, looked up at him beside her bed and nodded once. And together they settled down to wait for the long night surely coming on.

PETER TAYLOR

The Hand of Emmagene

(FROM SHENANDOAH)

    After highschool, she had come down from Hortonsburg
To find work in Nashville.
She stayed at our house.
And she began at once to take classes
In a secretarial school.
As a matter of fact, she wasn't *right* out of highschool
She had remained at home two years, I think it was,
To nurse her old grandmother
Who was dying of Bright's disease.
So she was not just some giddy young country girl
With her head full of nonsense
About running around to Nashville nightspots
Or even about getting married
And who knew nothing about what it was to work.

    From the very beginning, we had in mind
— My wife and I did —
That she ought to know some boys
Her own age. That was one of our first thoughts.
She was a cousin of ours, you see — or of Nancy's.
And she was from Hortonsburg
Which is the little country place
Thirty miles north of Nashville
Where Nancy and I grew up.
That's why we felt responsible
For her social life
As much as for her general welfare.

We always do what we can of course
For our kin when they come to town —
Especially when they're living under our roof.
But instead of trying to entertain Emmagene
At the Club
Or by having people in to meet her
Nancy felt
We should first find out what the girl's interests were.
We would take our cue from that.

   Well, what seemed to interest her most in the world
Was work. I've never seen anything quite like it.
In some ways, this seemed the oddest thing about her.
When she first arrived, she would be up at dawn,
Before her "Cousin Nan" or I had stirred,
Cleaning the house — We would smell floor wax
Before we opened our bedroom door some mornings —
Or doing little repair jobs
On the table linen or bed linen
Or on my shirts or even Nancy's underwear.
Often as not she would have finished
The polishing or cleaning she had taken upon herself to do
Before we came down. But she would be in the living room
Or sun parlor or den or dining room
Examining the objects of her exertions, admiring them,
Caressing them even — Nancy's glass collection
Or the Canton china on the sideboard.
One morning we found her with pencil and paper
Copying the little geometrical animals
From one of the oriental rugs.

   Or some mornings she would be down in the kitchen cooking,
Before the servants arrived.
(And of course she'd have the dishes she'd dirtied
All washed and put away again before the cook
Came in to fix breakfast.) What she was making
Down there in the pre-dawn hours,
Would be a cake or a pie for Nancy and me.
(She didn't eat sweets, herself.)
Its aroma would reach us

Before we were out of bed or just as we started down the stairs.
But whether cleaning or cooking,
She was silent as a mouse those mornings.
We heard nothing. There were only the smells
Before we came down. And after we came down there'd be
Just the sense of her contentment.

It was different at night. The washing machine
Would be going in the basement till the wee hours,
Or sometimes the vacuum cleaner
Would be running upstairs before we came up
Or running downstairs after we thought
We'd put the house to bed.
(We used to ask each other and even ask her
What she thought the cook and houseman
Were meant to do. Sometimes now we ask ourselves
What did they do during the time Emmagene was here.)
And when she learned how much we liked to have fires
In the living room and den, she would lay them
In the morning, after cleaning out the old ashes.
But at night we'd hear her out in the back yard
Splitting a fireplace log, trying to get lightwood
Or wielding the ax to make kindling
Out of old crates or odd pieces of lumber.
More than once I saw her out there in the moonlight
Raising the ax high above her head
And coming down with perfect accuracy
Upon an up-ended log or a balanced two-by-four.

There would be those noises at night
And then we noticed sometimes the phone would ring.
One of us would answer it from bed,
And there would be no one there.
Or there would be a click
And then another click which we knew in all likelihood
Was on the downstairs extension.
One night I called her name into the phone —"Emmagene?"—
Before the second click came, just to see if she were there.
But Emmagene said nothing.
There simply came the second click.

There were other times, too, when the phone rang
And there would be dead silence when we answered.
"Who is it?" I would say. "Who are you calling?"
Or Nancy would say, "To whom do you wish to speak?"
Each of us, meanwhile, looking across the room at Emmagene.
For we already had ideas then, about it. We had already
Noticed cars that crept by the house
When we three sat on the porch in the late spring.
A car would mosey by, going so slow we thought sure it would stop.
But if Nancy or I stood up
And looked out over the shrubbery toward the street,
Suddenly there would be a burst of speed.
The driver would even turn on a cut-out as he roared away.

More than once the phone rang while we were at the supper
    table
On Sunday night. Emmagene always prepared that meal
And did up the dishes afterward since the servants were off
On Sunday night. And ate with us too, of course.
I suppose it goes without saying
She always ate at the table with us.
She rather made a point of that from the start.
Though it never would have occurred to us
For it to be otherwise.
You see, up in Hortonsburg
Her family and my wife's had been kin of course
But quite different sorts of people really.
Her folks had belonged to a hard bitten, fundamentalist sect
And Nancy's tended to be Cumberland Presbyterians
Or Congregationalists or Methodists, at worst
(Or Episcopalians, I suppose I might say "at best.")
The fact was, Nancy's family — like my own —
Went usually to the nearest church, whatever it was.
Whereas Emmagene's traveled thirteen miles each Sunday morn-
    ing
To a church in the hilly north end of the County.
A church of a denomination that seemed always
To be *changing* its name by the addition of some qualifying adjec-
    tive.
Either that or seceding from one synod or joining another.

Or deciding just to go it alone
Because of some disputed point of scripture.

   Religion aside, however, there were differences of style.
And Emmagene — very clearly — had resolved
Or been instructed before leaving home
To brook no condescension on our part.
"We're putting you in the guest room," Nancy said
Upon her arrival. And quick as a flash Emmagene added:
"And we'll take meals together?"
"Why of course, why of course," Nancy said,
Placing an arm about Emmagene's shoulder.
"You'll have the place of honored guest at our table."

   Well, on Sunday nights it was more like we
Were the honored guests,
With the servants off, of course,
And with Emmagene electing to prepare our favorite
Country dishes for us, and serving everything up
Out in the pantry, where we always take that meal.
It was as though we were all back home in Hortonsburg.
But if the phone rang,
Emmagene was up from the table in a split second,
(It might have been her own house we were in.)
And answered the call on the wall phone in the kitchen.
I can see her now, and hear her, too.
She would say "Hello," and then just stand there, listening,
The receiver pressed to her ear, and saying nothing more at all.
At first, we didn't even ask her who it was.
We would only look at each other
And go back to our food —
As I've said, we were more like guests at her house
On Sunday night. And so we'd wait till later
To speak about it to each other.
We both supposed from the start
It was some boy friend of hers she was too timid to talk with
Before us. You see, we kept worrying
About her not having any boy friends
Or any girl friends, either.
We asked ourselves again and again

Who in our acquaintance we could introduce her to,
What nice Nashville boy we knew who would not mind
Her plainness or her obvious puritanical nature —
She didn't wear make-up, not even lipstick or powder,
And didn't do anything with her hair.
She wore dresses that were like maids' uniforms except
Without any white collars and cuffs.
Nancy and I got so we hesitated to take a drink
Or even smoke a cigarette
When she was present.
I soon began watching my language.

   I don't know how many times we saw her
Answer the phone like that or heard the clickings
On the phone upstairs. At last I told Nancy
She ought to tell the girl she was free
To invite whatever friends she had to come to the house.
Nancy said she would have to wait for the opportunity;
You didn't just come out with suggestions like that
To Emmagene.

   One Sunday night the phone rang in the kitchen.
Emmagene answered it of course and stood listening for a time.
Finally, very deliberately, as always,
She returned the little wall phone to its hook.
I felt her looking at us very directly
As she always did when when she put down the phone.
This time Nancy didn't pretend
To be busy with her food.
"Who *was* that, Emmagene?" she asked
In a very polite, indifferent tone.
"Well, I'll tell you," the girl began
As though she had been waiting forever to be asked.
"It's some boy or other I knew up home.
Or *didn't* know." She made an ugly mouth and shrugged.
"That's who it always is," she added, "in case you *care* to know."
There was a too obvious irony
In the way she said "*care* to know."
As though we ought to have asked her long before this.
"That's who it is in the cars, too," she informed us —

Again, as though she had been waiting only too long for us to ask.
"When they're off work and have nothing better to do
They ring up or drive by
Just to make a nuisance of themselves."
"How many of them are there?" Nancy asked.
"There's quite some few of them," Emmagene said with emphasis.
"Well, Emmagene," I suddenly joined in,
"You ought to make your choice
And maybe ask one or two of them to come to the house to see
    you."
She looked at me with something like rage.
"They are not a good sort," she said. "They're a bad lot.
You wouldn't want them to set foot on your front steps.
Much less your front porch or in your house."

    I was glad it was all coming out in the open and said,
"They can't all be all bad. A girl has to be selective."
She stood looking at me for a moment
In a kind of silence only she could keep.
Then she went into the kitchen and came back
Offering us second helpings from the pot of greens.
And before I could say more,
She had changed the subject and was talking about the sermon
She had heard that morning, quoting with evangelistic fervor,
Quoting the preacher and quoting the Bible.
It was as if she were herself hearing all over again
All she had heard that very morning
At that church of hers somewhere way over on the far side
Of East Nashville. It was while she was going on
About that sermon that I began to wonder for the first time
How long Emmagene was going to stay here with us.
I found myself reflecting:
She hasn't got a job yet and she hasn't got a beau.

    It wasn't that I hadn't welcomed Emmagene as much as Nancy
And hadn't really liked having her in the house.
We're always having relatives from the country
Stay with us this way. If we had children
It might be different. This big house wouldn't
Seem so empty then. (I often think we keep the servants
We have, at a time when so few people have any servants at all,

Just because the servants help fill the house.)
Sometimes it's the old folks from Hortonsburg we have
When they're taking treatments
At the Hospital or at one of the clinics.
Or it may be a wife
Who has to leave some trifling husband for a while.
(Usually the couples in Hortonsburg go back together.)
More often that not it's one of the really close kin
Or a friend we were in school with or who was in our wedding.
We got Emmagene
Because Nancy heard she was all alone
Since her Grandma died
And because Emmagene's mother
Before *she* died
Had been a practical nurse and had looked after Nancy's mother
In her last days. It was that sort of thing.
And it was no more than that.
But we could see from the first how much she loved
Being here in this house and loved Nancy's nice things.
That's what they all love, of course.
That's what's so satisfying about having them here,
Seeing how they appreciate living for a while
In a house like ours. But I don't guess
Any of them ever liked it better than Emmagene
Or tried harder to please both Nancy and me
And the servants, too. Often we would notice her
Even after she had been here for months
Just wandering from room to room
Allowing her rather large but delicately made hands
To move lightly over every piece of furniture she passed.
One felt that in the houses she knew aroung Hortonsburg
— In her mother's and grandmother's houses —
There had not been pretty things — not things she loved to fondle.
It was heartbreaking to see her the day she broke
A pretty pink china vase that Nancy had set out in a new place
In the sun parlor. The girl hadn't seen it before.
She took it up in her strong right hand
To examine it. Something startled her —
A noise outside, I think. Maybe it was a car going by,
Maybe one of those boys. — Suddenly the vase crashed to the floor.

Emmagene looked down at the pieces, literally wringing her hands
As if she would wring them off, like chickens' necks, if she could.
I was not there. Nancy told me about it later.
She said that though there was not a sign of a tear in the girl's eyes,
She had never before seen such a look of regret and guilt
In a human face. And what the girl said
Was even stranger. Nancy and I
Have mentioned it to each other many times since.
"I despise my hand for doing that," she wailed.
"I wish — I do wish I could punish it in some way.
I ought to see it don't do anything useful for a week."

   One night on the porch
When one of those boys went by in his car
At a snail's pace
And kept tapping lightly on his horn,
I said to Emmagene, "Why don't you stand up and wave to him,
Just for fun, just to see what happens, I don't imagine
They mean any harm."
"Oh, you don't know!" she said.
"They're a mean lot.
They're not like some nice Nashville boy
That you and Cousin Nan might know."
Nancy and I sat quiet after that,
As if some home truth had been served up to us.
It wasn't just that she didn't want to know
Those Hortonsburg boys.
She *wanted* to know Nashville boys
Of a kind we might introduce her to and approve of.
I began to see — and so did Nancy, the same moment —
That Emmagene had got ideas about herself
Which it wouldn't be possible for her to realize.
She not only liked our things. She liked our life.
She meant somehow to stay. And of course
It would never do. The differences were too deep.
That is to say, she had no notion of changing herself.
She was just as sure now
About what one did and didn't do
As she had been when she came.
She still dressed herself without any ornamentation

Or any taste at all. And would have called it a sin to do so.
Levity of any kind seemed an offence to her.
There was only one Book anyone need read.
Dancing and drinking and all that
Was beyond even thinking about.
And yet the kind of luxury we had in our house
Had touched her. She felt perfectly safe, perfectly good
With it. It was a bad situation
And we felt ourselves somewhat to blame.
Yet what else could we do
But help her try to find a life of her own?
That had been our good intention from the outset.

  I investigated those boys who did the ringing up
And the horn blowing. In Nashville you have ways
Of finding out who's in town from your home town.
It's about like being in Paris or Rome
And wanting to know who's there from the U.S.A.
You ask around among those who speak the home tongue.
And so I asked about those boys.
They were, I had to acknowledge, an untamed breed.
But, still, I said to Nancy, "Who's to tame 'em
If not someone like Emmagene. It's been going on
Up there in Horton County for, I'd say — Well,
For a good many generations anyway."

  I don't know what got into us, Nancy and me.
We set about it more seriously, more in earnest
Trying to get her to see something of those boys.
I'm not sure what got into us. Maybe it was seeing Emmagene
Working her fingers to the bone
— For no reason at all. There was no necessity.—
And loving everything about it so.
Heading out to secretarial school each morning,
Beating the pavements in search of a job all afternoon,
Then coming home here and setting jobs for herself
That kept her up half the night.
Suddenly our house seemed crowded with her in it.
Not just to us, but to the servants, too.
I heard the cook talking to her one night in the kitchen.

"You ought to see some young folks your own age.
You ought to have yourself a nice fellow."
"What nice young fellow would I know?" Emmagene asked softly.
"I'm not sure there is such a fellow — not that I would know."
"Listen to her!" said the cook. "Do you think we don't see
Those fellows that go riding past here?"
"They're trash!" Emmagene said. "And not one of them
That knows what a decent girl is like!"
"Listen to her!" said the cook.
"I hear her," said the houseman, "and you hear her.
But she don't hear us. She don't hear nobody but herself."
"Ain't no body good enough for you?" the cook said.
"I'd like to meet some boy
Who lives around here," the poor girl said.
And to this the cook said indignantly,
"Don't git above your raisin', honey."
Emmagene said no more. It was the most
Any of us would ever hear her say on that subject.
Presently she left the kitchen
And went up the back stairs to her room.

    Yet during this time she seemed happier than ever
To be with us. She even took to singing
While she dusted and cleaned. We'd hear
Familiar old hymns above the washer and the vacuum cleaner.
And such suppers as we got on Sunday night!
Why, she came up with country ham and hot sausage
That was simply not to be had in stores where Nancy traded.
And then she *did* find a job!
She finished her secretarial training
And she came up with a job
Nowhere else but in the very building
Where my own office is.
There was nothing for it
But for me to take her to work in my car in the morning
And bring her home at night.

    But there was a stranger coincidence than where her job was.
One of those boys from Hortonsburg turned out to run the el-
        evator

In our building. Another of them brought up my car each night
In the parking garage. I hadn't noticed before
Who those young fellows were that always called me by name.
But then I noticed them speaking to her too
And calling her "Emmagene." I teased her about them a little
But not too much, I think. I knew to take it easy
And not spoil everything.

    Then one night the boy in the garage
When he was opening the car door for Emmagene, said,
"George over there wants you to let him carry you home."
This George was still another boy from Hortonsburg,
(Not one that worked in my building or in the garage)
And he saluted me across the ramp.
"Why don't you ride with him, Emmagene?" I said
I said it rather urgently, I suppose.
Then without another word, before Emmagene could climb in
        beside me,
The garage boy had slammed my car door.
And I pulled off, down the ramp —
With my tires screeching.

    At home, Nancy said I ought to have been ashamed.
But she only said it after an hour had passed
And Emmagene had not come in.
At last she did arrive, though
Just as we were finishing dinner.
We heard a car door slam outside.
We looked at each other and waited.
Finally Emmagene appeared in the dining room doorway.
She looked at us questioningly,
First at Nancy's face, then at mine.
When she saw how pleased we were
She came right on in to her place at the table
And she sat down, said her blessing,
And proceeded to eat her supper as though nothing unusual had
        happened.

    She never rode to or from work with me again.
There was always somebody out there

In the side driveway, blowing for her in the morning
And somebody letting her out in the driveway at night.
For some reason she always made them let her out
Near the back door, as though it would be wrong
For them to let her out at the front.
And then she would come on inside the house the back way.

    She went out evenings sometimes, too,
Though always in answer to a horn's blowing in the driveway
And never, it seemed, by appointment.
She would come to the living room door
And say to us she was going out for a little ride.
When we answered with our smiling countenances
She would linger a moment, as if to be sure
About what she read in our eyes
Or perhaps to relish what she could so clearly read.
Then she would be off.
And she would be home again within an hour or two.

    It actually seemed as if she were still happier with us now
Than before. And yet something was different too.
We both noticed it. The hymn singing stopped.
And — almost incredible as it seemed to us —
She developed a clumsiness, began tripping over things
About the house, doing a little damage here and there
In the kitchen. The cook complained
That she'd all but ruined the meat grinder
Dropping it twice when she was unfastening it from the table.
She sharpened the wood ax on the knife sharpener — or tried to,
And bent the thing so the houseman insisted
We'd have to have another.
What seemed more carelessness than clumsiness
Was that she accidentally threw away
One of Nancy's good spoons, which the cook retrieved
From the garbage can. Nancy got so she would glance at me
As if to ask, "What will it be next? — poor child."
We noticed how nervous she was at the table
How she would drop her fork on her plate —
As if she intended to smash the Haviland —
Or spill something on a clean place mat.

Her hands would tremble, and she would look at us
As though she thought we were going to reprimand her
Or as if she hoped we would.
One day when she broke off the head of a little figurine
While dusting, she came to Nancy with the head
In one hand and the body in the other.
Her two hands were held so tense,
Clasping so tightly the ceramic pieces,
That blue veins stood out where they were usually
All creamy whiteness. Nancy's heart went out to her.
She seized the two hands in her own
And commenced massaging them
As if they were a child's, in from the snow.
She told the girl that the broken shepherd
Didn't matter at all,
That there was nothing we owned
That mattered *that* much.

    Meanwhile, the girl continued to get calls at night
On the telephone. She would speak a few syllables
Into the telephone now. Usually we couldn't make out what she was
        saying
And we tried not to hear. All I ever managed
To hear her say — despite my wish not to hear —
Were things like "Hush, George" or "Don't say such things."
Finally one night Nancy heard her say:
"I haven't got the kind of dress to wear to such a thing."

    That was all Nancy needed. She got it out of the girl
What the event was to be. And next morning
Nancy was downtown by the time the stores opened,
Buying Emmagene a sleeveless, backless evening gown.
It seemed for a time Nancy had wasted her money.
The girl said she wasn't going to go out anywhere
Dressed like that. "You don't think I'd put you in a dress
That wasn't proper to wear," said Nancy, giving it to her very
        straight.
"It isn't a matter of what you think
Is proper," Emmagene replied. "It's what he would think it
    meant —

George, and maybe some of the others, too."
They were in the guest room, where Emmagene was staying
And now Nancy sat down on the twin bed opposite
The one where Emmagene was sitting, and facing her.
"This boy George doesn't really misbehave with you
Does he, Emmagene?" Nancy asked her. "Because if he does,
Then you mustn't, after all, go out with him —
With him or with the others."
"You know I wouldn't let him do that, Cousin Nan," she said.
"Not really. Not the real thing, Cousin Nan."
"What do you mean?" Nancy asked in genuine bewilderment.
The girl looked down at her hands, which were folded in her lap.
"I mean, it's my hands he likes," she said.
And she quickly put both her hands behind her, out of sight.
"It's what they all like if they can't have it any other way."
And then she looked at Nancy the way she had looked
At both of us when we finally asked her who it was on the tele-
     phone,
As though she'd only been waiting for such questions.
And then, as before, she gave more
Than she had been asked for.
"Right from the start, it was the most disgusting kind of things
They all said to me on the telephone. And the language, the words.
You wouldn't have known the meaning, Cousin Nan."
When she had said this the girl stood up
As if to tell Nancy it was time she leave her alone.
And with hardly another word, Nancy came on to our room.
She was so stunned she was half the night
Putting it across to me just what the girl had told her
Or had tried to tell her.

    Naturally, we thought we'd hear no more about the dress.
But, no, it was the very next night, after dinner,
That she came down to us in the living room
And showed herself to us in that dress Nancy had bought.
It can't properly be said she was wearing it,
But she had it on her like a night gown,
As if she didn't have anything on under it.
And her feet in a pair of black leather pumps —
No make-up of course, her hair pulled back as usual into a knot.

There was something about her, though, as she stood there
With her clean scrubbed face and her freshly washed hair
And in that attire so strange and unfamiliar to her
That made one see the kind of beauty she had,
For the first time. And somehow one knew what she was going to
     say.
"I'll be going out," she said, searching our faces
As she had got so she was always doing when she spoke to us.
Nancy rose and threw her needle work on the chair arm
And didn't try to stop it when it fell on to the floor.
Clearly, she too had perceived suddenly a certain beauty about the
     girl.
She went over to her at once and said,
"Emmagene, don't go out with George again.
It isn't wise." They stepped into the hall
With Nancy's arm about the girl's waist.
"I've got to go," Emmagene said.
And as she spoke a horn sounded in the driveway.
"George is no worse than the rest," she said.
"He's *better*. I've come to like things about him now."
There was more tapping on the horn,
Not loud but insistent.
"He's not the kind of fellow I'd have liked to like.
But I can't stop now. And you've gone and bought this dress."

     Nancy didn't seem to hear her. "You mustn't go," she said.
"I couldn't live through this evening.
I'd never forgive myself." The horn kept it up outside,
And the girl drew herself away from Nancy.
Planting herself in the middle of the hall
She gave us the first line of preaching we'd ever heard from her:
"It is not for us to forgive ourselves. God forgives us."
Nancy turned and appealed to me. When I stood up
The girl said defiantly, "Oh, I'm going!"
She was speaking to both us. "You can't stop me now!"
The car horn had begun a sort of rat-a-tat-tat.
"That's what he's like," she said, nodding her head
Toward the driveway where he was tapping the horn.
"You can't stop me now!
I'm free, white and twenty-one.

That's what *he* says about me."
Still the horn kept on,
And there was nothing we could think to say or do.
Nancy did say, "Well, you'll have to have a wrap.
You can't go out like that in this weather."
She called to the cook, who came running
(She must have been waiting just beyond the hall door to the
    kitchen.)
And Nancy sent her to the closet on the landing
To fetch her velvet evening cape.
There was such a commotion
With the girl running out through the kitchen,
The cape about her shoulders and billowing out behind
Almost knocking over the brass umbrella stand,
I felt the best thing I could do was to sit down again.
Nancy and the cook were whispering to each other
In the hall. I could see their lips moving
And then suddenly I heard the groan or scream
That came from the kitchen and could be heard all over the house.

   I went out though the dining room and the pantry
But the cook got there first by way of the back hall door.
The cook said she heard the back door slam.
I didn't hear it. Nancy said afterward she heard
The car door slam. We all heard the car roar down the driveway
In reverse gear. We heard the tires whining
As the car backed into the street and swung around
Into forward motion. None of that matters,
But that's the kind of thing you tend to recall later.
What we saw in the kitchen was the blood everywhere.
And the ax lying in the middle of the linoleum floor
With the smeary trail of blood it left
When she sent it flying. The houseman
Came up from the servants' bathroom in the basement
Just when the cook and I got there.
He came in through the back porch.
He saw what we saw of course
Except he saw more. I followed his eyes
As he looked down into that trash can at the end of the counter
And just inside the porch door. But he turned away

And ran out onto the back porch without lifting his eyes again.
And I could hear him being sick out there.

The cook and I looked at each other, to see who would go first.
I knew I had to do it, of course.
I said, "You keep Miss Nancy out of here."
And saw her go back into the hall.
I went over to the trash can,
Stepping over the ax and with no thought in my head
But that I must look. When I did look,
My first thought was, "Why, that's a human hand."
I suppose it was ten seconds or so before I was enough myself
To own it was Emmagene's hand
She had cut off with the wood ax.
I did just what you would expect.
I ran out into the driveway, seeing the blood every step,
And then back inside, past the houseman still retching over the
    bannister,
And telephoned the police on the kitchen telephone.
They were there in no time.

The boy who had been waiting for Emmagene
In the car, and making the racket with his horn
Used better judgment than a lot of people might have.
When she drew back the velvet cape and showed him
What she had done to herself
And then passed out on the seat,
He didn't hesitate, didn't think of bringing her back inside the
    house.
He lit out for the emergency room at the Hospital.
She was dead when he got her there, of course,
But everybody congratulated the boy —
The police, and the doctors as well —
The police arrested him in the emergency waiting room,
But I went down to the Station that night
And we had him free by nine o'clock next morning.
He was just a big country boy really
Without any notion of what he was into.
We looked after arrangements for Emmagene of course
And took the body up to Hortonsburg for burial.

The pastor from her church came to the town cemetery
And held a graveside service for her.
He and everybody else said a lot of consoling things to us.
They were kind in a way that only country people
Of their sort can be,
Reminding us of how hospitable we'd always been
To our kinfolks from up there
And saying Emmagene had always been
A queer sort of a girl, even before she left home.
Even that boy George's parents were at the service.
Nancy and I did our best to make them see
George wasn't to be blamed too much.
After all, you could tell from looking at his parents
He hadn't had many advantages.
He was a country boy who grew up kind of wild no doubt.
He had come down to Nashville looking for a job
And didn't have any responsible relatives here
To put restraints upon him
Or to give him the kind of advice he needed.
That might have made all the difference for such a boy,
Though of course it wasn't something you could say
To George's parents —
Not there at Emmagene's funeral, anyway.

JOHN UPDIKE

The Man Who Loved Extinct Mammals

(FROM THE NEW YORKER)

SAPERS lived rather shapelessly in a city that shall be nameless. It was at a juncture of his life when he had many ties, none of them binding. Accordingly, he had much loose time, and nothing, somehow, better filled it than the perusal of extinct mammals. Living species gave him asthma, and the dinosaurs had been overdone; but in between lay a marvellous middle world of lumpy, clumping, hairy, milk-giving creatures passed from the face of the earth. They tended to be large: "During these early periods," writes Harvey C. Markman in his pamphlet "Fossil Mammals" (published by the Denver Museum of Natural History), "many of the mammals went in for large size and absurdity." For example, *Barylambda*. It was nearly eight feet long and half as high. It had a short face, broad feet, muscular legs, and a very stout tail. "It combined" — to quote Markman again — "many anatomical peculiarities which together had little survival value. One might say of this race, and other aberrant groups, that they tried to specialize in too many ways and made very little progress in the more essential directions." It was extinct by the end of the Paleocene. "Who could not love such a creature?" Sapers asked himself.

And who is to say what is an "essential direction"?

Barylambda was an amblypod, meaning "blunt foot." This order (or suborder) of ungulates had, Webster's Dictionary told Sapers, "very small smooth brains." The "small" was to be expected, the "smooth" was surprising. It was nice. The man who loved extinct mammals resented the way Markman kept chaffing the amblypods;

nothing about them, especially their feet and their teeth, was specialized enough to suit him. One could hear Markman sigh, like the sardonic instructor of a class of dullards, as he wrote, "At least one more family of amblypods must be mentioned: the uintatheres. By late Eocene time some of these grotesque creatures had attained the size of circus elephants. Arranged along the face and forehead they had three pairs of bony protuberances resembling horns. . . ." In the accompanying photograph of a *Uintacolotherium* skull, the bony protuberances looked artful, Arplike. Sapers didn't think them necessarily grotesque, if you tried to view them from the stand point of the Life Force instead of from ours, the standpoint of Man, with his huge, rough brain. Sapers shut his eyes and tried to imagine the selective process whereby a little bud of a bony protuberance achieved a tiny advantage, an edge, in battle, food-gathering, or mating, that would favor an exaggeration from generation to generation. He almost had it in focus — some kind of Platonic ideal pressing upon the uintathere fetuses, tincturing uintathere milk — when the telephone shrilled near his ear.

It was Mrs. Sapers. Her voice — alive, vulnerable, plaintive, his — arose from some deep past. She told him, not uninterestingly, of her day, her depressions, her difficulties. Their daughter had flunked a math exam. The furnace was acting funny. Men were asking her to go out on dates. One man had held her hand in a movie and her stomach had flipped over. What should she do?

"Be yourself," he advised. "Do what feels natural. Call the furnace man. Tell Dorothy I'll help her with her math when I visit Saturday."

"If I had a gun, some nights I'd shoot myself."

"That's why they have firearms-control laws," he said reassuringly, wondering then why she wasn't reassured.

For she began to cry into the telephone. He tried to follow her reasoning but gathered only the shadowy impression that she loved him, which he felt to be a false impression, from previous field work as her husband. Anyway, what could he do about it now? "Nothing," Mrs. Sapers snapped, adding, "You're grotesque." Then, with that stoic elegance she still possessed, and he still admired, she hung up.

Mammae, he read, are specialized sweat glands. A hair is a specialized scale. When a mammal's body gets too hot, each hair lifts up so the air can reach the skin. The bizarre *Arsinoitherium,* superficially like a rhinoceros but anatomically in a class by itself, may be distantly related to the tiny, furry hyrax found in nooks of Asia and Africa. The sabre-toothed tiger was probably less intelligent than a house cat. Its "knife tooth" (*smilodon*) was developed to prey on other oversize mammals, and couldn't have pinned a rabbit. Rabbits have been around a long time — though nothing as long, of course, as the crocodile and the horseshoe crab. Sapers thought of those sabre teeth, and of the mastodon's low-crowned molars, with the enamel in a single layer on top, that were superseded by the mammoth's high-crowned molars, that never wore out, the enamel distributed in vertical plates, and he tried to picture the halfway tooth, or the evolutionary steps to baleen, and his thought wandered pleasantly to the truth that the whale and the bear and Man are late, late models, *arrivistes* in the fossil record. What is there about a bear, that we love him? His flat, archaic feet. The amblypods are coming back. Joy! There was a delicate message Sapers could almost make out, a graffito scratched on the crumbling wall of time. His mistress called, shattering the wall.

She loved him. She told him so. He told her *vice versa,* picturing her young anatomy, her elongate thighs, her small smooth head, its mane, her spine, her swaying walk, and wondering, mightn't his middle-aged body break, attempting to cater to such a miracle? She told him of her day, her boredom, her boring job, her fear that he would go back to his wife.

"Why would I do that?" he asked.

"You think I'm too crass. I get so frightened."

"You're not especially crass," he reassured her. "But you *are* young. I'm old, relatively. In fact, I'm dying. Wouldn't you like to get a nice youngish lover, with a single gristly horn, like a modern-day rhinoceros, one of the few surviving perissodactyls?"

He was offering to divert her, but she kept insisting on her love, his bones crunching at every declaration. Rhinoceroses, he learned when at last she had feasted enough and hung up, had been backed with unguarded enthusiasm by the investment councils of the Life Force. Some species had attained the bulk of several elephants. There had been running rhinoceroses — "long legged, rather slender bodied" — and amphibious rhinoceroses, neither of them the ancestor of the "true" rhinoceros; that honor belonged to hornless *Trigonias,* with his moderate size, "stocky body," fourteen toes, and "very conservative" (Sapers could hear Markman impatiently sighing) dentition.

What is this prejudice in favor of progress? The trouble with his mistress, Sapers decided, was that she had too successfully specialized, was too purely a mistress, perfect but fragile, like a horse's leg, which is really half foot, extended and whittled and tipped with one amazing toenail. The little *Eohippus,* in its forest of juicy soft leaves, scuttled like a raccoon; and even *Mesohippus,* though big as a collie, kept three toes of each foot on the ground. *Eohippus,* it seemed to Sapers, was like a furtive little desire that evolved from the shadows of the heart into a great, clattering, unmanageable actuality.

His wife called back. Over the aeons of their living together she had evolved psychic protuberances that penetrated and embraced his mind. "I'm sorry to keep spoiling your wonderful solitude," she said, in such a way that he believed in her solicitude for his privacy even as she sarcastically invaded it, "but I'm at my wit's end." And he believed this too, though also knowing that she could induce desperation in herself as a weapon, a hooked claw, a tusk. Perhaps she shouldn't have added, "I tried to call twice before but the line was busy;" yet this hectoring, too, he took into himself as pathos, her jealousy legitimate and part of her helplessness, all organs evolving in synchrony. She explained that their old pet dog was dying; it couldn't eat and kept tottering off into the woods, and she and their daughter spent hours calling and searching and luring the poor creature back to the house. Should they put the dog into the car and take her to the vet's, to be "put to sleep"?

Sapers asked his wife what their daughter thought.

"I don't know. I'll put her on."

The child was fourteen.

"Hi, Daddy."

"Hi, sweet. Is Josie in much pain?"

"No, she's just like drunk. She stands in the puddle in the driveway and looks at the sky."

"She sounds happy, in a way. Whose idea is it to take her to the vet's?"

"Mommy's."

"And what's your idea?"

"To let Josie do what she wants to do."

"That sounds like my idea too. Why don't you let her just stay in the woods?"

"It's beginning to rain here and she'll get all wet." And the child's voice, so sensible and simple up to this point, generated a catch, tears, premonitions of eternal loss; the gaudy parade of eternal loss was about to turn the corner, cymbals clanging, trombones triumphant, and enter her mind. "Keep calm," Sapers told himself. One thing at a time.

"Then put her in the back room with some newspapers and a bowl of water. Talk to her so she doesn't feel lonely. Don't take her to the vet's unless she seems to be in pain. She always gets scared at the vet's."

"O.K. You want to talk any more to Mom?"

"No. Sweetie? I'm sorry I'm not there to help you all."

"That's O.K." Her voice grew indifferent, small and smooth. She was about to hang up.

"Oh, and baby?" Sapers called across the distance.

"Yeah?"

"Don't flub up any more math exams. It drives Mommy wild."

Giant and bizarre mammalian forms persisted well after the advent of Man. The splendid skeleton of an Imperial Mammoth, *Archidiskodon imperator,* exhibited in the Denver Museum of Natural History, was found associated with a spear point. Neanderthal men neatly stacked, with an obscure religious purpose, skulls of *Ursus spelaeus,* the great cave bear. Even the incredible *Glyptodon,* a hardshelled mammal the size and shape of a Volkswagen, chugged about the South American pampas a mere ten thousand years ago, plenty late enough to be seen by the wary, brown-faced forebears of the effete Inca kings. Who knows who witnessed the fleeting life of *Stockoceros,* the four-pronged antelope? Of *Syndyoceras,* the deerlike ruminant with two pairs of horns, one pair arising from the middle of its face? Of *Oxydactylus,* the giraffe-camel? Of *Daphoenodon,* the bear-dog? Of *Diceratherium,* the small rhinoceros, or *Dinohyus,* the enormous pig? Again and again, in the annals of these creatures, Sapers found mysterious disappearances, unexplained departures. "By the end of the Pliocene period all American rhinos had become extinct or wandered away to other parts of the world."

"After the horse family had been so successful in North America
. . . its disappearance from this hemisphere has no ready explanation."

Sapers looked about his apartment. He observed with satisfaction that there was no other living thing in it. No pets, no plants.
Such cockroaches as he saw he killed. But for himself, the place had
a Proterozoic purity. He breathed easy.

The telephone rang. It was his mother. He asked, "How are
you?" and received a detailed answer — chest pains, neuralgia,
shortness of breath, numbness in the extremities. "What can I do
about it?" he asked.

"You can stop being a mental burden to me," she answered
swiftly, with a spryness unseemly, he thought, in one so dilapidated. "You can go back to your loved ones. You can be a good
boy."

"I *am* a good boy," he argued. "All I do is sit in my room and
read." Such behavior had pleased her once; it failed to do so now.
She sighed, like Markman over a uintathere, and slightly changed
the subject.

"If I go suddenly," she said, "you must get right down here and
guard the antiques. Terrible things happen in the neighborhood
now. When Mrs. Peterson went, they backed a truck right up to the
door, so the daughter flew in from California to find an empty
house. All that Spode, and the corner cupboard with it."

"You won't go suddenly," he heard himself telling her; it
sounded like a rebuke, though he had meant it reassuringly.

After a pause, she asked, "Do you ever go to church?"

"Not as often as I should." *. . . no ready explanation.*

"Everybody down here is praying for you," she said.

"Everybody?" *The herds had just wandered away.*

"I slept scarcely an hour last night," his mother said, "thinking
about you."

"Please stop," Sapers begged. When the conversation ended, he
sat still, thinking, We are all, all of us living, contemporary with the
vanishing whale, the Florida manatee, the Bengal tiger, the whoop-
ing crane.

He felt asthmatic. The pages about extinct mammals suffocated
him with their myriad irrelevant, deplorable facts. *Amebelodon,* a
"shovel-tusker" found in Nebraska, had a lower jaw six feet long,
with two flat teeth sticking straight out. Whereas *Stenomylus* was a

dainty little camel. Why is a horse's face long? Because its eyes are making room for the roots of its high-crowned upper grinders. But even *Eohippus,* interestingly, had a diastema. Creodonts, the most primitive of mammalian carnivores, moved on flat, wide-spreading feet; indeed, the whole animal, Sapers had to admit, looked indifferently engineered, compared to cats and dogs. "The insectivores, however, have made very little progress in any direction" — with a sudden little surge of cathexis that shifted his weight in the chair, Sapers loved insectivores; he hugged their shapeless, shameless, fearful archetype to his heart. "Feet and teeth provide us with most of our information about an extinct mammal's mode of existence. . . ." Of course, Sapers thought. They are what hurt.

Biographical Notes

Biographical Notes

ALICE ADAMS has had her stories published in *The New Yorker, The Atlantic, McCall's, Redbook, The Paris Review, The Virginia Quarterly Review,* and other magazines. They have also appeared in *O. Henry Prize Stories* six times. She has finished three novels, the second of which, *Families and Survivors,* was nominated for a fiction award by the National Book Critics Circle in 1975. *Listening to Billie,* her third novel, will be published in 1977. Ms. Adams lives in San Francisco and is now working on more stories and another novel.

M. PABST BATTIN, who holds a M.F.A. in fiction writing and a Ph.D. in philosophy from the University of California at Irvine; teaches aesthetics and philosophy of literature at the University of Utah. She is the author of "Aristotle's Definition of Tragedy in the POETICS," in *The Journal of Aesthetics and Art Criticism,* and is currently writing on Plato's theory of art. "Terminal Procedure" is one of her first stories to be widely published.

MAE SEIDMAN BRISKIN has written an as-yet-unpublished novel and some short fiction and is now at work on a second novel. She lives in Palo Alto, California.

NANCY CHAIKIN graduated from the University of Michigan, where she won Avery Hopwood awards for short fiction and critical essays. She has reviewed for *The Saturday Review,* and her short stories have appeared in *Mademoiselle,* many quarterlies, three other *Best American Short Stories* collections, and *Fifty Modern Short Stories.* She writes a regular column for a Long Island weekly and has published in the *Christian Science Monitor.* She and her husband, a communications engineer, have three children and one grandchild. Mrs. Chaikin is presently at work on a novel.

JOHN WILLIAM CORRINGTON's publications include three novels, the latest of which, *The Bombardier,* was published in 1970; four volumes of poetry; and a collection of short stories, *The Lonesome Traveler.* He has received a National Endowment for the Arts Award, and his work appears in several anthologies of short fiction. A holder of degrees in both the liberal arts and jurisprudence, Mr. Corrington has been a professor of English, is a member of the New Orleans Bar, and has written articles on law and philosophy. He has also, with Dr. Joyce H. Corrington, written a number of screenplays, including *The Battle for the Planet of the Apes* and *The Killer Bees*.

H. E. FRANCIS' first collection of stories was published in Spanish translation in Argentina, the "other" world of both his life and fiction. Between 1963 and 1970 he spent half of his time teaching in the Universidad de Cuyo and half in the United States. Three times he was visiting Fulbright lecturer to Argentina. His collection, *The Itinerary of Beggars*, won the 1973 Iowa School of Letters Award for Short Fiction, and his stories and translations of Argentine literature have appeared in many magazines and anthologies. He is currently Professor of English Literature at the University of Alabama in Huntsville.

JOHN HAGGE, a graduate student in English at the University of Minnesota, is Books Editor of the *Minnesota Daily*. "Pontius Pilate" won the 1974 Nick Adams Short Story Contest sponsored by the Associated Colleges of the Midwest and judged by Professor Wayne C. Booth at the University of Chicago. At present Mr. Hagge is working on a first novel.

WARD JUST, 40, was born in Illinois and now lives in Warren, Vermont. He has published three novels, the latest of which is *Nicholson at Large*.

JOHN MCCLUSKEY is the author of a novel, *Look What They Done to My Song*, published in 1974. His stories and articles have appeared in a number of periodicals. He also edits *Juju*, a journal of research papers in Afro-American Studies. A member of the English Department at Case Western Reserve University, he lives with his wife and two sons in Cleveland. He is completing his second novel.

STEPHEN MINOT is the author of *Chill of Dusk*, a novel, and *Crossings*, a collection of short fiction. His stories have appeared in 14 periodicals including *The Atlantic, Harper's, Playboy, The Virginia Quarterly Review*, and *The North American Review*. They have been translated into German, French, and Flemish and have been reprinted in England. He is also a recipient of a Saxton Memorial Fellowship and is the author of *Three Genres*, a college text on writing, and *Three Stances of Modern Fiction*, coedited with Robley Wilson, Jr. In 1974–75 he served as Writer in Residence at The Johns Hopkins University. He is presently an Associate Professor at Trinity College, Hartford, where he has taught since 1959, and is completing a second novel, *Ghost Images*.

KENT NELSON was born in Colorado in 1943 and returned there to live after graduating from Yale and Harvard Law School, teaching at a maximum security prison in Massachusetts, and doing considerable traveling. He has written a number of short stories and one novel. In

1975 he won the Emily Clark Balch First Prize, awarded by *The Virginia Quarterly Review.*

CYNTHIA OZICK is the author of *Trust,* a novel; *The Pagan Rabbi and Other Stories;* and *Bloodshed and Three Novellas.* She has also published essays, poetry, criticism, reviews, and translations in numerous periodicals and anthologies and has been the recipient of several prizes, including the 1975 O. Henry First Prize for Fiction and the Award for Literature of the American Academy of Arts and Letters.

REYNOLDS PRICE was born in Macon, North Carolina, in 1933. He was educated at Duke and Oxford universities, and since 1958 he has taught for a part of each year at Duke. His first novel, *A Long and Happy Life,* was published in 1962 and was followed by three other novels, two volumes of short stories, and a volume of essays and scenes. He is now at work writing poems and a study of the origins of narrative.

MICHAEL ROTHSCHILD was born in Maine in 1947.

BARRY TARGAN was born in Atlantic City, New Jersey, in 1932. He was educated at Rutgers University, the University of Chicago, and Brandeis University, from which he received a Ph.D in English Literature. He has published short stories, poetry, and essays in such magazines and journals as *Esquire, The Southern Review, American Review, Salmagundi,* and *Quarterly Review of Literature.* Mr. Targan won the Iowa School of Letters Award for Short Fiction for 1975, and the University of Iowa Press published his colleciton of short stories, *Harry Belten and the Mendelssohn Violin Concerto,* in 1975. Mr. Targan lives with his wife and two sons in Schuylerville, New York.

PETER TAYLOR's fifth book of short fiction, *Collected Stories,* appeared in 1969; he is currently finishing a second story collection. In 1973 *Presences,* a group of one-act plays, was published by Houghton Mifflin. He lives in Charlottesville, Virginia, with his wife, the poet Eleanor Ross Taylor, and he teaches at the University of Virginia.

JOHN UPDIKE was born in Shillington, Pennsylvania in 1932 and attended Harvard College, graduating *summa cum laude.* He is the author of eight novels, five collections of short stories, three of poetry, and two of critical essays. He lives in Massachusetts.

The Yearbook of the American Short Story

January 1 to December 31, 1975

Roll of Honor, 1975

DIXON, STEPHEN
Streets. Harper's Magazine, August.

FREDERICK, K. C.
That Other Place. Epoch, Spring.

FRIEDMAN, B. H.
Moving in Place. Hudson Review, Winter.

GARDNER, JOHN
The Music-Lover. Antaeus, Spring-Summer.

GHISELIN, OLIVE
Mrs. Homo Sapiens. Michigan Quarterly Review, Fall.

GINGHER, MARIANNE
Variation on a Scream. Carolina Quarterly, Winter.

GLOVER, DOUGLAS
Horse. Fiddlehead, Winter.

GOLD, HERBERT
Meester Boris. Midstream, January.

GOLDBERG, LESTER
The Love Song of J. Paris Wladaver. Quartet, Fall-Winter.

GOODWIN, STEPHEN
God's Spies. Shenandoah, Summer.

HALL, JAMES BAKER
Hands. Hudson Review, Winter.

HARTER, EVELYN
The Landlady. Southwest Review, Winter.

HAUPT, ARTHUR
A Story. South Carolina Review, April.

HAWKES, JOHN
Dead Passion. Fiction, Vol. 4, No. 1.

HERMANN, JOHN
Candle of the Lord. South Dakota Review, Spring.
Ignoramibus. Carolina Quarterly, Fall.

HOFFMAN, WILLIAM
The Darkened Room. Sewanee Review, Fall.

HUMMA, JOHN
The Man Who Wrote Haiku. Denver Quarterly, Spring.

ISRAEL, PHILIP
The Bendorf Report. Carleton Miscellany, Vol. XV, No. 1.

KILLENHYI, MARIELLO
A Barrel of Snakes. Vis a Vis, May.

KNIGHT, WALLACE E.
Searchers. Atlantic, February.
Making History. Atlantic, October.

KRUMSIECK, HOWARD
The New Typewriter. Cimarron Review, January.

LAMPART, JACOB
The Muse of Ocean Parkway. Commentary, April.

MCMARTIN, SEAN
Everybody Should Own One. Quartet, Fall-Winter.

MCNAMARA, EUGENE
The May Irwin-John C. Rice Kiss. Malahat Review, October.

MCPHERSON, JAMES ALAN
Problems of Art. Iowa Review, Summer.

MARTIN, C. P.
A Warrior. Carolina Quarterly, Spring-Summer.

MINOT, STEPHEN
Ghost Images. North American Review, Winter.

MOLINARO, URSULE
Freud & Fraudulence. Ascent, Vol. I, No. 1.

MONKS, ELIZABETH GRAHAM
A Cure for Death. Yale Review, Summer.

NABOKOV, VLADIMIR
The Admiralty Spire. Playboy, February.

NELSON, KENT
The Tennis Player. Michigan Quarterly Review, Spring.
The Saint of Illusion. North American Review, Spring.
The Humpbacked Bird. Virginia Quarterly Review, Summer.

OATES, JOYCE CAROL
The Tempter, Fiction, Vol. 3, Nos. 2 & 3.
The Scream. Michigan Quarterly Review, Summer.
Blood-Swollen Landscape. Southern Review, Winter.
Corinne. North American Review, Fall.

OLIVER, CHARLES
White Butterflies. Kansas Quarterly, Winter-Spring.

PETSCH, NATALIE M.
Losses. Kansas Quarterly, Winter-Spring.

PONSOLDT, SUSAN
The End of the Season. Colorado Quarterly, Summer.

POWERS, T. F.
Tinkers. American Review, No. 23, October.

POWNING, BETH
That Good Night. Fiddlehead, Fall.

PRICE, REYNOLDS
Honest Hearts. Esquire, March.

PURDY, JAMES
Garnet Montrose and the Widow Rance. Fiction, Vol. 4, No. 1.

REYNOLDS, LAWRENCE JUDSON
Proceedings of a Judicial Inquiry. Greensboro Review, Winter.

RHEINHEIMER, KURT
Men in the Snow. Michigan Quarterly Review, Summer.

RUDOLPH, WILLIAM
Some Chapters in the Life of the American Practical Navigator. North American Review, Winter.

SAROYAN, WILLIAM
The Inscribed Copy of the Kreutzer Sonata. Atlantic, January

SAYLES, JOHN
1-80 Nebraska. Atlantic, May.

SCHULMAN, SONDRA
Golden Prince/Black Nothing. Massachusetts Review, Winter.

SHIELDS, JAMES
Down Snowballing. Carolina Quarterly, Fall.

SHREVE, ANITA
Silence at Smuttynose. Cimarron Review, July.

SNYDER, RICHARD
A Heraldry of Hands. Nantucket Review, February.

SOLUOSKA, MARA
Death By Water. Ohio Review, Spring.

SPENCER, ELIZABETH
Mr. McMillan. Southern Review, Winter.

STAPLES, GEORGE
Mohamed from the Djebet. Antaeus, Spring-Summer.

STOUT, ROBERT JOE
Medicine Creek. South Dakota Review, Winter.

TAUBE, MYRON
The Obituary, Kansas Quarterly, Spring.

TYLER, ANNE
A Knack for Languages. New Yorker, January 13.
The Artificial Family. Southern Review, Summer.

UPDIKE, JOHN
Separating. New Yorker, June 23.
The Chaste Planet. New Yorker, November 10.

VALGARDEN, W. D.
A Business Relationship. Fiddlehead, Spring.

VALIUNAS, ALGIO
An Aesthetic Distance. Michigan Quarterly Review, Fall.

WEGNER, ROBERT E.
Cleanse Me Cobalt: Let Me See Spring. Southwest Review, Spring.

WIEBE, DALLAS
For the Most Part. Fiction International 4/5.

WILKINS, KIRBY
  Indian Camp Exit. North American Review, Fall.
WILSON, ERIC
  The Interpreter. Massachusetts Review, Winter.

YATES, RICHARD
  Bellevue. North American Review, Summer.

II. Foreign Authors

AMIS, KINGSLEY
  Dear Illusion. Antaeus, Spring.

BACHMAN, INGEBORG
  The Barking. Ms., July.
BÖLL, HEINRICH
  Katharina Blum. Trans. by Leila Vennewitz. Fiction, Vol. 3, No. 2 & 3.

CARTER, ANGELA
  Master. Iowa Review, Summer-Fall.
CICELLIS, KAY
  Proportions. Shenandoah, Fall.

DALY, ITA
  Aimez Vous Colette. The Critic, May-June.

GARSHIN, VSEVOLOD
  A Night. Trans. by Eugene M. Kayden. Colorado Quarterly, Summer.
GORDIMER, NADINE
  City Lovers. New Yorker, October 13.

HAKKAS, MARIOS
  The Bidet. Trans. by Kay Cicellis. Shenandoah, Fall.

IOANNOU, GEORGIOS
  "Voungari." Trans. by Roderick Beaton. Shenandoah, Fall.

KLENOV, ANDREI
  The Son. Trans. by Bytas Dukas. Literary Review, Winter.

LENDAKIS, ANDREAS
  In the Noonday Heat. Trans. by Kevin Andrews. Shenandoah, Fall.

MISHIMA, YUKIO
  The Perfect Companions. Antaeus, Spring-Summer.

O'FAOLAIN, SEAN
  Liberty. Atlantic, April.
ONETTI, JUAN CARLOS
  Santa Rosa. Trans. by Hortense Carpenter. Chicago Review, Autumn.

REDGROVE, PETER
  The Glass Cottage. Hudson Review, Summer.

SHAHAR, DAVID
  The Dagger of Ali Ibn Masrur. Commentary, September.

TRACY, HONOR
  Via Dolorosa. Atlantic, December.

VALTINOS, THANASSIS
  August '48. Shenandoah, Fall.

WALKER, TED
  Cosher and the Sea. New Yorker, June 10.
  Underground. New Yorker, August 4.

Distinctive Short Stories, 1975

CROWE, JUDY
Happy Birthday. Four Quarters, Autumn.

CULLINAN, ELIZABETH
The Sum and Substance. Shenandoah, Summer.

DAGG, MEL
The Museum of Man. Fiddlehead, Fall.

DAVIDSON, AVRAM
One Red Rose. Playboy, September.

DAVIS, KENNETH S.
What Somebody Said to the Golden Girl. Kansas Quarterly, Fall.

DELORME, J. M.
The Golden Prey. South Dakota Review, Summer.

DEMARINIS, RICK
Medicine Man. Atlantic, January.

DILLARD, ANNIE
Five Sketches. North American Review, Summer.

DISCH, THOMAS M.
Getting Into Death. Antaeus, Spring-Summer.

EDELMAN, PREWITT
The Wall. Southwest Review, Winter.

ELKIN, SANLEY
The Franchiser. Fiction, Vol. 4, No. 1.

ELY, DAVID
Always Home. Playboy, August.

EVANS, SUSAN
Late Great American Hero. South Dakota Review, Spring.

FERGUSSON, HARVEY
The Enchanted Meadow. South Dakota Review, Winter.

GALLANT, MAVIS
Between Zero and One. New Yorker, December 8.

GANZ, EARL
Jewish Lightning. Iowa Review, Winter.

GASS, WILLIAM
I Wish You Wouldn't. Partisan Review, Spring.

GIFFORD, WILLIAM
A Little Company. Apalachee Quarterly, Spring.

GLYNN, THOMAS
Needle. North American Review, Spring.

GODWIN, GAIL
Nobody's Home. Harper's Magazine, February.
False Lights. Esquire, January.

GOLDBERG, GERALD JAY
The Secrets of Malaterre. Iowa Review, Winter.

GOYEN, WILLIAM
Bridge of Music, River of Sand. Atlantic, August.

GROVER, DORYS C.
The Bus From Winnemucca. South Dakota Review, Winter.

HALL, DONALD
The Figure of the Woods. Ohio Review, Fall.

HALL, JOHN C.
Stuart and Michael. North American Review, Summer.

HALLEY, ANNE
The Sisterhood. Shenandoah, Winter.

HANSEN, RON
The Jump. Carolina Quarterly, Fall.

HARLOW, ENID
Asthma Clinic. Ontario Review, Fall.

HARTER, EVELYN
The Publication Day Party. South Dakota Review, Summer.

HAWKES, JOHN
The Animal Eros. Antaeus, Spring-Summer.

HAYDEN, JULIE
The Lists of the Past. New Yorker, March 10.

HELPRIN, MARK
The Home Front. New Yorker, February 3.

HERBKERSMAN, GRETCHEN
Thor. Paris Review, Summer.

HEYNEN, JIM
Standing Alone. Cutbanks, Fall.

HILL, WOLF
Jericho and the Blue Roan. Michigan Quarterly Review, Spring.

HINCK, ROBERT H.
Letters to Action Central. Georgia Review, Summer.

HODGINS, JACK
Great Blue Heron. Prism International, Summer.

HOFFMAN, ALICE
Property Of. American Review, No. 23, October.

HOLTZMAN, HARRY
Sand Is Harder Than Chickens. MD, December.

HORNE, LEWIS B.
The Red Iris. Ontario Review, Fall.

HOWER, EDWARD
Foxy Lady. Epoch. Spring.

JONES, ANN
Silent Acres. Four Quarters, Autumn.

JONES, GEORGE
Sloan. North American Review, Spring.

JOYCE, WILLIAM
You Can't Lose With an Echo Harp. New Letters, Fall.

JULIAN, MARILYN
Cycloids: Two Wheels. Fiddlehead, Winter.

JUST, WARD
The Double Agent. Harper's Magazine, December.

JUVIK, THOMAS E.
What You Have To Be. Twigs, Spring.

KATZMAN, SARAH S.
Cry By the Picture. Literary Review, Fall.

KAYE, HOWARD
The Apotheosis of White Sauce. Cimarron Review, October.

KENNEY, SUSAN
Mirrors. Epoch, Fall.

KITAIF, THEODORE
Detainment. South Dakota Review, Summer.

KITTREDGE, WILLIAM
The Vineland Lullaby. Ploughshares, 2/3.
Kookooskia. Chariton Review, Fall.

KOCH, CLAUDE
The Block Collection. Four Quarters, Summer.

KUMIN, MAXINE
The Neutral Love Object. Virginia Quarterly Review, Winter.

LARSEN, ERIC
Fragments For the Death of My Grandfather. South Dakota Review, Spring.

LASALLE, PETER
Anything You Want. North American Review, Spring.

LEDBETTER, KEN
Idiots. Canadian Fiction Magazine, Spring.

LEFCOWITZ, BARBARA F.
Vivian's Uncle. Webster Review, June.

LIBERMAN, M. M.
I'll Keep You in Mind. Ascent. Vol. 1, No. 1.

LINDNER, VICKI
Conversation. Paris Review, Winter.

McHANEY, TOM
What the Heart Is For. Southern Humanities Review, Winter.

MADDEN, DAVID
Second Look Presents: The Rape of an Indian Brave. Fiction International 4/5.

MAI, WILLIAM
The Implement Man. Antaeus, Spring-May.

MAIN, J. M.
Miss Stilvey. Virginia Quarterly Review, Summer.

MAIROWITZ, RICHARD
  The Dregs. Fiction, Vol. 3, Nos. 2 & 3.
MAKUK, PETER
  Assumption. Sewanee Review, Winter.
MASTERS, HILARY
  The Moving Finger. Massachusetts Review, Autumn.
MATTHEWS, JACK
  The Project. Southern Review, Summer.
MAZORIE, JO ANN
  The Funeral Breakfast. Literary Review, Winter.
MELLA, JOHN
  Last Days. Carolina Quarterly, Spring-Summer.
MOORE, ELIZABETH
  Twin. Cimarron Review, October.
MORGAN, CAY
  The Rowboat. Cutbank 4.
MORRIS, REBECCA
  Irv Upstairs. Miscellany, Vol. XV, No. 1.

NABOKOV, VLADIMIR
  Christmas. New Yorker, December 29.
NELSON, KENT
  The Only Safe Place. Carolina Quarterly, Winter.

OATES, JOYCE CAROL
  The Widows. Hudson Review, Spring.
  Falling In Love, Ashton, British Columbia. Epoch, Spring.
O'BRIEN, DAN
  Eminent Domain. Sunday Clothes, Summer.
O'BRIEN, TIM
  Where Have You Gone, Charming Billy? Redbook, May.
O'NEILL, PATRICK
  A Night Out. Green River Review, Summer.

PARRA-FUGUEREDO, A.
  One on One: Skydiver vs. Henry Jones. Carolina Quarterly, Spring-Summer.
PETERSON, MARY
  Girl in a Boat. South Dakota Review, Summer.
PETROSKI, CATHERINE
  Beautiful My Mane in the Wind. North American Review, Fall.
  Drawer. Falcon, Winter.
POWERS, THOMAS
  Going for the Paper. Harper's Magazine, January.
PRICE, REYNOLDS
  Commencing. Virginia Quarterly Review, Spring.

REED, KIT
  Mr. Rabbit. Transatlantic Review, Spring.
ROCKHAM, JEFF
  Lila Watches. Kansas Quarterly, Winter-Spring.
ROGERS, LENORA K.
  A Dirty, Rotten Miracle. Graffiti, Fall.
ROSKOLENKO, HARRY
  Peshky. Fiction, Vol. 4, No. 1.
RUSS, JOANNA
  Daddy's Girl. Epoch, Winter.

SANDERS, THOMAS E.
  Ave Lutie. South Dakota Review, Spring.
SANTIAGO, DANNY
  A Message From Home. Playboy, October.
SAROYAN, WILLIAM
  How to Choose A Wife. Ladies' Home Journal, October.
SCHIFFMAN, CARL
  I Got Shoes. Four Quarters, Spring.
SCHMIDT, DOROTHY
  Gretchen Am Spinnrade. Kansas Quarterly, Fall.
SCHWARTZ, JOHN
  WPFK. Atlantic, November.

SCHWARTZ, SEIDE
Olympians. Apalachee Quarterly, Spring.

SCHWEITZER, LEN
The Horizon Beyond. Apalachee Quarterly, Winter.

SIEGEL, GERALD M.
A Most Fragile Friendship. Response, Summer.

SILMAN, ROBERTA
Company. Atlantic, May.

SINGER, ISAAC BASHEVIS
The Admirer. New Yorker, January 6.

SKEEN, P. PAINTER
Perspective. South Dakota Review, Spring.

SMITH, LEE
Passion and Crime. Carolina Quarterly, Winter.

SOLLID, JOHN
Night Wishers. Green River Review, Summer.

SPEYER, JUDITH
The Man With a Balloon in His Heart. New Yorker, June 10.

STANGE, KEN
Seven Days Out. Canadian Fiction Magazine, Spring.

STANTON, MAURA
The Robber Bridegroom. Ploughshares 2/3.

STONE, ALMA
I'm Waving Tomorrow. Esquire, April.

SULKIN, SIDNEY
The Secret Seed. Literary Review, Winter.

TAGER, MARCIA
Home Free. Fiddlehead, Summer.

TAMMINGA, FREDERICK W.
The Benediction. Fiddlehead, Fall.

TAYLOR, PETER
Three Heroines. Virginia Quarterly Review, Spring.

TRUDELL, DENNIS
A Tuesday. The Falcon, Vol. 6, No. 10.

VALE, KATHRYN
Legion. Carleton Miscellany, Vol. XV, No. 1.

VALGARDEN, W. D.
Snow. Malahat Review. January.

VAN NOPPEN, SALLY
Envy. Greensboro Review, Winter.

VIVANTE, ARTURO
The Children. New Yorker, March 10.

WAMPLER, MARTIN
Samantha: Two Stories. North American Review, Fall.

WARD, ROBERT
Farmer. Antaeus, Autumn.

WEATHERS, WINSTON
The Dancing Goat. Chariton Review, Spring.

WEAVER, GORDON
In the Dark of Summers Past. Carolina Quarterly, Spring-Summer.

WEST, PAUL
The Monocycle. Carleton Miscellany, Vol. XV, No. 1.

WILDMAN, JOHN HAZARD
Some Notes on Wiggins. Georgia Review, Summer.

WILSON, AUSTIN
The Refuge. Apalachee Quarterly, Spring.

YOUNG, KATHRYN
Leftovers. North American Review, Spring.

ZACHARIAS, LEE
Consumption. South Dakota Review, Spring.

II. Foreign Authors

BRYCHT, ANDRZEJ
The Funeral. Trans. by Kevin Windle. Malahat Review, January.

DAS, MANOJ
Farewell to a Ghost. Malahat Review, October.
The Last I Heard of Them Old Folks of the Northern Valley. Carleton Miscellany, Vol. XV, No. 1.
A Day in the Life of the Mayor. Ascent, Vol. I, No. 1.
A Night in the Life of the Mayor. Ascent, Vol. I, No. 1.

FINN, KONSTANTIN
Two Encounters. Trans. by Vytas Dukas. Literary Review, Winter.

FUENTES, CARLOS
The Doll Queen. Antaeus, Spring-Summer.

GARSHIN, VSEVOLOD
The Red Flower. Trans. by Eugene M. Kayden. Colorado Quarterly, Spring.

GORDIMER, NADINE
A Lion on the Freeway. Harper's Magazine, March.

GORIN, GRIGORII
Stop Potapov. Trans. by Vytas Dukas. Literary Review, Winter.

HATZIS, DIMITRIS
Outworn Symbols. Trans. by Roderick Beaton. Shenandoah, Fall.

HEALY, THOMAS
A Noble Moment. Transatlantic Review, Spring.

HENDERSON, MICHAEL
The Dead Bush. Webster Review, Fall.

KASDAGLIS, NIKOS
The Sponge Diver. Shenandoah, Fall.

LAURENCE, VINCENT
Tell Me Once Again You Love Me. Transatlantic Review, Spring.

NOVIS, LESLIE
Sliding. New Yorker, November 17.

O'BRIEN, FLANN
The Martyr's Crown. Antaeus, Autumn.

RAMOS, GRACILIANO
Caetes. Trans. by Bernadette Guedes. Chicago Review, Autumn.

SUAREZ, GONZALO
Getting Rid of Gusantemo. Malahat Review, October.

VASILIKOS, VASSILI
The Three T's. Trans. by James Merrill. Shenandoah, Fall.

Addresses of American and Canadian Magazines Publishing Short Stories

American Review (formerly New American Review), 661 Fifth Avenue, New York, New York 10019

Americas, Organization of American States, Washington, D.C. 20006

Ampersand Magazine, Ltd., 816 South Hancock Street, Philadelphia, Pennsylvania 19147

Antaeus, 1 West 30th Street, New York, New York 10001

Antioch Review, 212 Xenia Avenue, Yellow Springs, Ohio 45387

Apalachee Quarterly, P.O. Box 20106, Tallahassee, Florida 32304

Aphra, RFD, Box 355, Springtown, Pennsylvania 18081

Ararat, 109 East 40th Street, New York, New York 10016

Argosy, 205 East 42nd Street, New York, New York 10017

Arizona Quarterly, University of Arizona, Tucson, Arizona 85721

Arlington Quarterly, Box 366, University Station, Arlington, Texas 76010

Ascent, English Department, University of Illinois, Urbana, Illinois 61801

Aspen Leaves, Box 3185, Aspen, Colorado 81611

Atlantic Monthly, 8 Arlington Street, Boston, Massachusetts 02116

Bachy, 11317 Santa Monica Boulevard, West Los Angeles, California 90025

Boston University Journal, Box 357, Boston University Station, Boston, Massachusetts 02215

Brushfire, Box 9012 University Station, Reno, Nevada

Canadian Fiction, 4248 Weisbrod Street, Prince George, British Columbia, Canada

Canadian Forum, 30 Front Street West, Toronto, Ontario, Canada

Capilano Review, 2055 Purcell Way, North Vancouver, British Columbia, Canada

Carleton Miscellany, Carleton College, Northfield, Minnesota 55057

Carolina Quarterly, P.O. Box 1117, Chapel Hill, North Carolina 27514

Chariton Review, Division of Language & Literature, Northeast Missouri State University, Kirksville, Missouri 63501

Chelsea, P.O. Box 5880, Grand Central Station, New York, New York 10017

Chicago Review, University of Chicago, Chicago, Illinois 60637

Cimmaron Review, 203B Morrill Hall, Oklahoma State University, Stillwater, Oklahoma 74074

Colorado Quarterly, University of Colorado, Boulder, Colorado 80303

Commentary, 165 East 56th Street, New York, New York 10022

Confrontation, English Department, Long Island University, Brooklyn, New York 11201

Connecticut Fireside, Box 5293, Hamden, Connecticut 06518

Contributor, 30 East Sprague, Spokane, Washington 99202

Cosmopolitan, 1775 Broadway, New York, New York 10019

The Critic, 180 North Wabash Avenue, Chicago, Illinois 60601

Cutbank, Department of English, University of Montana, Missoula, Montana 59801

Dark Horse, c/o Barnes, 47A Dana Street, Cambridge, Massachusetts 02138

December, Box 274, Western Springs, Illinois 60558

Denver Quarterly, University of Denver, Denver, Colorado 80210

Dogsoldier, East 323 Boone Street, Spokane, Washington 99202

Ellery Queen's Mystery Magazine, 229 Park Avenue South, New York, New York 10003

Epoch, 252 Goldwin Smith Hall, Cornell University, Ithaca, New York 14850

Esquire, 488 Madison Avenue, New York, New York 10022

Event (Canada), Doughlas College, P.O. Box 2503, New Westminster, British Columbia, Canada

Event (U.S.A.), 422 South Fifth Street, Minneapolis, Minnesota 55415

Falcon, Mansfield State College, Mansfield, Pennsylvania

Fantasy and Science Fiction, Box 271, Rockville Centre, New York 11571

The Fault, 41186 Alice Avenue, Fremont, California 94538

Fiction, Department of English, City College of New York, 138th Street and Convent Avenue, New York, New York 10031

Fiction International, Department of English, St. Lawrence University, Canton, New York 13617

Fiddlehead, Department of English, University of New Brunswick, New Brunswick, Canada

Florida Quarterly, University of Florida, 330 Reitz Union, Gainesville, Florida 32601

Forum, Ball State University, Muncie, Indiana 47302

Four Quarters, La Salle College, Philadelphia, Pennsylvania 19143

Gallery, 936 North Michigan Avenue, Chicago, Illinois 60611

Gallimaufry, 359 Frederick Street, San Francisco, California 94117

Georgia Review, University of Georgia, Athens, Georgia 30601

Gone Soft, Salem State College, Salem, Massachusetts 01970
Good Housekeeping, 959 Eighth Avenue, New York, New York 10019
Graffiti, Box 418, Lenoir Rhyne College, Hickory, North Carolina 28601
Green River Review, Box 594, Owensboro, Kentucky 42301
Greensboro Review, University of North Carolina, Box 96, McIver Building, Chapel Hill, North Carolina 27401
Harper's Bazaar, 572 Madison Avenue, New York, New York 10022
Harper's Magazine, 2 Park Avenue, New York, New York 10016
Hawaii Review, Hemenway Hall, University of Hawaii, Honolulu, Hawaii 96822
Hudson Review, 65 East 55th Street, New York, New York 10022
Husk, Cornell College, Mount Vernon, Iowa 52314
Intellectual Digest, 110 East 59th Street, New York, New York 10022
Iowa Review, University of Iowa, Iowa City, Iowa 52240
Jeffersonian Review, P.O. Box 3864, Charlottesville, Virginia 22903
Kansas Quarterly, Kansas State University, Manhattan, Kansas 66502
Ladies' Home Journal, 641 Lexington Avenue, New York, New York 10022
Laurel Review, West Virginia Wesleyan College, Buckhannon, West Virginia 26201
Lifestyle, 572 Madison Avenue, New York, New York 10022
Literary Review, Fairleigh Dickinson University, Teaneck, New Jersey 07666
Lotus, Department of English, Ohio University, Athens, Ohio 45701
Mademoiselle, 420 Lexington Avenue, New York, New York 10022
The Malahat Review, University of Victoria, Victoria, British Columbia, Canada
Massachusetts Review, University of Massachusetts, Amherst, Massachusetts 01002
McCall's, 230 Park Avenue, New York, New York 10017
MD, MD Publications, Inc., 30 East 60th Street, New York, New York 10022
Michigan Quarterly Review, University of Michigan, Ann Arbor, Michigan 48104
Mississippi Review, Box 37, Southern Station, University of Southern Mississippi, Hattiesburg, Mississippi 39401
Ms., 370 Lexington Avenue, New York, New York 10017
Nantucket Review, P.O. Box 1444, Nantucket, Massachusetts 02554
National Jewish Monthly, 1640 Rhode Island Avenue, N.W., Washington, D.C. 20036
New Directions, 333 Sixth Avenue, New York, New York 10014
New Letters, University of Missouri, Kansas City, Missouri 64110
New Orleans Review, Loyola University, New Orleans, Louisiana 70118
New Renaissance, 9 Heath Road, Arlington, Massachusetts 02174

New River Review, Radford College Station, Radford, Virginia 24142
New Writers, 507 Fifth Avenue, New York, New York 10017
New Yorker, 25 West 43rd Street, New York, New York 10036
Nimrod, University of Tulsa, Tulsa, Oklahoma 74104
North American Review, University of Northern Iowa, Cedar Falls, Iowa 50613
Northern Minnesota Review, Bemidji State College, Bemidji, Minnesota 56601
Northwest Review, Erb Memorial Union, University of Oregon, Eugene, Oregon 97403
Occident, Eshleman Hall, University of California, Berkeley, California 94720
Ohio Journal, Department of English, Ohio State University, 164 West 17th Avenue, Columbus, Ohio 43210
Old Hickory Review, P.O. Box 1178, Jackson, Tennessee 38301
Ontario Review, 6000 Riverside Drive East, Windsor, Ontario, Canada
Paris Review, 45-39 171 Place, Flushing, New York 11358
Partisan Review, Rutgers University, 1 Richardson Street, New Brunswick, New Jersey 08903
Pathway Magazine, P.O. Box 1483, Charleston, West Virginia 25325
Penthouse, 909 Third Avenue, New York, New York 10022
Perspective, Washington University Post Office, St. Louis, Missouri 63130
Phylon, Atlanta University, Atlanta, Georgia 30314
Playboy, 232 East Ohio Street, Chicago, Illinois 60611
Ploughshares, P.O. Box 529, Cambridge, Massachusetts 02139
Prairie Schooner, Andrews Hall, University of Nebraska, Lincoln, Nebraska 68508
Prism International, University of British Columbia, Vancouver, British Columbia, Canada
Quarry, College V, University of California, Santa Cruz, California 95060
Quarterly Review of Literature, 26 Haslet Avenue, Princeton, New Jersey 08540
Quartet, 1701 Puryear Drive (Apt. 232), College Station, Texas 77840
Queens Quarterly, Queens University, Kingston, Ontario, Canada
Re: Artes Liberales, School of Liberal Arts, Stephen F. Austin State University, Nacogdoches, Texas 75961
Redbook, 230 Park Avenue, New York, New York 10017
Remington Review, 505 Westfield Avenue, Elizabeth, New Jersey 07208
Response, Box 1496, Brandeis University, Waltham, Massachusetts 02154
Roanoke Review, Box 268, Roanoke College, Salem, Virginia 24513
Rocky Mountain Review, Box 1848, Durango, Colorado 81301
Salmagundi Magazine, Skidmore College, Saratoga Springs, New York 12866
San Francisco Review, P.O. Box 671, San Francisco, California 94100

San José Studies, 174 Administration Building, San José State University, San José, California 95192

Saturday Evening Post, 1100 Waterway Boulevard, Indianapolis, Indiana 46202

Seneca Review, Box 115, Hobart and William Smith College, Geneva, New York 14456

Sense of Humor, P.O. Box 3088, Grand Central Station, New York, New York 10017

Seventeen, 320 Park Avenue, New York, New York 10022

Sewanee Review, University of the South, Sewanee, Tennessee 37375

Shenandoah, Box 122, Lexington, Virginia 24450

South Carolina Review, Box 28661, Furman University, Greenville, South Carolina 29613

South Dakota Review, Box 111, University Exchange, University of South Dakota, Vermillion, South Dakota 57069

Southern California Review, Bauer Center, Claremont Men's College, Claremont, California 91711

Southern Humanities Review, Auburn University, Auburn, Alabama 36830

Southern Review, Louisiana State University, Baton Rouge, Louisiana 70803

Southwest Review, Southern Methodist University, Dallas, Texas 75222

Spectrum, Box 14800, Santa Barbara, California 93107

St. Andrews Review, St. Andrews Presbyterian College, Laurinsburg, North Carolina 28352

Striver's Row, Department of English, Johns Hopkins University, Baltimore, Maryland 21218

Sumus, The Loom Press, 500 West Rosemary Street, Chapel Hill, North Carolina 27541

Sun & Moon, 4330 Harrick Road, College Park, Maryland 20740

Sunday Clothes, Box 66, Hermosa, South Dakota 57701

Tamarack Review, Box 157, Postal Station K, Toronto, Canada

Texas Quarterly, Box 7527, University Station, Austin, Texas 78712

Transatlantic Review, P.O. Box 3348, Grand Central Station, New York, New York 10017

Transpacific, P.O. Box 486, Laporte, Colorado 80535

TriQuarterly, Northwestern University, Evanston, Illinois 60201

Twigs, Hilltop Editions, Pikeville College Press, Pikeville, New York 41501

Virginia Quarterly Review, 1 West Range, Charlottesville, Virginia 22903

Vis à Vis, Division of Library Science, California State University, Fullerton, Fullerton, California 92634

Viva, 909 Third Avenue, New York, New York 10022

Wascana Review, Wascana Parkway, Regina, Saskatchewan, Canada

Webster Review, Webster College, Webster Groves, Missouri 63119

Western Humanities Review, Building 41, University of Utah, Salt Lake
  City, Utah 84112
Western Review, Western New Mexico University, Silver City, New Mexico
  88061
Windsor Review, University of Windsor, Windsor, Ontario, Canada
Yale Review, P.O. Box 1729, New Haven, Connecticut 06520
Yankee, Dublin, New Hampshire